BROKEN BONDS

THE CURSE OF SOTKARI TA: BOOK TWO

MARIA A. PEREZ

Published by: Maria A. Perez

Editor: Stephanie Hoogstad

Cover Design: Christian Bentulan

ISBN: 978-1-7351133-2-6

Ebook ISBN: 978-1-7351133-3-3

Disclosure: Consensual Sexual Content, Physical and Sexual Abuse/Violence

DEDICATION

The Curse of Sotkari Ta series features maternal figures and related themes. I dedicate Book Two to my aunt, Carmen, who fills that role for me and has gone above and beyond the call of duty, and to my wonderful sons Isaac and Jonathan, who made me a mom.

BOOKS BY THIS AUTHOR

The Curse of Sotkari Ta: Book One

Broken Bonds, The Curse of Sotkari Ta: Book Two

Montor's Secret Stash of Poems (A companion book to The Curse of Sotkari Ta series)

TAN ARANDA: A WARRIOR'S SONG

Aranda, my home
Blue, lavender and pink
A sunrise of majesty
To Aranda, we drink!

So sing a song now
Sing with me!
Oh, Tan Aranda
Our planet will be free!

Remember all
Remember well
What doomed our clans
To shame, in hell

Division sowed
Our broken bonds
A weakness felt
We must respond!

Jonjuri, the victors!
On to Victory!
Oh, Tan Aranda!
Our planet will be free!

Divided, we fell
To Lostai scum
Together, we rise
Beating the drum!

As moons shine
In deep purple skies
So shall we prevail
To claim our final prize!

Jonjuri, the victors!
Sail the lost red sea!
Oh, Tan Aranda!
Our planet will be free!

Let's join together
In red, green and gold
As birds take flight
Our destiny foretold

Our warriors are strong
Yellow skies ablaze
Unified forever
We seize our future days!

Jonjuri, the victors!
Watch the Lostai flee!
Oh, Tan Aranda!
Our planet will be free!

In days of yore
Our separate ways
Cast our sad lots
In deep malaise

But now our hands
We clasp and raise
We pump our fists
For glory days!

Jonjuri, the victors!
Unity, our key!
Oh, Tan Aranda!
Our planet will be free!

We form a quilt
Woven tight and strong
Our clans together
All sing this song!

Jonjuri, the victors!
Great gods, hear our plea!
Oh, Tan Aranda!
Our planet will be free!

1

MINA

Montor, my fiancé and captain of our spaceship, called an impromptu staff meeting. It still felt surreal sometimes to think of him in those terms, considering that back on Earth I had a husband and three children.

So much had happened since the Lostai kidnapped me two years earlier. When I thought about the time I had spent on the Lostai science station on Xixsted, my hands trembled, and my stomach churned. I was just a typical thirty-seven-year-old wife and mother. The scars on my body gave testimony to what I had been through. The thought that my family on Earth would never know what had happened to me weighed heavy on my soul.

We gathered in the main conference room of the *Barinta*, the name Montor had given this spaceship when we all agreed to become a part of the United Rebel Front. *Barinta* signified collaboration in Montor's native tongue, Arandan.

Montor stood before us, hands behind his back, chest puffed. Our son, Josher, sat on my lap. Josher at four months old was the size of an eight-month-old human child. Arandan children develop at an accelerated rate until they reach puberty at about seven years of age. After that, their aging continues at a rate similar to humans. Even at that young age, he was the spitting image of his father with lionesque features, slanted almond-shaped eyes, broad flat nose, thin lips, and soft fuzz on his skin. He only inherited amber-colored irises and rounded pupils from me; Montor's were yellow with feline vertical pupils.

"We should be landing on Penstarox in a few hours. Our schedule will change a bit as I have some personal news to share," Montor announced.

Our eyes connected, and for a moment Montor broke his formal captain persona with a wide, proud smile.

"Mina and I will be married there in a traditional Arandan wedding ceremony."

Foxor and Lasarta, Montor's foster parents, beamed at the news. Colora, the widow of Montor's old friend Jortan, winked at me. She had also become a good friend of mine. I offered a restrained smile to all of them. I loved Montor and was happy to marry him, but thoughts of my future also brought memories of my past and the grief of knowing I would never see my children on Earth again.

Kindor completed our small crew. He had kept to himself for most of the trip. Being a pureblood, original Sotkari Ta, he was mute and communicated only telepathically. Montor and I were also telepathic as a result of our embedded Sotkari Ta genes, but the rest of the crew was not, so Kindor used his tablet to communicate. Nodding to Montor and me, his expression polite, he typed in his reply and the tablet emitted audio.

"I am sure I speak for all of us here when I say we are honored to witness your wedding."

Montor thanked Kindor with a courteous nod of his own. Thankfully, they were doing their best to be cordial.

Montor continued with his announcements, returning to a more serious posture.

"This means we will need to stay a few days longer than anticipated before we begin our mission. We will remain domiciled on our craft, but you will be free to get familiar with the island and the *Tan Aranda* rebel base. It will please Mina and me that you, our closest friends and family, can share this joyous event with us."

Later in the dining area, Lasarta and I chatted about the wedding plans while eating dinner.

"Lasarta, what do you think of Montor's plan that we be married on Penstarox?" I asked.

"It is wonderful news, my dear. Penstarox is a tropical island in the southeastern quadrant. It must be pleasant weather at this time, not too hot."

"I would like to do my part to make everything be perfect but have no idea what is expected from the bride in Arandan culture. I am going to need some help."

Tapping my hand, she smiled.

"Of course, my dear. For all practical purposes, I am your mother-in-law. It is actually my duty to give you guidance in these matters, since you do not have an Arandan mother. First thing you need to know is that you are expected to give Montor an amulet as a wedding gift."

Without thinking, my fingers played with the amulet I wore around my neck, a gift from Montor, almost identical to his. People from Montor's clan maintained the tradition of wearing cords around their necks with amulets that are gifted to them on specific milestones during their life. At a minimum, everyone wore the amulet their parents gave them on their first birthday, but a person could have several cords with more than one amulet. Montor wore his twin sister's cord and amulet. She died as a child. Montor gave me his when I left him to escape the Lostai.

"You will bake a small cake the day of the wedding, placing the amulet inside. During the wedding ceremony, you both will share the cake, and you will present him the amulet while making your pledge to love him until your last breath. You need to learn to speak at least that pledge in Arandan."

I sighed, shaking my head.

"What is the problem?" she asked.

I had spent over a year as a prisoner on Xixsted, a few days on the planet Renna One, and six months in a remote village on Fronidia with Kindor's family. Now, we were heading to an island rebel military base. Let's just say, I didn't know where the nearest jewelry store was.

"I have no idea how or where to find an appropriate amulet."

Lasarta became thoughtful for a moment, and then her yellow eyes lit up.

"I think Foxor will be able to help. Montor does not know this because he was only a child at the time, but his father gave Foxor his amulets before he was taken away to be executed by Lostai military. Foxor wears all his amulets hidden under his shirt, so Montor has never seen them. One of them is the amulet that Montor's mother gave his father at their wedding. It is engraved with Montor's family name, and I am sure he will be thrilled to receive it from you."

"Lasarta, that sounds perfect," I said, excited for a minute until I grasped her words.

"Wait. Did you say Montor's father was executed by the Lostai?" I couldn't believe what I was hearing. "I was not aware. I thought he had died in The Clan Wars. I mean, I notice Montor does not like to speak about it. I assumed his father was a victim of the war...like maybe an explosion or in battle... something like that."

Lasarta shook her head, her expression solemn.

"It is emotionally distressing for Montor to get into the

specifics of how he lost his family. Avoiding the subject is easier than facing the fact that all his adult life he wore the uniform of the people responsible for his entire family's demise. Becoming a Lostai soldier helped Montor avoid feeling like a victim and led him to prosperity, but it was also the source of significant internal conflict. This is why he led a double life secretly helping the rebel cause. I, for one, am thankful he finally got rid of that disgusting uniform!"

Tears welled up as I digested another bit of Montor's history. My heart filled with compassion as I imagined the guilt and self-loathing he had buried deep down in his psyche. Who knows how long he might have continued living under that duality if he hadn't met me?

We landed in a clearing near a thick jungle. The Arandan sky looked different from those of Earth, Renna One, and Fronidia. Although breathable for all of us, traces of certain gases in the atmosphere caused the sky to be mustard-colored and the clouds to be a light blue and lavender. Our spacecraft was equipped with two small transport pods that we used to travel to the *Tan Aranda* rebel base. The small island was in the middle of a red ocean, subject to bad storms most of the year, thousands of miles away from any land. *Tan* signified "free" in the Arandan language. The rebels had stolen Lostai technology that allowed them to encompass the entire base in a force field that both protected and hid it from detection.

A young Arandan soldier dressed in a red-and-green military uniform with a gold sash across the chest greeted us. A patch with a picture of a bird with bright red, gold, and green feathers adorned his jacket. At the sight of it, I stopped to think. I had seen this bird before. Then it came to me. Colora had this same bird tattooed on her midriff. She wasn't just a chatty beauty salon owner. Underneath her effervescent personality lay the soul of a patriotic rebel.

The soldier escorted us to a conference room where refreshments and snacks were served. After we settled in, a middle-aged Arandan walked into the room, also dressed in uniform. Montor, who was sitting next to me, stood at attention, crossed his arms over his chest, and bowed. The Arandan did the same, so I concluded this was a salute. We all got to our feet, and Montor spoke in Lostai, which, for unfortunate reasons, was the only language that we all understood.

"All, this is Commander Portars. He manages the operations of this base."

"It is a pleasure to meet you," Commander Portars said, giving us all a once-over. "You are quite a mixed bunch. I suppose that is why we must speak in *that* language." A bit of annoyance laced his tone.

There was no denying we were a diverse group and, I imagined, interesting to take in at once. Montor and his foster parents had the typical leonine Arandan features. Montor, built like a heavy-weight boxer, stood at least six-and-a-half feet tall. Kindor was also tall at about six feet with an athletic build and could have passed for human if it hadn't been for his slate-colored skin and blue hair and lips. Colora's eyes had black sclera and tiny pink pupils, and her nostrils were two tiny orifices in the center of her face.

Montor nodded to Portars with an apologetic look I wasn't accustomed to seeing him display. Commander Portars ordered all personnel to come to the conference room. Once everyone assembled in the room, we all took our seats. Portars cleared his throat before addressing us.

"The first order of the day is to pay tribute to someone who, until recently, had remained anonymous. As we all know, not too long ago we lost a patriot, a brave soul who secretly served as our strategic leader. To keep them protected, he never divulged his family ties. Well, today we have among us someone who knew all about the risks he was taking and stood steadfast by his side. I am referring to Jortan's widow, someone who has suffered his loss without any recognition. We will correct this today. Please, Colora, may I request that you stand?"

This caught us all off guard. Sadness washed over me as I remembered the one time I met Jortan back on Renna One and how friendly and genuine he was. My chest tightened as I noticed Colora's eyes already brimming with tears. As soon as she stood, Commander Portars saluted her and gestured for the other soldiers to do the same.

"We would like to present a small token of our appreciation and respect to the widow of someone who was totally committed to the cause of *Tan Aranda* for many years and who gave his life to keep our secrets safe. Please, Colora, join me."

While Colora walked to the front of the room, I turned to see Montor's lips pressed in a tight line. He looked at no one. I'm sure he was afraid eye contact would cause him to lose control. Jortan was an old family friend.

I swallowed hard. Collective grief hung heavy in the air as Commander Portars placed a medal around her neck. Everyone bowed to her again, and she lost composure, crying openly, her chest heaving. Commander Portars placed his hand on her shoulder, an unusual gesture, inappropriate in Arandan culture. I was sobbing too by the time I heard Colora's voice loud and clear, speaking in Arandan. Although I didn't understand the language, the pride and strength rang true. Once her speech was complete, everyone in the room erupted in shouts and fist pumps.

"Montor, please stand. I also would like to announce that Montor has agreed to replace Jortan as our strategic leader."

My neck and shoulders tensed. Montor and I already had discussed and agreed that he would accept this position, but I couldn't help worrying about his safety. Everyone stood, faced Montor, and bowed.

My mind wandered to everything that Montor had explained to us about Jortan's involvement with the rebel movement. Before Jortan was murdered, he had spearheaded a new strategy for the *Tan Aranda* rebel group to regain control of Aranda through an all-out war against the Lostai. A significant fleet of battle crafts and other tactical technology had been built up with the funds Jortan had raised, as well as a militia of over ten million Arandans. Jortan's strategy also involved joining forces with three other groups in the sector engaged in rebellious activities against Lostai military rule. These included the Sotkari, the Rennans, and a relatively primitive people from a planet at the far end of the galaxy who called themselves the Namson. The movement's new name: the United Rebel Front. As strategic leader, Montor would also have the responsibility to liaison with these other insurgencies.

My thoughts were interrupted as I heard Portars announce, "In addition, we are happy to hear from Montor that we have cause to celebrate." He looked towards us. "We will be hosting a wedding ceremony."

I sat tall in my chair with Josher in my lap, trying to hide my insecurity. Portars was a proud Arandan rebel commander. As he walked over to me and bowed, I wondered what he thought about Montor choosing to marry someone outside of his race.

"You must be Mina. I hope we can meet your expectations in hosting this special event."

"We are very grateful that you allow us to celebrate our union in such an honorable place," I said, nodding back.

Commander Portars rewarded me with a genuine smile. Montor also smiled, and I heard his voice in my mind.

"Perfect answer, sweetness."

"Sweetness" was Montor's nickname for me because,

according to him, my eyes were the color of honey. It always warmed my soul to hear him use it with me.

Commander Portars turned his attention to Montor and continued, "Montor, as you know, we have here the other two Earthians who were rescued from Xixsted, the young male and the female child. The older male became ill, and we did not know enough about his physiology to save him. If we are successful in finding and taking over a transportal, the young girl would be the first in line to be returned home. We need someone on your crew to become familiar with all the research we have gathered about the Sotkari Transportals so that they can chaperone the child home."

"Commander, may I suggest the young Earthian male would be the perfect companion? Mina has explained to me that her people have not conquered space travel beyond their neighboring planet. Many Earthians still believe they are alone in the universe. Someone from another planet could not just show up there and walk around out in the open."

"The young male has made a commitment to stay and fight the war against the Lostai in repayment for how well we have treated him. I have already asked him about this, but he admitted he prefers not to be assigned the task of accompanying the child to Earth. He is not sure he will have the mental fortitude to return and honor his promise," explained Portars.

The young man's honesty was commendable, but it presented a dilemma.

"I guess, then, I will need to be the one to bring the little girl back to Earth," I said without giving it much thought.

Montor looked at me as if I had lost my mind and asked to speak with me in private. Our lack of experience with this mode of travel made for a risky mission, so I understood why Montor might be reluctant to assign me to the job. Commander Portars dismissed the group except for the *Barinta* crew. Montor and I walked to another room to discuss the issue.

"I am not comfortable with you taking on that responsibility," Montor said, cracking his knuckles.

"I thought you told me earlier you wanted me to help the child."

"She is very sad. I was referring to helping her come out of her depression, not accompanying her back to Earth."

"We agreed returning rescued children home was a priority, and in her case, even more so. Every one of us has accepted the risks of this mission. It is not fair to the others if you try to shield me. We would test the process first to make sure it is safe, right?"

"I do not like the idea at all," he said in a conflicted tone, turning away from me. I knew there was more on his mind than what he was letting on.

"Are you thinking that I might also be tempted to stay...that I might not return?"

He whirled around, fire in his eyes and a tremor in his voice.

"Well, let us review the situation." He stood with his hands on his hips. "There is a male on Earth who can claim you as his wife! You have children there. How could you not be tempted?"

I took his hands in mine and looked into his tormented eyes. I wasn't as confident as I sounded, but I owed Montor some assurance so he could be at peace.

"Josher is my son too, and I will never abandon him, or you. In a few days, you will be my husband and we will be a family. I have already made peace with the fact that I will never see my Earth family again. We should not make this girl wait any longer than necessary to reunite her with her parents."

He paced around for a few minutes, shaking his head and rubbing his neck. Drawing a deep breath and exhaling loudly, he stared down at me.

"I need to think further about this."

We returned to the conference room, and Montor told

Commander Portars that we were still deciding who on our crew would become the transportal expert. He made some other announcements to the *Barinta* crew.

"We will remain here for five days. During the third day, Mina and I must go on the traditional pre-wedding journey into the wilderness, and the wedding will be the following day. Please take advantage of your time here to learn as much as possible but also feel free to use the recreational areas on the base and explore this beautiful island. We will have a staff meeting each morning before leaving the *Barinta* for our assigned tasks."

While Montor wrapped up his comments, Commander Portars checked his handheld device for a message and then whispered something to Montor. A female Arandan walked into the room. I guessed she was about ten years younger than Montor and I, appearing about thirty years old. She sported the typical tall and perfectly proportioned Arandan body and wore a uniform but with a scarf across the left side of her face tucked under her military cap and the collar of her shirt.

"Everyone, allow me to introduce our newest crew member, Officer Lorret. She will be our medical officer," announced Montor.

Lasarta and Foxor looked at each other, and Colora appeared to be recalling a memory. Something was up. This Officer Lorret was no stranger to them. She saluted us and started to address us in Arandan. Portars whispered something to her, after which she switched to Lostai.

"I look forward to working with all of you and will be setting up meetings to get your medical history and first official physical on our database. Thank you." Nodding, she left the room.

Montor turned his attention to us, handing out schematics of the base's layout and maps of the island as he gave instructions.

"Kindor, please meet with the Senior Engineer so you can become familiarized with our navigational, environmental, and energy systems. Colora, I would like you to talk to the Communications Officer so she can update you on the contacts the United Rebel Front has made with the major planets in this sector. Foxor and Lasarta, please take care of whatever setup is necessary on the *Barinta* to ensure I can get fresh, home-cooked meals. You know how I hate reproduced food. We will meet again here for our midday meal."

I didn't have an assignment yet, so Montor suggested I assist Lasarta and Foxor. Before we left, I asked Foxor if I could speak to Lasarta in private, and we walked over to a corner.

"Lasarta, I know we have discussed what will happen during the wedding ceremony, but I feel like I should be doing a lot more to prepare. I just do not know exactly what."

"Mina, in our culture, the only other things the bride needs to worry about is to show up as beautiful as possible on the wedding day and be well rested for the wedding night. Family and friends are in charge of everything else," answered Lasarta with a giggle.

"Really? What about the journey in the wilderness that Montor mentioned?"

"Oh yes, I forgot to explain that to you. It is a survival adventure the groom and bride must go on before the wedding, meant to represent the journey in life you are about to take on as spouses. During your time out there, you must find the right moment to thank him for protecting you, and you need to give him a reason to thank you for taking care of him."

"OK, sounds straightforward."

"One more thing, Mina. From the moment that the bride and groom decide on the place and date of the wedding, the couple must abstain from sexual relations until the wedding. It is supposed to ensure the groom saves his vigor for that night. Do not be surprised if Montor decides to sleep in another room

until then. Lucky for him, it is only a few days. Poor Foxor had
to wait two lunar cycles, but he was so patient about it," Lasarta
said, laughing out loud.

"Oh my, another example of how much Foxor loves you," I
said, wondering if Montor could have waited two months.

There was something else on my mind, but I wasn't sure
how to approach the subject.

"Lasarta," I hesitated. "I have another question."

"Yes, yes, of course. What is it? Do not be shy."

"Officer Lorret." As soon as I mentioned her name, Lasarta
looked down. "You know her, correct?"

"Yes, dear, I do. I was surprised to find out she would be a
part of our crew."

Lasarta folded her hands while still avoiding looking me in
the eyes.

"Well, who is she?"

"A long time ago, about ten revolutions, she and Montor
were together. But it was short-lived. They were not a good
match. She was barely an adult, immature and very head-
strong. She wanted to lead Montor down a path that, at the
time, he was not prepared to follow."

Then she did look me straight in the eyes. "I would not
worry about it, dear."

So, they dated ten years ago.

I bit my lip and simply answered, "OK." Then I added a
random request. "I would like to learn to speak Arandan.
Maybe we can find some time each day for you to help me."

She smiled and stroked my cheek with the back of her hand
(an Arandan sign of affection).

"Of course, my dear. It would be a pleasure for me."

F oxor took me to the reproduction room and left me with a list of supplies that needed to be replicated while he and Lasarta ran other errands. At midday, I headed back to the conference room where we had first gathered. I found Colora, Montor with Josher in his arms, and Officer Lorret engaged in a lively conversation in Arandan, which reached a lull once I walked in. Officer Lorret excused herself and brushed past me to leave the room.

"Is it my imagination, or does she not like me?" I asked.

Colora remained quiet, but Montor was quick to reply.

"Your imagination, sweetness. She is just busy preparing to join us when we leave to Sotkar."

Foxor, Lasarta, and Kindor arrived, followed by Commander Portars. Food and drink were brought in for lunch. Before we started, Commander Portars addressed us.

"Montor, we have here the two Earthians whom we discussed should join your crew."

Officer Lorret returned accompanied by a young man and a little girl. Memories of my kids back home flooded my brain. I pressed a hand against my chest as if that could calm the accelerated heartbeat. The young man appeared no older than nineteen or twenty, only a few years older than my son Chris. He had smooth, dark skin and quite a muscular build for someone that age.

"Please introduce yourselves to our newest United Rebel Front squadron. You may speak in Lostai as some of them do not *yet* speak Arandan," instructed Commander Portars.

The young man saluted us and spoke in broken Lostai.

"Hello, Damari I named, hers Marcia."

We all greeted him in unison, and his eyes scanned the room. When he saw me, his smile revealed dimples, an infectious grin that made me smile back. He held the young girl's hand, but she was listless and didn't look at us.

Something caused Damari's expression to change. He looked as if he had seen a ghost and hastened to move the girl behind him in a protective stance. Clearly upset, he began shouting to Commander Portars in Arandan, pointing to...me? No, to Montor. I looked at Montor, and he appeared mortified, staring into his lap and covering his mouth.

"He remembers me from Xixsted. He is telling Portars that I am a filthy Lostai soldier," Montor said to me telepathically.

Commander Portars put his hand on Damari's shoulder and spoke to him in Arandan, trying to calm him down using a reassuring tone. It took a few minutes before Damari regained composure. Montor made space between us, inviting the young man and child to sit next to me. Damari only offered Montor an apprehensive nod as he sat down but wasn't shy with me at all.

"Mi glad fi see you. Mi never know seh mi would a see somebody from Earth again."

He spoke in Jamaican patois that I wasn't familiar with, so I gave him my undivided attention as he continued.

"Yuh talk English? Jamaica mi come from."

"Yes, I speak English. I'm from the United States, from Florida. My name is Mina. I was a hostage in Xixsted, like you."

"Nuh badda tell mi nutten bout dah place deh," he said, shaking his head.

It sounded like he didn't even want to hear the name Xixsted mentioned. I couldn't agree with him more.

"This is Montor, my fiancé. He helped us all escape that place, and the baby is our child."

"Him neva too nice to me when mi did deh deh. Nuff time him beat mi up."

I didn't understand the whole sentence, but it was clear that Montor had beaten him. I decided to lie to excuse Montor's bad behavior. I imagined how this strong, young man might have tried to stand up to him. Montor didn't take too well to people challenging his authority.

"Ummm, I'm so sorry to hear that. He was an undercover rebel spy, so he needed to play the part or the Lostai would suspect him."

In reality, keeping prisoners in line was one of Montor's tasks as the trusted assistant of Xixsted's cruel Commander Zorla.

"But believe me, he was the one who coordinated our escape from Xixsted." I turned my attention to the little girl. "Does Marcia speak English?"

"She talk English and Portuguese, but nowadays she nuh talk much."

Marcia appeared about six years old and had olive skin, dark eyes, and dark curly hair. She stared at her plate and began picking at her food.

"There was an older man with you, correct? What was his name?" I asked Damari.

"Him name Bernie. Him a good yute. Him dead a month ago, and now Marcia sad all the time."

Portars told us Marcia had become close to the third hostage from Earth, an older man. He apparently had reminded her of her grandfather. I turned my attention to Marcia.

"Hi, my name is Mina. You're a good eater. You definitely deserve dessert later, but if there is something on your plate that you don't like, you don't have to eat it. Like, for example, this vegetable here does not taste good to me at all."

She turned her head to look at me with such sad, dark eyes that it took all my willpower not to break down and cry.

"I don't like it either." It was barely a whisper.

"Well then, let's push it aside. I can serve you more of what you do like."

"Will I be in trouble?"

"Of course not! Have you been punished here with the Arandans?" I asked, looking around concerned.

"No, but I don't know if it's OK," she gave Montor a furtive glance and then averted her eyes, "in front of the monster."

I tried to contain my outrage as I spoke to Montor telepathically.

"These kids are terrified of you! What did you do to them?"

"I did nothing to her! Maybe she witnessed me roughing up the other one. I am sorry. What do you want from me? He was not following instructions, being cocky and confrontational."

"My heart breaks for them and what they have been through," I said, shaking my head.

"Just imagine how I feel! The good news is you are already rendering fruits on this mission. She is talking to you. I was told she had not spoken a word since the older Earthian died."

I turned again to Marcia.

"I know he seems scary and perhaps you have seen him be tough with others, but he was only pretending to trick the other people...the short, bald ones. Those are the real bad guys who took us away from our homes. He's the one who helped you escape that place. Look, he has a baby on his lap who is laughing and happy. He can't be a monster, right? Would you like to see the baby?"

"Mmmm. I think, no. It's a baby monster. And I remember now. He even told us his name was Monster."

I turned to Montor and made a face.

"Great, your name sounds like the word monster in our language," I said to Montor telepathically. He raised his eyebrows and looked away.

"No, actually, his name is Montor, not monster. You know, that is our baby. He is my boyfriend. We are going to be married," I said to Marcia.

"*Impossivel*," she said in Portuguese, shaking her head.

I took Josher on my lap, and Marcia cringed at first.

"Look at his eyes and then at mine, Marcia. What do you notice?"

I bounced Josher, and he giggled. Marcia inched closer to take a good look at him.

"I know. Your eyes are the same color, like *me!*"

Portuguese was close enough to Spanish that I understood.

"Yes, that's right, like honey. Not too many people have eyes that color, right? Montor's are—"

"Monster's eyes are yellow, like a dragon or a cat," she finished for me. "They're scary."

I decided to stop including Montor in our conversation.

"My baby's name is Josher. You know, he doesn't like that vegetable either. Tell me what you like the best and I'll serve you more of that."

"I like the meat and the bread!"

"That's Josher's favorite too!"

I spooned more of what she liked on her plate. Later, small individual sweet pies were served for dessert. Marcia liked them, so I gave her an extra one. While the adults (except me) enjoyed the strong after-meal Arandan coffee, I showed Marcia some of the small toys that we had brought along for Josher and asked her to help me entertain him. Josher soon won her over with his giggles and babbling. Most everyone got up to mingle and chat. I remained seated, distracted with Marcia and Josher, when I felt Montor's large hands on my shoulders. He bent over to nuzzle my hair and kissed me on the cheek while Marcia observed wide-eyed.

"Monster *is* your boyfriend," she acknowledged, an amazed look on her face. She became pensive for a moment. "You turned him into a nice monster, didn't you?"

She nodded, proud of herself for figuring that out all on her own.

I smiled.

"Yes, I did. That's why he helped us escape from the bad guys."

She looked up to him and smiled as well. His expression softened, and he knelt on one leg next to her, stroking her hair.

"Mina, please tell her I am so sorry for scaring her and assure her that will never happen again. Let her know we are all on the same team now. Tell her we will do our best to get her back home."

I relayed the message, and Marcia hooked her small arms around his neck. Montor caressed her cheek.

"Tell her I need to get back to the others," he said while gently extricating himself from her embrace. His eyes glistened as he excused himself and walked away. Although Montor's feelings ran deep, he didn't like to appear vulnerable or display his emotions outside of a very close circle of trust. Marcia's reactions moved him and consequently tugged at my soul as well. I wiped away a tear before Marcia could notice.

Before we could return to the *Barinta*, we still needed to resolve who on the crew would be assigned to learn about the transportals and eventually accompany Marcia back to Earth if we found one. I asked Lasarta to watch over Josher and Marcia while I joined the discussion.

"Mina, I was just suggesting to Commander Portars that Sotkari look enough like Earthians that Kindor could be our transportal expert and be the one to accompany Marcia back home. Kindor has agreed to do it."

"Kindor?" I said, shaking my head. "I do not think it would work. He is mute and does not understand any Earthian language. Also, he is not familiar with the geography."

Using his tablet, Kindor interjected, "I agree with Montor. This could be dangerous for Mina. I am sure I can learn the basics of the Earthian language between now and then. Plus, I really would not be interacting with anyone there. I only need to deliver Marcia back to her house."

"It will not work. He still will appear alien because of his skin and hair color."

"I do not understand. Damari and you have very different skin color."

"Yes, yes, but no one on Earth has grey skin. He would be very conspicuous."

The conversation reached a standstill. Montor's jaw clenched in frustration, his breathing getting heavier by the second. Determined that I not be assigned this responsibility, he lunged at Damari and poked him hard in the chest. Damari was caught off guard and fell back a step.

"You should be the one to go. Mina has a young child to take care of," shouted Montor, scowling.

"Stop it!" I grabbed Montor by the arm and tugged him hard towards me.

Everyone shared looks of disbelief. They were not used to someone putting Montor in his place, much less a female. I lowered my tone to try to diffuse the tension.

"Montor, I can take on this responsibility. I know I can. Damari has his reasons for being reluctant to commit to this assignment. If we want to have success, someone needs to embrace the role wholeheartedly. I can be that person."

Commander Portars chimed in with a stern voice but kind eyes. He placed a hand on Montor's shoulder.

"I understand your concern, Montor, but we all have made sacrifices. Your betrothed has a brave and dedicated soul. We need people like her engaged in our cause."

Montor inhaled and exhaled slowly to control his anger. I locked eyes with him.

"Montor, I want to help Marcia get home as soon as possible. She deserves that."

At the mention of Marcia's name, he lowered his eyes and relented.

"OK, let us plan on Mina being our crew's expert on the transportals. However, if later we find a better candidate for travel, I reserve the right to make my recommendation."

"Of course, Montor," said Portars.

Although I had closed the discussion, and despite my arguments, I also secretly found the prospect of traveling to Earth troubling.

I can't worry about that now. Marcia's parents must be heartbroken. We need to get her home.

After lunchtime, everyone resumed their duties. I left Josher with Montor and walked to a room designated Transportal Research, where I met Officer Xartor and Officer Na Nar, a male and female Arandan couple about my age. In my mind, I nicknamed them the Transportal Nerds. As a part of the Lostai Empire for decades now, Arandans were required to learn the Lostai language. The Transportal Nerds were fluent but with an accent. I was thankful they made a point to speak slowly as they explained the details about the transportals.

The Arandans had learned the location of four of these doorways to other worlds located far outside of their star system, but they suspected there were others closer by in their own quadrant. The four that they knew about were all on planets with extraordinary magnetic fields prone to electromagnetic storms like those on Fronidia. These transportals occurred in nature when certain magnetic fields pressed against each other and merged, but additional technology was required to take advantage of their potential for space travel. Lostai military guarded these portals to ensure they were used for their purposes only. However, every now and then, crime organizations and large corporations paid the Lostai vast sums of funds to use them as well.

As they shared this information, Xartor and Na Nar transferred to my tablet all the reference material they had put together so far.

"We hope we have organized our research in a way that is easy for you to understand," said Xartor. "You must be excited at the prospect of visiting your home planet."

He didn't know much about my background and was trying to be sociable, but his words only reminded me of the conflict tearing at my soul.

Our newest crew members returned to the *Barinta* with us that evening, and we assigned them quarters. We put Marcia in the room next to ours. I thought she might be afraid to sleep alone, but she insisted she was a big girl and used to sleeping in her own room. I was curious about Marcia's Sotkari Ta abilities. Holding her hand, I summoned my strongest motherly feelings and asked Marcia what she felt.

"I feel safe. I like being with you," she replied.

In return, I sensed her trusting energy. I showed her how to communicate telepathically. It was remarkable how quickly she grasped the concept and executed it.

"So, you see, if anything concerns you, we can talk to each

other even if we are in separate rooms. Montor and I believe Damari can do this also, but you need to be able to figure out who's who in your head. Every day, I can teach you a little more, if you like."

"Wow, Mina. We're like superheroes with special powers, right?"

"Yes, something like that, but even superheroes need to get some rest, so it's time for you to go to sleep."

I choked up when she hugged me, so I made sure she didn't see the tears in my eyes. When the Lostai took me from Earth, my son Bobby was nine years old, still young enough to want me to tuck him in each night. We would say prayers together first. I wondered if Josh (my husband on Earth) was taking care of this or if this part of Bobby's childhood was lost forever after my disappearance.

As Lasarta had predicted, Montor told me he was going to sleep in another room because he would be too tempted to break his promise of abstinence. I'd miss his strong embrace at night, but it was not an exaggeration on his part. It had been only weeks since we reunited after I had been hiding in Fronidia for six months. We were definitely still in honeymoon mode. After Montor left, I put Josher to sleep and then focused on studying the reference material that the Transportal Nerds had given me. The day had been an emotional one, and after a while, I felt I could use a glass of wine to relax before bed. I walked to the lounge and heard hushed voices that made me quiet my steps.

I peeked in the entrance and saw Officer Lorret sitting on a bench and Montor in front of her on one knee. There was no one else in the lounge. He eased the scarf to the side to expose her whole face. She looked down as if embarrassed, so I couldn't see her face, but I did see Montor caress her cheek with the back of his hand. It seemed like they were sharing a tender moment. Pangs of jealousy rocked me. He was my fiancé, she was his ex-girlfriend, and this just felt too intimate. I wondered why he hadn't mentioned anything to me about his previous relationship with her. I considered strolling in casually to see their reaction but decided against it.

I'll ask him about it tomorrow.

I returned to my room and into bed, telling myself not to jump to conclusions on what I had just witnessed. Morning greeted me with a headache since I didn't sleep well at all, but there was no time to dwell on it. I got Josher ready, checked on Marcia, and took them to the dining area for breakfast. Next stop was the conference room for our daily staff meeting. Montor arrived soon after. He approached me and caressed my cheek, as was his habit first thing every morning.

"Good morning, sweetness."

"Hello, how did you sleep?" I asked, searching his face for any unusual reaction.

His lips curled into a mischievous grin, and he bent to kiss my cheek.

"Not so good. I missed you."

I didn't get any guilty vibes from him, so I blurted out what was on my mind.

"Montor, last night I left the room to get a glass of wine, and I saw you talking to Lorret." I tried my best to keep my tone neutral.

He straightened up with a jerk.

"Yes, we spoke for a bit."

"I know you and she dated. I am surprised you did not mention that to me before adding her to our crew." I tilted my face up to study his expression. His eyebrows furrowed, and I detected impatience in his yellow eyes.

"That was a long time ago." He couldn't avoid rolling his eyes. "There is nothing about her that you should worry about."

The fact that my questions irked him only made me

wonder even more what they were talking about, and I still didn't know why he hadn't mentioned her to me. Before I could press him on the issue, others entered the room, and he took his chance to dismiss our conversation. I sighed, annoyed at him for leaving me with unanswered questions, but vowed to bring up the topic again the next time we had privacy.

After the meeting, we boarded the pods to head back to Penstarox. I purposely chose not to board the same one as Montor and spoke very little with the others. When we arrived at the base, Commander Portars immediately asked Montor to meet with him. Everyone else dispersed to their assigned stations. As I headed over to meet with the Transportal Nerds, Kindor grabbed my hand and pulled me aside. I prayed no one saw him. In Arandan culture, it was inappropriate for a male to touch a female who had a partner. I heard his concerned voice in my mind.

"Mina, are you OK? You seem distant. I thought I noticed some tension between you and Montor when I walked into the conference room."

I put Josher in his rolling playpen and asked Marcia to watch him.

"Kindor, you know me too well. Let me ask you, have you spoken to Officer Lorret?"

"Yes, she met with me yesterday afternoon to get my medical history, and she performed a physical examination."

"What do you think of her?"

He cocked his head with a quizzical expression.

"I find her to be very professional. She explained to me that she was not able to complete her medical certification but has many years of experience. Why do you ask?"

"Well, she does not like me at all. Lasarta, Foxor, and Colora all know her because she and Montor had a romantic relationship years ago...and...and last night..." I hesitated.

"What, Mina?"

I explained to him what I had observed between Montor and Lorret in the lounge. He remained thoughtful for a few minutes before reacting.

"Mina, let us imagine you and I were to go our separate ways, I found you ten revolutions from now, and you were covering a scar on your face. It would be normal that, as a concerned friend, I would be interested to know what happened. As much as a part of me might enjoy you having problems with Montor, you probably are reading too much into this."

"Maybe, but the thing that bothers me the most is that he has not told me anything about her. He could have advised me we are taking on a crew member with whom he once had romantic ties. Why has he not mentioned it?"

"Well, I can see where you would be curious about that. Find the right moment and ask him."

"Yes, that is exactly what I intend to do."

"OK, Mina. Remember, I am always here for you if you need me."

"Thank you, Kindor. Just talking to you helps."

I walked to the Transportal Research room with Marcia and Josher in tow. It was a busy day as I tried to absorb as much information as possible regarding the transportals while taking care of the children. Montor and Commander Portars did not join us for lunch. Kindor, Officer Lorret, and Colora were sitting together when I arrived. I sat by them. Kindor put Josher on his lap, taking advantage of the opportunity to spend time with him.

"Mina, tomorrow you and Montor will be going on that journey into the wilderness thing, correct?" asked Colora.

"Yes, I do not know what to expect. Did you do the same when you married Jortan?"

"Yes, I did. Not really my thing. Getting all grimy and sweaty and such, but Jortan insisted, and I was willing to do anything for him. Well, first thing when you get back, you and I have an appointment. I will need to get you ready for your wedding. You will require plenty of attention after spending all that time roughing it in the outdoors."

Officer Lorret did not say much and focused on her meal, but just before I got ready to return to my work, she addressed me. It was the first time she had even acknowledged me.

"Mina, I am afraid I will not have time to conduct your physical before your wedding, so I will set a time once we are in flight again. I will also examine your son at that time."

I smiled, thanked her, and tried to be friendly.

"Officer Lorret, if there is anything I can do to help you get acclimated to your new quarters or position on the *Barinta*, please do not hesitate to let me know."

"Yes, of course. Montor told me the same, but I have experience in living under harsh conditions, so I am sure I will not have any issues."

I nodded politely and gathered the children.

"I must get back to my duties."

I didn't see much of Montor the rest of the day either. In the evening, he came to play with Josher for a bit and then advised I should get to bed due to the early start the next day.

"Montor, I feel like we left our conversation this morning open-ended. I would like to talk more about it."

There's that impatient look again.

He turned away from me, as if trying to reset his expression before turning back and answering me.

"Tomorrow, we will have plenty of time to talk as we walk in the jungle."

"I guess." My face scrunched up. Montor ignored it.

"Mina, I will see you tomorrow just before sunrise. Lasarta will take care of Josher. Dress comfortably as we will be doing quite a bit of walking. Bring an extra set of clothing and whatever you think you need to be comfortable for sleeping overnight in the outdoors. Keep in mind, though, it is better to travel light as we will be carrying everything we bring on our backs. Goodnight, sweetness."

He bent over to kiss me on the lips before rushing out of the room.

3

KINDOR

I accompanied my typical morning meal of bread, cream, and tea with thoughts of Mina. I should not have allowed myself the luxury of thinking about her, but it was inevitable.

Will she be safe sleeping overnight in the thick Arandan jungle? Strange, the customs of these people. Of course, she will not be alone. They will be together.

Mina's quick decision to marry Montor was somehow my fault. Had I not gone into her room that night and propositioned her, maybe she would have stayed longer with my family. Or if Karixta, my jealous ex-girlfriend, had not informed Lostai military that Mina was alive and in Fronidia, we would not have needed to rush off and leave.

I once advised Mina not to second-guess her destiny, so why am I indulging in these doubts? Had I not met her, if all this had not happened, I would not be involved now in liberating my planet from Lostai rule.

War was about to engulf the whole sector. In all honesty, if I had been so lucky as to be Mina's partner, I would have wanted to celebrate my wedding sooner rather than later too.

"Eating alone?"

I looked up. Officer Lorret sat across from me with her food tray. I glanced at her before I continued eating quietly. Not in the mood for socializing, I was pleased that Officer Lorret did not speak for a long while. Then she broke the silence.

"It seems you and Mina are close. I saw you take her by the hand yesterday morning. Luckíly, Montor did not see you."

Montor was proud of his physical strength, but I was sure my expression made it clear that he did not intimidate me at all. She chuckled.

"Have you known her for a long time?"

Lorret did not understand sign language, so I typed in my tablet and audio emitted with my replies.

"Her shuttle crash-landed near the small village where my family lived. She had intended to reach the refugee center in the capital city of Fronidia but got caught in an electromagnetic storm that veered her way off course. She lived with us for six lunar cycles."

"Interesting. Are all people on your planet mute?"

"No, only those of us who are fully evolved."

"Fully evolved, huh. Sounds like a pretty snobby way of referring to oneself."

"I do not mean to be pretentious. It is merely the reality of things. We call ourselves Sotkari Ta. I am a pureblood Sotkari Ta because all my ancestors are fully evolved. If we train properly, we have the abilities of telepathy, telekinesis, healing, mind control, and, most importantly, blocking."

She appeared more focused on her meal than on my reply but caught the tail end of it and, I believe out of courtesy, asked, "What is blocking?"

"We can stop others with telepathic abilities from accessing our minds. Some of our population is known as Sotkari Pasi because they are telepathic but can speak out loud and lack the other abilities. Others have none of these abilities."

Lorret continued to be unimpressed.

"Really? So much power and yet your people allowed the Lostai to take control of your planet."

She is just as annoying as Montor. Are all Arandans the same? Well, Lasarta and Foxor seem nice enough.

"The Lostai took advantage of our divisions. Some Sotkari Ta who were upset with the Sotkari government assisted them. The Lostai are also ruthless at blackmail. They will find someone vulnerable in your family and threaten them if you do not comply with their orders."

She looked down to her lap for a second, then corrected her posture. When our eyes met again, any emotion from her expression had been deleted. "So, you said your family lives in Fronidia now? How long have they been there?"

"My family stayed as long as possible in Sotkar trying to help in the struggle to regain control of our planet. My grandparents, aunts, uncles, and siblings were all killed or taken away by the Lostai. Finally, my father brought my mother, niece, and me to Fronidia. He went back to find my sister and was also killed. That was twenty revolutions ago."

Lorret tucked at the scarf that covered half of her face and for the first time her expression softened.

"The Lostai are an immoral race. It will be good if our peoples can join together and take back control of our planets."

"Would you like to try my Sotkari tea?" I asked, feeling a little more at ease. She nodded yes, and I brought a carafe and two fresh cups.

It was an off day at Penstarox. I decided I might as well relax a bit and get to know her better, especially recalling Mina's comment about Lorret's previous relationship with Montor.

Maybe I can acquire some information for Mina.

"It is much sweeter than I am accustomed to, but I like it," Lorret said.

"Since when do you know Montor?" I asked.

She furrowed her brow.

"What makes you ask that?"

"Mina saw you two talking the other evening. She was not too happy about it."

She smirked at first, but her expression became nostalgic, yellow eyes looking through me.

"Montor and I dated a long time ago. It was a brief relationship. I was too young. That was ten revolutions ago. I am surprised he is marrying Mina. She is so...different."

She tried to sound diplomatic, but it was clear she did not think Mina worthy of Montor. On this point, we would have to agree to disagree. I considered him to be arrogant, crude, and vulgar, lacking, in my mind, when it came to honor and integrity, but they did seem to have a powerful connection, and I believed he truly loved her. Although Mina and I had forged a special bond, it was only a platonic friendship, and I respected her choice.

"Montor is very lucky to have Mina as a partner. Anyone would be."

Lorret's eyes narrowed, an impatient look on her face that showed she could not disagree more.

"They have nothing in common."

"They both have a full set of embedded Sotkari Ta genes."

"Oh yes, I heard something of this. The young Earthians we rescued also have these embedded genes. I am curious how this came to be."

I poured us a second cup.

"When the Lostai invaded Sotkar, many of our elder scientists escaped to other sectors and even other galaxies. They feared our people's evolution would be thwarted or that we might even go extinct, given the Lostai slaughtered many of us in the beginning who refused to work with them. No other species in this galaxy had exhibited these abilities. The scientists figured out how to embed their genes in the embryos of unsuspecting people on planets with less advanced technology. They used invisible energy pulses transmitted randomly from outside the host planet's atmosphere. Usually, it was a one-time spread only affecting pregnant females at a very specific stage of pregnancy. Their children passed those traits to their offspring."

Now, I had her undivided attention.

"Amazing. So, Mina and Montor have the same abilities as you?"

"They have the same potential, but it requires training and following a lifelong regimen of practice. A Sotkari Ta elder mentored Montor since his childhood. I must admit he is very skilled. Mina only recently became aware of her abilities."

"I see." After a second or two of silence, she changed the subject. "I guess we all are supposed to be getting ready for tomorrow's wedding." She could not hide the irritation in her eyes.

"That is true. I have no idea what to expect. Is there a dress code?"

"The females will all wear red, but considering we are on a rebel base, I am sure all the men will dress in full military regalia."

"Hmm. I do not think it is respectful or appropriate that I wear an Arandan military uniform. I would like to wear something representative of my people, but I think the reproducer on this spaceship is limited."

"No worries, we can go in the transport pod to a nearby city and be back by evening."

Her offer surprised me.

"Is it safe for me to be walking around your cities? I do not want to attract the attention of any Lostai patrolling the area."

"The Lostai presence on Aranda is limited to the capital cities. It should be fine, but let us check with Commander Portars."

We took a transport pod to Penstarox and found Commander Portars giving Colora a personal tour of the facilities. They seemed startled to run into us.

"Is everything OK?" Commander Portars asked. "I expected everyone to be resting today. I...I...uhhh...was just showing Colora the defense systems and holographic rooms that we put in place with Jortan's fundraising and donations."

"Everything is fine, sir. Kindor is looking to acquire appropriate attire for tomorrow's wedding. I suggested that I could take him in the transport pod to the nearest city," explained Lorret.

A notification on Commander Portars's tablet distracted him. He checked the screen and shook his head, appearing concerned.

"Problem, sir?"

"Some bad weather is coming through sooner than expected. I think it may impact Montor's calculations for his jungle trek."

Does this mean Mina might be in danger?

I tapped my tablet to communicate.

"Will it be dangerous for them in the jungle?"

"Hopefully not," he replied, but his concerned expression did not allay my worries. "I do not think you should travel off the island today. We have upgraded our databases. Kindor should find our reproducers here adequate for his needs."

"Yes, sir," Lorret said. "Come, Kindor. I'll take you to the main reproduction area."

I fought the urge to ask the Commander more questions about the problems Montor and Mina might encounter in the jungle.

As we walked to the reproduction area, Lorret asked, "So, what do you have in mind for tomorrow?"

"I think I would like to wear the traditional Sotkari military uniform, dating from the time we first battled against the

Lostai. It might seem a little old-fashioned, but it feels right for me."

The database did have a record of the uniform I wanted. It was royal blue with a white sash around the waist and a smaller one around the neck. The tight-fitting jacket sported two rows of shiny silver-toned buttons down the front. Lorret convinced me to try it on and model it for her. I was completely out of my element.

Does she think I am like Montor, who always struts around like a bird during a mating dance?

I looked everywhere except at her, embarrassed as she studied me.

"Do not be so shy. You have a nice physique," I could hear the smirk in her voice, "for an alien. The fit accentuates your broad shoulders, and the color complements your blue eyes and hair. I think it is an excellent choice."

"OK, good," I said hastily. "What would you like to do now?"

"Well, since we cannot travel off the base, let us use one of the holographic rooms so I can show you some of the natural beauty of Aranda."

After our holographic explorations, we shared dinner. We seemed to be at the onset of an unlikely friendship. I enjoyed her company. She confided a bit more of what happened between her and Montor back when they dated. I was not sure what to make of it, but I decided I would share with Mina when she got back.

4

MINA

We began our trek into the jungle at the crack of dawn. It took us about two hours to traverse the clearing where we had landed the *Barinta* and enter the jungle. The coloring of the plants, trees, and vegetation differed from those on Earth. Instead of green, the leaves, vines, and stems boasted various shades of orange, the tree trunks, mostly olive-toned. We came across an array of flowers and fruits in every remaining color. Montor pointed out that I should avoid a shrub with blue thorny flowers that caused a nasty rash. The crisp cool breeze didn't match the lush flora. I had expected higher temperatures and humidity. Montor explained that during other times of the year the weather in this area was very hot with months of continuous rainstorms. We were lucky to have arrived during the short autumn-like season with cooler temperatures and rain limited to a few hours per day.

We walked without much catching my attention other than the sounds of birds, insects, and our boots crunching the jungle floor. Montor used a laser gun to clear a path through the thick vegetation. Every few steps, a break in the canopy allowed rays of sunshine to sneak in. Montor was on some sort of timetable because he kept us going for about four hours straight until I asked if we could stop to rest. We sat down, and he peeled some fruit he had gathered on the way. Instead of carrying bottles or canteens of water, we used small thirst-quenching pods. As we ate the fruit and sucked on the pods, I remembered we never finished our conversation about Lorret. I took advantage of the break to ask him.

"Montor, the fact that you didn't tell me about Lorret is still on my mind, and you seemed irritated when I asked about it. Why? I mean, you must admit that it is natural I would be curious, especially when I saw you talking to her privately and caressing her cheek."

He inhaled deeply and cracked his knuckles, looking everywhere except at me.

"As you already know, Lorret and I had a romantic relationship, but that was a long time ago, and there is not much more to say about it."

"But why did you keep that from me?"

"I did not want anything to upset you right before our wedding."

"You have something bottled up inside regarding your previous relationship with her. I think you should tell me, so I do not reach the wrong conclusions. That would most definitely ruin my mood for the wedding."

His whole face turned into a scowl, clearly uncomfortable discussing this topic.

"I should have never pursued her. She was barely an adult, and I was much older. Even at that young age, she was already a rebel committed to freeing Aranda from Lostai rule. I guess that was what attracted me to her. Of course, she had no idea I was a Lostai soldier, or she probably would have killed me in my sleep. Lorret could not understand why I was not willing to openly join the Arandan rebel forces and fight the Lostai, considering..."

He hesitated.

"Yes, considering what?"

His lips pressed into a line, and he shook his head before continuing.

"I might as well tell the entire story, now that you have me baring my soul." He gulped hard. "Mina, the Lostai murdered my family. Lorret knew this. Her family was from our clan. She had heard the story of what happened to them from an older family member."

Gosh, I feel guilty now. As Lasarta had mentioned, he's upset to admit he knowingly served in the same Lostai army that murdered his family. This isn't about Lorret.

I didn't want to betray the fact that Lasarta had already confided this to me, so I pretended this was the first I had heard of it.

"Oh Montor, I understand now why this is a tough thing for you to discuss." I took his balled fist in my hand and rubbed my thumb across his knuckles, trying to comfort him. "You do not need to expand on the topic."

He continued anyway.

"Lorret was disappointed that I would not join the rebel forces with her and ended up accepting a risky mission as an assistant medic on the front lines of an area where Arandans and Lostai were openly fighting each other. I never heard from her again until recently when I first met with Commander Portars. He talked to me about a medic stationed at Penstarox that had requested to be assigned to a crew with an active role in our cause. He did not know our history and decided she should join us."

Our eyes met, his filled with pain.

"When you saw us talking, she was filling me in on what happened to her. The Lostai captured and punished her for resisting arrest, scarring her face as they did your back. I must admit this has brought about guilty feelings in me, making me wonder if I had joined the rebellion back then, maybe I could have protected her. Other Arandan rebel forces eventually rescued her, and she has been working as a doctor on Penstarox ever since."

I felt like someone had shoved a small ball in my throat.

Wait. Maybe this is about Lorret after all.

"Montor, do...do you have feelings for her? As you once told me, you can have an active role in Josher's life without having to marry me."

His expression became impatient again, and instead of replying, he looked up to gauge the position of the sun.

"We must be on our way. We need to reach the river by midday."

He stood and began walking without saying a word. I caught up with him.

"Is that the end of this conversation? You did not answer me. Do you want to be with her?"

He stopped dead in his tracks and crossed his arms.

"Mina, sometimes you can be so self-absorbed."

"What do you mean? We were in the middle of a conversation."

"Do you ever consider stopping and looking at things from my point of view?"

He sounded cranky and sarcastic, so now I walked ahead, ignoring him. Grabbing my arm, he stopped me and made me turn around to face him.

"Do not be rough with me!" I said, yanking my arm out of his grip.

His expression reflected so many feelings at once. Worry, anger, impatience.

"Mina, while you are interrogating me about Lorret, have you thought about what I might be feeling at the dawn of our wedding? Let us examine my position for a moment. First of all, I have led my close friends and family to believe you are a widow because in my culture it is dishonorable to take another male's partner without fighting for her. My relationship with you is as if I were taking advantage of a disabled person. Your Earth husband has no chance to defend his position. Furthermore, let us think about what might happen if our mission is successful. It is likely we will find and take control of some of the transportals. We may find a path back to your planet and ask you to accompany someone like little Marcia back home. Then what? Will you come back to Josher and me or be tempted to stay there and reunite with your Earth family?"

His breathing became heavier now.

"Do you know the most shameful thing that can happen to an Arandan male is for his spouse to leave him without even having a chance to fight for her? As if I do not feel dishonorable enough for having spent my whole adult life as a Lostai soldier. Yet I am willing to take the risk of facing all this dishonor and shame to be with you and have you as my wife. Of course, I cannot share this with anyone. I have to keep this worry buried deep inside."

He avoided my eyes.

"I have told you before. I will not abandon my husband and child," I said in a quiet voice.

He grabbed me by the shoulders and stared down at me, his words filled with venom.

"Well, is that not exactly what you will be doing if you ignore the chance to reunite with your Earth family?"

How dare he throw that in my face!

Every day, I struggled with the gut-wrenching choice between staying with Josher and the possibility of returning to my Earth children, between falling in love with Montor and knowing I left a husband on Earth. His comment angered me. I stepped closer and shoved him hard with the full force of my frustration. He was caught off guard by my sudden violence and had to take a step back to regain his balance. I even surprised myself as I glared up at him, my whole body shaking with rage, each syllable spoken at a higher pitch.

"You have no idea how I suffer each and every day not knowing what has become of my Earth children and how much I miss them. The guilt of one day possibly having to choose between them and Josher is killing me, but I love him too. Truthfully, he needs me the most right now. Why are you torturing me and torturing yourself?"

Before I could stop myself, shouting morphed into crying. I brought my hands up to cover my face. He pulled my hands away.

"Yes, I am tortured, Mina. You have done this to me, so please do not ask me if I want to be with any other person. I only wish to be with you."

As I stood there looking up into his troubled yellow eyes, and despite my anger, my soul exploded with love for him. I was happy with the family that he, Josher, and I had formed, but my pounding heart also held another truth. He had hit a raw nerve. It had been two years since the Lostai kidnapped me.

My love for Montor is strong, but I'm not sure how I'll react if I find myself back home. Why hurt him with that truth when returning to Earth is still so improbable?

Instead, I put my arms around his waist and pressed my face against his chest.

"Montor, I accepted your marriage proposal because I love you. Yes, my Earth family will always occupy an important part of my heart, but now my place is at your side. You do not have to worry. I will not leave you."

I stood on my toes to reach my fingers around his neck, and he bent down to kiss me on the lips.

Cupping my face in his hands, he whispered, "Mina, what

am I going to do? I did not expect to develop such powerful feelings for you. As an adult, I never felt fear until I met you. Now, my heart, my honor, my whole destiny is in your hands."

Our eyes remained locked for a few seconds until, shaking his head, he checked the sun's position again and raised his voice. "We should get going."

The way to the river was up a rocky hillside. Before reaching the top, I already could hear gurgling, splashing water. Once there, I couldn't believe my eyes. The steep mountainous wall on the other side of the hill dropped at least a hundred feet to a violent rush of red, foamy liquid bordered by giant rocks and boulders extending as far as I could see.

"Montor, the view is spectacular, but how are we crossing?"

He pointed sideways to a bridge.

We walked across the top of the hill for another half hour to reach it. Once we arrived, I was flabbergasted again. The dilapidated swinging bridge was a sorry sight with several of the rusty slats missing and a flimsy railing. I guessed the bridge stretched on for at least two miles.

"This seems risky," I said in a worried voice.

"I went over it yesterday just fine, but," he looked at the sky again, "the weather is changing more quickly than I had expected. We need to hurry before the storm comes through. I can carry your backpack."

"No, let me carry mine. Lasarta explained the backpacks represent how we need to share the burdens of married life. Plus, it is not a good idea for all our supplies to be with one of us. I will do my best to keep up with you."

"OK, sweetness, then let us not waste any time."

Back on Earth, I hated crossing these types of bridges. I used the mental strength I had developed from my Sotkari Ta training to stay focused and ignore the fear. Although looking down made me nervous, I needed to stay aware of which slats were missing. We kept a quick pace for about fifteen minutes until dark clouds rolled in, reminding me of the sudden thunderstorms that were common in Florida. Wind picked up and it began to pour. I shuddered with each clap of thunder. The slats became slippery, and the bridge rocked violently. Montor turned back to check on me and didn't realize there were several slats missing in that spot. The poor visibility, the momentum of the swinging, and the loss of balance created the perfect equation for the worst possible scenario. Montor fell through the empty space to the rushing river below. Midair, he threw off his backpack.

"Mina, grab it!" I heard his voice in my mind. "I can swim to the other side. Meet me there."

I used my telekinetic abilities to bring the backpack into my arms and throw it over one shoulder while carefully jumping over the space Montor had just fallen through. Having surpassed the first hurdle, it took all my willpower to avoid worrying about whether Montor could survive a drop into a raging river from that altitude. Instead, I remained focused on getting to the other side. The bridge continued to swing, but there were hardly any more missing slats. Disregarding the whistle of the wind and the rain flooding my eyes, I maintained the consistent rhythm of my boots hitting the slats. The extra backpack taxed me, and I was out of breath. After a half hour, I saw the other side. Seeing the end of the bridge helped steady my nerves. It took me another ten minutes to get there. I ran several yards down the hill to secure the backpacks and came back to the edge to scan the river below for any sign of Montor.

I called out to him telepathically, overcome with anxiety when I received no reply. The mountain wall was not as steep and smooth as the other side. I decided to descend to the river and get a better look. As I started down, I heard his voice in my mind.

"Mina...did you...make it...over...the bridge?"

"Yes! Should I climb down to help you? Where are you?"

No immediate reply, but I discerned his form approaching the riverbank. The river waters rushed as if on a life-or-death mission. Favoring one arm, he grabbed onto a boulder to steady himself and pulled out of the raging water. I didn't wait another second to start down climbing, alternating looking for hand and foot holds on the rocks and keeping an eye on Montor's location. I made it to the riverbank and quickly headed towards him. He had not reached the shore yet and was resting on the boulder when he caught sight of me.

"Mina, do not go into the water! The current is strong, and there are river creatures that can harm you. I will get to you...only...need...to...catch my breath."

After a few minutes, he stood on the boulder and surveyed the area. Having identified a viable path by stepping on rocks and boulders, he made it to the edge. I ran to him.

"Are you OK?" I asked, out of breath.

"Yes, I am fine. We need to get away from here before the river swells."

His ripped left shirtsleeve revealed a big gaping wound. I covered my mouth. Blood flowed out in a way that made my stomach churn.

"My God, you're injured!" I shouted in English.

Montor cocked his head, not understanding, and then I repeated it in Lostai. Without thinking twice, I took off my shirt and used it to create a tourniquet. The icy rain shocked my skin.

"Sweetness, now is clearly not a good time to seduce me."

He tried to joke, but I could tell he was weak. At a slow pace, I helped him climb up the ledge. We reached the top and scampered down the hill, where I grabbed the backpacks.

"I need to tend to your injury. Is there a good place for us to take cover, or should we camp here?"

"Let us go farther into the jungle where the canopy can shield us a bit from the rain."

We walked for another half hour and used the portable reproduction device in Montor's backpack to create a good-sized tent. Although this trip was meant to be rustic, we were allowed certain leeway in using technology. Once we were sheltered from the elements, I looked for the medical kit. The instruments were similar to the ones from my Lostai military training. One device took a snapshot of the patient's DNA and physiology and served as a diagnostic tool. It sent information to a large rectangular object that looked metallic but was pliable. The Lostai called it a healing pad. The sheet adhered to the wound and repaired tissue, muscle, tendons, nerves, and even bones.

I didn't say much as I worked on repairing Montor's injury. The whole process took about half hour. By then, the rain had tapered off. In the meantime, I helped Montor to clean up and change into dry clothing. He was weak from blood loss, so I reproduced a thick soup and made him drink plenty of water. After he ate, I peeled off the pad. To my relief, the wound had healed nicely.

It was only then that I became conscious of my own shivering in my wet pants and undershirt. I felt Montor's hand on my shoulder.

"Sweetness, thank you so much for taking care of me, but now you must take care of yourself, or you will get sick."

I changed clothes under the scrutiny of Montor's watchful eyes.

"Mina, it is not nice to tease me, getting nude like that when I cannot have you."

"Calm down, big boy. You need to rest. Tell me, how did you get injured?"

"There is a carnivorous animal that swims in the river called a *tomdarox*. If they feel you are intruding in their territory, they will attack."

I sat close to him and leaned my head on his shoulder.

"I was so worried for you, Montor."

"I thought I had to worry about keeping you safe. Instead, you have taken good care of me. I remember how, the first time we were together, I quickly reached the conclusion that we could be an unstoppable pair. I was right on target."

He put his arms around me and kissed me slowly with such tenderness that I lost my breath. Once I regained my composure, I asked him about the remainder of the trip.

"We have had enough excitement for one trip and have fulfilled at least half of our purpose. We can relax here the rest of the afternoon. As soon as the sun is up tomorrow, we will head back. I do not expect it to be rainy in the morning, so going over the bridge again should not be a problem. We will be back nice and early, so you can get yourself ready for the wedding."

I encouraged Montor to take a nap and save his energy for the trek back the next morning. I also rested but, after a few hours, woke up needing a bio break, and the tent did not come equipped with such facilities. I stepped out of the tent, turned off the force field to go further in the brush for privacy, and turned it back on to protect Montor as he slept.

While I took care of business, the sound of twigs snapping caught my attention. I hurried to finish and pull up my pants.

Whatever it is, it's coming quick and getting close.

As I went to grab my laser gun, I sensed a sudden *whish,* and something knocked me down. My head hit a rock, leaving me dazed and disoriented.

I regained consciousness to find myself crushed under an enormous creature, a dull pain and cold sensation on my collarbone. Blood covered my chest, and I began punching the animal like a maniac.

Intimidating roars replaced predatory silence. The large bearlike body was covered in wet black fur with a moldy odor. Putrid breath and wild red eyes completed its terrifying appearance. Fear impeded my ability to focus and call upon my telekinetic abilities. When I tried to scream, no sound came out of my throat. A few more creatures stalked behind the one on top of me. Finally, I found my voice and shouted out to Montor.

I saw laser fire, heard yelps, and smelled burnt fur. The creature that had me pinned turned around to assess what was happening to the rest of the pack. It stomped all over my body with its heavy paws, ripping the cloth of my shirt and raking my skin with its claws. The pressure its weight exerted on my chest and throat and the energy I spent trying to fight it off me made me lightheaded.

The laser fire came closer, and the creature slumped off me. Strong arms lifted me up and I knew I was safe. Back in the tent, it was Montor's turn to tend to my injuries. Lasarta's instructions regarding the importance of expressing gratitude for each other on this trip came back to mind.

"Montor, I am so thankful I can always count on you to protect me. I am sorry. I should have known better than to go outside of the force field."

"I feel terrible, Mina. I did not think those creatures would come out of the river after us. I am not so familiar with the animals of this area."

I winced as he cleaned my wounds and thought about the bruises that surely would mark my body the next day, our wedding day.

"I cannot believe this has happened and that you will have to see my body damaged this way on our wedding night."

He stroked my hair.

"Do not worry, we will have you all healed up soon, but even if we did not have the medical technology, you are always perfect in my eyes."

His answer reminded me of the permanent scars on both our bodies. When I escaped from Renna One with Montor's help, I had to injure him to make it look like he had been ambushed.

"Montor, the Lostai purposely left my back scarred so I could remember their punishments, but why did you not properly erase the scars of when I was forced to injure you?"

"When you left Renna One, besides the dress that you will wear tomorrow, the scars were the only thing I had left of you, so I preferred to keep them."

I rubbed his cheek with the back of my hand. He worked tirelessly the next few hours attending my injuries. Sure enough, by evening, I felt better with no evidence on my body of my encounter with the *tomdarox*. We cuddled on a thin mattress with our laser guns nearby. I heard animal howls and growls in the distance but felt secure in Montor's arms.

"I love you."

"I love you more, Mina."

5

MINA

Anxious to get our wedding day going, Montor had us heading back to the base before the sun was up. The Arandan sunrise treated my eyes to a spectacular battle of colors. Lavender, blue, and pink streaks crept over the horizon, consuming the dark purple night. Bluish, smoky gas clouds lined in gold glided across the sky before a blood-red ball of light popped out, allowing the daytime yellow sky to finally win the war.

The approach to the bridge brought back memories of the previous day's incidents, and my stomach knotted up. Luckily, no wind or rain made for an easy crossing. As we walked through the jungle, Montor explained that three holographic rooms on the military base would be used for the wedding activities: one to simulate an Arandan temple, one for the banquet, and one for our wedding night. Tradition required us to spend the night in the same location where the ceremony was held. He asked if I preferred a particular location to simulate for our wedding night. I thought about how many places even on Earth I had not yet visited, and here he was asking me to pick among so many possible planets and star systems.

"Honestly, I have been to such few places in this...actually, any galaxy."

"But is there an ambiance you prefer?"

"I have always loved the ocean and the beach."

"Perfect," he said, a wide smile showing his approval. "My clan's ancestral territory has an extensive ocean coastline. We will simulate one of the beaches that is well known across the galaxy for its beauty."

"Sounds wonderful, Montor. I very much am looking forward to seeing it."

"Mina, there is something else we should talk about. In our culture, an elder male of the bride's family accompanies and delivers her to her new husband. It can be her father, her older brother, or even an uncle."

"Yes, we have a similar tradition on Earth."

"Well, since you have no family members here, we need to assign a surrogate for that duty. The closest you have to such a family member is Kindor. I mean, you lived under the same roof with him for quite some time without being in a romantic relationship. Right?" He emphasized the last word and quickly added, "I plan to ask Kindor to take on that role for the wedding. What do you think?"

As benevolent as the request sounded, I knew Montor was still at least a little jealous of Kindor and looked forward to rubbing our marriage in his face. I supposed Kindor harbored some resentment towards Montor, too. I didn't want to offend anyone and felt presumptuous trying to explain my concern.

"I do not know. I would hate to put him in an uncomfortable position."

"Why would he feel uncomfortable? I thought he would be honored," asked Montor with the most innocent expression he could muster. "Well, I suppose if you dislike the idea, I will have to ask someone else, perhaps Commander Portars. It could not be Foxor as he is considered of my family. Hmmm, I wonder if Kindor would actually be offended that we did not ask him."

"I'm torn on this, but you bring up a valid point." I rubbed my face with both hands, conflicted. "Maybe it might be easier for me to ask Kindor, but I am afraid he might agree just to please me."

Montor's brow furrowed, and he sucked his teeth with impatience as I danced around the fact that Kindor was in love with me.

"This should not be such a big deal. And you wonder why he irritates me. What is the problem, Mina?"

"I do not want to hurt his feelings."

The line between his brows became deeper.

"Our wedding is not news to him or to anyone. Do you think he is hoping you will change your mind?"

"No, no, but I know how you can be sometimes."

He pretended to be offended.

"I have no idea what you are talking about."

Of course, he did.

I took a deep breath.

"OK, go ahead and ask him but promise me you will be polite. If you notice he is uncomfortable with the idea, do not press him on it or become sarcastic."

"Sure, Mina. Of course."

I detected a tinge of mischief in his eyes and hoped he would keep his promise.

We arrived back to the *Barinta* before midday. Montor delivered me to Colora and left, explaining that I would not see him until the wedding ceremony, which was scheduled for just before the typical dinnertime hour. Before I submitted myself to Colora's care, I baked the small cake that would be part of our wedding vows exchange. Foxor had already given me the amulet to place inside.

When I returned to Colora, I explained to her everything

that happened during our time in the jungle. She carefully examined my entire body for any bruises or blemishes that Montor might have missed before she set out to give me the ultimate skin, hair, nail, and massage treatments. These were all meant to relax me, but it was of no use. In a few hours, I would pronounce words of lifelong commitment to a new husband. Yet far away on Earth, a man wondered what happened to his wife.

Can I really just slough off my past like dead skin and move on?

The time to head out to the military base arrived fast. Colora did an exquisite job, styling my hair and applying makeup and a shimmering lotion all over my body.

"Mina, you look even more stunning than the day I first met you. I need to finish getting ready myself now. Someone is waiting to escort you to the base. I will follow in the other pod once I am done," said Colora.

I grabbed the cake and walked to the pod docking area. Kindor faced away from my direction and turned around as soon as he heard my steps. He was dressed in a royal blue military uniform I wasn't familiar with. I later learned it was a traditional Sotkari military uniform dating from the time they battled against the Lostai. He wore his hair slicked back and tied into a tail with a white band, making his chiseled features even more prominent. The blue color of his clothing complemented his gorgeous eyes. I was always taken aback whenever I realized how handsome he was.

He had never seen me dressed and made up for this type of occasion and literally tripped over his feet, causing me to look away, embarrassed for the both of us.

"*Kantarext!*" he exclaimed.

"What? What is it?" I asked.

He slapped his palm against his forehead and then stood stiffly, putting both hands on his hips.

"Mina, you have me feeling like an adolescent meeting a

beautiful female for the first time. You look amazing. Hurry, let us go before I decide to do something crazy."

I couldn't help but smile at the compliment.

When we arrived at the base, Kindor went over what to expect, although Lasarta had explained most of it to me already. Someone contacted Kindor to confirm that everything and everyone was in place, so we walked over to the holographic room that simulated an Arandan temple. As we entered, we found people lined up in queues facing each other. All the males were dressed in Arandan military uniforms. All the females wore elegant, long red dresses with flowing tails. Colora was the only exception wearing a cropped red blouse and long skirt, exposing her midriff and the tattoo I now understood to be a symbol for the Arandan rebel movement.

Montor stood in front of one of the lines, a towering figure dressed in a more regal version of the Arandan military garb with precious metal and jeweled ornamentation. Brushed out hair gave him an even wilder look than usual. He carried himself with his typical swagger. There was no doubting his personal magnetism and blatant sexuality. As always, I was drawn to him and already fantasizing about our wedding night. Directly behind him were Foxor and Lasarta, her hand in the crook of his bent arm as couples did on Earth in more formal gatherings. I searched for Josher and saw he was also dressed in military uniform, carried by Officer Lorret. I hadn't seen him since two nights before. My heart swelled with pride at how handsome my little prince looked. Behind them were Commander Portars and Colora, standing as a couple, which made me wonder if he was married.

My side of the line started with Damari and Marcia. She also wore an elegant red dress and carried a red bag. He cradled a chunky piece of red crystal in his hands. I placed the cake inside the bag. He smiled at me and she giggled.

"Mina, are you a queen, and Mr. Monster your king?"

"Not really, but you, sweetie, are a beautiful princess."

Soldiers stationed on the base, either standing as couples or individuals, filled in the rest of the lines.

As Kindor and I walked up in front of Damari and Marcia to face Montor, he gave me a once-over and smiled to Kindor, and I heard his voice in my mind.

"Sweetness, my heart is skipping beats. Make sure your Sotkari Ta brother is not trying to kill me." After a pause and becoming more serious, he added, "No, really, Mina, your beauty leaves me breathless."

We took our places in front of each line. A long white table in the center of the room had golden plates with something glistening on them and an iron pot. Behind the table stood an Arandan priestess in a red tunic and two musicians, one playing a harp-looking instrument and the other some type of percussion. A six-person choir accompanied them. The priestess, the musicians, and the singers were real people, but the inside of the temple itself was a holographic image.

As they chanted and sang, each line promenaded around the room, resembling the lines in amusement parks. We started out facing each other but then marched in opposite directions. The queue wound back and forth from the middle to the ends of the room and across to the other side. There were spots where we met up with the other line.

As we walked, a faintly irritated look crept across Kindor's face. I spoke to him telepathically.

"What is the problem?"

"As usual, your future husband never misses an opportunity to provoke me."

"Why? What did he say?"

"He thanked me for delivering my sister to him and said that now he and I will be like brothers."

"Do not always assume the worst. Maybe he means it."

Kindor pulled a face.

"Mina, you know very well that he does not."

"Well, what did you say?"

"What I always tell him. He better make you happy."

As we promenaded around the room, I marveled at how the holographic technology made the temple feel so real. Huge red scrolls with black writing draped the white walls. The floor simulated red marble-like stone. Different to what I was accustomed to seeing in Christian religious buildings on Earth, there were no sculptures, paintings, or images of any sort.

When we faced Montor again, he stared at my cleavage through the revealing cutout in the front of my dress. He licked his lips in a lascivious manner.

Kindor shook his head with disgust and said to me telepathically, "That creature cannot conduct himself with decorum even at his own wedding."

I laughed nervously but noted that as we got closer to the center table, Montor became more and more reverent. By the time we traversed the entire room and faced each other in front of the table, the mischief had left his eyes. He was stone-faced.

The music and singing stopped. The priestess made a proclamation, after which Kindor was to finish delivering me to my future husband. Her words hit me like a whack across the face. Eighteen years earlier, I had become Joshua's wife, and as far as I knew, we were still married. Yet here I was, galaxies away, taking the same oath of lifelong commitment to someone else. An adrenaline rush began to cloud my mind, overwhelming me with the desire to run out of the temple and keep running until my legs no longer worked. I looked into Kindor's blue eyes and couldn't believe the thought I transmitted to him.

"Take me out of here. I love you!"

His eyes became as wide as saucers, but after a minute, he answered telepathically.

"Mina, if I thought for a second that this were anything other than last-minute jitters, I would challenge Montor to a duel right this minute, stop his heart from beating and his lungs from breathing before he could take one swing at me, and take you far away from here where we could be together forever, but that is not what you want me to do. I have seen you with him. The truth is, unfortunately for me, you two have a connection that I was not able to create in all the time we spent together."

My face flushed with chagrin. My thoughts were not meant for Kindor at all. He didn't know the real source of my conflict, but his words centered me. I was here for a reason. I did love Montor, regardless of whatever quandary afflicted my soul.

"What did I ever do to deserve you, Kindor? Thank you for steadying me. I do love you, though. I guess in a different way."

"And I will always love you, Mina," he answered as he nodded to Montor, who offered his arm to me.

I took hold of Montor's arm, and he momentarily rubbed my hand with his free one, sending electricity through my veins. Everyone remained quiet as the priestess continued her speech. She asked Marcia for the red bag, took out the small cake, and placed it on one of the gold plates. I broke it into two pieces, putting the amulet on the plate, and fed one piece of cake to Montor. He did the same to me.

Thank goodness! The cake is moist and delicious.

Montor recognized Foxor's recipe. After smiling at me, he turned to nod to Foxor. I cleaned the amulet with a small cloth placed on the table for that purpose.

The priestess took a yellow crystal from one of the gold plates and rubbed it first on my upper arm and then Montor's. It numbed my skin. Next, she took a circular metal device and pressed it against the numbed area on my arm, causing a slight tingle but no pain. Chanting began again, and when she lifted the device from my arm, red characters branded my skin. She repeated the same with Montor. When she was done, the device had seared "*Mina*" in my handwriting onto Montor's arm. A few days before, without explanation, Montor had asked me to sign my name on the display of his tablet. Now, I understood its purpose.

Conflicting emotions built up in me again. I had no other tattoos or markings on my body. From that point on, his name would be burnt into my skin forever, and mine on his. Every milestone towards my union with Montor felt like I was attending my own funeral and rebirth. The old Mina was dead. I deeply grieved for her and everything she had lost, but I looked forward with excitement to the reborn Mina and the vibrant, sexy relationship she was forging with her new husband, bonding with him over fighting a common enemy.

6

MONTOR

The branding ritual shook Mina. I did not read her mind to learn this. Her expression said it all.

Is she having second thoughts?

I had been to other weddings before, so it annoyed me how stiff and vulnerable I felt at my own. During the procession, I tried to conceal my nervousness with jokes in poor taste. Fighting the temptation to search Mina's mind, I distracted myself by focusing on the ceremony, but I could barely stop my hands from shaking.

Using a metal rod, the priestess broke the red crystal into many pieces and poured them into the iron pot in the center of the table. She used the metal rod again to stir the crystals, and flames erupted.

"Lock it," said the priestess, referring to the bracelet I had gifted Mina when I asked her to marry me. I was a robot following her instructions.

The priestess verified that the bracelet could not be unfastened and dropped the tiny key into the flames. After some time, she extinguished the fire by placing the blue crystal in the pot. When she dumped the contents onto one of the plates, only charred crystal and a warped, melted piece of metal fell out, confirming the key had been destroyed and the bracelet could not be removed from her arm. The guests fist-pumped and shouted. Every nerve in my body stood on end but in a good way now, feeling that much closer to being bonded to Mina until our last breath.

The next step was for Mina to present me with an amulet and make a pledge of eternal love spoken in Arandan. To my relief, the nerves she had exhibited before disappeared. My mind raced wondering what she planned to give me or say. She looked up at me with those spectacular honey-colored eyes.

"As your mother did to your father, Montor, I present to you this gift as a symbol of my love. I will love you and stay by your side as your partner and the mother of your children until I take my last breath."

Proud at how well she pronounced the words in Arandan, I untied the knot on my cord and examined the amulet before stringing it on. I could not believe my eyes as I studied the amulet's old-fashioned style. Mina's words were not symbolic. She had given me the actual amulet my mother had gifted my father. Our family name and crest were engraved on it.

How can she possibly have this?

My father should have had it on when he died and was cremated.

Shermont! Leave it to Mina to throw me off balance.

I recalled how Lostai soldiers had beaten my father and used their *zirems* to deliver painful burns. When he turned to look at us one last time, he told us to remember that we came from a proud line of Arandan poets, warriors, and teachers. They dragged him off, and I called out to him, "*Ta Ri, Ta Ri.*" Other soldiers warned my mother to silence me, and she covered my mouth.

Holding onto the table to steady myself, I thought about all the years I had served in the Lostai military. My father would have been disgusted to see me wear that filthy uniform.

Mina looked vexed again as the ceremony took an unexpected turn. Instead of thinking about Mina's sexy body, tears streamed down my face in a way they never had in all my adult life. I turned to Lasarta and Foxor. Foxor nodded, and I realized he must have safeguarded the amulet all this time.

Must get my emotions under control.

Closing my eyes, I conjured up a happy memory of my father, having to go way back to my early childhood to find one. He was teaching me the rules of a popular Arandan sport because I wanted to play with my older brothers. I held on to that image and faced the crowd. They all looked confused except Lasarta and Foxor, who were also crying. It was time to tell these people my truth.

"See here, everyone. My beautiful wife-to-be has surprised me with something truly special...something that has touched me deeply. She has presented me with my own father's amulet. My father, a patriot who was executed by the Lostai for standing his ground and defending his family. The Lostai took me as a child because of my special abilities and forced me to become one of their soldiers. I became the same scum that decimated my family and my clan. Unbelievably, for many years, I actually embraced that part of my life, enjoying the power and luxury. Yes, it is true, I always secretly helped my rebel Arandan brothers, but I lived a dual life and hated myself for it. It is only fitting that the female who eventually stole my heart is a strong person of conviction who refused to submit to the Lostai and their evil plans. She has motivated me to leave that life for good. I have a young son, and the Lostai military is hunting my bride, so it is not the right time for me to leave them and lead you into battle. However, we will do our part to aid the rebellion and stand against the Lostai."

I turned to face Mina and placed my hands on her shoulders.

"She is not of Aranda and may be short of stature, but she has the soul, strength, and loyalty of an Arandan warrior. I pledge to love her and protect her, the mother of my son, until my last breath."

Silence.

Hushed whispers.

My hands tightened on Mina's shoulders, but I stopped before I hurt her.

It took a minute or two for my words to sink in until, to my relief, fist pumps and shouting erupted again like a volcano. The priestess smiled and gave us permission to show our affection for each other. I stroked Mina's cheek, and she did the same to me. This marked the end of the ceremony, but I leaned over and whispered to the priestess.

"May we also show our affection in the way of her people?"

She extended her arms, signaling her permission.

I bent over, my fingers caressing her neck. We *kix*, first a slight touch, and then I pulled her closer to me, enjoying the taste of her tongue and lips. A roar of approval filled the room.

With Mina's hand warm in mine, we walked out the entrance and to the next holographic room where the banquet hall was simulated. Protocol required we greet and thank the guests as they filed in. The first ones to walk through the doors were Foxor and Lasarta. I bowed so Lasarta could stroke my cheek. Mina wanted to embrace them, a sign of friendship in her culture. Lasarta agreed without a second thought, but Foxor, true to Arandan tradition, requested my permission first. I never imagined I would one day find myself huddled together this way for a simultaneous four-way embrace with my foster parents. We Arandans only embraced our lovers.

"Thank you, thank you, for help with the cake recipe and

the amulet and just everything. I do not know how to repay you for your kindness," Mina said in a tremulous voice.

"All we ask is that you take care of our foster son and give him plenty of true love for the rest of his life, to compensate for all he has missed out on until now," answered Lasarta, stroking her cheek.

Colora and Commander Portars walked in next. He saluted me, and Mina insisted in hugging Colora too. Damari approached us with his ever-present smile, and Marcia skipped by his side. He surely had a moment of lunacy as he hugged Mina effusively, followed by a loud *kix* on the cheek. I tapped him on the shoulder and shook my head, controlling the urge to hurl him across the room.

"What do you think you are doing? Have you lost your mind?"

Unbelievably, Mina waved her hand, as if disregarding my disapproval.

"Oh, never mind him. He is just giving you a hard time," she said to Damari.

Lucky for Damari, Marcia distracted me by tugging at my jacket and gesturing that I pick her up. She put her arms around my neck and said something to Mina.

"Marcia says you look very handsome today."

I could not help but smile and gave her a *kix* on the cheek as Mina had instructed me was appropriate to do. I put her down so she and Damari could continue inside before I remembered my irritation with him. Several soldiers came in after, saluting and greeting us. Kindor and Officer Lorret, carrying Josher, arrived almost at the end. Kindor entered first, grabbing my forearm in the typical Sotkari salutation. He was smart enough to defer to Arandan tradition and only nodded to Mina, but she searched my eyes and requested telepathically that I grant her permission to embrace Kindor, too. I gave up trying to impose Arandan customs on her.

Is there any wish that I would not grant her?

"Go ahead, you two. Disrespect me openly in front of my friends and family," I said telepathically to them both, trying to keep my tone pleasant.

I summoned more self-control as Kindor pulled her close and she looked into his eyes. Perhaps they were communicating, but I tapped her on the back to signal that was enough when she pressed her face against his chest and lingered a second too long. Officer Lorret handed Josher to me.

"Mina, you are a very unconventional but beautiful Arandan bride. I wish you both a long life together," she said in a, I must admit, dry tone.

I decided Mina should have to concede me some leeway too, so I caressed Lorret's cheek, and she reciprocated.

After the last few people walked in, I got a drink for Mina and me and led her to the stage set in front of the room. Before addressing the guests in Arandan, I explained to her first telepathically in Lostai, "Sweetness, I am raising a toast to you and your stunning beauty."

I did not expect her to say anything after I was done and was ready to leave the stage when, to my surprise, she spoke in Arandan.

"Today, I am fortunate enough to forge a union with a proud member of the Ventamu Clan. I will stand by his side with our son, and together we will do our part to help free Aranda and this sector of filthy Lostai rule!"

It was not common for Arandan females to make this kind of bold toast, especially at a wedding.

Mina, what have you done now? How will these people react?

I saw Lasarta's smiling face in the crowd. She must have instructed Mina to say this. As a proud Arandan patriot, she lived vicariously through Mina's ability to not be so tied down by Arandan tradition.

After a few seconds of awkward silence, Commander

Portars lifted his glass and repeated Mina's words, "Let us free Aranda of filthy Lostai rule!"

Mina's subtle ability to charm people never ceased to surprise me. I stood behind my bride with my hands on her shoulders in solidarity, and soon, everyone chanted, "Free Aranda of filthy Lostai rule! Free the sector of filthy Lostai rule!"

Even Officer Lorret smiled at Mina, in spite of herself.

"My wife, you are truly a blessing. You have even won over these proud people," I told her telepathically.

We stepped down from the stage, and there were no more formalities. Everyone circulated freely around the room, getting food and drink and mingling. Musicians took the stage and began to play. Soon, people were dancing.

I joined Commander Portars, Foxor, and other soldiers while Mina took Josher to the table to feed him. Within a few minutes, she approached me.

"Sweetness, is everything OK?" I asked.

"Yes, of course. I was talking to Colora and asked her to translate what you said at the wedding when I gave you the amulet."

"Yes?"

"It left me wondering if I had done the right thing, surprising you with that amulet, provoking you, perhaps, to talk of things you would have preferred to keep private. I thought it would be a precious gift to you, but maybe I should have advised you ahead of time about it. I am so sorry if I put you in a bad position. I had no intention of hurting you."

I pulled her close and lost myself in her eyes.

"Mina, everything turned out perfectly. It was healing for me to say those words. They needed to be said. These soldiers had considered me to lead them into battle. I had confessed my story to some of the top leaders of the rebellion, but the rest of the command and soldiers were unaware. Imagine if they found out later on their own that I used to fight with the Lostai military. I needed them to know everything about me to earn their trust in whatever mission we take. You gave me the perfect opportunity and have nothing to worry about. It was hard at first but liberating when I was done."

"Oh, I am so relieved to hear that."

"And something else that I would like to point out. The fact that Foxor gave you that amulet to present to me shows the affection and trust he feels for you."

"That makes me happy, as I have come to care for Lasarta and Foxor very much also."

Having put that concern to rest, Mina was more at ease, and we both continued spending time separately with the different guests. Later, I found her and invited her to dance as several guests cheered us on. We spent a while on the dance floor and joined in on a group folk dance. As the dance wound down, I pulled her close. She looked up to me, her heartbeat still accelerated from the upbeat dance steps. Her gorgeous amber eyes stared at mine, as if asking what would come next.

"Mina, as much as I am enjoying my time here with you, I am ready for us to be alone."

She ran her palms over my sleeves and squeezed my biceps.

I love it when she becomes flirtatious.

"Me too. Are we supposed to formally say goodbye to everyone?"

My hands ached with the desire to touch all her curves.

"No," I could not wait another second. "Once we hand Josher over to Lasarta, we can quietly slip out. The party will continue without us."

7

MINA

Montor and I walked into the next holographic room. The second the doors closed behind us, we found ourselves in the foyer of what appeared to be a small beach house. The foyer led to a sitting area, the dining room, and the entrance to a master bedroom, equipped with a spa tub and bathroom. One of the bedroom walls and the ceiling were made of a transparent material, so we had a clear view of the sky, ocean, and sand. Several candles lit the room. A tall mattress lay directly on the floor, dressed in light red silky sheets and soft blankets with several pillows.

"Are we able to actually go outside and step in the sand?" I asked.

"Yes, of course."

Montor used a handheld device from one of the side tables to cause the entire back wall to disappear. I slipped off my shoes, and he took my hand as we walked out of the bedroom right onto the beach. Two full moons illuminated the deep purple Arandan night sky, their light reflected across the vast red ocean and the brownish-pink iridescent sand. Soft waves slapped against the shore. A slight breeze released a curl from my updo, and the sand felt cool on my feet.

"I am awestruck."

"I hoped you would like it."

"Are you kidding? It is breathtaking. Can we put our feet in the water?"

"Yes, Mina, everything is as if it were real. We can swim in the ocean."

I stopped in my tracks.

"Wait. We cannot go into the water with these clothes on."

My toes curled in the sand as he smiled at me seductively.

"I like the way you think, sweetness. You are right, we should undress."

He led me back into the bedroom, and his hands raced to the zipper of my dress. Lasarta had begun to teach me basic Arandan, and I'd made a point to learn certain phrases for some situations I'd anticipated.

"No, I am easy...you first...I will help," I said.

He stroked my cheek and flashed that smile again, making me second-guess my plan.

"I like how you sound in Arandan."

He followed my instructions and sat in a comfortable chair by the mattress. I unfastened the gold sash across his chest, folded it, and placed it on the side table. Next, I unbuttoned his jacket, took it off, and also folded it carefully. Tapping his foot in exaggeration, he pretended to be impatient at the fact that I was in no rush. I ignored it and unbuckled his belt, pulled out his shirt, and unbuttoned it. He took it off. Again, I folded it, and finally, we were down to his undershirt. I pulled it over his head, but this time, instead of folding it, I tossed it across the room.

Montor laughed out loud at my antics. I stopped my silliness and stroked his chest. His eyes closed as even the slightest skin contact flooded our bodies with potent sexual energy.

Having undressed him from the waist up, my attention turned to his lower half. I knelt on the plush red carpet to unfasten his boots and remove his foot coverings. As usual, I was impressed with his well-pedicured feet and toenails and decided to give him a quick massage.

In a quick motion, he stood, now that his patience truly had reached its limits. He pulled his legs out of his pants, immediately followed by his underpants. I looked up at his glorious nudity. It always felt like the first time. In a matter of seconds, he pulled me to my feet, whipped me around, and unzipped my dress. The bodice slipped off my shoulders, and the dress fell to my feet. I wore nothing underneath.

"See, I told you I was easy," I said softly, still speaking in Arandan.

He let out a low groan, his hands on my waist, bending over to slide his tongue along the back of my neck. I became playful again and ran back out to the beach. He chased after me, lifted me off my feet, and walked into the ocean. The lukewarm water felt silky with a curious fragrance to it.

"The oceans and rivers on Earth are blue like those on Fronidia and Renna One. Why is the water here red?"

"It contains a certain mineral that gives it this color and is also said to be excellent for the skin. However, try not to swallow any as it might upset your digestive system."

Splashing around and playing chase games like children was fun, but Montor finally said, "Mina, I cannot wait any longer."

We returned to the room and rinsed off in the spa tub. After we dried up, he carried me to the bed and sat staring at my nakedness.

"Mina, I plan to worship your body tonight like never before," he whispered. "I will make love to you the way Arandans do."

He took one of my feet in his hands, licking between my toes. I moaned softly as they curled.

"I will start here and travel up to here," he leaned over and slid his hand up between my thighs. "And I will remain feasting here for a while."

I gasped and whispered, "Yes."

He moved farther up the mattress, his fingers walking to my nipple, squeezing it between his thumb and forefinger.

"Then I will spend some time here," he said.

I moaned louder, and he caressed my cheek.

"Eventually, I will end up here, and then I will make us one. After that, we will improvise. What do you think of my plan?"

By now, his voice was deep and husky. His dark pupils dilated so that barely any of the yellow irises were visible.

"It suits me just fine," I whispered.

He executed his plan to perfection, and I praised him in whispers. He encouraged me not to hold back.

"No risk of waking Josher here, Mina. We are alone. Let me know if you enjoy what I am doing," he growled.

My shouts became louder and higher-pitched each step of the way until he completed his titillating journey. We fell asleep with satisfied smiles and dampened bodies. After a few hours, I awoke, turned to face his chest, and kissed him there.

Montor's eyes opened, glowing in the dark room. He asked with a lusty smile, "Mina, can I have you again?"

This time, there was no plan. We rolled around the bed laughing, kissing, and caressing each other until we fell off onto the carpeted floor. I ended up on top.

"Now, you are mine, my handsome Arandan warrior!"

I rode him slowly at first, progressing to a steady gallop until I was out of breath. He flipped me over facedown to finish what I started. My voice was spent, and delirious tears ran down my cheeks. It took us time to recover, but we finally got back on the bed. I slept until a lavender mist peeked over the horizon, a signal that sunrise was approaching. Kissing my neck, he stroked me from my thighs to my breasts. Now alert, I turned to embrace him.

"My king, again?"

"I cannot get enough of you, sweetness."

Every inch of my skin tingled.

"I think I would like to make love to you as Earthians do. I will start here," I said, kissing his lips, then parting mine and encouraging him to do the same so we could taste each other.

"Then I will move down here," I continued, kissing his chest and abdomen.

"And then here..."

He gasped as I took his member into my mouth. I pleasured him, and he shouted words in Arandan that I didn't understand. He pulled me back up, and we faced each other side by side, our legs entangled. He grabbed hold of my hips and pushed inside me hard as I shouted his name.

I ordered him when to go deeper and when to go faster. He panted like an animal, groaning with his last thrusts. We fell into deep sleep, this time for several hours, the sun high in the yellow Arandan sky when our eyes opened.

After thanking Commander Portars and his staff for their hospitality, we took off in the evening. We had two routes to choose from. On one, we were more likely to encounter Lostai military. On the other, we risked running into marauders from a nearby star system that called themselves the Bertau. We decided the Lostai were the greater risk. The Bertau rarely utilized large spacecraft. Instead, their strategy was to create blockades with several small ships at once. Based on our chosen flight plan, the trip to Sotkar was scheduled to take thirty-five days.

Our small crew soon fell into a busy routine and a certain camaraderie. Montor, Kindor, Damari, even little Marcia, and I shared a few hours together daily on our Sotkari Ta physical and mental workout regimen. Kindor and Montor led us in meditation and in teaching us new Sotkari Ta skills. Lasarta, who had been a schoolteacher, taught Kindor, Marcia, and me how to speak and understand the Arandan language of Montor's clan and the dialects of other clans. She said afterwards we would move on to reading and writing. We spent time together practicing our assignments, which resulted in Kindor learning to understand and telepathically communicate some basic English phrases and Marcia and me learning some Sotkari. Marcia, who had refused to learn any new language since she had been taken, was also learning Lostai.

Kindor helped Foxor to maintain the garden and small livestock. We all spent time doing research on our respective areas of responsibility and updating the rest of the crew periodically. Montor led us all, even Lasarta and Marcia, in military training, including the use of weapons and how to pilot the spaceship and shuttles. Officer Lorret trained us all in first aid. Colora informed us about the different races of the sector and their customs and civics. Everyone helped in taking care of Josher.

Montor established a rotation for nighttime and mealtime watch shifts. Other than those on duty, we mostly ate our meals together except for Kindor and Officer Lorret, who were engaged in an unlikely friendship and usually sat together separate from the rest of the group. Kindor taught her Lostai sign language, and they learned Arandan sign language together.

During a breakfast with Colora one day, she jokingly observed, "They are very different but share one thing."

"What?" I asked.

"Unrequited love," she said with an exaggerated sigh, placing both her hands on her chest for effect.

72 MARIA A. PEREZ

I glanced in their direction, shook my head, and turned back to her.

"Colora, you certainly have a flair for drama."

I looked back again and saw that Lorret laughed while Kindor held her hand, showing her how to position certain fingers for a sign.

"But I am glad he is finding other people to connect with here," I added and rushed through my meal to get an early start on my daily routine.

Montor required strict discipline with our workouts and duties but encouraged us to use the lounge and bar area, the observation deck, or the holograph room in our free time. Every sixth day, we relaxed to take a break from our busy routines.

Sometimes, Montor and I also shared our evening meals separate from the crew and a glass of wine or a drink before retiring. During this time, I practiced my Arandan and taught him some English. We had a friendly competition on whether Josher's first words would be mother or father or some other word altogether.

On the second rest day, Lasarta suggested she take care of Josher so Montor and I could use the holograph room to spend time alone together. I prepared a picnic basket, and Montor brought two bottles of wine and a blanket. He simulated a riverside forest similar to his old property in Renna One. We walked hand in hand for a long time and found the perfect spot under a gigantic tree near the river to set our blanket. I sat against the tree with my legs outstretched, and he lay with his head on my lap. It didn't take long for him to shut his eyes, and I let him nap for a while. He was putting in longer hours than the rest of us, creating the new strategy for the rebel forces and tactical plans for the different situations our crew might face. Although he continued to display his typical self-confidence in front of the others, I knew he felt the pressure of having the responsibility not only for our safety but also for the destinies of so many rebel soldiers.

He awoke hungry, so I broke out our snacks, and he popped open the wine. We ate. We drank. We slowly undressed and gave each other massages. We kissed and made love. We drank more wine and made love some more.

As we lay staring up to the cloudless sky, he said, "Mina, it is mind-boggling to me that all the luxuries and females and power I used to have never brought me the contentment I feel now. Even with all the challenges we face," he turned to look at me, "I am happier than I have ever been."

I met his eyes.

"You deserve happiness, Montor."

"Mina?"

"Yes?"

He hesitated and looked to the sky again.

"Are you happy?"

I caressed his cheek.

"Yes, my king, of course. We are together, our son is doing well. We are united on the same mission."

"But as I look back at my time as a Lostai soldier, it makes sense that I am happier now because I hated what I had become, but you..."

Again, he searched my eyes.

"What?"

"You were perfectly happy before on your planet, right?"

I stretched my neck, rolled my shoulders, and took a deep breath.

"Why do you bring this up, Montor?"

"I am afraid of losing you, Mina."

His whole demeanor was so different than his usual confident posture. As usual, he only gave himself permission to be vulnerable in private with me.

"I told you once before, you are stuck with me."

"You did not answer my question."

"We have had this talk before. In general, I was happy, yes, but what does it matter? That is in the past, a past I cannot dwell on. I am focused on the present. In my present, I am happy too. I have a loving husband whom I care very much about and who has given me a beautiful son. Montor, you know I love you."

My reply assuaged whatever was troubling him. He licked the palm of my hand and placed it over his heart. I cuddled close to him, and we napped the rest of the afternoon.

When we returned to pick up Josher, he pointed to me and said, "Ro...Ro...ma...sta!" which meant "mother" in Arandan. I hugged Josher and gave Montor a smug look as he rolled his eyes jokingly.

Lasarta had a mischievous look.

"We have been practicing," she said, giggling.

She had made sure "mother" was his first word and may have had an ulterior motive for doing so. The implications of us finding a transportal and me being the one assigned to return Marcia to her home on Earth were not lost on anyone.

One week later marked Josher's five-month birthday. I made a point to celebrate each month's birthday, even though Arandan tradition didn't acknowledge any such milestones until a child celebrated what they called his first revolution. At five months, Josher was close to the size of a one-year-old human child, and suddenly, his development accelerated.

That day, I made a special meal including Josher's favorite food, and Foxor baked a cake. We gathered around the table, Josher sitting between Montor and me. Especially fond of a sweet flat bread Arandans accompanied most of their meals with, Josher surprised us by tapping his father on the arm and pointing to the plate of it.

"*Taristo...bomar, bomar, bomar.*"

Taristo meant father and *bomar* meant bread. Montor beamed, saying something to Lasarta and Foxor in Arandan, and then reached over to hand Josher some bread.

I stopped Montor just before he placed the bread on Josher's plate and asked in Lostai, "What is the word for please in Arandan?"

"*Namit,*" answered Montor. "Why do you ask?"

"Well, we should teach him manners. He should get into the habit of saying please and thank you."

Montor shook his head, his brow furrowed. Foxor and Lasarta looked equally disturbed.

"That is a very strange suggestion, sweetness. A child should never have to beg his parents for food."

I started to clarify but stopped short, realizing this was one of the cultural differences Montor and I would need to figure out as we raised Josher, a child with two very different heritages.

In a matter of days, Josher started calling Kindor "*Faristo*" or "*Fa Kindor*" and Colora "*Somasta*" or "*So Colora,*" which meant "uncle" and "aunt." He also learned how to say grandma and grandpa to Lasarta and Foxor, "*Lo Romasta*" and "*Lo Taristo*" or "*Lo Ro*" and "*Lo Ta*" for short. Soon after, he began speaking short phrases, and everyone gushed over him. Now that he had started to speak, my bond with Josher grew even stronger.

The only thing Montor and I relished more than our private holographic getaways was our time playing with Josher. He took his first steps playing a holographic warrior game with his father, where as a team they faced a holographic rival. I thought these games were weird for a toddler, but I agreed to play the part of referee. Montor admitted he was starting Josher a little young but assured me this type of game was normal in the upbringing of Arandan male children.

Montor pretended the opponent was getting the best of him and called out to Josher for help. There was no real danger as I insisted the holographic game be set to "safe" mode.

"Josher, *yomurati Ta Ri, yomurati!*"

Josher stumbled and fell several times, his frustration and fear evident as the holographic rival punched and kicked his father. I was ready to intervene when he stood, took several quick steps to reach his father, and began punching the opponent.

Montor was beside himself with pride telling Lasarta and Foxor the story, especially when they commented on how Josher was physically almost identical to him at that age. I prayed we could guarantee him a different childhood from the one his father had faced.

8

MINA

Early one morning after our daily staff meeting, Montor received several transmissions from a group of seven small spacecraft. Our sensors scanned two occupants in each of the crafts. A cacophony of voices transmitted simultaneously in accented Fronidian. They must have determined our ship was registered in Fronidia. Montor set the communication on audio only.

"Identify yourself."

"This is the recreational craft *Barinta*. I am on my way to Sotkar to pick up its owners," Montor said.

The *Barinta* was outfitted with special shields that prevented its passengers from being scanned. They had no way of knowing how many of us were aboard.

"Well, a toll must be paid to pass through here," one voice replied.

"Charged by which government? This is free space not claimed by any planet," answered Montor.

"Have you not heard of the Bertau? Whoever is unlucky enough to run into us must pay a price," another voice said.

"Even though this is a recreational craft, it is equipped with powerful weaponry. I am prepared to defend myself."

"Our ships are small, but I am afraid you will be no match for all of us. I suggest you comply with our toll," a third voice said.

"What is the toll?"

"We will come on your craft and look around to see what might be of use to us. Prepare your docking station to receive our shuttle."

Weapons exchange between the *Barinta* and the seven of them was risky. With arms crossed, Montor paced the room like a caged animal. I could almost feel his mind working on a plan. His brows were drawn together, anger and concern on display.

"Fine," answered Montor, controlling his tone to hide any emotion.

"Make sure you are unarmed when we meet you."

All eyes were on Montor as we absorbed his instructions. He told all of us to hide in the holographic room because it had its own set of shields. We would be undetectable by any screening instruments they might bring on board. Back on Aranda, Montor had retrofitted the holographic room to camouflage the entrance and made it appear as a wall. The room also possessed video and audio equipment that displayed other areas of our craft, so we could see what was happening once the Bertau boarded. Montor planned to use his Sotkari Ta skills to manipulate the mind of their leader into allowing us passage without further incident. The tricky part was that the Bertau included people of many different races who had turned to a life of crime, so we didn't know what to expect and whether their minds or bodies were accessible to telepathy. If things didn't go according to plan, Damari was supposed to come out and help Montor. Kindor communicated telepathically in conference mode, telling Montor that he would be the better choice for backup. Montor simply answered, "No, you are in charge of watching over my family and the rest of the crew."

Before we left, I approached Montor and hugged him.

"Please be careful," I whispered to him, my head against his chest.

He tilted my chin up.

"Everything will be fine. Now go."

We rushed to the room. Once inside, tension stiffened our bodies. With eyes glued on the viewer, we saw seven heavily armed beings of average height and stocky build, apparently one from each Bertau craft, walking out of the docking area. They had long wild hair, red markings on their light skin, and long animal-like snouts. Montor was almost a foot taller than any of them, and they made a point to look him up and down, obviously assessing his strength.

"I am on a tight schedule, so let us make this quick. Who of you is in charge?" asked Montor.

"None of us, we decide everything as a team," they replied in chorus.

Not good news for us. More than one person's mind would need to be manipulated.

"I see. So, where do we go from here?"

Montor's body language didn't betray any emotion other than growing impatience.

"We would like to see what handheld weapons you carry."

This was also not good news for us because we had brought from Aranda an arsenal of weapons to offer to the Sotkari rebel group.

"There's not much here in terms of weapons. I only carry what I use for my personal protection."

As they walked, I saw Montor's brow furrow in concentration. One pirate whirled around to face the others.

"Perhaps medicine and food would be a better choice."

Another one agreed, but the remaining five were not

convinced. It was obviously taking a lot of mental effort for Montor to manipulate more than one person at a time. Colora looked at Kindor and me.

"I have a bad feeling about this. Montor will not be able to manipulate all their minds at once. I have read information on this particular race. They are called Rondoo. They are ruthless, greedy anarchists who do not accept any leader among themselves, which causes them to take forever to make decisions. My guess is once he shows them around, they will grow impatient in not being able to agree on what to do. Instead, they will try to kill him and claim the whole craft for the Bertau."

Kindor spoke to me telepathically and signed for Colora's benefit.

"I know he ordered that I stay here, but I think I have a solution. Similar to what we did when we escaped from the Lostai in Fronidia, we could render these pirates unconscious and hold them hostage until they let us through. Once we are far enough from their territory, we can send them off on their shuttle on autopilot. Between Montor and me, we can accomplish this. I can get near them and communicate my plan to Montor telepathically."

"I have learned how to do that too. Would not three be better?" I said.

Kindor pointed his finger at me, eyes narrowed, his face frozen in a stern expression.

"No! Montor would not forgive me if I allowed you to be exposed to danger. I would not forgive myself either."

I didn't like being rebuked like a child.

"OK, but if it looks like you are having trouble, I am going out to help and leaving Damari here. He is not as far along in his Sotkari Ta training, but he is physically stronger and can defend the crew here if needed. Another thing to be aware of is that once you step out, you will show up on their sensors if they decide to scan for other passengers."

"I will have to be quick, then."

Kindor walked out of the room. We watched the video of him rushing down the corridors towards Montor and the pirates. Montor was leading them somewhere. With Kindor just a few feet behind the pirates, we could see by the clench of Montor's jaw and the anger in his eyes the exact moment when Kindor communicated with him telepathically. Clearly, Montor was upset that his orders had not been followed.

In the next moments, two of the pirates fell to the floor. One of the remaining five dove to the ground to check on his fallen comrades. The other four scattered, shouting in their language. Some of their weapons flew into the hands of Montor and Kindor or across the room. Two other pirates lost consciousness, but the three still standing ran down a corridor, still armed.

Montor and Kindor ran after the pirates but were unable to disarm them. They began exchanging laser fire. To render several people unconscious as well as perform telekinesis was mentally taxing, not to mention maintaining focus while running and dodging laser fire. I knew they needed help.

Before anyone could stop me, I ran out of the holographic room. The sound of weapon fire and footsteps led me to the observation deck. I spotted two of the pirates and, using my telekinetic abilities, disarmed them, smashing their weapons against the wall. After causing one of them to lose consciousness, I called out telepathically to Montor and Kindor, letting them know my location and what I had accomplished. The conscious disarmed pirate looked around. He didn't see me and ran out of the observation deck. I tried my best to focus and make him also pass out, but I started feeling dizzy and needed a few minutes to recover.

I remained hidden, hoping Montor and Kindor would catch him. Counting off in my head how many pirates had been rendered unconscious or disarmed, I realized there was still a third one possibly armed out there. While I scanned the area, a hand covered my mouth, and a laser gun poked my side. I concentrated and caused the weapon to fly across the room while I elbowed the pirate and turned to face him. Recovering in a second, he tried to punch me, but I ducked and aimed a kick to the groin. He dodged the blow, then lunged at me. I struck him in the face, and he promptly countered with a punch to my stomach that left me gasping for air.

Taking advantage of me doubling over, he kicked me, and I fell to the ground dazed. Pinned under his heavy body, I blocked my face as he rained blows to my head. His hands broke through and wrapped around my neck. My training kicked in. I planted my feet on the ground with my knees bent and trapped one of his legs with one of mine. Grabbing his arm with both of mine, I steadied myself to lift my hips and attempt to roll him, but he tightened his grip on my neck. I gasped for air.

Oh God, I need to get him off me. Don't let me pass out!

The prayer barely formed in my mind when his grip lightened and he fell over. I looked up to find Montor staring at me, worry and frustration evident in his yellow eyes. He pulled me up and asked if I was OK. I nodded yes, and one second later, Damari ran into the room. Montor looked at him incredulously.

"What are you doing here?" Yellow eyes blazed with fury.

"She in trouble. I came for help," answered Damari in his broken Lostai.

Montor's voice started as a whisper and ended like thunder.

"So, let me see. You have left my son and little Marcia in the protection of an elderly couple and two defenseless females!"

"I...I thought...Officer Lorret said she—"

"Officer Lorret is a medic, not a soldier!"

Poor Damari was a picture of chagrin as he rubbed his forehead, trying to figure out what he could say to appease Montor.

I met his eyes and told him telepathically in English, "He's furious. It's best not to answer him now."

Damari replied with a quick nod and rushed back to the holographic room. Montor then looked at me tight-lipped.

"Go back to the holographic room, too. All the pirates are now unconscious. We will discuss this later."

I returned to the holographic room, where we watched the monitor as Montor and Kindor cuffed the seven unconscious pirates and moved them to one of the conference rooms equipped with a video communications system. After sending Kindor to join us, Montor contacted the Bertau spacecraft and let them see on the viewer that their fellow pirates were disabled.

"What is the meaning of this?" said one of the Bertau.

"Letting you board my craft was a trap. The environmental settings here include a gas I am immune to but can be deadly to other species. Right now, even though unconscious, your fellow crew members are still alive as I have created a separate environmental setting in this room that is suitable to them."

"This is an outrage!" said another voice.

Montor laughed before his lips curled into a snarl. He pulled out a weapon that delivered an electric burn called a *zirem*. I shuddered recalling the punishments I had received on Xixsted with that very weapon.

"I am considering whether I let your comrades die of suffocation or torture them slowly."

"That would be unwise. We will fire on your craft," said yet another.

"I am able to target at least four of your crafts at one time, so at best, three of you will survive. And for what? A damaged craft that you cannot even board," said Montor.

Radio silence. Finally, they replied as a chorus.

"What do you want?"

"I want safe passage through this area today and in the

future. As a gesture of good faith, I will return your crew members with their weapons and gift you five more laser guns."

After a few more minutes of silence, someone replied, "How do you propose to return them to us?"

"We are very close to Sotkar. I will move them to the shuttle still unconscious and put the shuttle on autopilot after I am safely within Sotkar space limits."

"Why should we trust you? How do we know they are not already dead?"

Montor shut his eyes for a moment and roused one of the pirates, shaking his shoulder. The pirate, realizing he was cuffed and that the others were passed out, shouted something incomprehensible.

"I am on a strict schedule and need to be on my way. What is your answer?" pressed Montor.

They agreed to Montor's proposal. After he rendered unconscious the one he had awoken, he called for Damari to come out to help him carry the pirates to the shuttle and then sent him back to the room with us. As he had agreed, Montor loaded on their shuttle any of their remaining functional guns and the additional ones he had offered. We remained in the holographic room until we entered Sotkari space and he released their shuttle. It took about six hours. By then, we were all mentally, and some of us physically, exhausted. We all ate our dinner quietly, relieved at having surpassed the danger.

Montor was in a nasty mood. When he and I retired to our room, he cradled Josher in his arms and rocked him to sleep. Shaking his head without saying a word, he inspected my neck, which had already begun to bruise. I hadn't even thought to have Officer Lorret check me. He then lay down with his back to me for the first time since we had begun sleeping together. For the second time in one day, I felt like a chastised child. Turning towards him with my face touching his back, I intertwined my legs with his, told him I loved him, and closed my eyes. He replied with a gruff "OK." In the next morning's staff meeting, he was livid.

"We need to have an important discussion. We were lucky yesterday to get through an emergency without any major injuries," he said while walking over to me, poking my neck and making sure everyone saw the dark bruises and finger marks.

Heat flowed from my neck to my face and ears. Mortified, I wished I could leave the room. Kindor covered his mouth and looked away. Others squirmed uncomfortably in their seats.

"This is only the first of many dangerous situations we will face, and I do not know how we will be successful if I have a crew that does not heed my instructions! Does anyone here want to challenge my authority and take charge of this spacecraft?"

Montor's voice increased in volume with each phrase. We all crumpled in our seats, shoulders hunched, chins dropped as he took his time to scan each of us.

"I gave specific instructions on what should happen if things did not go as planned, and you all decided to do the opposite. I do not know what you were thinking! In the end, my wife was almost strangled to death, and the most defenseless ones on our ship, my son and Marcia, were left unprotected! How can I keep you safe if you cannot follow simple directions?"

Damari stared at his feet. A thick silence filled the room.

Montor continued berating us until Lasarta spoke up.

"Son, I think you are wrong."

"Lasarta!" Foxor shouted at his wife, hoping his stern stare would be enough to quiet her.

Montor's expression was first one of irritation and then shock. Lasarta ignored Foxor, walked over to Montor, and placed her hands affectionately on his shoulders.

"Montor, please do not misunderstand. You are the best leader we could ask for, and I know you worry very much for our safety. My concern is that you are trying to take care of us as if we were babies. The pressure will soon be too much for you. I was your mother's best friend since we were children. I knew her to be wise, and since she cannot be here, I speak on her behalf. You need to change the way you are approaching all of our roles, or you will make yourself sick."

Foxor's expression changed. His wife's words were right on target.

"I think you are trying to shoulder all the responsibility for our safety in an unrealistic way."

Her arms outstretched, gesturing towards us as she continued.

"We all knew the risks we were facing when we agreed to go on this journey. We were successful yesterday because we have strong, capable, brave people on our crew who were ready to jump into action to protect each other. Yes, you are correct to expect that, in general, we need to follow your instructions, but we cannot be robots blindly following directions that no longer meet the challenges of the situation at hand. Is that not the reason why you have been training us? By the way, before I forget, I need to make something clear. As a female, I can attest to the fact that my husband is quite healthy, strong, and definitely not yet elderly."

I tried my best to suppress a smile when Foxor's jaw dropped at the innuendo of her last comment. Montor's body froze, and he grimaced before looking away.

"I also think you need to set a chain of command so if, for some reason, you are incapacitated or absent or in some kind of trouble, we know who can make decisions. I would suggest Mina be your second-in-command. After you, she has the most formal military training and, as a mother, the most to lose if things go wrong, but that is your decision to make."

Everyone was quiet for a few minutes until Montor, lips pursed, stroked Lasarta's cheek.

"Lasarta, what a shame it is that our people are so backwards when it comes to female and male roles. You could have been a brilliant commander of armies or chancellor for our government. I am so lucky to have you. As much as I hate to admit it, you are right in everything you have said. Perhaps had we stayed with my original plan, things might have turned out worse. I was too focused on trying to shelter everyone from danger in an unrealistic way. I should apologize for my bad attitude and scolding."

We all took a collective deep cleansing breath, our eyes lighting up with a renewed feeling of confidence and synergy. I smiled to myself.

OK, good. We're not complete failures.

Later in the staff meeting, Montor created the chain of command that Lasarta suggested. He put it to a vote, and everyone except Lorret agreed I should be second-in-command (she voted for Kindor). I had tried to be friendly towards her, but she had snubbed most of my overtures. At that point, I didn't really care if she liked me or not, but she was a part of the crew. I needed to earn her respect. An adrenaline rush jolted me as the burden of taking on the role as Montor's First Lieutenant felt a bit overwhelming.

I'll have to double up on my tactical and physical training.

The hierarchy of command continued with Kindor, Lasarta, Foxor, Lorret, Colora, and finally Damari. After the incident with the Bertau, Montor also created a special compartment in the holographic room to hide the weapons we stored on board. The remaining leg of our trip transpired without incident, and soon we found ourselves on Sotkar.

9

MONTOR

When the *Barinta* arrived in Sotkari atmosphere, Lostai border control hailed us. I could not help but get irritated at seeing how much more control the Lostai maintained on all major governmental matters on Sotkar compared to how lax they were in Aranda. They thought we Arandans too inferior and primitive to be much of a threat. The stupid Lostai would soon learn the hard lesson that they should not have underestimated us.

Everyone except for Colora and Kindor moved to the holographic room. Colora identified herself as a Fronidian citizen and Kindor as a legal Fronidian resident since that provided them certain protection when dealing with the Lostai. Per our plan, she informed the border agent that she had rented the *Barinta* for vacation travel with Kindor as her pilot and security guard.

I hated hiding like a coward while the agent boarded our craft to look around but swallowed my pride for everyone's safety. The idiotic agent became agitated once he realized Kindor was Sotkari Ta and ordered him not to move from his position as the agent and Colora inspected the craft. I imagined tearing the agent limb from limb as he arrogantly inspected my ship. After passing the inspection, we landed on Tremoxtar Mor, a giant island home to several vacation and recreational resorts.

The Sotkari insurgents were not as well organized as the Arandan rebel forces. Commander Portars told us Jortan had established communication with this group before his death. Before leaving Aranda, we had sent an encrypted message to their leader, Kaonto Brimoa, to let him know to expect us. The insurgent base was on the small island of Marimbo Tu, where Kaonto lived with his family. Similar to the rebel base on Aranda, an isolated island helped keep them under the radar of Lostai military. We did not want to expose his family in any way and, for that reason, did not land our conspicuous spaceship on Marimbo Tu. Instead, they flew us in from Tremoxtar Mor on a transport pod.

The pilot took us down in the middle of a heavily wooded forest cleared to make space for a few small buildings. Someone was waiting for us as we piled out of the transport pod.

"Greetings. I am Kaonto."

I stepped forward, and we grasped each other's forearms in the typical Sotkari salutation. Younger than I had expected, he wore his hair short and sported a beard, unusual for Sotkari Ta males. His bright turquoise hair and eyes set against his dark grey skin made for a striking appearance.

"It is an honor to meet you. My name is Montor. I speak Sotkari, but unfortunately, not all of my crew does. The one language we all speak—"

He finished the sentence for me, switching to Lostai.

"Is Lostai. I understand. The Imperial Language, as we refer to it here. Although it is frustrating to have to use their language, hopefully it symbolizes that we have other things in common."

I introduced everyone else, and he led us into a conference room in the largest building. We sat around an oval table where sweet Sotkari tea and snacks were served.

"Montor, I appreciate you using the transport pod to get here. This island is not only an insurgent base but is also where I have chosen to live to hide my son from the Lostai. Neither my wife nor I have any evolved Sotkari abilities, but somehow my young son is exhibiting telepathic behavior."

I looked towards Kindor and asked him telepathically, "Is this possible?"

Kindor typed into his tablet, where his words were translated to audio as we did not know whether Kaonto understood sign language, and neither did Foxor nor Lasarta.

"I first heard of this phenomenon ten revolutions ago and have been researching and following the trends ever since. Because most Sotkari Ta either left Sotkar or were killed or kidnapped during the Lostai occupation, many assumed they eventually would become extinct on their home planet. However, the fact that children with enhanced abilities are spontaneously being born of non-Sotkari Ta or Pasi parents is proof that the Sotkari as a species are still going through a process of evolutionary change despite the displacement of generations of Sotkari Ta people from this planet."

"Kindor, you are mute, so I must assume you are Sotkari Ta," Kaonto asked.

"Yes, I am a pureblood Sotkari Ta," answered Kindor.

Lorret glanced to the ceiling ever so briefly. I also exercised extreme self-control to suppress the sarcastic words that crossed my mind. She and Kindor had become friends, but snobby Sotkari behavior can put any Arandan off.

"Well, I must say, I am honored," replied Kaonto, wide-eyed and visibly impressed. "Because my son has these abilities, I am eager to learn about the history of the early Sotkari Ta and their teachings. I am deeply concerned that the Lostai are still rounding up as many Sotkari Ta children they can find and taking them to military bases to be assimilated into their forces. I have made it my mission to do whatever I can to help our people regain control of their planet and secure the safety of our evolved brothers and sisters."

His patriotic sentiment provided the perfect segue for me to introduce the idea of the United Rebel Front.

"Our Arandan rebel troops have strengthened. We are committed to regaining our independence and are looking to join forces with your group. We have brought hand weapons and the equipment needed to set up a shield around your insurgent base."

He stroked his beard and sighed deeply before replying.

"I was saddened to learn of what happened to Jortan. I harbored a lot of respect for him and what he was trying to accomplish."

Clearly, he was wary of my proposal.

Colora spoke up.

"I am Jortan's widow. We can honor him by continuing his vision."

"It is hard for us. The Lostai are completely in control here. I know in Aranda you have a very organized rebel army, but our people are afraid, especially those with children displaying enhanced abilities," Kaonto replied, looking away for a moment.

"We believe that united we have a better chance to defeat the Lostai and take back control of all our respective planets." I stood to give emphasis to my words. "We need to move from mere protesting to an all-out revolt and declare independence from the Lostai Empire."

"What we need first is to energize the people here. They are too used to feeling hopeless," said Kaonto.

Kindor also stood as he typed in his tablet.

"The Sotkari should be a proud people. They are on an

evolutionary journey, and they need to get out from under the yoke of the Lostai to reach their full potential."

Oh, suddenly he is a revolutionary. Where has he been all this time? Well, I suppose now is as good a time as any.

"Yes, but we have so few people who can speak to this fact and can explain the history. Those who do exist prefer to not call attention to themselves for fear the Lostai will intimidate and destroy their families," explained Kaonto.

This sparked an idea in my mind.

"My mentor, Kaya, is a Sotkari Ta elder who currently lives here on Sotkar. I think we should reach out to her. She and Kindor could go with you and meet with the people."

"Did you say an elder?"

"Yes."

Kaonto smiled, and I knew we had convinced him.

"OK, I will organize meetings with the patriotic underground groups I am in contact with."

I left the meeting with the task of visiting Kaya and asking if she would be willing to accompany Kindor and Kaonto on a road trip around the major metro areas of Sotkar. It was imperative that we convince these people to join us in taking a stand against the Lostai.

We returned to Tremoxtar Mor and secured lodging at a modest hotel. Mina, Josher, Marcia, and I shared a two-room suite. Foxor and Lasarta stayed in another room. Colora and Lorret shared a room, as did Kindor and Damari. I transmitted a message to Kaya's contact codes asking if she could meet us. Mina and I talked as we lay in bed.

"I am so excited by the idea of seeing Kaya again. She was so kind to me. I wonder what she will think about us being together," said Mina.

"Actually, I already shared some things with her about us," I answered.

"Wait till she sees Josher," Mina said, hugging me.

I knew that in Mina's culture not all embraces are about sexual contact, but usually that was all it took to make me hard for her. I *kix* her on the forehead, got up, closed the door to the room where Josher and Marcia were sleeping, and returned to bed. She knew me well by then. Lucky for me, we were like-minded. It did not take much for me to get her in the mood, and soon, our bodies were joined.

The next morning, I received a reply from Kaya saying she was available to meet us. She lived in a rural, mountainous area called Solaro. Mina, Kindor, and I flew there in one of the *Barinta* transport pods. We brought Josher and Marcia with us.

Kindor and Mina were both jumpy with anticipation as we walked up to the small rustic house. Kaya opened the door, and her eyes widened.

"My goodness, I am speechless," Kaya said telepathically in Lostai, smiling at her own joke.

We all heard each other's voices in our minds in conference mode. Mina and Kaya grasped each other's forearms.

"Mina, I always hoped to see you again," Kaya said.

Kaya was responsible for setting off all that had happened between Mina and me. For many revolutions, the Lostai coerced Kaya into training their hostages in unleashing Sotkari Ta abilities. After killing her son, they threatened to harm her daughter-in-law and granddaughter if she did not comply. Mina was her trainee on Xixsted. Kaya had introduced us and put the idea in my head of helping her escape the Lostai.

Again, Mina fell into her Earthian custom of embracing people, as she usually did when she was overcome with feelings of friendship and gratitude, forgetting it was very unusual for the rest of us. Kaya indulged her for a bit, and I rescued her by handing Josher to Mina. As I lowered my head in reverence, she reached up to put her hands on my shoulders, and we locked eyes.

"Son, it is so good to see you."

When the Lostai brought me to Xixsted as a child, Kaya trained me too, but she went beyond that role and was like my second foster mother. We had been through a lot together, and emotions ran strong between us. Yet no one would have guessed that we had not seen each other in a while.

"I am also glad you are doing well."

Kaya turned back towards Mina and caressed Josher's cheek, acknowledging the Arandan form of showing affection.

"And this must be young Josher. Mina, after you left to Fronidia, Montor shared with me how you two had fallen in love. Honestly, I was not surprised, given the embedded Sotkari Ta genes you both have. He was inconsolable when he thought you were lost."

Must she get into those details in front of Kindor?

"You cannot imagine how happy it made me to hear you found each other again and that you are married," Kaya continued. "But the most wonderful news was to learn you had a child together."

With a tender expression, Kaya took Josher in her arms.

"What a handsome boy. My goodness, the exact image of his father!" she said. "And this young girl is the one that you helped escape from Xixsted, right, Montor? Please explain to her I cannot speak out loud."

Zorla, the Xixsted commander to whom I reported had ruthless plans in mind for little Marcia. She reminded me of my twin sister who died as a child. It was bad enough they had separated her from her family. I could not let them damage her further.

"I hear you in my head!" the little Earthian girl replied with confidence.

Mina had been training Marcia in telepathy, and as they practiced different language skills, she had picked up some Lostai.

"That is wonderful. You are a very smart young lady," said Kaya.

Kaya then turned to Kindor, who was waiting his turn to introduce himself. He extended his arm to Kaya.

"My name is Kindor Grahmon. It is an honor to meet you."

They held each other's wrists and entered a trance, their eyes closing for a moment.

Once she reopened her eyes, Kaya exclaimed, "Kindor, we must trace your roots. I am sure we are related."

Is there any relationship of mine that Kindor will not encroach upon?

Kaya said to all of us, "Where are my manners? Please come in."

She served us tea and freshly baked biscuits. I spoke of everything that had happened since Mina found me in Fronidia, as I had only told Kaya the basics. I did not talk of the time Mina spent in Fronidia before she decided to look for me. Mina filled in the gaps.

"As you know, we staged a scene that suggested rebel forces had ambushed Montor and rescued me from his command. In reality, he put me on a shuttle on autopilot to Fronidia. I traveled alone, and during the trip, I realized I was pregnant. My destination was the capital city on the northern continent next to the refugee center, but I encountered bad weather that caused my shuttle to crash land far away from my target."

Mina and Kindor smiled at each other as she recounted how they first met. I controlled my expression to not appear rude, but this story always made me want to punch Kindor in the face.

"Kindor saved my life, and since I needed to keep a low profile, I lived with his family during my pregnancy and Josher's first months."

We finally came to the topic of unifying Sotkari, Arandan, and other insurgent movements against the Lostai. I explained

Kaonto believed the first step towards a Sotkari rebellion was for the people to reconnect with their roots and embrace the inevitable evolutionary journey their race was facing.

"These people must learn not to be afraid of the Sotkari Ta and Pasi that continue to be born in their population. They need mentors to teach them how to reach their full potential. We suggest you and Kindor, as pureblood Sotkari Ta, go with Kaonto to meet with these groups in the cities to motivate them, but we can only ask. I am not sure if you would be up to it," I said.

Kaya's reply was immediate.

"It is an excellent idea, and I would definitely like to be a part of it. How long would this trip be, Montor?"

"Kaonto estimates about thirty days. After that, our small crew needs to continue to other phases of our mission, but we hope to have set the foundation for a strong rebel force here on Sotkar that will collaborate with the Arandan and other forces as one united army against the Lostai."

"Will Kindor be staying in Sotkar to continue to mentor the youth here after you leave?"

The question caught me off guard. Kindor irritated me to no end, but as a powerful Sotkari Ta, he was handy to have around.

"Ummm, he would have to speak to what his wishes might be. I had hoped he would continue as part of our crew and be a liaison between the Sotkar rebels and the other groups."

Mina seemed dumbfounded by my reply. I never denied to her I was jealous of the close friendship she shared with Kindor, but as captain of the *Barinta*, I needed to be practical.

"The idea of mentoring the youth here would be a rewarding role, but I would prefer to remain on the *Barinta*. I could still serve my people in the liaison role that Montor just mentioned," Kindor replied.

Kaya remained pensive for a few minutes with her fingers

pressed against her temples before she said, "Montor, I look forward to going on this tour, but my concern is that we should have a younger person who can continue to mentor the people on an ongoing basis."

"Do you know of another Sotkari Ta who might be willing to take on this role?" I asked.

"Well, it just happens I have recently reconnected with the daughter of my husband's niece who is Sotkari Pasi. I think she would be perfect for this role, especially since she can speak both telepathically and out loud, and she also knows Sotkari sign language. Her name is Kimbra. She could help create a bridge between all Sotkari people attending those meetings. I will contact her and see if she is willing."

As we continued to discuss various topics, Kindor and Kaya discovered they were, in fact, related. Kaya was the cousin of his paternal great-grandfather.

"What great news," I said, this time not able to avoid rolling my eyes. Mina shot me a warning look.

We made plans to meet Kaya again and fine-tune the details of the road trip, this time with Kaonto and, we hoped, Kimbra.

10

MINA

The second meeting with Kaya, Kaonto, and Kimbra went well. Kimbra made quite an impression on us. When I first saw her, it occurred to me that perhaps someone in her family tree was not Sotkari because other than her dark blue lips, she could have passed for human. Shorter than any of the Sotkari women I had met so far, she stood only a couple of inches taller than me, with a curvy but fit figure like how Colora often described mine. Her dark blue eyes and curly hair appeared almost black, and her creamy white skin had no grey tinge to it.

Although she was younger than Kindor, Montor, or me, more along the lines of Lorret's age, she won us over with her articulate expression and charismatic personality.

"I am a devout student of Sotkari and Sotkari Ta history and rituals. Your mission to rescue hostages and get them back to their homes is of special interest to me," said Kimbra, her eyes welling up. "The Lostai kidnapped my Sotkari Ta sister when she was a child, and we have not heard from her since. We cannot allow the Lostai to continue their crimes against our people."

"Kaya, thank you for recommending Kimbra to us. It is clear she is an excellent choice to help us motivate and mentor the Sotkari people," said Kaonto.

Kaonto hammered out the details of the trip. Although he was sure the groups they would be meeting with were trustworthy Sotkari patriots, the tour would have its risks. Montor asked they apprise us daily of their progress and let him know immediately if they perceived any danger. In the meantime, the rest of us would remain on Tremoxtar Mor continuing our research, planning our next steps, and actually taking it easy, as there would be very little time to relax once we left Sotkar. It wouldn't be a good idea for the rest of us, especially for Montor and me, to roam Sotkar in the open.

Montor asked for some private time with Kaya before wrapping up the meeting. As they stepped into another room, he glanced at Kindor, who seemed to be engaged in a telepathic conversation with Kimbra. Raising his eyebrows, Montor communicated to me telepathically.

"Looks like your Sotkari friend is quite taken by her."

Kindor did appear to find Kimbra charming, and I was unprepared for the slight jealousy that swept over me. The same thing happened when I saw him sharing meals with Lorret. Truthfully, I considered his friendship something special and kind of missed the days when I was the sole center of his attention.

When we arrived back to Tremoxtar Mor, Montor told me he had asked Kaya for recommendations on where to go for a sort of after-wedding getaway. She recommended a small village in a remote area with no Lostai presence not too far from her home.

"Kaya said it is a quaint village with traditional Sotkari shops, taverns, and markets, bordered by lush woods and a river," he said, twirling one of my loose curls around his finger. "She suggested we rent a house in the area and gave me references of who to contact there. We can ask Lasarta and Foxor to take care of the children for a few days."

A sly smile curved his lips. That look always got me going. I slid my hands up his arms to reach his shoulders, getting a good feel of his hard biceps along the way. Coaxing him to bend down, I brushed my lower lip across his. He followed my lead, parting his lips so that our tongues could play like I taught him. I pulled back slightly to make eye contact.

"I think that is an excellent idea."

The next day, Kindor, Kaonto, Kaya, and Kimbra set out on their trip.

"We wish you much success," Montor said. "Please send me updates often."

I searched Kindor's eyes and communicated with him telepathically.

"Be vigilant, Kindor. The fact that there are so many Lostai around makes me nervous."

"Of course, but Kaonto says we will avoid the places where we are likely to run into them. I must admit, I am looking forward to spending time with Kaya and having such an active role in getting my people back on their feet. Kimbra is very excited about it too."

I glanced towards Kimbra and nodded.

"Yes, you all make an excellent team. Montor and I are going to spend some time alone in a small village near Kaya's house. I like the idea of getting to know your planet."

Kindor's eyes shifted, and he took a moment before replying.

"Yes, I hope you enjoy your time there. Oh, it seems Kaonto is ready to go. See you soon, Mina."

"Goodbye, Kindor."

After they left, Montor and I packed our things. Now that it was time for us to head to the small village of Rovera, I felt a bit of trepidation at leaving Josher behind.

"Do not worry, Mina. Foxor and Lasarta have instructions to remain within the hotel grounds, and I have arranged for Kaonto to assign three of his officers to guard the children. I would not leave Josher or Marcia if I thought they were in danger."

It touched my heart to know he was as concerned about Marcia as he was for his son.

Although not fancy, the spacious house Montor rented was equipped with everything we needed to be comfortable. We dropped our bags off and took a quick walk in the woods. My eyes devoured the bright, colorful Sotkari landscape. The countryside popped with fluorescent vegetation. Their flowers and leaves appeared to have been accentuated with highlighters. A vibrant purple hue covered the nearby mountain range, and the river ran an intense indigo. The vivid blue hair and eyes of the Sotkari people matched their environment. The only drab thing on this planet was their grey skin.

Night fell during our stroll. The river came to life with fish and microorganisms that gave off phosphorescent light. Trees with orange, purple, and blue flowers glowed in the dark. The magical aura left me breathless.

When we arrived back at the house, I prepared a quick snack of toasted Sotkari dark bread with butter cream, smoked meat, and fruit and poured us each a glass of wine.

"This was a nice idea, Montor. Thank you," I said as we sat next to each other on a small sofa in the main resting room.

I caressed his cheek. He leaned into my hand, took it in his, and brought it to his lips, running his tongue across each finger.

"Yes, sweetness. I thought since everything for us has always been so rushed and busy, we could take advantage of this downtime."

"I agree. We have had so few opportunities to simply enjoy each other's company."

"Kaya told me the village of Rovera is currently celebrating one of their most beloved holidays. I have always thought the Sotkari to be a little stuffy. I would like to see how they behave when they are enjoying festivities. This house also comes with a watercraft that we can use on the river. The woods are safe, no dangerous wild creatures, only small animals that I can hunt and we can cook together."

I fed him a slice of fruit.

"That sounds wonderful, my king."

By the time we finished eating, the temperature had dropped, and I rubbed my arms to warm up.

"You are cold. I know how to fix that," Montor said with a quick kiss.

Centered in the resting room, metallic plates filled with different colored crystals and a pitcher surrounded an empty circular stone pit. Montor got up, scooped out some crystals, dumped them in the pit, and then poured the liquid from the pitcher over them. The crystals lit up with flashes of blue, orange, and red and emitted a soft crackling sound as they generated heat without any smoke. Montor dimmed the rest of the lighting so the only illumination in the room came from the pit.

"Oh my, I like that. I want a better view," I said, mesmerized as I moved off the sofa to sit on the floor closer to the pit.

Montor joined me, leaning his back against the furniture. He pulled me sideways onto his lap, pressed my head gently against his chest, and stroked my hair. I relaxed, enjoying the feel of his hard pecs and the beating of his heart.

This is perfect.

Montor inhaled deeply, his pupils enlarged with excitement. I reached up to stroke his neck. He bent his head, and our lips touched.

"Mmmm...nice," I said.

"Mina, I love you so much," he murmured and nibbled on my lips until I let him slip his tongue in to meet mine. His hands were all over my body now, greedy with desire.

"I love you too, Montor."

My heart pounded in my chest, aching with anticipation.

I turned to face and straddle him. His fingers softly traced my collarbone and then the edges of my low-cut dress. I leaned back, and he buried his face in my cleavage, his breath warming my skin. The floor, covered in thick rugs, was comfortable enough. We decided to spend the night there.

The next morning, after breakfast, we took another brisk walk in the woods.

"Mina, thinking back on what you mentioned last night, I realized I have never asked you any details about your family, whether you have siblings, parents, what your job was. I avoided this so I would not have to share stories about my family and perhaps to not hear about your—"

His jaw clenched for a moment.

"—the father of your Earthian children. But the best example I have of a loving marriage is from Lasarta and Foxor. I see that there are no secrets between them. They also know each other's favorite things and their peeves, their strengths and weaknesses. I know it has taken them a lifetime, but this quiet time together is at least a start for us. What do you think?"

"Yes, of course. That is exactly what I was referring to."

As we explored more of the forest, Montor and I shared life stories we really had not spoken about in depth before. Some topics were painful, but we got through them. He started by explaining how the Lostai invaded his clan's homeland when he was four years old, which would have been the equivalent mentally and physically of a human eight-year-old.

"I was always hungry after that and never able to sleep because of the continuous explosions. The Lostai moved our family to a labor camp except for my older brother, who escaped to secretly join a militia."

I looked down, a lump in my throat. His words made me recall how we were required to visit a mining labor camp on Renna One where the Lostai forced prisoners from different planets into slave labor. I witnessed a human woman crying out for help because her son had died and the Lostai had simply thrown his body on a junk pile.

Montor interrupted my thoughts as he continued, "I was too young to understand much of what was going on. I realize now that my parents tried to shelter my siblings and me from how precarious our situation was. My father became a leader figure at the labor camps, bravely requesting from the Lostai wardens basic necessities and fair treatment for all the prisoners. Lasarta and Foxor were my parents' best friends, and I remember them always being there too. I idolized my older brother and dreamt about when I would be old enough to join him in the militia. He was Jortan's best friend."

He looked up to the sky before completing his words.

"We never saw my brother again, though we received word he had died in the war. Mother was so depressed after that."

I was horrified hearing the details of what happened to Montor's family. When he spoke of his twin sister, his voice became choked and tears flowed freely. This fierce warrior broke himself down into vulnerable pieces right in front of my eyes. I wanted to protect him from this terrible memory, to take him into my arms and soothe him somehow. Being so much taller than me, the best I could do for him was hold both his hands in mine.

"Montor, maybe that's enough for today," I said.

"No...no...another day, I might not have the courage to talk about it." He wiped away his tears and smiled sadly before continuing. "She was my twin, but shorter than me...very cute... followed me everywhere even though she was not strong enough to play the same games. When she fell ill, a basic antibiotic could have saved her, but the Lostai warden refused to provide any."

He paused as if to pay her silent homage.

"She died, and the warden quickly tired of my father's demands, executing him soon after. My mother was injured in a mining accident and could no longer work. The Lostai warden ordered any adult not fit for work to be killed. That left only my other older brother, my older sister, and me. This brother had always been the most disciplined of us in following rules, never engaging in any mischief."

I sensed he needed some space, so I let go of his hands. He looked down pressing his fingertips against his forehead as memories continued to flood his brain.

"I remember we used to tease him for being so good, saying he should become a priest. After my mother died, he snuck out of the labor camp to get food for me and my older sister. The Lostai cut off his hands and feet before killing him as punishment. They made my older sister and me watch as a warning."

Montor covered his mouth and turned away, a tremor rocking his body. I hugged him as he took a minute to compose himself.

"I loved my older sister the most. She took care of me after my mother died, and soon she was dead too. When all my family was gone, Lasarta and Foxor, who had lost their own two children, took me as a foster child. After about one revolution, the Lostai discovered I was Sotkari Ta and took me to Xixsted for training."

I thought about my son Bobby, who was nine years old when the Lostai kidnapped me. Montor would have been just a little older mentally and physically when he was taken to Xixsted.

"At Xixsted, I met Kaya. The Lostai assigned her to train me in unleashing my Sotkari Ta dormant abilities, as they did with you. She could not openly show me physical affection, but as soon as I learned how to communicate telepathically, I recognized her kindness. She constantly reassured me, made sure I was well cared for, and had me transferred to her quarters so I would not have to sleep alone."

Montor told a story of how Kaya once caught Lostai soldiers beating him and killed the three of them on the spot with her mental abilities. He never found out if or how they punished her for that. I finally understood the extent of the bond they shared. Unfortunately, she could not always be with him, especially as he grew into a teenager. I learned he was claustrophobic.

"The Lostai soldiers constantly berated me, calling me 'vermin' and saying that I came from a primitive people. They punished me by putting me in a small crate like an animal and leaving me in a dark room for days."

Tears welled up in my eyes. I couldn't imagine a young person living through so much heartbreak and torture.

"Montor, it is despicable how they tried to break and humiliate you."

"I was so lucky Kaya cared for me. She tried her best to research Aranda and teach me to be proud of my heritage. She instilled in me the Sotkari Ta discipline of constant self-improvement and explained to me that I was special and possessed outstanding abilities and potential. As I grew stronger, physically and in my Sotkari Ta abilities, my Lostai soldier peers came to fear and respect me."

I looked up, and our lips met in a slow, gentle kiss. When we separated, he smiled. We walked again, and he continued to offer snippets of himself as we chatted.

"Mina, just so you know, I very much dislike a vegetable called *gotumi*. Some Arandans consider it a delicacy, but it is mushy and smells horrible."

I laughed.

"OK, I will make a note of it."

My biggest surprise? This strong, cantankerous, arrogant creature that I loved wrote poetry. I didn't know he had a secret stash of poems, many of them about me, some written since the time we were separated. We sat on a boulder by the river to rest. After much insistence on my part, he stared across the river and reluctantly agreed to recite one, first in Arandan and then translated to Lostai. He said it was titled "Surrender":

All my life I was loyal to no one
Now her supple body is the land I fight for
Her billowing hair is my flag
Her amber eyes form my crest
Her gentle laughter sings my battle hymn
Victory is her cheek against my chest
I have won and lost this war
She made me both her prisoner and patriot

Overcome with emotion, I sat in silence. No one had ever written a poem about me before, that I knew of. Teary-eyed again, I reached up to tilt his face towards me. He tried to be aloof but couldn't hold my gaze.

Looking down to our interlaced hands on his lap, he asked, "Do you like it? It is not very good...just something I do when I am feeling inspired."

"It is beautiful. I wish I could express what I am feeling in a poem like that. All I can say is that I love you, Montor, more than I ever thought possible. I am so lucky to sleep in your embrace each night."

He gathered me in his arms, our kiss more passionate this time as moans brewed in my chest.

"Let us get back to the house, Mina. I want to *kix* you everywhere."

The next morning, I made him a hearty breakfast of meat-and-vegetable omelet, crackers, and tea. I served it on a table on the front porch, and we sat next to each other, continuing the conversation from the afternoon before.

"You know, Mina, at first it was hard, the things we spoke about yesterday, but I am glad I opened up to you. I know I can be difficult sometimes and do not pretend to excuse my bad behavior, but hopefully knowing my history helps you understand me a bit more."

"You have been through a lot," I said, squeezing his hand.

"Now, it is your turn. Tell me of your family and your life back on Earth."

I talked to him about my parents' broken marriage, how my mother died soon after in a car accident, and that I became a mother figure for my sisters.

"Similar to Josher, my first pregnancy was unplanned. Josh and I got married, but he broke my heart when he left newborn Chris and me to join a military branch of my government called the *Marines*. He was too young and not ready for married life. I only saw him a few times in the next six revolutions. It was a lonely and frustrating time for me. During one of those visits, we conceived our second child, our daughter, Amber. She looks a lot like me. Her eyes are the same color as mine."

He looked into my eyes.

"I never would have left you alone with two young children," he said in a soft voice.

I stopped short of telling him not to be judgmental and continued, "Josh eventually returned from the military more mature and ready to take on his responsibilities as a father and husband—"

"So, your previous husband was a soldier like me, correct? He knows how to fight and defend himself?"

I knew exactly what was running through his mind.

"I do not like when you let your thoughts go down this path, Montor. Yes, he was in an active combat zone for several years, and although he is not as tall as you are, he is strong and fearless. Nothing intimidates him. He is a master in martial arts, skilled in hand-to-hand combat, and knows how to use several hand weapons. I am glad you will never meet each other. He would not be one to back down."

Montor's yellow eyes took on a ferocious glare that unsettled me but promptly was replaced by a calm resignation.

"And neither would I. This is of comfort to me. At least in my imagination, or if we ever did meet, he would be a worthy rival and we could fight for you with honor. I would not use any Sotkari Ta capabilities, only my skills as a soldier."

I changed the subject by talking about the special relationship I shared with my father and how although he was disappointed that I got myself into a commitment too early in life, he helped support me financially and emotionally during those first lonely years of my marriage. I described my sisters and best friend, and when I began talking about my children, it was my turn to lose composure. Montor hugged me and stroked my hair as I wept.

"Mina, I wish we could have met under other circumstances. Now that we are together and have Josher, I understand your pain. I cannot imagine what it would be like to be separated from him...or from you."

"Now you have an idea," I whispered in between gasps, "of the battle I face each day."

We spoke frankly of our strong connection and sexual affinity.

"Montor, I have never experienced with Josh what I feel with you."

His male ego inflated.

"What can I say, sweetness."

I pulled a face.

"Do not be so cocky. We know the Sotkari Ta genes are the reason for our good chemistry. Plus, I only have Josh to compare you to."

"Well, I had many sexual partners before I met you, sweetness, and no female has affected me like you have. This is more than just genetics, Mina. I love and admire you deeply, and that is what makes everything else so intense."

He had made himself vulnerable to me once again, and I forgot about his earlier smugness. I leaned against him, running my fingers over his thick locks.

"Well, you make me feel like a joyfully fulfilled lunatic every single time, my king."

He ran one hand from my waist to my thigh, pulling me closer.

"And you, my dear, are a sexual addiction." He stopped to think for a moment, his other hand moving under my blouse. "Our intimacy is like being under the effects of some powerful drug that slowly engorges my mind, body, and soul and then causes me to explode into innumerable satisfied pieces."

I laughed out loud.

Is that the poet coming out?

"What?" he asked, suddenly serious.

"Nothing," I answered innocently, but I couldn't suppress a smile. "I guess I have never heard it expressed that way."

After the third day of being on their road trip, we heard news from Kindor. He said all was going well with plenty of enthusiasm from the people attending the meetings. We also touched base with Lasarta and Foxor, who said they enjoyed the downtime and playing with the kids. Our minds were at ease.

On a sunny day when the river wasn't too choppy, Montor introduced me to the watercraft. I was all smiles as we climbed into what looked like an oversized speedboat with a retractable cover. The colorful fish and sea creatures that populated the river could be viewed through the transparent floor. We packed blankets, pillows, snacks, water, and plenty of wine. When we first started out, Montor put up the cover so we were completely enclosed and protected from the splashing water. He instructed me to strap on security belts. It didn't take long to figure out why.

In a matter of seconds, Montor had us rushing across the river. My heartbeat accelerated with each violent bump as he pushed the craft to its speed limit. I held on tight to the armrests, my body jerked around every few minutes as if on a wave runner. Several miles downstream, the river dropped into a cascade. Although I trusted his ability to navigate the craft, I couldn't contain my loud, high-pitched screams as he rushed for the edge at full throttle. I was out of breath while he was in his element. His broad smile and laughter displayed his large canines in a way I'd seen very few times. We held on as he let the craft fly off the edge and land in the wide plunge pool fifty feet below.

The craft included flight ability, so we were never in danger of losing control while in the air, but I didn't know that at first. After the dive, we lifted off from the plunge pool in a vertical pattern, flew to the original river level, and traveled back to our point of origin. By then, it was almost dusk. We unstrapped, retracted the cover, and broke out the snacks and drinks, while drifting peacefully. The sunset was a spectacular splash of orange, lavender, and gold but timid compared to what followed. Once the sky darkened, the water and surrounding woods lit up like an amusement park. The fish and creatures of every imaginable color glowed brightly in the dark, as did many of the insects that flew about and certain strange flowers that bloomed in phosphorescent colors only in the moonlight. The water that during the day was dark blue now appeared interspersed with streaks of neon green and purple.

Montor looked around and gazed into my eyes. His voice deep, he asked, "Mina, what would you say if I suggest we spend the night right here? I am sure we would be safe."

"I am always safe with you," I said, blowing him a kiss.

"What is that?" he replied with a startled look, not being familiar with the gesture.

"Well, since I cannot reach you from here, I blew you a *kiss*."

He stood from the seat and spread some of the blankets on the small standing space. Then he placed the pillows on top and sat on the boat floor. He offered me his hand to guide me down to the blankets, pulling me onto his lap.

"You can reach me now, sweetness," he said as he touched my lips with his fingers.

I smiled and kissed him, reaching over to grab some other blankets to cover us. I knew by the look on his face that we would soon be without our clothing. The unexpected neon colors, drinking wine straight out of the bottle, making love in too small of a space, sleeping cuddled on a river under a blood red Sotkari moon—it all made for a magical night.

The next evening, we visited the village. People of all ages crowded the streets, eating, drinking, singing, and dancing. Trees and storefronts were strung up with multicolored lights. Street vendors, live music, people dressed in costumes, and marching bands completed the festive scene. Shops and taverns stayed open late. We tried something from every other shop or vendor, sampled drinks in several taverns, and asked strangers to teach us their traditional dances. There were also kiosks where people played betting games and a central area for holographic simulations for children. We learned the festivities would continue for a couple of weeks and decided to bring our entire crew to the house after a few more days on our own so we could all enjoy some time together in the enchanting environment.

11

MONTOR

As much as I enjoyed having Mina to myself, it was good for the rest of the team to join us and enjoy the festivities in Rovera. The Earthian girl, Marcia, especially enjoyed the holographic centers for children, and Damari spent most of his time using the watercraft. The adults bonded over nights of dancing and drinking, except for Lorret, who mostly offered to mind the children when we were out late.

After three weeks, we returned to the hotel in Tremoxtar Mor. No sooner than we had arrived, Mina insisted I show her what she called "Montor's secret stash of poems." I was hesitant at first, but she found them very romantic, which led to vigorous love making. One of her favorites, a short one, titled "Bond":

Hand in hand we go
Against all odds we struggle
A forever bond

Another week transpired until Kaonto and the road trip team returned. I called us all together to hear Kaonto's summary of their travels.

"Everything went smoothly until the third week. That particular night, we had a larger group than usual and gathered in a theater. We were wrapping things up when a squadron of Lostai law enforcement barged in demanding an explanation for why so many of us were assembled late at night. I identified myself as the person in charge of the gathering. They were about to take me into custody. Luckily, Kimbra convinced them we were engaging in a religious ritual. She saved me from what probably would have been a very uncomfortable interrogation."

Kaonto looked in Kimbra's direction and nodded as a sign of appreciation and recognition. A shy smile swept across her face.

"Why did Kindor not just manipulate the mind of their leader?" I asked.

"Kindor and I were communicating telepathically, and he said if my story did not work, then as a last resort he would use mind control," explained Kimbra.

Kindor, as usual, portrayed himself as someone who always took the moral high ground. I do not have such concerns when dealing with filthy Lostai bastards.

Kaonto continued to give his report.

"Other than that time, we had no issues with the Lostai. We traveled to ten major cities in the western hemisphere in thirty days." He stood proud, chin high and shoulders back with an enormous smile. "An amazing fifty thousand new recruits have enlisted in the Sotkari insurgency. Among those are thirty young Sotkari Ta that had been in hiding. We identified and put in place in each city a rebel leader who will be our point of contact."

That was good news but only the first of many important steps. Other than the small insurgent group Kaonto had founded, there were virtually no Sotkari with military training. The Lostai had dismantled the Sotkari armed forces when they took over Sotkar, and those who had fought against the Lostai during the invasion were either dead, kidnapped, or exiled. The Lostai-imposed law prohibited any Sotkari to own or possess weapons.

I stood and joined Kaonto in addressing our group, taking a moment to make eye contact with each person. "Take pride in what you have accomplished. You have set the groundwork for changing the course of our history."

Kaya and Lasarta both locked eyes with me. Their proud smiles brought back memories of how my mother looked when I played sports with much older boys and excelled at school. I transmitted to Kaonto's tablet an official pact of collaboration approved by the Arandan High General while continuing my explanation.

"We have taken a great step forward. Next, we must work on training and fundraising. I will have Commander Portars send Arandan squadron leaders to train your troops, but this will be a gradual process to avoid gaining the attention of the Lostai. The Arandan trainers will need to come individually and on separate spacecraft at different times, pretending to be visiting Sotkar on vacation or business."

"This is the true birth of the United Rebel Front," said Kaonto, visibly moved. "I confess I have withheld some crucial information that I must share with you, now that we are allies in this revolution."

Hmmm...Withholding information...not a good way to start an alliance.

"I know the exact location of the nearest Sotkari trans-portal. One of our newly inducted Sotkari Ta rebels retrieved the secret information by reading the minds of Lostai security personnel. The transportal is on a small planet with breathable atmosphere named Dit Lar about ten days travel away from Sotkar. Dit Lar is uninhabited except for the Lostai personnel in charge of executing the transportations and maintaining the equipment. Expect three large Lostai security spaceships guarding the planet."

The color drained from Mina's face the minute she heard Kaonto's words.

Why?

In spite of what she had always insisted, the possibility of returning to her planet weighed heavily on her.

How is that supposed to make me feel?

Both her reaction and the fact that Kaonto had held back this information irritated me. As everyone digested what he said, I did my best to hide my feelings.

"I see. OK, I will share this intelligence with Commander Portars. It is clear that now Dit Lar will be our next stop. Please transfer to Mina's tablet all the information you have regarding this transportal. And Kaonto, I assume that going forward there will be more transparency between our two groups."

Kaonto nodded and went on to emphasize the importance of a second road trip to the eastern hemisphere to continue the momentum they had achieved in adding new recruits to the insurgency.

"Kindor, I would like to invite you to remain on Sotkar and continue working with Kimbra and me on the recruitment and training."

Everyone looked in expectation to Kindor for his answer. This time he was more hesitant with his reply than when Kaya had asked a similar question. Kimbra and Officer Lorret were feigning disinterest, but their body language told a different story. I chuckled to myself as I realized what was going on.

Kindor, you blue-haired Sotkari scoundrel! You pretend to be so immaculate, and here you have two females vying for your romantic attention. Well, at least that means you might stop pining for my wife.

No sooner did the thought cross my mind than I saw him lock eyes with Mina, and my smile disintegrated.

I could not help the sarcasm in my tone as I communicated to her telepathically, "Seems as if your Sotkari friend has been getting around with the females, but as usual, I see him staring at you. What is going on? Is he consulting his answer with you first? Are you his personal advisor now?"

An impatient tilt to her head made it clear Mina did not approve of my tone.

"He is a little conflicted and not sure he is ready to leave us yet. He feels he can be of great help to his people here but believes you would prefer it if he stayed to help you keep our crew protected," Mina replied.

"That presumptuous snob...and he claims I am the arrogant one? You must mean he is not ready to leave YOU yet. So, what did you tell him?" I said, going from sarcasm to anger.

"Watch your tone, Montor. I told him it is not fair for us to hold him hostage with the idea that he needs to help protect us. You, Josher, and I are the only true fugitives here. That is our problem. On the other hand, in either role he will provide an important service to his people. If he decides to stay with our crew for a while longer, he can return to Sotkar to work with the trainees at any time in the future. I advised him not to worry about what other people want and do whatever he is most comfortable with."

My leadership role required me to constantly control my impulses. I would have liked to knock Kindor off his chair, but instead, I patiently waited as he took another few seconds to think about it before typing an answer in his tablet. He said he preferred to remain with the *Barinta* crew for the time being and serve as a liaison between the Sotkari insurgency and the other rebel groups. Kimbra stared at her hands while Officer Lorret leaned back in her chair, letting a sigh of relief slip out.

Later that day, Mina and I considered what lay ahead of us. With the intelligence we received from Kaonto regarding the location of the nearby transportal, we knew that our next stop would be a dangerous one. We did not even get to the topic of her possible trip to Earth. Just taking control of Dit Lar would be difficult enough for the United Rebel Front. Fighting off the military forces the Lostai would surely send to take it back would be even more challenging, marking the beginning of all-out war against the Lostai.

This sparked a new round of soul-searching for Mina and me as we revisited the gravity of taking our young son into what would soon become a war zone. We always knew that it could come to this, but our trip to Sotkar had been so successful that it was no longer a possibility but a reality. We considered the options of Josher remaining with Kaya in Sotkar or sending him back to Fronidia with Lasarta and Foxor. The potential of the Lostai tracking him down was ever-present, and we would also be putting in danger anyone who harbored Josher. After talking it through, we decided the three of us should stay together.

Before leaving Sotkar, Kindor, Mina, the children and I visited Kaya to bid her farewell. At her house, we all communicated telepathically as a group.

"I am so fortunate to have been able to see you two and your son happy together. Finally, my training can count for something good. As you know, I am probably down to my last few revolutions and am not sure if I will be here to congratulate you on your victory, but my spirit will be with you always," said Kaya.

I did not like to hear her say such things.

"Ahhh, do not say that, Kaya. You are still strong and healthy as ever."

She placed her hands on my shoulders.

"Son, be careful. Things are going to get dangerous in this sector. I pray the Farthest Light guides you in all your next steps."

Next, she placed her hands on Mina's shoulders.

"Mina, may you find happiness with your new family. I know it has been at a terrible cost, but I think you were destined to be here."

Finally, she picked up Josher in her arms and looked deep in his eyes. Tears came down her cheek. Mina's jaw dropped, and Kindor smiled. My heart jumped as I heard my son's voice in my mind for the first time.

"*Lo Ro Kaya,*" he said, which meant "Grandmother Kaya" in Arandan.

"I cannot believe he called out to me telepathically! So young! This one is going to be something special," Kaya said.

Before we left, Kindor gave Kaya the contact codes for his mother and niece.

"I know they will appreciate connecting with an Elder pure-blood Sotkari Ta that also happens to be a part of our family line," he said.

I inferred from Kaya's reply that Kindor apparently had mentioned something about a priest's prophecy.

"The priest was correct. You have already started on a journey to becoming important in the history of our people. I am grateful that the Farthest Light led us to each other."

How humble he is. Now, he is going to fulfill a prophecy.

Again, I suppressed my body language to hide my sarcasm

while Kindor nodded reverently and replied, "I am the one who is thankful and honored to have met and learned from an Elder."

We left Sotkar early the next morning. Kaonto sent two small Sotkari rebel crafts posing as merchant ships to accompany the *Barinta* with ten Sotkari insurgents on each of them a few hours behind us to avoid being conspicuous.

In our morning staff meeting, Mina informed us regarding the transportal.

"The transportal itself is a laboratory inside a cave in the mountainous area on the northwestern quadrant of the planet Dit Lar where the geomagnetic energy that fuels the jumps can be harnessed. The Elder Sotkari scientists were the first to discover the rare metallic meteorites that had fallen to the planet's surface thousands of revolutions ago and combined them with natural geomagnetic fields and manufactured technology to create a pathway to faraway star systems and galaxies. They recreated these transportals across star systems on their quest to escape the Lostai as well as embed their DNA in as many different species as possible. The equipment used to transport a person is mobile. In order to travel to the designated destination and then return or jump to a third destination, travelers need to carry a handheld device that is charged with geomagnetic energy. A jump can be initiated from any location if the device is charged, but as this energy becomes depleted, the device needs to be returned to Dit Lar to recharge."

I took over addressing the team.

"Thank you, Mina. The United Rebel Front has developed two secret weapons that the Lostai are not aware of. The first is a special shield that allows our battle crafts to be undetectable by Lostai sensors. The Lostai will not be able to detect our crafts until they are in visual range. Secondly, we have developed long-range torpedoes that can be fired with precision from much longer distances than before. The plan is for our forces to launch a surprise attack against Lostai security and establish a perimeter around the planet Dit Lar to defend it from the Lostai military that will surely arrive to confront the invasion."

The route for the battle crafts traveling from Aranda to Dit Lar was straightforward and unlikely to encounter Lostai interference. However, the opposite was true for us, as the trip from Sotkar to Dit Lar took us through areas heavily patrolled by the Lostai.

On the fourth day of our trip, Lostai space patrol contacted us. As we had done with the Lostai border agents on Sotkar, we all hid in the holographic room, leaving Colora and Kindor to deal with the two-man Lostai patrol as we monitored them via the viewer. Like before, Colora said she was on a rented craft on vacation and that Kindor was her security guard. The patrol agents requested access to our docking bay and boarded. Colora led them to a conference room where they asked politely for her identification codes. One of them punched the codes into his tablet while the other kept an eye on Kindor. Once they got the readout, their demeanor changed. They scrolled through some screens and then showed Colora something on the display.

"We know this Lostai soldier is of your acquaintance. We believe he has failed his duties by aiding a fellow soldier who left her position without permission and is considered a fugitive of the law. Have you been in contact with him in the last lunar cycle?"

My jaw, my fists, my whole body clenched with tension. I hated putting Colora in this position. She did a good job of looking at the screen with interest and pretending to be shocked.

"Oh, yes, I know him. This is Montor, but I was not aware that he is aiding a fugitive. I have not seen him in a long time. Honestly, I have no idea where he might be. He visits Renna One often. He has property on that planet. You might start there."

The other Lostai that had been observing Kindor took the tablet from his partner and punched something else in. After a few seconds, he pointed at the display. I did not like the looks on their faces as they spoke amongst themselves in a hushed tone.

"Is this your husband?" they asked.

Colora looked indignant. She continued to put on a good show.

"You must mean my deceased husband. He was murdered within the territory limits of Lostai space, and I still am waiting for Lostai law enforcement to solve the crime. What? Did Montor have anything to do with it?"

They grabbed each of her arms roughly, and the second Lostai said, "You are coming with us. It has been determined that your dead husband was an insurgent conspiring against the Lostai Empire. I would not be surprised if there is a connection with Montor's disappearance. You will need to appear before a court and give detailed testimony."

"I am a Fronidian citizen and am protected by law. You cannot take me by force."

"We can and we will. We do not recognize the laws you are referring to."

She tried to pull her arms from their grip, but the second one pointed his weapon to her head and Kindor waited no longer. In slow motion, he turned towards them, and in two seconds, both Lostai fell to the ground.

I have to admit, he is good.

Mina and I rushed out of the holographic room, asking the others to stay but remain vigilant.

When we arrived at the conference room, I asked matter-of-factly, "Are they dead?"

Kindor replied with a shocked expression, "Of course not! Only unconscious."

"Well, you might have to start getting used to more permanent solutions," I said.

Kindor shook his head while I checked that Colora was OK. We needed to quickly decide on a plan of action. I assumed the Lostai patrol had already signaled to their command that they had stopped us. That meant their commanders were awaiting news and ready to send more patrols. I checked the navigation console to review maps of the area.

"We need to avoid the Lostai sending reinforcements here. I should get on the Lostai patrol craft with these idiots and, pretending to be one of them, radio in that they have apprehended me and that the situation is under control. There is a large moon nearby with breathable atmosphere. I will land their craft on the moon, and once we have waited a bit to confirm that the coast is clear, I will contact you to come get me."

Mina's response was immediate.

"Absolutely not! I do not agree with leaving you behind, subject to being taken prisoner by the Lostai. There must be another way. Why does it have to be you? Should not the captain remain on his craft?"

Time was of the essence, and I did not appreciate her second-guessing me.

"I am the only one here that speaks Lostai like a native, without any accent...and I know Lostai military protocol and how to pilot their craft. Do you have any other ideas?"

"But why do you need to land on the moon? Why could you not radio in from their craft and send them off on autopilot?"

"I am concerned their command might send more patrols this way if they do not get regular updates from these guys. Then we will all be in trouble, including the Sotkari rebel crafts that are coming behind us. Even if I were to kill them now, that would only cause their command to question why they are not replying."

Kindor interjected, "I guess it was good I did not kill them after all."

The last thing I need from him now is this unusual sarcasm, but he is right.

"Mina, truthfully, there is some risk that I might be captured, and if so, I want to establish as much space as possible between their craft and the *Barinta* so that you have a chance to get away. I plan to say the viewer is damaged, but if they do not believe it, I may have to awaken these two pieces of crap and manipulate their minds. For all these reasons, I need to get with them on their craft and head away from the *Barinta*. The two Lostai alone are no match for me, and I will make up some excuse for why we need to land on the moon."

I knew by the way she was rubbing her forehead that the thought of leaving me alone with them terrified her, but she understood my rationale, and neither she nor Kindor could come up with another viable option. She embraced me with tears welling in her eyes.

"Listen, you better not get any crazy ideas of us leaving you behind. This crew needs their captain, and I need my husband. We will monitor your navigation constantly. If you need help, let us know and we will all go in for a rescue."

"OK, sweetness, but buckle up. Remember, in my absence, you are the captain, and the crew will look to you for leadership," I said to her in a stern voice.

She looked up at me, and I cupped her face with both my hands. We *kix* as if our next stop was the bedroom. For a moment, I almost forgot what was going on. I took a deep breath and looked towards Kindor, having to trust him now with those I loved the most.

"Please keep my family and the crew safe."

Kindor nodded and helped me cuff the two Lostai and carry them back to their craft.

12

MINA

Colora and I looked at each other. The worry in her eyes only made me more aware of my queasiness. I crossed my arms to hide my trembling hands. We notified the rest of the crew to come out of the holographic room and informed them of Montor's plan. All eyes were on me, awaiting orders.

Time to set aside my fears and assume my role as second-in-command.

Lasarta immediately requested permission to retire to her room to pray. I put Kindor in charge of the scanners to keep track of the Lostai craft, the Sotkari ones trailing us, and any other activity in the area. I asked Colora to man the communications system.

"Please contact the Sotkari escorts to let them know what is going on and advise them to be on high alert."

After about two hours of navigation away from the *Barinta*, Montor contacted us and let us know that, so far, his plan was working. I put him on the viewer so we could all see as he updated us. The two Lostai were slumped in their chairs, unconscious.

"I had to awaken these two idiots so that their commander could see me in their custody. You should have seen their faces. They could not remember bringing me on board their ship." He doubled over laughing. "Anyway, the Lostai Patrol Command is waiting for me to be brought in to the nearest Lostai military station. As soon as we were off the viewer, I put these guys back to sleep again and will soon be landing on the moon. If there is no Lostai activity in the area, you can come to the moon and pick me up."

I forgot about protocol and ended our conversation on a personal note.

"Montor, please be careful. I will see you soon...I love you."

We were all relieved things were going according to plan. I notified the Sotkari escort, telling them to continue to Dit Lar and to let us know if they run into any other Lostai patrol on the way. Setting course for the moon at maximum speed, it took us about half hour to get there as our ship traveled faster than the smaller Lostai patrol craft. We established an orbit waiting for Montor to contact us again and give us coordinates for landing. The atmosphere around the moon was chaotic with electrical storms and strong winds.

A half hour went by with no news from Montor. By then, he should have landed and contacted us with his coordinates. I kept asking Colora if there was any incoming transmission from the Lostai patrol craft. My pacing probably made everyone else feel just as nervous as I was, but anxiety got the best of me. Against my better judgment, I even attempted to establish communication with the Lostai patrol craft. Finally, after receiving no replies to several hails, I gave the order to land.

We had no idea where Montor had landed. Kindor informed me he was no longer picking up the Lostai patrol craft's signal on the scanner. I considered the possibility that the electromagnetic storm was interfering with our sensors. I needed to make a decision, now.

"Kindor, would you agree a transport pod is better suited for a search and rescue since it can fly close to the surface and give us a visual?"

"Yes, but this stormy weather could pose a problem."

Words formed in my mind clipped and quick.

"Something has not gone according to plan. Otherwise, he would have contacted us by now. I need to do something. I am going down there. You are the next in command. Stay here and protect the children and crew. I will call if I need you."

His face contorted with worry, but he knew better than to try to change my mind.

"OK, Mina, but be careful and keep me updated."

When I took off, grey hail, some the size of apples, pelted the transport pod.

It didn't take long to locate the Lostai patrol craft. I found it crash-landed on its side against a mountain, partially buried by a rockslide. My heartbeat accelerated at the sight of rocks being hurled in the air, and I knew it meant Montor was trying to get out from under the rubble. I landed and the ground shook, rocking the pod. Between the wind, seismic activity, and my nerves, I could barely reach the communication controls to contact the *Barinta*.

"Kindor!" My breathing was shallow. "I have found the Lostai patrol craft, and it is trapped under a rockslide. Here are the coordinates. Come immediately. I need your help to rescue Montor. Hurry!"

Kindor acknowledged and confirmed he was on his way.

The pounding of my heart and in my head made me dizzy as I jumped out of the pod and ran full speed to the crash site, already focusing my mind on moving rocks out of the way. I reached the craft and could hear nothing other than the sounds of crackling electricity, swirling wind, hail, and rocks crashing to the ground. It was a relief that I could make telepathic contact with Montor.

"Montor, are you OK? Kindor will be here soon, and between the three of us, we will get rid of all these rocks!"

"Mina, what are you doing here? You need to leave."

"What do you mean, what am I doing here? Once I did not hear further from you, I realized you might be in trouble. We need to get you out of there."

There was a strange tone to his voice in my mind, so weak that a sick feeling crept into the pit of my stomach.

"Mina, you must leave immediately. When Lostai crafts crash, they send out a homing signal. Reinforcements are probably on their way here now!"

"There is no way I am leaving you here. I will order Kindor to go back and take the *Barinta* away from here, but I am staying."

"Listen to me. Not only is there danger from the Lostai, but there is seismic activity on this moon. The tremors may cause more rockslides. Also, my legs are broken and possibly my back too. I feel a strange numbness. I will not be able to run or fight."

"You do not need to run. The pod is right here. I can help you in."

After a few minutes of silence, I heard his voice again, his tone impatient now.

"Why are you so stubborn?"

"What are you saying? Let us not talk so much and focus on moving the rocks."

"Mina! Leave, please. They will capture all of you and Josher. There is not a minute to spare!"

My head hurt, and I found myself gasping for breath.

"No! I will not!"

I continued to focus on removing the rocks as I agonized over whether I should have Kindor turn back or not. After a period of silence, Montor's voice entered my mind again, stronger now, with an arrogance and unpleasantness that reminded me of when we first met.

"Mina, you are doing a terrible job as second-in-command. Listen carefully. I think I am not getting out of here, so it is time I own up to something I have done, something you most likely will not be pleased with."

"What? We have no time for this."

The movement of rocks slowed down. He had stopped working on them, so now it was only me. A painful vibration assaulted my brain as I alone concentrated on lifting the heavy rocks away from the patrol craft as fast as I could and dropping them a few feet away.

"You do not love me, Mina."

"Huh? Of course, I do. Have you hit your head?"

"I have manipulated you from the very beginning, made you think you felt things that you did not."

"Montor, I know you are making this up to make me leave. It is not going to work."

It took a lot of effort to move the huge rocks and keep the telepathic connection.

"No. Think about it. You have sometimes wondered whether we have rushed into our relationship and marriage, especially considering your ties on Earth, right? I hate to disappoint you, my dear, but I manipulated you from the first night we were intimate to the day I proposed marriage to the present. I made you believe you were in love with me, but those are not your true feelings at all. I mean, I do not know who you really love. Perhaps it is your Sotkari friend."

"Do not bring Kindor into this!"

Time stopped for me.

Could it be true?

I stood there, hail falling around me in hard clunks, hitting my body and face. The rocks were no longer being moved. I licked my lips and tasted blood.

With a tremor in my voice, I answered, "You are lying. Tell me you are lying."

"Unfortunately, my dear, it is true. The Sotkari Ta chemistry between us is real, but love...no...not at all. How did you express it once? Ah, yes...I got into your head...to make you think you did. I hate to admit it, but I do not love you either."

Now, my whole body shook.

"I cannot believe it. How could you pretend? Everything has been so real."

"Yes, well, I am efficient that way. Please do not take my bad behavior out on our son. Promise me you will take care of him. Do not leave him, Mina. A boy who grows up without his mother becomes a hard person with no soul, usually without remedy. I would not mind if you married Kindor. He would be a suitable guardian."

"You idiot, shut up! I am not marrying anyone. I am married to you. Why, why would you say such a thing?" I froze in place, shaking my head. "No. I will not listen to this nonsense. This is clearly you trying to confuse me."

"At first, it was just physical. I desired you, and I liked the challenge of making you forget any loyalty to your husband. Then you came back with my son. I knew he needed his mother, and I wanted to make sure you would not abandon him."

"Abandon my son? Are you crazy? I would never...I cannot believe...What?"

I was confused and incoherent and not feeling like myself. A deep loathing washed over me, as if I had two personalities. It didn't make sense, but I couldn't control it.

"Montor, you are an evil person with no integrity or honor. What you have done is despicable. I hate you."

"Good, Mina, that is good. The lives of everyone on the *Barinta*, including our son, depend on what you do right this second. Do not be stupid. I am telling you the truth. Leave. Now!"

I heard the second pod landing. My senses dulled. Tears flowed down my cheeks and mixed with blood from the cuts on my face, creating a salty, metallic taste in my mouth. Kindor ran towards me, and the rocks flew through the air again at three times the pace they had before. It was humbling to witness the power wielded by this unassuming being. He looked at me perplexed as I walked in the opposite direction towards my pod and communicated to him, "Let him rot in a Lostai jail cell. You were right about this creature. He has no honor."

Despite my comment, Kindor ran to the craft, and rocks continued to fly from the area at a fast pace. I turned to watch him. He placed his hands against the exposed portion of the patrol craft hull, and I assumed he was communicating with Montor. Whatever Montor told Kindor must have been upsetting because he ran his fingers through his hair, staring at me long and hard, before turning to face the patrol craft again. He placed one hand on the hull, gesticulating with the other in a way that appeared as if he were arguing. Finally, he took a deep breath and pressed fingertips to his temples. Usually, this was a sign of exerting an extreme level of mental strength. After a few minutes, he came running back to me.

"I have repaired his legs, and his back has no permanent damage. We must leave now."

I said nothing and walked to my pod like an automaton.

"Mina, are you OK?" Kindor asked. "Maybe you should leave that pod here and ride with me."

"I am fine." My voice sounded hollow and foreign.

I didn't look back once at the crash sight as the pod lifted off the moon's surface.

Everyone was waiting anxiously by the shuttle bay as we walked in. No words came out of my mouth as I continued to the main conference room, the door closing behind me. I pounded my fists against the table until the pain was unbearable and then put my head down, my cheek against the cold tabletop. I sat there for a long time doing nothing other than repeating the same scene with Montor over and over in my head until a hollow grief consumed me.

When I stepped out of the conference room and into the main navigation area, I saw that Kindor apparently had taken charge and ordered that we lift off. I hadn't even noticed we were already outside of the moon's atmosphere and well on our way to Dit Lar. Everyone was there except Lasarta and the children. They looked at me as if I were a strange animal in a zoo. Kindor was tight-lipped.

Jutting out my chin and without looking at anyone in particular, I said, "I am emotionally unable to properly command this crew, so I hereby transfer all my duties and powers as captain to Kindor."

I took a step towards the corridor that led to the living quarters when Officer Lorret approached me and blocked my way.

"How can someone with powers like yours be such a coward," she snarled at me, her face full of contempt.

She appeared ready to strike me, so Kindor stepped between us. Because of her height, she was able to look at him, eye to eye. Her voice trembled with rage.

"And you...I am sure you are just salivating...ready to claim her...You bastard, we do not know if her husband is even dead yet."

Kindor's jaw dropped. Ice flowed through my veins. My speech was slow and my voice deep. I didn't bother to look up at her and kept my hands folded in front of me.

"You know nothing about me or what I have been through. Speak to either of us like that again, and I will cause your lungs to explode. Now, please get out of my way."

Officer Lorret clenched her jaw but moved aside. I assumed Lasarta had the children in her room, so I walked there, doing my best to get under control. When Lasarta let me in, I realized it was already evening as the children were sleeping. She looked tired, her eyes red and puffy.

Gesturing that we move into the next room to not awaken the children, she asked, "Mina, how are you? You have not tended to the cuts on your face. Come to the bathroom and I will see what I can do until you can get to the infirmary."

She used gauze and an antiseptic ointment to gently wipe off the dried blood and disinfect the cuts. We then sat down in the resting area of her quarters. I began to feel like myself again, as if a veil had been removed from my eyes.

"Thank you. I need to apologize. You were left as captain once I summoned Kindor. At a minimum, I should have debriefed you when we returned."

"No worries. You were distraught. It was understandable. Kindor explained everything to us."

"What did he say?"

"The Lostai patrol craft apparently had crash-landed into the side of a mountain and then was partially buried by a rock-slide. He said you all tried to remove the rocks, but Montor insisted you return because of the homing device that was automatically activated by the Lostai craft."

"Yes, Montor also had leg fractures, which Kindor repaired before we left."

"You are very strong, Mina. I know it must have been difficult to leave Montor there for the safety of the crew and the children. I admire you. I...I think I could not have done it."

I looked down, biting my lip.

"Do not praise me, Lasarta. I was not strong in that way. I was ready to order Kindor back here to take you all away from this moon while I remained with my husband to face whatever was coming together, but something happened down there. First, Montor confessed that he did something, something terrible to me."

She stood and put her hands on my shoulders while I remained sitting.

"Mina, consider what you are about to say. I have grown quite fond of you, but my loyalty and love for my foster son are unconditional."

I sighed deeply.

"Yes, Lasarta, I know. Although I was confused for a moment, I am pretty sure now he was not telling me the truth. I think he was just trying to convince me to leave."

Her expression softened as she sat by my side again and took my hand in both of hers.

"Tell me, Mina, what happened?"

I had hoped to remain composed, but tears filled my eyes even before I spoke my next words.

"Montor told me that from the beginning, he has been manipulating my mind to make me feel that I love him. He said at first it was only to satisfy his male ego, just on a whim."

Lasarta remained silent as my voice became tremulous.

"Then he said once I returned with Josher, he continued the farce because he was afraid I would abandon my son."

I choked up, my voice high-pitched as sobs forced their way between my words.

"But that is not all. The worst thing...the worst is that he said he never really loved me either."

"But Mina, you just said you do not believe this, right?" Lasarta interrupted in a somber voice. "It is obvious he said all of this to convince you to leave him behind. He made the ultimate sacrifice."

"Yes, but then I felt anger and hatred towards him. I bet anything he was manipulating me at that very moment. I know for a fact he has done this to me once before, and I have told him I consider it a violation. If he so easily falls back into that habit, sometimes, I do not know what to think."

"Mina, I have no doubt that Montor loves you. Just the fact

that he agreed to marry you even though you have a husband on Earth—a husband that is very much alive—is proof of this."

I could only imagine how wide my eyes were at that point.

"Yes, we know you are not a widow. Montor told us the truth just before the wedding. He was seeking Foxor's counsel on what for us Arandans is a delicate issue. To take the wife of another male without giving him an opportunity to fight for her is dishonorable. It was a hard step for Montor to take. Foxor reassured him that the most important thing was your feelings for each other. I remember Montor spoke like someone deeply in love."

This internal conflict Montor harbored about my husband on Earth was not news to me, but the fact that he had swallowed his pride to discuss it with his foster parents confirmed how seriously he took our commitment to each other. Lasarta's words revealed another of several sacrifices Montor had made for our love. My lips trembled as tears streamed down my face. He didn't deserve my harsh words. Doubting his feelings for me even for a few minutes felt like I had committed a stupid betrayal.

"In my last words to him, I said he was an evil person and that I hated him."

I slipped my hand out of hers, buried my face in both of mine, and continued to cry, my whole body shaking, overwhelmed with the force of grief. She rubbed my shoulders, trying to console me. We remained like this for a while until I wore myself out. I looked sideways at her, rubbing my forehead.

"What am I going to do now?"

"Mina, I am grieving just like you that we had to leave Montor behind, but the correct action was to hurry out of there before the Lostai arrived. Montor knows what it is like to be an orphan. He does not want that for Josher. My foster son has found himself in difficult situations before. He is powerful, resilient, and resourceful. The Lostai will try to get as much information from him as possible. They will not kill him, as they are not willing to lose such a powerful asset. Instead, they will attempt to force him back on their side. My guess is they are going to try and capture someone he cares about to use as leverage. We need to avoid this at all costs. Once we are in a safe position, we can focus on getting Montor back."

13

MONTOR

My life is a mess
A cluttered chaos of love
You in the center

"Chaos of Love" from *Montor's Secret Stash of Poems*

I cursed everything in the heavens and down below. My voice bounced off the walls of the damaged patrol craft like sonic booms. Nothing irked me more than to owe that Sotkari yet another favor. With his Sotkari Ta abilities, he repaired the fractures in my legs and helped remove more of the rocks that had all but buried the Lostai patrol craft I was trapped in. There was not enough time for him to get me out. Lostai Patrol Command had already received a distress signal, and patrols in the vicinity could arrive at any moment. I explained to Kindor the grave danger Mina, my son, and the rest of the crew were in. We could not risk the Lostai finding them. I made him promise he would waste no time getting the *Barinta* out of orbit and away from this moon.

I hurt Mina with my words and hated myself for it, but she was so stubborn. The worst thing I said to her is that I did not love her. *Shermont!* I even told her that Kindor might be a suitable partner for her. She called me an idiot and said I had no morals or something along those lines. I could take that. I never made myself out to be a scrupulous person. Then she said she hated me and told Kindor she hoped I rotted in a Lostai cell. Those words stabbed my heart like a knife to the chest.

The truth is Mina's love is the greatest thing that has ever happened to me.

I pushed my pain and worries aside for the moment. My main concern was how to deal with the Lostai that were about to arrive. I could not risk communicating with anyone, and so hours went by at an agonizingly slow pace.

The two Lostai soldiers that had attempted to take me into custody were already unconscious when we crash-landed. I used my mental abilities to cause their organs to stop functioning. Ha! They were dead. Thanks to Kindor, my legs were functioning fine, but my back hurt and I had a few cracked ribs. I used the medical equipment on board to repair my ribs and contusions. Still, I was not in the best shape for hand-to-hand combat and decided to hide in the back of the craft to catch whoever was coming by surprise. I took the hand weapons that belonged to the filthy dead soldiers with me and waited. Timing would be crucial. I needed to kill them before they could communicate back to Lostai Patrol Command.

The faint sound of spacecrafts landing in midst of the heavy hailstorm put me on alert. I soon heard banging on the outer hull. They would either have to move enough rocks to access the entrance or carve out a piece of the hull. The banging stopped. The key to my escape would be that they not call for reinforcements. Itching to jump out of my hiding spot and face them, the sound of a photon beam and an explosion further frayed my nerves. They had come in larger crafts outfitted with weaponry. I lay down to appear unconscious.

The hatch opened and two Lostai patrol officers stepped into the craft. Using my mental abilities, I caused them to lose consciousness and stopped their hearts from beating. Grabbing a weapon, I ran outside and came face to face with two more patrol officers. Taken by surprise, those idiots did not even have time to draw their weapons. One second later and they were also dead. I got the name of one officer from his identification tags and continued to survey the area to assess my situation. There were two large shuttlecrafts. They had used the photon beam to disintegrate the rocks that were blocking the entrance to the craft. After checking both shuttlecrafts and finding no other patrol officers, I initiated an audio only transmission to Lostai Patrol Command.

"Sir, this is Officer Morax," I said, reading the dead officer's name off his tag. "The bad weather here has affected our video systems. We attended to an automated distress call from the patrol craft that was carrying the prisoner, Montor Ventamu. The other patrol officers have perished, but we have Montor in our custody and will proceed to take him to the closest Lostai military station."

"Yes, excellent work. You should use a stunner to keep him unconscious as he has extraordinary mental abilities."

What a moron.

"Yes, sir. That is what we have done."

I put one of the shuttlecrafts on autopilot and sent it to the Lostai military station and boarded the other shuttle, bringing all their hand weapons with me. My next important decision was to identify a destination. I could have tried to catch up with the *Barinta* and reunite with my crew and family. My wife might not have been too happy that I survived after all the ugly things I told her, but that was not my chief concern. I did not want to draw the Lostai military close to them, which meant getting to a safe place as far away from the *Barinta* as possible.

Fronidia was a good choice since that planet's government was distancing themselves from the Lostai and their expansionist policies. I could hide in the Arandan immigrant enclave where no Lostai would dare to go for fear of being lynched. The normal route would have taken thirty days. Instead, I took a more direct path dangerously close to a nebula that cut travel time in half and avoided running into more Lostai. It was a risk I needed to take.

I had not traveled this far totally alone in some time. Although concerned about letting my guard down, I needed rest to regain strength and start healing. Trusting the notification system to let me know if there was another craft in the area, my sleep occurred in spurts. I could not relax completely.

What could Mina be thinking right now? Does she really hate me?

I loved Mina like I had loved no female before. A glorious mystery, sex with her was like an addictive drug, but my attraction was more than just physical. She was strong, loyal, and kind, and an excellent mother to our son.

Hopefully, one day I will be able to explain my actions.

I lied and manipulated her mind to protect her and get the *Barinta* off that moon as soon as possible. My survivor instinct guided my choices, sometimes in not the most upstanding way. By now, the effects of manipulating her mind had probably worn off, but she would still resent that I took over her thoughts. She often reminded me how even Kaya was against mind control.

I wondered if the *Barinta* would continue to Dit Lar. War was about to break out. If the United Rebel Front were successful in gaining control of Dit Lar, Mina would be asked to test the transportal and perhaps even use it to take little Marcia back to Earth. Although I acknowledged that would be wonderful for Marcia, dark thoughts percolated at the idea of Mina making that trip. She always said she would never leave me or Josher, but I had hurt her feelings and confused and angered her.

Might she change her mind? What will be her reaction when she finds herself back on her home planet, perhaps only hours away from her Earthian children?

14

MINA

My heart felt like it was dragging around a load of blocks, but I couldn't waste time feeling sorry for myself. I needed to be strong and focus on repairing the crew's morale and camaraderie. The morning after my talk with Lasarta, I called a staff meeting and declared myself fit to resume my duties as captain.

"I know we are all upset because we were not able to bring Montor back. I myself felt the emotional strain, and I regret if I offended any of you in the process. However, we need to remain focused. Kindor, by any chance did you monitor for any Lostai craft heading to the moon?"

He shot me a confused look, then replied, using his tablet so all could understand, "We did. Soon after we left the moon's atmosphere, two crafts landed."

"Did they subsequently take off, and if so, were we able to track their destinations?"

"Yes. One appeared to be heading towards another moon about ten days' travel away from Dit Lar. The trajectory of the second is unclear."

"I need you to share this information with Arandan

command and research everything you can about Lostai presence on that moon."

"Are we Montor rescue?" asked Damari. His Lostai was not getting any better.

"Yes, we are, but first we must complete our mission on Dit Lar with the transportal."

Kindor cocked his head, his eyes meeting mine.

"I thought you said he should rot in a Lostai jail cell," he said to me telepathically.

I felt my brows knit together.

Is he questioning me?

"I was upset and may have jumped to conclusions. Of course we need to get him back," I answered.

Kindor raised his eyebrows but communicated nothing else.

After the meeting, we went about our regular schedule. I stopped by the dining area to get some hot tea. Lasarta had prepared a special blend that helped calm my nerves. Officer Lorret walked in and asked if she could sit with me. I eyed her with suspicion but gestured for her to go ahead.

"Mina, I apologize for my behavior yesterday. I was way out of line," she said, her voice back to its typical monotone.

"No need to apologize. We were all upset with what happened. We all said things we should not have," I answered.

"I lost control because I was reminded of when the Lostai captured me. They can be so ruthless. You probably cannot understand, but in any event, I am very sorry."

I stood and untucked my shirt.

"Lift my shirt in the back and take a look."

Confused, her eyes opened wide, and she shook her head.

"Go ahead," I insisted.

She did, and I heard her catch her breath at the sight of the ugly scars on my back.

"Lorret, I was kidnapped, ripped away from my family and

my home, and held prisoner in a Lostai science camp for more than one revolution. They punished and humiliated me. I was forced to train and become one of their soldiers until Montor helped me escape. I understand your rage very well," I said plainly.

Lorret said nothing at first, but when we both sat again, she leaned over and touched my face, carefully inspecting where the chunks of hail had cut my skin.

After a few moments, she said, "Please come with me now to the dispensary so I can eliminate these scars before it is too late, and we should take advantage to get your physical done and documented."

"Oh, so you are finally going to do that for me?"

She furrowed her brow and I laughed.

"I am joking. That is fine."

As we walked toward her office, she said, "Mina, to be truthful, I disliked you from the moment I heard about you and even more so when I saw you for the first time. I could not understand how one of Aranda's most handsome, eligible bachelors, the first male I had ever been intimate with, was betrothed to a weak, puny alien."

Puny?

I pulled a face. She continued.

"Then I learn Montor has served in the detestable Lostai military for all his adult life. Because of you, he finally decided to leave all that behind and join the Arandan rebel force, something that I had begged him to do revolutions ago." She shook her head. "Well, then my disdain for you was complete."

Where is she going with this?

"Lorret, I thought we were finally getting on better terms with each other."

A tentative smile crept across her face. She hadn't smiled much since I'd met her.

"Then Kindor explained about Sotkari Ta and how you

three have special abilities. He did not tell me how you came to know Montor. When Kindor speaks of you, he limits himself to talking about the time you lived with his family...He has a thing for you...Well, you must know, of course."

She sighed and shrugged before continuing.

"Montor did not tell me much of how he met you either, and I did not care to know. I guess what I am trying to say is, I never knew until just now how much you also have suffered at the hands of the Lostai. I realize now that we have something in common, that you are not weak, and there is much more to you than meets the eye. I am ready to forget my previous opinions about you...and be a friend."

"Thank you, Lorret. You are an important part of this crew. To be successful, we all need to be loyal to each other, and I would be honored to count you among my friends."

I passed my physical with flying colors, and Lorret erased the scars from my face. Once she dismissed me, I contacted Commander Portars to get a status update on our plan to take over Dit Lar and the transportal. He explained that the rebel attack and formal declaration of war were scheduled to be launched in two days.

The *Barinta* was not expected to be involved in the battle itself. We were ordered to stand by at about a day's distance from Dit Lar to wait for confirmation that the Arandan forces had taken out Lostai security and were successful in maintaining the perimeter. At precisely the same time on Aranda, there would be a full-on attempt to overthrow the Lostai and retake control of utilities and key government installations. All related Lostai personnel would be taken into custody, followed by a formal declaration of independence from the Lostai Empire. The Sotkari insurgency would also hit several Lostai law enforcement installations on Sotkar simultaneously. We had not yet made formal contact with the rebel movement on Renna One, but once news got around about what was happening, they might, on their own, also launch attacks on the Lostai. If we were lucky, the chaos of hitting the Lostai on several fronts at the same time would give the rebels an upper hand.

I also asked Commander Portars if they had any information regarding the moon where we suspected Montor had been taken. He said it was a Lostai military station, but he didn't have positive confirmation yet that Montor was there.

"Mina, we need to discuss something else. We are going to do everything in our power to recover Montor, but in the meantime, we need to assign a replacement."

"Umm, with all due respect, Commander, we had already decided the line of succession for the *Barinta*, which makes me captain."

He cleared his throat before continuing.

"Yes, I know, but Mina, we chose Montor as our Strategic and Liaison Officer for the United Rebel Front because of his qualifications. Also, you may not agree or understand, but our protocols do not allow for a female to occupy such a position."

I worried about where this conversation was going.

"Well, we do have a male Arandan on board who can temporarily act as captain—Foxor—and I have become well versed on everything related to the transportals."

"Foxor is not qualified to dictate the strategy for our forces or help us create liaisons with other groups."

"Ummm...You know, Kindor was key in energizing the Sotkari community..."

Portars cleared his throat again, and I got the distinct feeling he was trying his best to be patient with me.

"Yes, he was, but he was following Montor's direction. Mina, we still want you to be our lead with the transportals as well, but we need to send you a qualified Arandan male to direct you all in your functions and take on the strategic lead until we get Montor back."

There was no convincing Commander Portars otherwise.

He informed me Montor's replacement would be traveling on a small spacecraft and delivered to the *Barinta* the next day. The matter was out of my hands. I let everyone know about my conversation with Portars.

"I do not like it," Lorret said. "I love my people, but some of these Arandan commanders can be narrow-minded." Foxor and Lasarta agreed.

Her comment made me even more uneasy, but there was nothing else for us to do other than continue our daily schedule as usual. While Josher, Marcia, and I ate dinner, they asked for Montor a few times. I told them he was on a special trip and would be back in a few weeks. Of course, Josher was too young to understand and continued to call out for his father. Eventually, I was able to distract him. At bedtime, I wished someone could do the same for me. I missed Montor's arms around me, pulling me tight against his body, kissing my back, and whispering sexy Arandan words in my ear. I prayed he was still alive and devising a plan on how to survive and escape from wherever he was.

Montor's replacement, named Sortomor, arrived early the next day. He was a few years older than Montor and me but still with the typical Arandan strong, muscular build. Once he was assigned quarters and settled in, he called a meeting.

He began, "I know you are still reeling from having lost Montor—"

"We have not lost him. We have just not rescued him yet," I said.

He pursed his lips and raised his voice.

"Do you routinely interrupt your captain?" His eyes narrowed as he glared down at me.

"Sorry," I said, looking away so he couldn't see the irritation on my face.

"You are right, we are trying to rescue him, and we will. I was about to say, we have lost his leadership for the time being.

I know this is not a true military craft and you are not proper soldiers. Commander Portars wanted to take advantage of Montor's vast knowledge and experience, and that is why he agreed to this unusual arrangement. However, I only know how to manage soldiers in a true, strict, Arandan military fashion. You will need to get accustomed to my style."

After we each explained our duties and our schedule, he reassigned Foxor as second-in-command, followed by Kindor and Damari. He also created a strict schedule adding typical Arandan boot camp training and eliminating most of the free time we used to dedicate to practicing our language skills or playing with the children. All domestic-type duties were assigned to the females, so now the males no longer helped us in taking care of the children, the garden, or the livestock. Kindor, Damari, and I would have to wake up extra early to fit in our Sotkari Ta regimen. Sortomor set strict times for meals and retiring at night, rules about where we could be and when, and limited time for us to meet casually. Everyone was still numb from what happened with Montor, so we didn't question his changes.

At the end of the day as I was passing through the lounge area on the way to my quarters, I came across Captain Sortomor with Foxor, Lasarta, and Lorret sharing some drinks. I walked over and asked in a cheerful voice, "So, are we celebrating your first day aboard the *Barinta*? I guess I missed the invitation."

Lasarta looked embarrassed. Something was off.

"Well yes, we are, but this is fine, aged Arandan brandy, which I am sure is too strong for your alien tastes. That is why you were not invited," Sortomor replied, a chill in his voice as he looked down at me.

Anger boiled up inside me, but I remembered the bitter Arandan coffee I could never stomach and decided against challenging him.

"I see. Very well then. Enjoy and good night," I replied as politely as I could muster.

To my surprise, Foxor interjected.

"I have seen Montor share this type of brandy with Mina plenty of times. Come Mina, let me pour some for you. If it is too strong, we can add ice or mineral water," said Foxor while making eye contact with Sortomor, as if daring him to intervene.

Sortomor raised his glass with a fake smile.

"Of course, have at it, if you dare."

I took mine straight, raising the glass close to my face and smiling as I looked up at Sortomor. I knew the color of my eyes rivaled that of the liquor in the glass. Montor had complimented me on that plenty of times. I breathed in the aroma and swirled the drink carefully in the glass before sipping. It turned out to be quite smooth.

"This is very good. Montor has shared a similar brandy with me. I believe it was a rare bottle of Tromozar Ristor. This one is *almost* of the same quality."

Foxor's expression showed he was pleased, albeit surprised, at my knowledge of Arandan spirits. I held Sortomor's gaze and could tell he was intrigued. This time, he couldn't help but give me a genuine smile.

"I am glad you like it," he said, the brandy smoothing his voice.

Proud of myself, I had a second serving, thanked everyone again, and excused myself. Colora was in my quarters, watching over the kids. By the time I arrived, the alcohol exposed my outrage.

"*Grimah!*" I shouted, pacing with my arms crossed. It was a Lostai word that literally meant to fornicate but was used as an expletive somewhat along the lines of damn or fuck.

Colora pulled back to study my expression, not quite knowing whether to chuckle at my obscenity or worry.

"That Sortomor is so annoying. I do not like him already. Did you know he called a little celebratory toast exclusively with the Arandans?"

Colora nodded, stroking her chin.

"That does not surprise me. Jortan used to tell me stories about him. Sortomor was not his favorite person, for sure. He is a fervent patriot but a bit to the extreme. In fact, he is a racist," replied Colora.

"Well, I guess that explains a lot."

"Yes, he is critical of Arandans who marry people from other planets," she said, her lips pursed, "and he was not in favor of Jortan's idea of collaborating with other rebel groups. He would say each planet should wage their own war against the Lostai. He is also very ambitious. I am afraid that once he gets used to occupying Montor's position, he might not be so willing to give it back."

15

MINA

After Colora left us and Josher fell asleep, I spent some time talking with Marcia. Over the last few weeks, I had been explaining our mission to her and that we were close to finding a way to return her to Earth. Now that this journey could be only a matter of days away, I wanted her to be familiar with the details and what to expect. She was eager to return home but also had grown close to all of us, especially Montor and me.

"Will Mr. Monster be back from his trip soon? I want to see him before I go back home."

Hearing her mention his *name* with so much affection, having to explain to her it was not likely he'd be back in time, and seeing her disappointment intensified my own grief.

"Honey, he would have loved to, but he is on an important mission that we hope will help a lot of other children get back home just like you."

"I'm happy you're coming with me. My mom and dad will like you a lot."

"And I would love to meet them too, but remember what we've already discussed. I'll stay close by until you secretly tell me that everything is OK, but I can't let them see me, and I can't stay. I need to come back to take care of Josher."

"Don't you want to go home, too?" she said, looking up at me through a filter of innocence.

I cleared my throat.

"Well, honey, this is my new home. I need to come back here, and I have an important job. I need to help other kids like you get back to their families."

"You're brave, Ms. Mina, like a superhero. I hope you can at least come visit me one day."

I kissed her forehead and told her it was time for bed.

Sleep eluded me for most of the night, and I woke up groggy but faithfully got ready for our—now early morning—Sotkari Ta workout routine. Lasarta also was punctual in arriving to take care of the kids. Before we started our exercises, I told Kindor and Damari about what had happened with Sortomor and Colora's input about him. We all agreed we would be vigilant and cautious in our dealings with him.

At midday, Sortomor summoned us to one of the conference rooms and connected the viewer to some of the news streams broadcasted from various points in the sector. We even brought the children so that no adult would miss it.

"Look, all of you, the fight for freedom has begun." Sortomor stood even taller and straighter than usual.

The split screen displayed different scenes, the first one showing shackled Lostai personnel being taken from various government offices across Aranda. Another showed military installations obliterated under heavy bombing. The scenes changed quickly to show other locations. We saw Arandans flooding the streets, somehow having found traditional Arandan banners that had long been outlawed by the Lostai Empire.

Sortomor pointed to yet another scene.

"At this precise moment, these five Arandan battle crafts are firing on the Lostai security forces guarding Dit Lar."

I was overcome with pride and emotion, as if this were my own planet driving out cruel invaders, the same invaders that put me through hell. I hoped one day my son would learn about this important moment in history and know his parents were a key part of it.

As the videos flashed across the screen, I couldn't help clenching my fist and shouting in English, "Yesss!"

Everyone glanced at Sortomor, apparently worried he would reprimand me for my outburst and usage of my language. It irritated him enough to have to speak in Lostai for Kindor's and my benefit. Instead, he cocked his head with that intrigued look, and although he didn't understand the word, he got the sentiment.

He, Foxor, Lasarta, and Lorret joined in the fist pumping and shouted in Arandan, "*Jonjuri!*" which meant "victory."

Colora covered her face with her hands, and I heard a quiet sob. I imagined she was thinking of Jortan and how he should have been here to witness this. The harsh reality that Montor was not with us either hit me in the gut, and tears trickled down my cheeks too. Lasarta placed her hand on my shoulder. Using his tablet, Kindor asked if any news was being transmitted from Sotkar. Sortomor turned away, and I caught him rolling his eyes. I could have swallowed my pride if he insulted me, but I wouldn't put up with him being disrespectful with Kindor. I walked over and grabbed his arm.

"Remember, the only reason we know of the location of the Dit Lar transportal is because of the intel shared by the Sotkari insurgency, so I suggest we show some respect," I whispered.

Sortomor turned to find me staring up at him defiantly. His impatient expression reminded me a bit of Montor. Well, I had tamed one Arandan warrior; I figured I could tame another. Everyone else remained silent.

I'm not going to let it go.

"Well?" I insisted, raising my eyebrows.

Sortomor huffed but changed the transmission channel to show images from Sotkar. We didn't expect anything as spectacular as what was happening on Aranda, thinking perhaps we might see some news of an explosion here or there. Instead, we witnessed an all-out revolution. Droves of civilians stormed the government installations and utility companies. Kindor's eyes glistened. I understood his emotion. He had played an important role in his people's first real attempt in decades to free themselves from Lostai rule. Hugging him would have been seen as extremely inappropriate in the eyes of the Arandans, so instead I communicated with him telepathically.

"Kindor, I want so much to embrace you right now, but I should not in front of these people. I know this must be a profound moment. I am happy to share it with you."

"I wish I could share a gesture of affection with you too, Mina, because I would not be on this journey had I not met and rescued you that day," he replied.

I returned to my seat, and we watched a few minutes longer until Sortomor turned off the video abruptly to address us.

"This is an exciting moment for all of us, but we must keep in perspective that this is only the beginning. You can be sure the Lostai will not roll over and accept us taking back control of our planets. They will strike back, and it will be hard. We need to expect that and not let anything affect our resolve to keep fighting."

We all nodded in agreement. A transmission came over the communication system for Sortomor. He took the call privately in the captain's office while we waited for him to return.

"That was Commander Portars. He says we have taken control of Dit Lar. The Lostai soldiers that were on or guarding the planet have been taken prisoner. Our forces also have already located the transportal site. He has authorized us to make our way there as soon as possible. Kindor, he also requests that you send a message of gratitude to the Sotkari insurgency for sharing their intel."

Sortomor made a point to look at me before he continued.

"He also said the bravery of the Sotkari civilians has inspired the Arandan rebel forces. They are sending reinforcements and supplies to aid them in their fight."

We all turned to smile at Kindor in recognition. A sensation that I could only describe as pure joy coursed through my body. I glanced towards our hands, which were casually set on the table, and noticed he had moved his hand ever so slightly so that two of our fingers touched. I met Kindor's eyes to acknowledge the connection. It was only for a matter of seconds as Sortomor immediately ordered that we set a course for Dit Lar and dismissed us to our regular duties. Dit Lar was one day's travel away.

At the next day's morning staff meeting, Sortomor showed us on the viewer images of Dit Lar, which was now mere hours away. My heart jumped as I realized Lostai battle crafts were approaching the perimeter established by the United Rebel Front.

As usual, I forgot to keep my place and shouted out, "Should we be this close? We can easily be targeted."

"We have perfectly good defense systems, and I have volunteered to help. You females should leave to pray while we males man the weapon and defense controls."

Lasarta and Colora gathered the children and left without argument, but Officer Lorret and I looked at each other with one shared thought. Her eyes begged me to say something.

I pulled my shoulders back, steadied myself, and glared up at him so that he could see that I meant business.

"You will be short-handed if you attempt to take us into the mix with just you four males. I have military training, am familiar with everyone's expertise here, and Montor has made sure that I can man every position on this bridge. You are putting the life of my son at risk, so I will not be relegated to a corner. Lorret has military experience and should be here in case we suffer injuries."

Lorret barely hid her satisfaction as Sortomor was at a loss for words. His eyes blazed with displeasure, and for a moment, I wondered if I had pushed my luck with him.

Foxor chimed in, "Captain Sortomor, forgive Mina's approach. Her people's culture is very different from ours, but the truth is we need their help."

Sortomor took a deep breath, covering his mouth. The air thickened with tension. With a long exhale, he replied, "Very well, you and Lorret will take charge of our defensive systems and sensors. What can the Sotkari do?"

"Umm, if I may suggest, Captain, because we can share a telepathic connection and will not waste time with translations, I think Kindor should be with me on defense and sensors. Lorret can help you on the weapons array, Foxor can monitor the ship's operating systems, including environmental and propulsion, and Damari should be at the helm and controlling navigational systems."

Foxor turned away to conceal his smile.

Sortomor's lips formed a tight line before shouting, "You heard her. Everyone, take your positions."

We all moved to our assigned stations.

"Damari, flank the Sotkari ships and remain in a holding pattern," ordered Sortomor, referring to the two smaller Sotkari ships that had accompanied us earlier.

I worried Sortomor was all too ready to get us involved in a battle we were not prepared for.

"Sir, exactly what are our orders?" I asked.

He whirled around as if guessing my thoughts and snapped at me, "Our role is to be on alert and jump into action if needed. Do you have a problem with that?"

If that were the case, it wouldn't suit us to have him distracted, so I silently shook my head "No," keeping my eyes on the sensors. So far, we had not attracted the attention of the Lostai crafts because they had their hands full defending themselves. The Lostai were not aware that in addition to the crafts orbiting the planet, the Arandans had battle cruisers armed with new long-range torpedo systems at a considerable distance outside of their sensor range.

Without warning, the Arandan battle cruisers picked off the Lostai spacecrafts. As I observed the fiery explosions and debris field, I considered how the Lostai weren't given the option to surrender or turn back. First, it felt like a ruthless tactic, but then I remembered the Lostai wouldn't show any mercy either.

Several hours went by with no change in the situation. We took turns having our meal breaks. As Lorret and I finished eating, Sortomor activated the alert system, and we rushed back to our stations.

"Sir, what has happened?"

"We had no choice but to reroute the battle cruisers to defend other vulnerable positions. We are back to using traditional weapons here."

I checked the sensors. My chest tightened. There were still several Lostai crafts trying to break through the perimeter around Dit Lar.

Sortomor received new orders. The two Sotkari ships and the *Barinta* were to maintain a rapid orbit around Dit Lar and fire against any Lostai engaged in battle with our forces. The idea was to help them without drawing the full force of the Lostai battleships. Well suited for this strategy, the two small Sotkari ships zipped around engaging in a variety of loop, roll, and zoom maneuvers to distract the Lostai. We didn't have the same maneuverability, but while we were at Penstarox, Montor had beefed up the *Barinta* shields. This provided us the ability to withstand prolonged bombardment while returning fire.

Also, our state-of-the-art propulsion system allowed us to travel at the same speeds as the fastest battle crafts.

As soon as we targeted the Lostai crafts, we drew their fire. The first hit came with a slight vibration and thud. We all looked at each other for a moment.

That wasn't too bad.

A deafening boom accompanied the second hit. The whole spacecraft shook. Those of us standing held on and braced ourselves to avoid falling on the floor. Having never been in such a situation, my whole body tightened in fear. I could almost feel the color drain from my face.

OK, that one was definitely scarier!

I contacted Lasarta via our internal communication system.

"Lasarta, how are you and the children?" I gasped.

"Josher does not know better, but little Marcia is definitely rattled. I told her we were having a fun race against other ships in the area."

"Oh, good idea. I think we are going to have more of these, so you all should strap into safety seats."

We continued to get blasted, and it was all we could do to stay standing.

"Mina, shields status!"

"Still holding, sir. No damage to the hull so far."

While Sortomor barked orders to Lorret to fire on targets, I focused on maintaining a seamless coordination among Kindor, Foxor, and myself to divert energy between shields, sensors, propulsion, and weapons systems, keeping them at optimal levels. Damari did a good job of accelerating and decelerating at a moment's notice to keep the Lostai confused.

During our third orbit around the planet, we were fired upon by two Lostai crafts simultaneously. The *Barinta* rocked, and all of us standing fell to the floor. Kindor helped me up, and I scrambled back to my station. Loud warning alarms and flashing lights signaled danger.

"Sir, our shields our down by a quarter portion. We cannot sustain many more hits like that."

"Tell us something we do not know, Mina," growled Sortomor.

I bit my tongue and instead addressed Lorret.

"Our strikes are paced much too slow. You need to hit our targets with two quick blasts."

Sortomor looked at me in disbelief. I knew what he was thinking.

How dare she give an order!

Lorret disregarded Sortomor and replied, "I need much more power for that, Mina."

"OK, the moment you have the target, give me a signal, and I will divert a burst of energy from sensors to the weapon delivery system. It is risky, so you better reward me. At a minimum, I want the filthy Lostai ship disabled." As if Sortomor wasn't irritated enough with me, I switched to English and told Damari, "Once Lorret does her thing, I'll give you some extra juice too, so you can punch it and get us out of the area quick."

We didn't have to wait long to try out my new tactic.

"Mina, I have a target. Give me the power boost now!" shouted Lorret.

"OK, here you go—"

"Stop!" Sortomor roared, lunging at me. "Have you lost your mind? Why are you giving orders on my ship? I will have you locked up—"

Everyone froze. We paid for the distraction.

Lorret's target, a Lostai battlecruiser, pounded us with two blasts that sent us all, including Sortomor, to the floor again. Warning lights flashed and alarms blared once more.

Damari was the first to return to his station.

Foxor rushed to help Sortomor up.

Sortomor pushed him away. "Leave me. I can get up on my own."

"Damari, get us out of here, now!" I shouted, pulling myself to my feet and running to my station to redirect power to propulsion.

Damari shot a look at Sortomor.

"Yes, yes, of course. Do it!" Sortomor said while still getting his bearings.

Damari's quick maneuvering saved us from being nailed again by the Lostai ship.

Our reprieve didn't last long.

"I see another one," said Lorret. The urgency in her voice was no exaggeration. We were on borrowed time unless we did something quick.

Sortomor glared at me. "If your plan fails, we will have no shields. It will be the end of us, but go ahead."

"Lorret, here is your energy. Make it count."

We held our breath.

It must have been the longest three seconds of my life. Lorret targeted what she believed to be the most vulnerable spot with our double-whammy tactic. Her precision paid off. The Lostai ship exploded into two large chunks amid flashes of red, gold, and orange.

"Damari, let's go!" I screamed in English.

We barely missed colliding with the debris field. Once we were in a safe position, everyone except Sortomor shouted in celebration and fist pumped. He rolled his eyes at me and said, "OK, Mina, let us see how many times we can get away with this."

Sortomor relaxed once he saw the strategy was working. We orbited the planet seven times achieving quality strikes against the Lostai ships.

On our eighth orbit, Kindor communicated to me, "Mina, there are only three Lostai ships remaining in the area, and they are retreating."

I relayed the information to Sortomor, who contacted the

battalion commander for Operation Dit Lar and relayed a message back to us.

"Team, the Lostai have retreated. In the next day or so, we should be cleared for landing. Great job to all of you. We will be able to tell our grandchildren that we took part in this historic battle."

Breathing a sigh of relief, I requested permission to see the children.

"Lasarta, Colora, we have secured Dit Lar. They have retreated."

I hugged the kids so hard that Marcia giggled, exclaiming, "Have we been extra good today?"

"Yes, you have, and we have won the race."

She waved her hands in the air and shouted, "Yippee," in English while Colora, Lasarta, and I shared a relieved look.

Later, as I got Josher ready for bed, a new worry crossed my mind.

Is it possible the Arandans used their new long-range weapons against the military station where we suspect Montor might be held?

Our room contained a private communications console and viewer that Montor used as needed for official business. I dared to contact Commander Portars directly at that late hour.

"Commander Portars, I am sorry to contact you like this, but I was thinking about the long-range weapons we were using against the Lostai and am worried if Montor might be in danger."

Although puzzled by my call, he indulged me. Lucky for me, everyone was in good spirits after our victories that day.

"Mina, I understand your concern, but you can rest assured that we did not target any Lostai military installations suspected of holding Arandan, Sotkari, or any other hostages. The plan is to mount rescue missions first, take the Lostai as prisoners, and then either destroy or take control of those sites."

"Sir, I am so glad to hear that. How many have we freed so far? Do we have any news on Montor?"

He gave me the condescending look that came so easily to most Arandan military officers.

"No, my dear. We will not be able to send any rescue missions for a few days, and there is no way to confirm where Montor might have been taken."

I looked at my lap, and he must have taken pity on me because his tone turned fatherly.

"Do not worry, Mina. We will find him and bring him back safely to his family."

The next day after our staff meeting, Sortomor called me into the captain's office.

"Mina, sit down. My understanding is that our first order of business on Dit Lar will be to use the transportal to return the Earthian female child that we have on board back to her home location and that you are going to accompany her. I can see why you and Damari would be our first choices for this mission, but I cannot help but wonder why you and not Damari?"

"Well, Damari was approached first, but he admitted to Commander Portars that if he found himself on Earth, he was not sure he would have the resolve to return. We need someone to come back to confirm that the process works and that the child was delivered to her family safe and sound."

"I see," he said, standing and rubbing his chin as if deep in thought. "I have learned that you have children on Earth from a previous marriage. Is that correct?"

I glanced at my folded hands and then met his eyes.

"Yes, that is true."

"Quite frankly, I would think it would be even harder for

you as a mother not to succumb to the temptation of staying there and reuniting with your family."

"Yes, but as you know, I have a young Arandan son and husband with whom I pray I will soon be reunited. Although it breaks my heart to be separated from my Earthian children, it would be equally devastating if I did not return to my new family. It is an almost impossible decision, but if I weigh both situations, the truth is Josher, being a baby, needs me more right now, and until the Lostai are completely defeated, he is in danger."

"I guess you are referring to the fact that the baby has the same enhanced abilities as you and Montor?"

What is going through Sortomor's mind?

"It is hard to tell to what extent, but he has already shown telepathic abilities. The Lostai want to capture as many Sotkari Ta individuals as possible to use them as weapons of war or for breeding. I need to protect my son from them."

"And what if, unfortunately, Montor is not rescued, would it not be easier for you to take Josher back to Earth with you?"

I caught myself rubbing my hands and stopped. Sortomor was forcing me to talk about the difficult decision that I had suffered through many times before. Having to repeat it out loud yet again took a toll on me. I didn't want to reveal my emotions to him, concealing despair behind deadpan eyes.

"No, my people have not had contact with races from other planets. My son would be an oddity there. I will not put him through that. His appearance is Arandan. I want him to be brought up in an Arandan community, to learn about and be proud of his heritage."

Sortomor crossed his arms and paced around, nodding thoughtfully, until he stopped to stare down at me.

"I see that you have carefully thought this through. Will you remarry? I suppose, based on what you want for your son, you would look for another Arandan male as a mate."

Where is he going with this line of questioning?

"Umm, no, I have no more love to give to any other male. I am done with romantic relationships. I will not remarry."

He placed both hands on the table and leaned over so his face was inches from mine, as if he were interrogating a prisoner.

"Yes, I know you care very much for Montor. I was at your wedding," he said, his speech slowing and his voice deepening in a way that made me uncomfortable, "but who will be a father figure for Josher? Who will show him what it means to be a proud Arandan male? Who will teach him the ways of his ancestors?"

His yellow eyes intimidated me at first, until I felt the heat of anger.

Why does he feel the need to involve himself in my personal affairs?

"With all due respect, Captain, that is none of your business."

He straightened up, surprised at my bravado and displaying that intrigued expression that I had provoked at other times. His demeanor changed to a more formal tone and manner.

"Perhaps I have surpassed my boundaries. I suppose you are still our best option to accompany the Earthian girl home and come back to report to us. As you mentioned, getting your feedback is crucial so that we can cement our knowledge of how these transportals work. We will continue with the previous plan then. If the transportal has not been damaged, you will take the girl back tomorrow. No need to waste time."

"Tomorrow? That seems a bit reckless. I assumed there would be tests to be done, some trial runs before we make such a long trip, and also—"

"You and Marcia *are* the trial runs. We are aware of several Arandan children being held on nearby Lostai military bases. I want to find out as soon as possible that the process works so we can prioritize getting them back to their families safely. We do not know how long we will hold on to Dit Lar, so we need to make haste."

Marcia and I were nothing more than indispensable lab rats to him. I wasn't about to let him get off so easily.

"Do you have so little faith in our troops?"

For a moment, he looked offended, but then his eyes narrowed again. Before I could swat his hand away, he stroked my cheek with a quick movement and stepped back.

How dare he touch me that way!

"I am not sure what Montor saw in you, my dear. You are such a disrespectful female. I do have every hope that we will have an enduring victory, but I am merely being pragmatic and considering all risks. Now, you are free to leave. We should be landing on Dit Lar in one hour."

I got up and turned my back on him without another word, irritated and rattled by the odd turn of our conversation and concerned at how soon the trip to Earth would be upon me.

16

MINA

The Arandan regiment guarding the perimeter around Dit Lar sent a few soldiers to inspect the *Barinta* before clearing us for landing. Operation Dit Lar was led by an older Arandan, Commander Larmont, whose squadron, made up of much younger soldiers, looked up to him with great respect. He invited us to a debriefing held in a large room inside a cave that served as the operations base. Some soldiers under Larmont's command had attended my wedding on Penstarox and were upset to hear about what happened with Montor.

Larmont explained that the Lostai damaged some of the transportal equipment once they realized they were under attack, but Arandan experts were already working on repairs. When he introduced the experts, I was pleased to see he was referring to the Transportal Nerds that I had worked with in Penstarox. Later in the day, Lasarta and I prepared a special banquet to feed all the soldiers as well as our crew, about sixty people in total. It reminded me of my days at Kindor's restaurant, and my stew was as popular as it had been back then.

To my dismay, as soon as The Transportal Nerds informed

Larmont that they had completed the required repairs, Sortomor announced to everyone that Marcia and I would attempt the trip to Earth first thing the next day. Socializing and drinks followed dinner, but I knew I should get some rest. After everyone was fed and the dining area cleaned, I retired to my quarters with Josher and Marcia. The next day's mission had me unsettled, and I was furious Sortomor wasn't allowing more time to prepare. My head ached with too many questions.

Will I successfully deliver Marcia to her family safe and sound?

What will it feel like to use the transportal?

How will I react when I find myself back home?

Will I be able to make the return trip?

What should Marcia tell her family about what has happened to her this whole time she's been away?

What will happen if she shares her experiences with her friends?

Would some extra zealous journalist eventually expose her?

Would she be treated like a freak?

Would she be allowed to live a normal life?

Would government authorities get involved?

Maybe no one will even believe her story.

Sortomor cared very little about any of this and left those concerns to me. I decided we couldn't keep Marcia from telling her family everything she had experienced but advised her to ask them who else she should talk to about it. I wrote a note for Marcia's parents that would corroborate her story, signing the letter as "Mina" without any last name out of respect to Montor. Based on our marriage, I carried his surname, and according to Arandan tradition, a family's surname was never spoken or written, except for certain exceptional milestones such as a birth, death, or marriage.

To Marcia's Parents:

My name is Mina, and I am happy to return your beautiful daughter to you. After you get over the shock and joy of having her back with you, you will obviously want to know what happened to her during all this time that she has been away. She is going to tell you a story that is very hard to believe, but every word is true. Thankfully, other than having gone through the experience of being separated from her family, she has not been harmed.

Marcia was kidnapped by beings from another galaxy that can travel across space to our planet. She was taken because she has some special abilities that she will tell you about. I know all this because I was also kidnapped. You can research missing persons' reports. I was taken from Florida. Someone else named Damari was taken from Jamaica. There are many more who I have not met.

We were held hostage in an alien science base in a star system far from Earth. War is being waged against these kidnappers, and we have begun rescuing hostages and returning them home. Marcia is hopefully the first of many. For reasons too long to explain, I am not able to remain on Earth but want to leave you this note so you don't think your daughter has somehow been brainwashed to tell this fantastic story. I know it sounds like something out of a sci-fi movie, and it will be your decision if you share this with anyone or keep it to yourself. Maybe you will find too hard to believe what is in this note and will choose to come up with some other explanation. Perhaps, over time, Marcia will display to you some of her exceptional abilities and you will realize the veracity of what you are reading here. In the meantime, enjoy your wonderful daughter. It was a pleasure knowing and caring for her during the time we had together.

Regards, Mina

After finishing the letter, I took a sedative tea to help me get to sleep.

The next morning, Lasarta came to my quarters early. She found me with Josher on my lap. I couldn't stop rocking, hugging, and kissing him. With a heavy heart, I spoke to Josher in English and sang him the Barney "I Love You" song. He knew some verses and sang them with me. Although she didn't understand the words, Lasarta sensed what I was going through. She sat next to me and stroked my cheek.

"Mina, what you are doing for Marcia is a brave and honorable thing. I am sure everything will be fine."

"I wish we had a practice run, perhaps from one end of this planet to another or to a closer location. Sortomor sees us as disposable test specimens." My voice lowered to a whisper. "I wish Montor were here."

It was more like talking out loud to myself, rather than replying to Lasarta, but she answered anyway.

"So do I, my dear, but I promise we will take good care of Josher until you get back. Then we can focus on finding my foster son, and everything will be back to normal."

I nodded, and we remained silent for a few minutes so I could regain my composure before picking up Marcia in her quarters. She was already washed and dressed.

"I'm ready for my trip back home!" she said to me in English with a wide, energetic smile.

There's nothing like the optimism of an innocent child.

We walked to the conference room where Sortomor was about to start our regular morning staff meeting. It gave everyone the opportunity to wish me luck and say goodbye to Marcia, a bittersweet moment that left everyone teary-eyed. Kindor requested permission to accompany me to the transportal site. Sortomor was reluctant at first but allowed it.

We met with Commander Larmont and the Transportal Nerds at their operations base inside the cave. Based on their research, the Transportal Nerds determined a person could carry objects while traveling through the transportal. We decided I should carry a weapon for self-defense in case we ended up in a hostile environment.

Please God, don't let that happen.

Larmont handed me a small but deadly pistol called a *vimor* that delivered narrow radioactive beams with precision. I also packed a small bag with thirst pods, snacks, and first aid supplies in case something didn't go as planned. We didn't know whether we would arrive during summer or winter, day or night, so we wore thermal jackets. The pocket of magnetic field needed to open the portal was generated using a piece of equipment the size and shape of a laptop. We nicknamed it a *hanstoric,* or "jumper" in Arandan, and I needed to keep it with me throughout the trip.

The *hanstoric* controlled the complete process from storing the magnetic field that energized the transportation and initiating the "jump" to displaying the interactive maps that pinpointed the target destination. We suspected the Lostai had enhanced the equipment with the ability to detect Sotkari Ta brain waves, but The Transportal Nerds had not devoted any time yet to research that functionality. Montor had previously explained to the Transportal Nerds where and how the Milky Way and Earth's solar system were represented on the Lostai star maps. The displays reminded me a bit of Google Earth. You tapped a location and zoomed in to specific target coordinates.

Luckily, Marcia knew the general location of her neighborhood, her home address, and the names of nearby important streets. She said her mother had helped her memorize them using a song.

Good job, Marcia's mom!

The Transportal Nerds started me out with an image of our galaxy and then our solar system. Next, I identified Earth, continued to zoom in to North America, then New York City, then Queens, and further in detail until I found the exact neighborhood in Astoria that Marcia was from. There were no names of cities or streets on these images. It took a while, but I had spent enough holidays and vacations with my grandmother in New York City when I was growing up to be familiar enough with the area and figure it out. Marcia helped me identify her building, and I then zoomed in to find an inconspicuous spot for us to "land." In reality, we would more likely be appearing out of thin air. Once we locked in the location, one of the readings showed the equivalent of thirty Earth hours. We weren't sure but assumed this referred to the time the *hanstoric* could store its magnetic properties before having to be returned to the crystalline cave to recharge. It was our best guess of the time limit I had to complete the trip.

Once we were finished with our preparations and with Larmont's final approval, the Transportal Nerds and three Arandan soldiers accompanied Marcia, Kindor, and me down one of the tunnels to the transportal site. From the cave's first large room, several tunnels and passageways led deep into smaller rooms, some of which detained Lostai prisoners in holding cells, and at the very end, the walls became crystalline. Here was the laboratory where we would initiate the "jump." This part of the cave lit up and sparkled as daylight shone through the smooth transparent blue and orange rock.

"Wow, Mina, I've never seen anything like this," said Marcia in awe.

Before initiating the process, I hugged Kindor and hoped the Transportal Nerds wouldn't snitch on me. Luckily, Marcia did the same, so even the Arandans would have to acknowledge it was innocent enough.

"Mina, I will be standing right here tomorrow awaiting your return. I know everything will go to plan. The Farthest Light will guide your way."

"Thank you, Kindor. I pray for the same."

Our understanding was that any person or thing within a certain circumference of the *hanstoric* would be transported. The Arandans and Kindor stood back well outside of that area as I held Marcia close to me and said a silent prayer before tapping the final command. We perceived no sounds, no incredible flashes of light or electromagnetic activity, or any strange bodily sensations. Traveling through the transportal was like falling into oblivion with no concept of how much time had passed.

My eyes opened to find us standing in an alley next to the five-story building Marcia called home. If making the "jump" had been a void, once we arrived, I became a basket of emotions. It took five deep breaths to calm my heartbeat. The *hanstoric* screen displayed the equivalent of twenty Earth hours. I wasn't clear if this meant a certain amount of time had gone by or simply the time remaining before I needed to recharge. In Astoria, Queens, New York City, I had no idea of the date or time, but dusk was falling and even with the jacket, a chilly wind made me shiver.

"Marcia, how do you feel?"

"Umm, fine."

She hugged me hard, so I guessed she was equally affected. We walked to the street and stood in the building's main entrance. Luckily, there weren't many people out on the sidewalk.

"I'm going to walk back to the alley, but I'll be keeping an eye on you. Ring the bell to your apartment. If they come down to get you, I will remain hidden. You need to telepathically let me know everything is ok. If they let you in, tell me, and I will follow you up the stairs, but I will stay one flight behind. Same thing, though. I won't leave until you confirm you are with your parents and all is OK. Also, remember you can't tell them I'm here right away. Later, you can tell them everything, but I can't meet them now. Understood?"

"Yes, Mina."

I got on one knee and held her close.

"You have been a very brave girl. I'll miss you so much. I hope one day we can meet again and that everything goes well with you."

"I'll miss you too. Thanks for bringing me home," she replied, wrapping her arms around my neck and kissing my cheek.

My throat knotted up, and I could barely say, "OK sweetie, time to go."

She nodded and walked up the stoop, disappearing in the vestibule to ring the doorbell of her apartment. My breathing became short and quick as if I had run a mile. Without any way of keeping track of Earth time, I started counting in my head to sixty, one minute, another minute, and at five minutes, the door burst open. A blond man with Marcia in his arms, and an olive-skinned woman ran down the front steps, looking up and down the street. I quickly stepped farther into the alley and hoped they hadn't seen me. Marcia's voice entered my mind, elated but concerned at the same time.

"Mina, I'm so happy. Everything is great. I'm with my mom and *papai*. They're asking who brought me home so you should leave."

"OK Marcia, God bless you. Remember to give them the note I gave you and pay attention to their advice on when and who you can talk about everything that happened to you."

I continued down the alley to the adjacent block. Strolling down the sidewalk, I brushed the tears from my eyes to take in the sights and sounds of the neighborhood before slipping into another alley. The hot dog stand made me wish I had a couple of dollars.

Do I even remember what they taste like?

The *hanstoric* suddenly felt heavy. I bit my lip and studied the display, unclear on how to interpret the fact that the device initially started off with thirty and now it showed twenty.

Does this thing have juice for another jump?

The idea crept into my mind like a virus invading my body, bringing on both nausea and an adrenaline rush. I found myself zooming in to the state of Florida and staring at an aerial view of my home on the display. The possibility of catching a glimpse of my children was irresistible.

I didn't remember consciously tapping the display. This

time arrival was even more jarring. On top of the momentary disorientation, there was no way I could have prepared for what it would feel like to be in my old backyard. Judging from the temperature and how darkness had fallen, I estimated it was around seven or eight in the evening. My heart exploded in my chest. No one seemed to be in the area or watching me as I finally walked to the dining and living room windows.

Nothing there.

I tiptoed to the other side of the house to each of my children's bedrooms. Their beds were neatly made, and everything was in its place.

Odd.

Usually, their rooms would look like this only one hour per week, immediately after I had cleaned them. I walked back and looked into the kitchen room window. It occurred to me how lucky I was that our dog Coco hadn't started barking yet.

But where is Coco?

I scanned the remaining rooms and within seconds froze. Josh was sitting in the recliner in the family room watching TV. As impossible as it seemed, my heart beat even faster.

Is he alone?

Seeing the woman's figure in the kitchen caused me to lose control over my emotions. My head pressed against the wall as tears ran down my cheeks. Over two years had gone by since I was taken. It would be logical that he had looked for companionship. I had no right to judge. Hell, I had fallen in love with Montor, remarried, and given birth to another child, for heaven's sake. Still, I grieved as if someone dear to me had died. Curiosity then got the better of me.

I wonder what she looks like.

She was serving food onto plates, and when she turned to bring them to the small table in the kitchen nook, I saw her face.

It was not anyone I knew. Tall, fair-skinned, and blond, she looked nothing like me. Not knowing why I even made that observation, I peered closer to the window and honed my vision between the blinds to be sure there was no one else with them. No, she and Josh were definitely alone. She put her hand on his shoulder, letting him know dinner was ready. It was hard to interpret, at first not necessarily romantic but with a soft squeeze that denoted a certain familiarity. Josh was engrossed in whatever he was watching, and her hand went from his shoulder up his neck, running her fingers through his hair. A small, pained noise escaped my throat as I bit my fist.

He looked up at her, smiled, and went to the table. They sat across each other and began to quietly eat. I was afraid of what else I might see.

Will he reach over and take her hand? Will they stop at some moment and gaze into each other's eyes? Will they have a glass of wine and later head to the bedroom?

No, I couldn't stand to watch them anymore. I stepped away from the window and walked further into the backyard.

Where are my children? It's possible Chris is away at college by now, but what about Amber and Bobby? Where is Coco?

I convinced myself there was a logical explanation.

Most likely, they're with one of my sisters. It's possibly winter or spring break. They could be visiting family.

My eyes blurred with tears. I blinked them away as I considered making another jump. The *hanstoric* display showed the equivalent of fifteen Earth hours. These readings frustrated and confused me. Going from New York to Florida, a relatively short trip, had reduced the figures by five, half the amount it had taken to travel across galaxies. Either distance wasn't a factor, or I wasn't interpreting the readings correctly. Continuing to jump to other locations without knowing exactly how the magnetic field was being consumed proved too risky. I thought about Josher and knew it was time to return to Dit Lar.

Maybe once I have more experience with the hanstoric, I can come back and try to see my other children, but now is not the right time.

My fingers flicked across the screen. About to tap in the final command, I looked back towards the house. Josh's head turned in my direction. I gasped as he stood from the table and rushed towards the glass sliding doors. Shutting my eyes, I pressed my finger to the display. When I opened them, I found myself back in the crystalline cave with Kindor standing in front of me, his hands on his hips and a look of relief brightening his face.

17

MINA

"Mina, you had us all worried! Based on their calculations, Officer Xartor and Officer Na Nar expected you here yesterday." Kindor's alarmed tone annoyed me.

The Transportal Nerds stared at me, their eyes full of expectation. I handed them the *hanstoric* and hurried out of the lab. Irritated, cranky, and in no mood to talk, I ignored Kindor as he followed me. Finally, he grabbed my arm to force me to turn and face him.

"Mina, is everything OK? Did Marcia make it safely to her parents?"

What is wrong with me?

"I am sorry, Kindor. Everything is fine. I am just a little tired. Yes, the trip was a success. I saw her parents. It was great to see them together."

"How was it to travel that way?"

"We did not feel anything at all. It was unbelievable. One moment we were here, and the next, we were there."

Kindor bent over and cocked his head to look me in the eyes.

"Mina, did you encounter any problems that prolonged your trip?"

I looked away and rushed through my reply.

"I will give you all the details later, but right now, I would like to see Josher. Let the Arandans know I will give them a full report by tomorrow or later. My goodness, I do not even know what time it is."

He furrowed his brow but didn't insist.

"No problem. I will take you back to the *Barinta* now."

Although I would have preferred not seeing Sortomor at that precise moment, protocol required that I report to him as soon as I arrived at the *Barinta* before seeing anyone else. He was directing the morning staff meeting attended by Lorret, Foxor, Colora, and Damari. To Sortomor's displeasure, a collective "Mina!" disrupted his meeting as soon as I walked in the room. They all left their seats to welcome and congratulate me. I gave a brief description of the trip to the point where I left Marcia safe with her parents.

"Captain Sortomor, may I be excused to spend time with Josher?" I asked.

"Fine, but I want a full documented report by the end of the day."

I made a beeline for the kitchen, where I found Lasarta singing an Arandan folk song to Josher while preparing dough for bread. The minute he saw me, Josher jumped up and down in his playpen, extending his arms.

"*Ro Ma, Ro Ma!*"

I picked him up, whirled him around, and hugged him tightly to my chest. Lasarta dropped what she was doing and rushed over.

"Mina, I am overjoyed to see you. My prayers for your safe return have been answered. How is Marcia?"

"Happily back with her parents."

"That is wonderful. Josher has been a very good boy."

"I am going to take him to the holographic room to play a bit. Then I will need to bring him back as Sortomor has requested I document a full report of my travels."

Playtime for Josher and me was different than when he played with his father. Instead of warrior and martial art scenarios, I set up the holographic room to simulate a play yard with an age-appropriate obstacle course. At eight months old, Josher was physically and mentally the equivalent of a human boy more than twice his age. Before we started, I sat on a bench with him on my lap and kissed his forehead.

"*Ro Ma* missed you."

He giggled and stroked my cheek. I looked into his eyes. Although Josher's eyes were shaped as his father's, they expressed a gentle calmness, opposite to the turbulence in his father. I kissed him again.

You deserve to be safe and happy. I owe you that.

Hugging him, I asked, "What would you like to play first? Obstacle course, Hide n Seek, or Simon Says?"

I had taught him the English names for these games.

He turned away for a moment as he pondered the question. It provided the perfect opportunity to wipe away the tear that had started its way down my cheek.

"Hide n Xeek!" he exclaimed, pronouncing it almost perfectly.

After a few hours with Josher, I returned him to Lasarta so I could freshen up and work on the report everyone was waiting for. I asked her if there had been any news about Montor.

"Unfortunately, no. Foxor asked Sortomor, and he said there was no news, but..."

"What?"

"Maybe...maybe you should contact Portars directly, my dear. Foxor suspects Sortomor is not interested in whether Montor is found or not."

"I am not surprised, Lasarta. Colora told me Jortan

mentioned to her that Sortomor was power-hungry. However, it would be inappropriate for me to contact Portars directly now that Sortomor is captain of the *Barinta*. Would it not be easier for Foxor, who is next in command, to approach Portars?"

"No, Foxor would be expected to know better than to do that, but you, you are the distraught wife who is desperate for news of her husband. You might be forgiven the indiscretion."

"I see. OK, I will contact Portars."

Lasarta placed her hand on my shoulder, and I looked up into her misty eyes.

"You will be the first to know whatever information I can get from Portars," I assured her.

"Thank you, my dear."

Back in my room, I began to document my trip and confronted a dilemma.

Should I mention the second jump I made to Florida?

If I mentioned the fact that I made a second jump to my old home, people who believed me to be a widow might conclude it was an inappropriate risk but reasonable for a mother to want to check on her children. On the other hand, Foxor and Lasarta knew my first husband was alive. If they suspected I saw him, it was logical that they would question my motives. Excluding that information would skew further research on how the transportal process worked, which would be unfair and unsafe for everyone who was counting on this technology to get back home. I decided to include a complete report of what I did and submitted it to Sortomor, Portars, and the Transportal Nerds.

Once I got that out of the way, I gave thought to when and how would be the best way to approach Portars. He was such a busy man. I couldn't simply interrupt his daily routine. Montor had mentioned once that Portars was an early bird who usually took some personal time in the morning to have a cup of tea and read or engage in some other recreational activity before starting his workday. I resolved to contact him early the next morning.

At bedtime, I brought Josher to sleep with me rather than in his crib and spent a long while caressing his head, playing with his hands, and talking and singing to him. With an ever-growing vocabulary, he constantly asked for his father. Food was his next favorite topic. Now, he also asked for Marcia.

Finally, I said, "Time to rest, *honey.*"

He pushed himself on top of my torso, nesting his face upon my heart, perhaps still remembering the beating sound from the womb. I sang him the same bedtime song I had sung to all my children.

"Baa, baa, black sheep, have you any wool? Yes, sir, yes, sir, three bags full..."

Early the next morning, I sent a transmission to Portars from the console in my room, as I did the previous time. He accepted my transmission request right away.

"Mina, I read your report last night. I am gratified to learn we were able to return the Earthian girl to her family and that you returned safely. I must say, however, I am surprised you contacted me directly. Usually, I would not accept such calls, but—"

"Yes, I know, and I am sorry. I appreciate you agreeing to talk to me. Commander Portars, have you any news of Montor?"

"Has Sortomor given you any update?"

"Actually, no. Foxor asked him, and he replied that there was no new information."

"Hmm, that is strange."

"Commander, I am desperate to know anything about my husband's status. I am about ready to take a shuttlecraft and go looking for him myself!"

"Well, that would be very unwise, my dear. You do deserve

to know the truth. Maybe Sortomor was looking for the right time to tell you."

I braced myself for whatever he was about to say.

"What, what is it?"

"The same day you left on your trip, we raided the military station where we suspected Montor might be. We found the Lostai held several hostages there, but Montor was not among them. With the help of one of the Sotkari Ta insurgents that Kaonto sent us, we interrogated the Lostai soldiers we took into our custody. It is unbelievable what those Sotkari Ta can do manipulating people's minds. The Lostai spilled all their secrets in a minute...very valuable resource...please relay my appreciation again to Kindor—"

"Commander, please, what did you find out?" I said, trying not to sound disrespectful.

"Oh yes, sorry. They told us that once they received the signal that the other craft had crashed, they sent two shuttle-crafts with two soldiers in each of them to retrieve Montor on the moon. Lostai Patrol Command received what they thought was a transmission saying their soldiers were on their way with him in custody. Instead, one craft arrived empty on autopilot and the other never returned. When they sent another crew to the moon, they found their soldiers dead, so apparently Montor has escaped."

While Portars explained this to me, my hand flew to my chest as if to control my heartbeat. With each word, it traveled up my neck and finally covered my mouth as tears of relief filled my eyes. To control my emotions, I folded my hands tightly on my lap again.

"This is wonderful news. Now, all we have to do is go find him," I said.

"Yes, my dear, it is good to know he escaped, but we have no way of tracking him. It would be easier for him to return to us. If he has not done so, he must deem it not safe yet. You know our whole sector is a war zone now. No doubt, the Lostai are trying to find him too. I am guessing he has found a place to hide and is keeping a low profile until we have turned the tide of the battle further to our side."

"I would guess Fronidia is the safest place. We should go check there."

"I suppose you could suggest that to Sortomor. As captain of the *Barinta*, that would be his decision to make."

"But the *Barinta* is Montor's craft. He purchased it. As wife and heiress to his property, I must insist that his safety and reuniting him with his family should be the priority."

Portars's expression changed. He had given me a certain amount of leeway in our conversation, but in his mind, as a female subordinate, I had crossed a line.

"Mina...As. I. Just. Said. You should discuss this with your commanding officer. When Montor agreed to put the *Barinta* at the disposal of the United Rebel Front, it ceased to be a civilian craft."

"OK, Portars, I understand. I certainly appreciate your patience with me and your willingness to share this information."

Then frustration got the best of me, and sarcasm slipped into my voice.

"That is more than what I can thank Sortomor for. I hope in the future he will be more forthcoming with me and not guided by his own ambitions."

Portars pressed his lips into a fine line.

"Good luck, Mina," were his last words before he cut off the transmission.

I realized it was time for the staff meeting and headed over to the conference room. Sortomor greeted me with a shark-like smile.

"Glad you could make it," he said in a condescending tone.

Everyone's head whipped around, making me feel like I was tardy and he'd been talking about me behind my back.

"Did you change the meeting start time?" I asked, flustered.

"Yes, I did, but I decided to let you have a little extra rest time. I am sure yesterday was a strenuous day for you. Meanwhile, I shared your report with the team," he answered with a glint in his eye that made me uncomfortable.

The rest of the team, especially Lasarta and Foxor, seemed stiff with tension.

Oh my God. He purposely told them about my second jump to my old home in Florida!

I sat, and no one made eye contact with me. Sortomor continued the meeting, explaining that the *Barinta* would travel to Renna One to attempt a collaboration with the rebel group there, as we had done on Sotkar. He informed us that young hostages found in nearby Lostai military stations were being taken to Dit Lar to begin the process of returning them to their home worlds. I should have been enthusiastic about these missions. Instead, I was frustrated that he mentioned nothing about rescuing Montor.

Sortomor turned to me, his lips pursed, and said in his most authoritative tone, "Mina, you and your child will remain on Dit Lar to either accompany these hostages back home or train other chaperones, depending on what is practical."

This caught me off guard. I immediately didn't like the idea.

"No. I would rather remain traveling with the *Barinta*. Maybe that will give me a better chance of finding my husband, since you are not especially concerned about his fate."

Sortomor glared at me in disbelief, his tone ominous as he asked, "What did you say to me? Are you refusing a direct order?"

"I am not a soldier! I am an upset wife and mother who has lost her husband. I will not have you ordering me about!" I shouted back, defiant.

Sortomor walked towards me in long, quick strides with his jaw clenched and his hands in fists. I was not sure what he planned to do. He stopped dead in his tracks when Kindor jumped out of his seat, giving him a warning look and obstructing his path towards me. Sortomor's eyes narrowed, and his lips curled into a snarl.

"I cannot imagine what is going through both your minds, but I am the captain of this craft and I decide what happens with it and its passengers. Mina is remaining on Dit Lar!"

Using his tablet, Kindor communicated that he would stay with me on Dit Lar to help care for Josher while I executed my duties.

"Fine, go ahead and be the most powerful babysitter on record if that is what you prefer. I do not want either of you on my craft, anyway."

"This is not your craft!" I shouted even louder, angry tears rolling down my face. The emotional rollercoaster of the last few days had taken a toll on me.

He pointed at Kindor and me.

"I will not tolerate mutinous behavior and insubordination amongst my crew. Mina thinks she is the only one with personal problems and that it is appropriate to put her issues above our quest for freedom!"

Sortomor paced now with swagger, gesticulating in exaggeration, relishing every word that came out of his mouth.

"That is why she put our mission in jeopardy when she decided to go visit her Earth family. Apparently, they are more important than her Arandan family and our struggle. With that extra jump, she risked not being able to return and report to us on the transportal process. At best, she behaved recklessly, but maybe there is something more nefarious."

He narrowed his eyes for emphasis.

"Maybe her plan was not to return at all, but she changed

her mind because she did not like what she found once she got there!"

Of course, I hadn't included in the report the details of what I found at my old home, but his words made me feel guilty, as if he knew. I slammed my fists on the table and stood.

"That is not true!"

"After dropping Marcia off, did you make another jump to visit your old home? I am only informing what you documented yourself!"

"Yes, but—"

"This conversation is over. I have more important issues to worry about. Gather your things and report to Commander Larmont first thing tomorrow morning. After that, the *Barinta* will head out."

I looked around for support, surprised to find no one was speaking up. Lasarta and Foxor both stared blankly at the floor. Clearly, the news of my trip to Florida upset them. Colora seemed to be searching her thoughts, and Lorret was stone-faced.

Who knows what Sortomor told them before I arrived?

He continued the meeting without further disruption while I shrank more by the minute. When the meeting was over, Kindor searched my eyes as I walked back to my quarters.

"Do not worry, Mina. Everything will work out."

18

MINA

After the meeting, I had no choice but to go about my regular chores. Later in the day, I met Lasarta in the kitchen to help with dinner. She was unusually quiet.

"I spoke to Commander Portars about Montor," I said, breaking the silence, and went on to explain what Portars told me about Montor's apparent escape.

"I am so relieved to know my foster son escaped the Lostai."

"Yes, I know, but I am worried that he is still in danger, potentially having to defend himself all alone in the midst of a battle zone. My guess is he went to Fronidia. What do you think?"

"That is a possibility."

"Lasarta, I need to do something, but what?"

"I know. Foxor and I feel helpless too, but we cannot get too reckless and put ourselves in danger. Then Montor's sacrifice would have been for nothing."

I covered my eyes with the palms of my hands and shook my head. This was not what I expected from brave, strong-minded Lasarta.

"Are we giving up already? If one of us were in his place, I am sure he would do anything possible to find us. Lasarta, I miss my husband. I want him by my side."

Lasarta didn't reply.

Maybe I should have lied on that report after all.

"Lasarta, are you upset with me? Did I do something wrong?"

Her eyes remained glued to the vegetables she was slicing, but I could almost feel the gears of her mind turning. Finally, she spoke to me without raising her eyes.

"Mina, were you able to see your children?"

I breathed deeply.

"No, they were not home. Their rooms appeared as if they had not been there for a while. Perhaps they are living with my sisters."

"I see."

"I just wanted a glimpse of them. Is it unreasonable that I was hoping to at least see that they were OK?"

"No, I could understand that. Did you find anyone else at home?"

"I saw my first husband."

Lasarta put the knife down and scowled. She had never looked at me like that before.

"Did you speak to him?"

"No, of course not. I kept hidden outside, looking through the windows. It was dark."

She picked the knife up again and resumed her work, but her exhale sounded controlled.

"Was he alone?"

I gulped.

"He was having dinner with another female. I do not know who she is. They were alone. I could tell by her gestures that their relationship is more than friendship."

I covered my mouth as my eyes watered. She put the knife down again, sat on a nearby chair, and called me over to sit by her. The frown vanished. I leaned my head on her shoulder, and next thing I knew, I was crying. She stroked my hair, which was very uncharacteristic of her.

"Mina, let us talk about this. No one can deny you have been through a terrible ordeal since the moment the Lostai ripped you from your family," she said in a kind voice.

"I think it is just the shock of being on Earth and seeing him after all this time, but I do understand it is normal for him to move on, like I have."

"Have you?"

"I have remarried. I have another male's child. You assured me yourself that you believe the love Montor and I share is real."

"Yes, I did say that, and while I am sure Montor loves you, now I wonder whether you really have moved on. You seem very upset. You owe it to yourself and Montor to explore your feelings and be brutally honest. It might be difficult, but I will help you."

Wait, is she looking to pull some dark truth out of me?

I examined her eyes. They were still kind.

"I love Montor and miss him terribly. Had he not manipulated me, I would have stayed there with him. Lasarta, I would give my life for his."

"Yes, but why? Are you sure you are not using Montor as a substitute for your previous husband, or maybe you have settled for Montor because you need a father for Josher, or maybe you know you cannot return to Earth with a child that looks so obviously alien?"

I took another deep breath and recalled all the soul-searching I had done during the last month and even when I was back on Fronidia with Kindor's family.

"Lasarta, even though it is true that once Josher was born, I realized I could not return to Earth, I did not need to marry

Montor to fill the gaps you mentioned. This is kind of private and I do not know if you have noticed, but Kindor—"

"Kindor loves you. Only a blind person would not see that."

I blushed.

"OK, well, if I merely wanted to fill a void or find a father for Josher, Kindor would have been perfect. Quite honestly, he has a much more easy-going personality than Montor. He is honorable and kind, and he cares very much for Josher. I do not mean to sound presumptuous, but Kindor would have loved for me to see him as a romantic partner. Even though we have some sort of connection, I do not feel for him in that way. On the other hand, with Montor...there is something special between us."

"I understand what you mean, but that chemistry could just be a result of the Sotkari Ta genes you both have."

"Kindor has Sotkari Ta genes too," I said, shaking my head to emphasize my point.

"OK, let us discuss Josher. No one would guess that his mother is not Arandan. Except for his eyes, he looks exactly like his father. Maybe you were inclined to marry Montor because you were concerned about Josher's sense of identity. Kindor might love Josher as a father, but he looks nothing like him. Josher would have eventually questioned his roots."

"Yes, it is true I want Josher to be proud of his ancestry and to have a relationship with his father, but Montor and I agreed we did not need to marry to provide a good environment for Josher to grow up in. Montor was committed to being present as Josher's father and ensuring our safety, regardless of whether he and I were a couple. We wanted to be together because we care for each other."

"So, you are saying that for all these reasons, you are sure you love Montor. Let me ask you one last question. If you did not have Josher and you would have found your previous husband alone in the house, would you have tried to talk to him, maybe even stay or perhaps made a plan to go back and be with him?"

She left me speechless, hitting it right on the money with that last question. I focused on my feelings for Montor, the loyalty he inspired in me, and our mind-blowing intimacy. I recalled how I once asked him to escape from the Lostai with me and how much I missed him after I left Renna One alone.

Then I thought about Josh and our years of ups and downs together, how I had been faithful to him for six years, raising our older children alone while he was figuring out what he wanted in life. Once he came back, even though our relationship wasn't the same as in the beginning, he had been determined to make it up to us and forge a family with strong bonds.

It hadn't taken Montor long at all to decide what he wanted. Of course, he was older than the age Josh had been when we first met. Still, Montor had taken many risks and made sacrifices for me.

Would Josh have done the same?

Hopelessly confused, and to my horror, I didn't have a clear, honest answer to Lasarta's question.

"To specifically answer your question, I cannot deny that if Josher did not exist and my previous husband were alone, I would have been tempted to talk to him. I am not sure what could have happened. My soul feels split. Do you think, Lasarta, that it is possible to love two males at the same time?"

She stood up and walked around, a worried expression on her face. Crossing her arms, she looked me in the eyes.

"I do not know, my dear. Maybe. Truly your situation is out of the ordinary. However, I do know you can only live one life at a time. Which life are you going to live? I respect your honesty, but you need to make a choice and stick with it. Do not play with people's feelings, Mina."

I was quiet again until a feeling of clarity washed over me.

"Wait, I understand why you asked the question, but it is

rhetorical," I said, my voice reflecting a new confidence.

I stood up and met Lasarta's gaze.

"The truth is, on the one hand, my previous husband appears to be in a new relationship. On the other hand, I will not abandon Josher nor allow him to live in a hostile environment, deprived of his culture and ancestry."

My shoulders relaxed, and my breathing became lighter.

"In the end, even those things do not matter. The most important truth is this. I love Montor. I am sure of it, and you must believe me, Lasarta."

I hugged myself.

"I miss him so much right now. Sadness consumes me because I do not know where he is and whether he is safe. Yes, a piece of my heart will always belong to my previous husband but in the same way that a person still loves someone who has passed on. Montor is my present, and I am aching to be reunited with him."

Lasarta smiled, but her eyes flashed a warning.

"But to be fair to Montor, it needs to be a choice that harbors no resentment, no mulling over what might have been."

"Resent Montor? Oh, no. I could never. Actually, I feel the opposite. He rescued me from a terrible fate. If he had not helped me escape the Lostai, I would probably be dead by now."

She stroked my cheek.

"And in a way, you rescued him too," she said with a resolute posture and expression. "Mina, I do believe you. So, while we travel across the sector, Foxor and I will try to find information on Montor without Sortomor knowing. I am sure Lorret and Colora will help us. I will stay in contact with you and keep you informed."

Another thought came to my mind that made me sad again.

"Lasarta, what if Montor reaches some crazy conclusion

that we are better off without him and does not even try to reunite with us? I mean, he made me so upset the last time I saw him that I said ugly things to him. What if he thinks I do not want him back?"

"At that time, he was focusing on keeping everyone safe. I am sure he knows we all are hoping for his return. He must wish to be back with his son and wife, but if he believes the Lostai are tracking him, he will conclude it is best to stay away from us. We will need to have faith in our prayers and be patient."

She walked back to the counter to continue her work but then turned around.

"And Mina, one more thing. This easy transportation to and from your planet concerns me for the future. You probably will feel the need to try to see your children again, and I cannot say I fault you. If you choose to do that, you need to make sure it is in such a way as not to compromise your relationship with Montor. I anticipate this will prove very difficult. Falling in love with you has put Montor in what normally would be an untenable situation for an Arandan male. Do not underestimate what a jealous Arandan male is capable of and how much our culture's principles of what is dishonorable means to Montor."

"Yes, I understand. If I ever try that again, I will make sure he has no reason to doubt my loyalty. Lasarta, thanks for your friendship. I know you love Montor so much, and you must sometimes wish your foster son had picked someone easier to be with."

She waved me off.

"Mina, when it comes to love, sometimes difficulty forges the strongest bonds."

"You are truly wise."

I walked over and hugged her, and she shrugged as if we had just had a simple conversation about what to make for dinner.

19

MONTOR

What do I hear murmuring?
My soul admitting
How much
We miss you

"Murmurs" from *Montor's Secret Stash of Poems*

I t took me thirteen days to arrive on Fronidia. I owned a small house in the Arandan enclave there. After seeing a doctor and purchasing some basic supplies and groceries, I remained at home for several days, keeping a low profile and regaining my strength.

Plenty had changed in the sector since I left my family. I poured myself a shot of *stampu* while I watched the newscasts. Aranda and Sotkar had declared themselves independent from Losta and taken control of utilities and other governmental facilities. I wished someone were here to celebrate with me.

Slamming my glass down on the table, I remembered my old friend.

Ahhh...Jortan...shermont! You should have been here to witness this.

The Lostai officials that used to be in charge of those offices were incarcerated. The United Rebel Front had taken control of the small planet Dit Lar where we learned a transportal was located. War engulfed the entire sector. The Lostai government was not ready to lose the empire they had amassed over the last hundred or so revolutions.

My house was small and simple but outfitted with a sophisticated communications system that allowed a secure channel to the United Rebel Front. I spoke directly with Commander Portars.

"Montor, when we invaded the Lostai military station on Nexori, we learned from interrogating the Lostai prisoners that you had escaped their military officers. We knew nothing else. Where have you been?" asked Commander Portars.

"I am in Fronidia, healing from my injuries and planning my next steps. You are the only person I have reached out to."

"I am certainly glad you are well."

"What can you tell me about the *Barinta*?"

"They were on their way to Renna One, but there were too many Lostai battle crafts en route for them to proceed safely, so they turned around and are heading to...Fronidia, actually... umm, but your wife and son are not with them."

Every muscle in my body clenched.

"What? Where are they?"

"We put Sortomor in charge to replace you. He decided she should remain on Dit Lar with her son to continue transporting freed hostages back to their home worlds. The transport of the young Earthian girl was a success. Sortomor, though, also disciplined her for insubordination...her and her Sotkari shadow."

He hesitated for a moment before continuing.

"Montor, I only say this because I have a great respect for you, but his attachment to her and your son is a bit, shall I say, perturbing. If the boy were not your spitting image, I would have thought him to be the father."

My fists clenched even tighter. His insinuation could be no clearer.

"I know what you mean, sir. I would have ripped his head off a long time ago, but I owe him a debt of gratitude. He has saved my family's lives more than once, and now even I owe him my life. Had he not come to my aid, I would have been in a Lostai prison camp or dead already."

Commander Portars nodded, his eyes avoiding the screen for a moment.

"I see, a strange situation for a proud Arandan male like yourself to be in. Anyway, I can tell your wife is quite loyal to you. First, she called me directly instead of going through Sortomor. I tolerated it because of the friendship you and I share. She asked about you, made a case that we should go search for you in Fronidia, and even said she was ready to get on a shuttlecraft and look for you herself. I advised her against that and told her to take it up with Sortomor, her commanding officer. I was patient with her at first, but then she became demanding. I tried my best to remain polite."

I shook my head like a parent receiving a complaint about how their child had misbehaved. Secretly, I was proud of her tenacity, and my heart swelled with love. She was much more loyal than Portars could ever know, finding it in her heart to be my advocate despite my harsh words. I was relieved that she had seen through the lies and apparently forgiven me for manipulating her mind.

"Then when Sortomor ordered Mina to Dit Lar, she openly disrespected him in front of the crew saying that she would remain on the *Barinta* to better her chances of finding news of your whereabouts. She told him he had no right to be ordering her about and that the *Barinta* was not his. The Sotkari became aggressive when Sortomor tried to get her in line. He also requested to accompany her to Dit Lar and watch over your son while she makes her trips. Sortomor was reasonably upset and banished both of them from the *Barinta*."

I knew Sortomor to be a power-hungry racist, and I did not like the idea of him being overzealous in his commanding role with a small group of civilians that included my wife and foster parents.

"I will speak to him about it next time I see him," I said.

Portars knew me well enough to understand I was not referring to an apology. Humility did not make up part of my personality. He started to say something and then changed his mind.

"On another subject, you mentioned you were thinking through your next steps. What have you decided? Will you rejoin your family on Dit Lar or go back to the *Barinta*?" he said.

"I think neither. As much as I miss my wife and son, I am concerned that going back to them now would put them in more danger. The same goes for my foster parents and friends on the *Barinta*. Zorla, my ex-commander on Xixsted, has been promoted within the Lostai military ranks, and I am sure he is particularly upset that I have turned against him. Even worse, he knows I am part of the rebellion now and that I have invaluable information. Zorla might make it his priority to capture someone he can use as leverage against me. Portars, that is why it is very important that no one, not even my family, know of my whereabouts. Please promise me you will be discreet. You have already seen how stubborn my wife can be."

"Of course, but let me ask you, does this mean you will remain in Fronidia?"

"No, I will not sit here hiding while everyone that I care about is engaged in the war against the Lostai. I need to think of a way I can be useful without drawing attention to my family."

Portars smiled.

"I thought you would say that. I might have a suggestion."

The next day, Portars sent me a *Vona* craft captured in battle from the Lostai. The *Vona* model was a small craft known for its maneuverability and speed. Its size did not allow for heavy torpedo-type weapons, but it could fire plasma beams with extreme precision capable of destroying much larger vessels.

He ordered his most trusted officer to pilot the craft to Fronidia. A passenger came along with the officer: a recently freed Namson who had been a Lostai prisoner for two revolutions. His name was Tzarst. He spoke heavily accented, broken Lostai, croaking every time he searched for the proper words, but I could piece together most of what he said. Seeing his light in my mind, I realized he had embedded Sotkari Ta genes. It would take us one lunar cycle to arrive at his planet, so we had plenty of time to get to know each other, and I planned to train him.

The next day, Tzarst and I set out on the *Vona* to the Namson planet. Tzarst had been the leader of his *marz*, which I understood to be the equivalent of a city or province. The Namson were a race different from any I had encountered before. Tzarst stood upright but was amphibious in nature, rather than mammalian. He explained that he had lungs but could also breathe under water through his smooth, slick, slimy skin. Long spindly fingers and toes, small openings for nostrils, huge eyes, and no body hair at all completed his frog-like appearance. I tried to hide any reaction when I saw he wore no shoes, but I did not do a good job of it. He looked down at his feet.

"Namson no use footwear. Help body temperature in tune with." He waved his arms around, not knowing the word for environment, but I understood.

"No problem," I said, thankful I detected no strange body odors.

After a few days of travel together, I had no doubt Tzarst was highly motivated to force the Lostai out of his *marz*. I exposed him to the idea of thinking beyond his clan or province and uniting with other leaders to get the Lostai off his planet entirely.

"I must be frank, Tzarst. My mission is to organize the Namson guerillas into one united front and provide military guidance."

"For I thank United Rebel Front return me home. I agree your mission."

Portars was pleased to hear that Tzarst was on board with our plans.

Even though I wore a mask and cloak to hide my identity during the entire trip to the Namson planet, I was able to gain Tzarst's trust. Over stories of our home worlds, hatred of the Lostai, and shots of *stampu,* we became friends.

20

KINDOR

After our farewells, Mina, Josher, and I reported to Commander Larmont. He debriefed us on the hostages that had been rescued from the recently raided Lostai military stations. They were six Arandan adolescents, four younger Sotkari children, and two children and one adult from Tormix, a planet with which I was unfamiliar.

Commander Larmont fully expected the Lostai would attempt to retake Dit Lar. A typical strict Arandan military leader, he requested we formally incorporate into his squadrons and join them for drills and training. I perceived a genuine affection between him and his subordinates, no hidden agenda, and a deep commitment to protect everyone under his command. Mina believed him to be a fair and honorable leader. She immediately requested permission to devote any free time to search for Montor, and he agreed to help her as long as his troops were not endangered.

Larmont put Mina in charge of caring for the rescued children's physical, mental, and emotional wellbeing while they waited to be reunited with their families. She was well suited for that responsibility and kept them comfortable and in good spirits. It also distracted her from worrying about Montor. I did not like to see her so sad but was secretly happy to have her and Josher to myself. Even though Mina saw me only as a good friend, I relished our time together.

Officer Xartor and Officer Na Nar returned to their lab on Penstarox. Arandan command did not think it wise that the only three rebel experts in transportals be in the same location. They took one of the *hanstorics* with them to reproduce more, and Mina kept three on Dit Lar. Officer Xartor and Officer Na Nar also had on their agenda to visit any transportal sites that the United Rebel Front might capture in the future. Mina asked them to keep their eyes and ears open for any news regarding Montor and to inform her of anything they learned.

After one week on Dit Lar, Mina made her second trip using the transportal. Although Aranda was close enough to Dit Lar to make the trip in ten to twenty days, depending on the type of spacecraft, that area of space had become a war zone. Since Mina had made it to her home world and back safely, the transportals were deemed to be a much safer and quicker mode of travel, especially for children. Mina still did not have a good grasp on how the magnetic field stored on a *hanstoric* was consumed, but she estimated it took three days after each trip to recharge. Because the Arandan adolescents were from opposite sides of the planet, she would require several trips to return all six of them.

I went to the cave to wait for her. Last time on her trip to Earth, she left and arrived in a silent, blinding flash of light. She also arrived one day later than what was expected, causing me extreme anxiety. My nerves were just as frayed during this second trip. This time, she arrived early.

"Mina!" I could not control my excitement. Her smile warmed my soul.

"Hello, Kindor. How is everything?"

"Good. I have one of the soldiers watching over Josher. Let

us go get him and have the evening meal so you can tell me about your trip."

We picked up Josher and went to her quarters to have a private meal.

"So, how did it go?" I asked.

"Really well. I had no need to hide in Aranda like I did on Earth, so I brought the children right to their front doors and met their families. You can imagine how happy these parents were to get back their children. They invited me in, quickly put together a feast, and called family. A celebration ensued with me as the guest of honor. I felt like a celebrity."

"Well, you are doing a very noble and brave thing. Do you understand the *hanstoric* readings any better? This time, you arrived earlier than expected."

"No, I am still not clear what those figures mean. For example, a third of the charge was expended when I traveled back to my planet, and yet half of the charge was used up this time even though the distance from here to Aranda is shorter. In three days, I am going back with two more children. I will continue to monitor the readings and see if I can make some sense of these numbers."

An uneasiness crept under my skin at the idea of Mina making several trips using the transportal without really understanding those readings.

"Mina, maybe you should train one of Larmont's soldiers to take over for you."

She nodded but did not reply right away.

"I will train one of the soldiers as a backup plan, but I will continue to take the children myself unless it is a very dangerous situation. I have established a rapport with them and want them to feel safe throughout the whole process. I also want to train you."

I did not have an issue learning how to use it, but I could tell there was something specific on her mind.

"Why me?"

"I am going to leave a *hanstoric* with you. If something happens while I am away and you think Dit Lar is in danger of falling back under Lostai control, I want you to promise me you will transport yourself and Josher to a place you deem safe."

"But Mina, what would happen to you?"

"That is not important. The most important thing is Josher's safety. You will take him somewhere where the Lostai cannot get to him. I do not want you to tell me where."

"Why would you not want to know? How will you find us?"

"Kindor, I do not want to take the chance that the Lostai could get Josher's location from me through torture or another medium. I do not want to be pessimistic, but it is a possibility. Remember what Larmont told us the other day."

The conversation upset me, but she was right to be concerned. The Lostai leadership had gained approval from their constituents to spend more resources on the war. They were distributing false propaganda that rebels were aiming to take over the Lostai home world. Larmont had requested another three hundred United Rebel Front soldiers to help defend Dit Lar against any possible Lostai incursion.

I looked down, rubbing my forehead. Mina took my hand in hers and tilted her head to force me to look into her eyes.

"Kindor, promise me, if something like that happens, you will take Josher away from here. I do not want to know where. I just want to feel secure he is somewhere safe with you. Promise me."

"Yes, Mina. I promise."

By the time Mina completed two more successful trips to Aranda, people began to refer to her as The Chaperone. She liked the ring of it. The rescued children and Larmont's soldiers took to calling her that too.

One evening a lunar cycle after we first arrived on Dit Lar, we were eating in Mina's quarters when she received a call from Lasarta. Mina put the transmission on her viewer.

"Lasarta, I am so happy to talk to you. How is everyone? Are you on Renna One?"

"Mina...and Kindor, it is wonderful to see you too." She became serious. "I hope I am not calling at a bad time."

"No, not at all. We just finished eating," answered Mina.

"Oh good. Umm, we never made it to Renna One because there was too much fighting going on between United Rebel Front and Lostai battle crafts in the area. We are taking refuge for a few days in Fronidia until Sortomor decides what to do next. I have news about Montor."

Mina caught her breath, covering her mouth with her hands before settling them in her lap.

"What is it? Tell me."

"Since we are here in Fronidia, Colora requested permission from Sortomor to check her house and take care of personal affairs. She also went to the Arandan enclave there to ask about Montor and learned that he had been there in the previous weeks"

Mina jumped from her seat.

"And where is he now?"

"We do not know. He spent some time in the house he owns there but has since disappeared, leaving no information of his whereabouts."

Mina started pacing. She punched the palm of her hand.

"I knew it. I always believed he was in Fronidia."

"Yes, and it gives me solace to know he seems to be alive and well. He surely must be torn between reuniting with his family and keeping any Lostai as far away from us as possible," said Lasarta.

"I am happy and worried at the same time. Even if he is evading the Lostai, there is no way Montor would be content to stay in hiding. If I know my bellicose Arandan husband well enough, he is going to make a point to engage the Lostai military in some fashion."

"You are probably right, my dear. I will continue to pray for him. How is Josher?" said Lasarta.

I had nothing to contribute to the conversation, so I left to retrieve Josher from his crib.

"Oh my, how long has it been? Only one lunar cycle, and he seems to have grown so much."

I sat Josher on my lap. He reached for the screen and called out to his foster grandmother.

"*Lo Ro. Lo Ro.*"

They exchanged words in Arandan, and Josher continued to babble.

"Yes, he is doing well. Everyone here spoils him, especially the soldiers who have children of their own on Aranda. Even Commander Larmont makes time to play with him. Josher has turned into everyone's foster child," explained Mina.

The minute she spoke those words, Mina bit her lip and lowered her eyes.

Lasarta looked to her lap as well.

No one said anything for a few minutes. When Lasarta faced us again, there was sadness in her eyes.

"That is good. I am sure it would please Montor to know everyone is helping out in his absence."

Lasarta signed off, and Mina remained despondent.

"Kindor, I wish I knew where he was and if he is safe."

I felt awkward wiping the tear that started down her cheek.

"Do not worry, Mina. I am sure he is fine."

21

MONTOR

Days turn into nights
Rainy season floods the land
Cool weather follows
Time goes on as we revolve
Only my love stays steady

"Seasons" from *Montor's Secret Stash of Poems*

Upon entering the Namson atmosphere, we were met with three Lostai security crafts. Since we were in an official Lostai military ship, they wasted precious time asking for my security codes, which allowed me to shoot all three of them down without warning and quickly land. We took what we needed and set the self-disintegrate mechanism to leave no evidence of our craft or whereabouts.

The eight-day hike through the dense jungle proved tough. I took off the cloak but kept the mask on and had trouble breathing. Thick humid air congested my respiratory system, and perspiration drenched my clothing the whole time. Tzarst had no issues at all with the environment, his physiology obviously well adapted to his home planet. Strong thunderstorms rolled in during the evening hours, providing some respite from the heat. Insects the size of my fist flew about. I used them as target practice, pulverizing them with my *lizon* ray gun.

Eat this, you flying piece of crap.

Tzarst took some mud, mixed it with the leaves of an orange-colored plant, and spread it all over his exposed skin as a repellant.

"Better you do same as me," he suggested, nodding in an exaggerated manner. "They sting, you die."

The village appeared out of nowhere. One minute, I was zapping vines and vegetation, and the next, we walked into a circular area comprised of ten-by-twenty rows of two- and three-story stone structures, a plaza in the center, and a sizeable open field. The only vehicles on the few cobblestone streets were carts drawn by domesticated beasts. It was as if I had traveled back a thousand revolutions in the past. Tzarst explained his province included seven additional similar villages farther into the jungle and a portion of a river.

We waited until after dusk when the only people remaining outside were eight Lostai soldiers standing guard, two each at the north, south, east and west borders of the plaza. Looking through a long-range ocular device, I smiled seeing their forlorn expressions. The Lostai scum obviously missed the cold weather of their home world.

"They do not seem too happy. We should take them out of their misery," I said.

"What you plan?" asked Tzarst.

"I need to get closer to them. Use the *lizon*, on second level only, to render them unconscious but not to kill. Take as many of them out as you can."

During our trip, I instructed him on the use of advanced hand weapons but was still wary of his ability and how well he could handle the weapon with his long spindly fingers.

"Be careful not to hit me."

"When?"

"You will know."

In the time we spent together during our trip, I learned to understand his expressions, which were mainly through his body language as his facial features barely changed. When he was worried or agitated, his long fingers moved constantly. He caught himself, grabbing one hand with the other, and nodded to me. I pushed his nervous behavior out of my mind, put the cloak back on, and walked out into the clearing towards the central plaza.

The Lostai soldiers noticed me immediately, and once I was within earshot, they shouted, "Hey, you, show your face! What are you doing outside past the curfew hour?"

I raised my hands in the air and closed my eyes. When I opened them, all their weapons were strewn about and out of their reach. Four of them were unconscious on the ground. Tzarst took care of the other four. Our sudden attack prevented them from calling for help. That advantage would only last until someone in their line of command checked in on them. I sorted through their identification tags, determined which one of the eight was the group leader, cuffed him, and killed the remaining seven.

"You kill unarmed, unconscious prisoners...no remorse," Tzarst said, bobbing his head side to side, which I had learned was a sign of disbelief, fear, or shock.

"Tzarst, unfortunately, we are at war and at a total disadvantage against our enemy. Now is no time for mercy. They would not think twice about killing you, me, or our families." Scanning the area, I focused on the task at hand. "OK, we need a holding location for this Lostai piece of crap."

I grabbed the group leader's tablet, pressed his finger on the screen to unlock it, and left him unconscious on the ground for the time being. Tzarst led me to a home and requested entry by using a brass knocker mounted on the wooden door. The antiqueness of everything dumbfounded me. I had only seen similar structures in recreational holographic imaging. The door opened, and a Namson of shorter stature stood there making a strange guttural sound before embracing Tzarst. I could not tell by the shape of the body or clothing if it was male or female, but I knew it was someone important because they remained embraced for a long while. Finally, they separated and Tzarst turned to me.

"Montor, she mother of my offspring. Her name, Forinza."

He also said something to her in his native language that I assumed explained who I was. I nodded, as is customary in Arandan culture when addressing a married female. She jumped, wrapping her arms and legs around my torso as her spindly fingers and toes dug into my back. I flailed my arms and turned to him to apologize with his spouse still attached to me. Tzarst made a raspy noise that I have learned to associate with humor.

"No problem, no problem, friend. She just happy I home," he told me.

Once Forinza finalized her embrace, she led us into the house, where I met Tzarst's four children. Tzarst asked his wife about the rules and structure that the Lostai had imposed. In the meantime, I studied the Lostai group leader's tablet for all the log entries and communication with his commanding officer.

We learned that every morning at dawn, the Lostai soldiers rounded up all able-bodied adults, except for mothers with young children, from the eight villages that made up his province and forced them to harvest precious stones from the riverbed. These stunning, rare stones were sold across the galaxy to fund Lostai military costs. I had kept the group leader alive to manipulate his mind and control how he answered any incoming communication from his line of command, but a new problem presented itself. They would certainly be alerted if this group did not meet up the next morning with the rest of the province for the normal labor routine.

"Tzarst, please ask your wife who, if anyone, among the Namson in the village has taken a leadership role."

Their language was a mixture of croaks, guttural sounds, and whistles that seemed quite animated accompanied by their extreme body movements. Tzarst turned to me.

"She say Lostai coordinate with her brother."

We went to Tzarst's brother-in-law's house to let him know what was going on. His name was Vermist. After the initial shock of seeing Tzarst and making introductions, Vermist showed us to the building the eight Lostai had been using as their lodging and command center. We locked up the unconscious group leader in one of the holding cells the Lostai had set up on the first floor while we discussed our next steps. Tzarst served as a translator for Vermist and me.

We came up with a plan, but Vermist was reluctant to upset the stability of the province. His head bobbed side to side as he spoke to Tzarst.

"Vermist not so sure, good idea," Tzarst said to me, his fingers fidgeting.

"His people are being enslaved. Does that not bother him?" I answered.

"He say at least now children eat and no more slaughter."

"Ask him, have the Lostai kidnapped any of the villagers, any children?" I instructed Tzarst.

Vermist listened and replied while pressing his fingertips against the back of his head, a sign of sadness.

"He say Lostai take many children, two revolution past, but no more."

"Tell him it is only a matter of time before the Lostai do another Sotkari Ta brain wave sweep. Then any children born since that time with embedded Sotkari Ta genes will be in danger."

I approached Vermist and put my hand on his shoulder while Tzarst translated for me.

"The people of my planet and another planet called Sotkar have joined forces to rise up against the Lostai imperialists. We call ourselves the United Rebel Front. We cannot allow them to continue to take our children! You will not be going at it alone. The United Rebel Front will send technology to help you."

Vermist was quiet for a few minutes. Tzarst launched into an impassioned speech in their language and patted Vermist in the chest as his voice elevated. Vermist's fingers moved in that nervous way, but finally with an exaggerated nod, he agreed to our plan.

Before I accepted this mission, Portars had promised me that soon after I arrived at the Namson planet, he would send an Arandan crew with weapons and communication and shield technology to support their insurgency. The crew would simulate an emergency landing to avoid anyone linking me to the Arandans and keep my identity a secret as long as possible. In the meantime, we needed to avoid attracting attention from Lostai troops.

The next morning, I brought the group leader back to consciousness and manipulated his mind. The idiot did not even remember there had been seven other soldiers under his command or question who I was. Villagers assembled in the plaza as usual, and the group leader took them to the river. During the previous evening, we had trained Vermist and four other villagers to use the weapons I had taken away from the Lostai soldiers. When we arrived at the meeting site at the river, the eight Lostai group leaders separated from the group. Tzarst, Vermist, and the other Namson we had trained shot and killed the Lostai soldiers while I rendered unconscious all their group leaders.

The next few days were mentally exhausting as I controlled the minds of the eight group leaders to ensure they continued to communicate normally with their line of command. This could not continue indefinitely. Eventually, someone would question why the shipments of precious stones were no longer arriving. Plus, my mental abilities were close to exhaustion. I needed a rest.

Commander Portars kept his promise. On the fourth day, a formidable Arandan battle craft landed and fought off the Lostai who attempted to board their craft. Afterwards, they erected a shield around the area. They brought with them a cargo of replicators, shield and communication equipment, handheld and ground-to-air weapons, and three transport pods. Within two days, we enclosed all eight villages under a protective shield and set up a communication network, after which the Arandans left the Namson planet with strict orders to maintain silence regarding their mission. At that time, we killed the eight Lostai group leaders.

The days that followed were busy. I identified a Namson leader from each of the eight villages that would report to Tzarst. We asked them to recruit soldiers who would leave the villages to join forces with other guerillas. I let them decide the selection process but suggested they maintain a balance to keep a strong contingent protecting the province while the guerilla was away. We set up a training schedule to teach every able-bodied adult who was not busy caring for children how to use the new technology, apply military tactics, and engage in hand-to-hand combat. Since no one knew my identity, they called me The *Zateim*, which meant "chieftain" in their language. I began a slow process of figuring out if there were any Sotkari Ta individuals. The Lostai had been thorough in their last sweep. I only encountered two elderly males, whom I trained anyway as they were eager to be helpful.

In less than one lunar cycle, the Lostai tried to attack the province from space, but the shielding system held well. Afterwards, they sent pods to shoot at us from within the atmosphere, but we countered with the ground-to-sky weapons system provided by Commander Portars and forced them to retreat. By the end of my first lunar cycle on the Namson planet, Tzarst and I led a small group in the transport pods to the next nearest province. We found there a similar setup of eight Lostai soldiers per village. Using the same strategy as before, we regained another complete province.

The communications system allowed me to maintain contact with Commander Portars. Fueled by our success in taking a second province, he authorized Arandan shuttlecrafts to return to the area we now controlled and provide more equipment and weapons. The Namson guerillas we had heard about were operating on the opposite side of the planet, but even the common villagers I had met so far were brave, intelligent, and thankful. They were ready to pay forward their liberation and help the next province be rid of the Lostai.

22

MINA

I prayed each night for Montor's safety and avoided depression by keeping the remaining children cheerful until the time came to transport them home. After the Arandans, I accompanied the Tormixians back to their planet. Although I was not familiar with their world or people, the transport was made easier by coordinating with their government. Next in line were the Sotkari kids. I contacted Kaonto to coordinate and took advantage of our conversation to get an update on how the rebellion was faring on Sotkar.

"Mina, it is wonderful to hear from you. Have you heard any news regarding Montor?" said Kaonto.

"It is good to talk to you, too. Yes, we recently learned he made a stop in Fronidia, so although it is tough not having any idea where he is or what he is doing, at least we know he is alive. How is the rebel movement doing on Sotkar?"

"Mina, I need to be honest. There has been much bloodshed, and sadly, many civilians have lost their lives. In our case, the fighting is not limited to battle crafts in Sotkari space. As you know, there was a large Lostai presence on our planet when the revolution was declared: security agents, patrol officers, military personnel, government officials, all of them armed. In most cases, our people are facing them with clubs, knives, agricultural tools, and in some cases, their bare hands. It is amazing, though, to see all Sotkari on our planet, regardless if they are Ta, Pasi, or not, united in this fight."

"Kindor will be so proud of how committed your people are to the cause. We have to make sure their sacrifice is not in vain. Are the Arandans still helping you?"

"Oh yes, and we are so grateful. In spite of our limitations, the insurgency has held its ground, except on the southwestern continent, where the Lostai have regained control with the help of a group of Sotkari Ta from Fronidia. I cannot believe they would go against their Sotkari brothers. On the positive side, Fronidia has since canceled the treaty of friendship with Losta, stated it wants to remain neutral, and has enacted a law forbidding any Fronidian citizen from getting involved in the war."

"That is good news."

"So, I hear The Chaperone will be returning some of our children soon," he said, smiling.

I laughed when he called me by that name and most probably blushed a bit, too.

"Yes, Mina, The Chaperone has become quite famous in this sector. Soon, they will be writing songs about you. You have captured the imagination of the people who are awaiting the return of lost family members. You are almost as famous as The *Zateim*."

"What is that?"

"Oh, you have not heard about The *Zateim*? Are you familiar with the Namson? They are from a planet that is at the outer edge of the sector. We know very little about these people because they have no advanced technology, but a large population of them are embedded with Sotkari Ta genes. That is why the Lostai established military stations there and keep it heavily guarded. *Zateim* means 'Chieftain' in their language, and they are referring to a mysterious person who has recently assumed a leadership role in their militia."

"What is the mystery about?"

"No one knows where this chieftain came from or who he is. He wears a mask and cloak to hide his identity. They treat him like a god because he is teaching them all manner of military tactics, hand-to-hand combat, and, interestingly enough, Sotkari Ta training. In one lunar cycle, they have successfully pushed the Lostai out of two provinces."

My curiosity was piqued.

"Interesting. Has no one from the United Rebel Front made contact with this person?"

"We learned about The *Zateim* from a group of Arandan soldiers forced into an emergency landing on the Namson planet. Now, the United Rebel Front is working with The *Zateim*, having secretly landed a few shuttles there with weapons and other technology."

"And he still keeps his anonymity?"

"Yes. I suspect he is not a native of that planet. The Arandans who first reported this said The *Zateim* is much taller than the average Namson."

Kaonto's eyes narrowed as if a thought had just crossed his mind. I knew what he was thinking.

"Kaonto, do you think it could be him?" I don't know why I whispered. We had privacy.

"Your guess is as good as mine, but we should keep our suspicions to ourselves. The *Zateim* is going to great lengths to keep his identity a secret."

We left the topic of The *Zateim* at that and moved on to discuss the details of my two upcoming trips to Sotkar. Later that evening when I met up with Kindor, I told him about my conversation with Kaonto.

"Kindor, I cannot get the idea out of my head that this mysterious *Zateim* person might be Montor. If some Namson hostages are rescued and brought here to Dit Lar, I will have a chance to visit that planet and inquire about The *Zateim,* perhaps even meet him in person."

"That would be a dangerous endeavor. That planet is under Lostai control."

"Yes, but Kaonto said with the help of The *Zateim,* they have already pushed the Lostai out of two provinces, and they are receiving help from the United Rebel Front. I tell you, Kindor, from this day on, I will be hoping and praying every single day for Namson hostages to be brought here."

Months went by with no further news from the *Barinta* or anything related to Montor. I constantly showed Josher video images of his father, grandparents, and the rest of the *Barinta* crew to keep their memories alive for him, but he asked about them less and less. It was just Kindor and me now, the two people who had always been a constant in his life. Of course, the soldiers and Larmont still doted on him.

My schedule kept me busy and allowed my mind little time to wander until bedtime. Alone in my bed, sadness, anger, frustration, and loneliness took over. I missed Montor's strong embrace and his cocky manner. My body ached for his touch. I also thought about my children on Earth. Making another trip there would be out of the question before reuniting with Montor and discussing it with him.

23

MINA / MONTOR

MINA

During my fifth month on Dit Lar, the first freed Namson hostages arrived. They were two young children and a young adult male found on a Lostai battle craft captured by the United Rebel Front. The prospect of soon traveling to their planet and inquiring about The *Zateim* filled me with hope and anticipation.

That evening, as I rocked Josher to sleep, I mused out loud, "Sweetie, I think I know where your father is, and I'm going to find him. It's time our family be reunited."

The next day, I wasted no time in making plans for my first trip to the Namson planet. I discussed the trip with Kindor, and he tried to convince me to have the Arandan soldier that I had trained go in my place. I knew he worried every time I made a transportal trip, but he was getting on my nerves.

Has he gotten so used to having Josher and me to himself that he doesn't want me to find Montor?

"Mina, I know so far the transportal has proven to be reliable, but there are still many risks. You are not clear yet on how the magnetic energy on the *hanstoric* is depleted or how far or how long you can go before having to return. I fear your curiosity regarding The *Zateim* might lead you to push those limits. You could be stuck on that planet without any immediate way to return. If you insist on going, maybe I should go with you."

"No. Have you forgotten what you promised me? Your job is to keep Josher safe and get him off this planet if there is an emergency. Kindor, everything will be fine."

He pressed his lips together in defeat.

"OK, are you taking the three of them back at once?"

"No, I do not have experience transporting that many people at one time."

He folded his arms across his chest and shook his head in frustration.

"That is just an excuse to guarantee a second trip."

"Kindor, enough. You are beginning to try my patience."

I could count on the fingers of one hand the times that we had used an impatient tone with each other. Clearly, the same thought ran through his mind because he uncrossed his arms and changed his expression to appear less confrontational.

"Who are you coordinating with on that planet?"

"The Namson people do not have a central planetary government that I can coordinate with. Commander Portars put me in contact with a Namson that the Arandans had rescued who recently returned to his planet and has regained control of several provinces. Maybe he is working with The *Zateim*."

The evening before transporting to the Namson planet, I followed my typical pre-trip routine of preparing a special meal for Josher and Kindor and spending some recreational time with them. When Kindor arrived at my quarters for dinner, he found me in high spirits.

"You guys are in for a treat," I said with a smile. "A ship

arrived from Aranda today and brought some fresh *goria* fruit, so I was able to actually bake a real pie."

"I love pie!" said Josher with enthusiasm.

Josher was almost one year old and communicated both verbally and telepathically, mainly in Arandan, which was what he heard from the soldiers around him. Kindor and I spoke Arandan at only a very basic level but enough to keep up a conversation with Josher, whose vocabulary also included a smattering of Sotkari, English, and Spanish words. Kindor and I still communicated telepathically in Lostai, the one language we both were fluent in. It was the language of our enemy, so I made a point not to teach it to Josher. I hoped that by the time Josher was an adult, he wouldn't be living on a world that forced him to use that language.

After eating, we asked permission for access to the holographic equipment that the Dit Lar soldiers used for training exercises. Josher at this very young age already showed a preference for anything that simulated hand-to-hand combat and martial arts. He was supposed to be physically and mentally the equivalent of an Earthian or Sotkari child twice his age, but he was more the size of a tall three-year-old human. Big for his age, even for an Arandan child, he would grow up to be tall like his father. We watched him as he kicked, punched, and flipped his holographic opponents, fantastical creatures of his own height.

"Mina, do you not think this might be too aggressive a game for a toddler?" Kindor asked.

"I find it a little odd too, but Montor told me it is perfectly normal in Arandan culture to learn self-defense from an early age. He began teaching Josher as soon as he started walking."

Kindor rolled his eyes, and I shot him a disapproving look, so he only added, "Well, I am glad we have started to teach him the Sotkari Ta regimen."

"Yes, me too, and he seems to enjoy it. Another good thing

about this game is that he will sleep soundly. Look, he is yawning already."

We came back to my quarters and put Josher to sleep. I served some Arandan brandy. Kindor had taken a liking to it. Same as Montor, he said the color reminded him of my eyes.

"Kindor, I must admit my heart is exploding in anticipation. I cannot wait to reach the Namson planet to try and find this *Zateim* person. My gut tells me it must be Montor."

"It could be anybody. Do not be too disappointed if it is not him, and Mina, do not be careless about how much time you spend there. Remember, most of that planet is still run by Lostai military and the natives have no technology. If you are not able to return, you will be in grave danger. I know I have been repeating this to you over and over, but I worry for your safety."

I took his hand in both of mine, something I only did in private as the Arandans would find it inappropriate for a married female.

"I promise to be careful."

MONTOR

After four lunar cycles on the Namson planet, I received news from Commander Portars that the United Rebel Front had found three Namson on a captured Lostai spacecraft. The two children and young adult male were on Dit Lar waiting to be transported home.

"Montor, these hostages come from an area still ruled by the Lostai. Obviously, it is not safe to transport them there. We will provide The Chaperone with a location within one of the provinces you have under Namson control," he said.

"The Chaperone?"

"Your wife. That is what people call her these days. Should we give her your contact codes?"

I had not considered the possibility of seeing her. It took me a minute to find my words.

"Montor?"

"Umm, she should train one of the soldiers to make the trip. It is dangerous here."

"That is her decision to make, Montor. She has been caring for the children on Dit Lar while they await their turn to be transported and has established a bond with them. She is adamant that she should be the one to accompany them. So, do we give her your codes?"

She is as stubborn as usual.

"No, it is best if she remains ignorant of my whereabouts. She can coordinate with Tzarst."

24

KINDOR

Mina arrived back from the Namson planet a few hours later than expected. I had already put Josher to sleep in my quarters. The first thing she did was go check on Josher, pressing her lips gently against his forehead as he lay asleep. Only after that did she greet me with an embrace. This was another Earthian form of affection Mina only used with me in private. I knew it was nothing romantic because she had done this before as a sign of friendship with males, females, and children alike. Still, being able to hold her so close, even for just a few seconds, was one of the things I most looked forward to. I poured us each a glass of brandy and asked about her trip.

"Everything went according to plan. It is inspiring to learn how the Namson have reclaimed seven provinces from the Lostai in only four lunar cycles. I met with one of their leaders named Tzarst. He spoke Lostai since he used to be a prisoner in one of their military stations. He is also Sotkari Ta. The only sad thing is that the hostages are from another area on the planet that is still under Lostai control, so they will need to remain in Tzarst's village for the time being."

"Well, at least they have their freedom and are back with their own people."

"Yes, yes. They were so grateful, and Tzarst's mate introduced them to a family whose son had been kidnapped some time ago. They will care for the young child until it is safe to return him to his province, and the older male decided to join the guerilla."

"That is good, and did you learn anything about The *Zateim*?"

"Well, because I do not speak their language, I was limited on who could provide me some input, but I did ask Tzarst. He said his people revere The *Zateim*. They feel they owe him everything, their freedom, their dignity. They will do anything for him, and so far, the only thing he has asked for is that they help maintain his anonymity."

If this is really Montor, I can only imagine how much more conceited he has become with all this adoration.

"I see. So you did not get to meet him."

"No, apparently he was on a mission with a group of their guerillas in the process of liberating another province. I took Tzarst into my confidence and told him why I was so curious. I confessed my husband was missing, that I would do anything even to spend a few moments with him or at least know he is safe. I explained that I suspected The *Zateim* might be my husband."

"Hmm, and what was his reaction?"

"He did not give any other details, but he told me he expected The *Zateim* back in seven days. I said I would return at that time with the third Namson child. I begged him to talk to The *Zateim* about me and perhaps arrange a meeting."

"Do you believe he will?"

"I think so. Although he did not say much, he seemed moved by my request."

Mina retired to her quarters, leaving Josher with me to not

disturb his slumber. It took me a while to fall asleep. The *Zateim* had captured my imagination as well. In the solitude of my bed, I hoped Mina would not get to see him, and I prayed the Farthest Light could forgive my selfishness.

The alarm system woke us early the next morning. We were under attack yet again. This was the third time since we had been on Dit Lar. We followed the now familiar routine. Mina rushed to my quarters to pick up Josher, gathered the other children, and headed to the crystalline portion of the caves. With two *hanstorics* in hand, she stood ready to transport herself, Josher, and the other children at any second. Bormat, the Arandan soldier she had trained on how to use the trans-portals, met her there. Between the two of them, they could transport all the children to Aranda if needed. I was expected to join Commander Larmont's troops to man one of the ground-to-air missile controls and use my Sotkari Ta abilities to help in any way possible.

Three Lostai battle crafts rained photon blasts on our base from outside Dit Lar's atmosphere. It seemed that it would be another failed attack on their part until a section of our shields system suffered a breach. Our missiles disabled one of their ships, forcing it to retreat, but another remained in orbit while the third landed in the unprotected area. Larmont called for United Rebel Front reinforcements while a troop of about nine hundred Lostai soldiers stormed our base. Larmont's squadron faced them bravely. I left my post at missile control and joined them. Using my Sotkari Ta skills, I disarmed and rendered unconscious as many Lostai soldiers as possible. We were able to keep the other Lostai craft from landing, but on the ground, we were outnumbered three to one. A group of Arandan soldiers formed a barrier around the entrance to the caves. Lostai long-range snipers were slowly picking them off.

Our situation appeared grim, and I prayed Mina would escape in time. I knew she would wait until it was clear that we had lost control of the base. A thunderous sound interrupted my thoughts, and the ground shook beneath us. An Arandan battalion carrier rushed through the atmosphere at an unsafe speed and somehow landed in one piece near the battleground. Everyone turned to look at the same time, stunned by the amazing feat. Hundreds of Arandan and Sotkari soldiers swarmed the area. The fight continued, but now we were more evenly matched.

Flashes of light, the harsh sounds of weapon fire, and all the shouting overloaded my senses. I had never been in the midst of a battle where so many people's lives were being extinguished at the same time. An Arandan soldier tapped my shoulder and handed me a phasor gun.

"I know you are doing your Sotkari Ta mind thing, but it would not hurt if you could also shoot some Lostai soldiers dead while you are at it."

The weapon was cold in my hands. I had never killed a person before and hoped these warriors could not see my hands tremble. Although I was not a soldier, I had joined Larmont's squadron in their daily drills and training. I knew what I was expected to do, was capable of executing it, yet I struggled. Thoughts of my father came to mind. Like me, he also hated violence and confrontation. As much as he strived for a diplomatic solution with the Lostai on our planet, he ended up witnessing the brutal killing of many of his family members anyway. Eventually, he himself lost his life at the hands of the Lostai.

As these thoughts paralyzed me, the soldier who handed me the gun fell to the ground, a perfect circle burned into his torso. He was very young, barely an adult, a son who would never return to his mother. I shuddered and, fueled by rage, stepped out of cover. Targeting the closest Lostai soldiers with the weapon while simultaneously disarming others using telekinesis turned out to be an efficient tactic. The area in my range of fire turned into a Lostai graveyard. The Arandans cheered me on as I crisscrossed the cave entrance, continuing my carnage. When I took a moment to rest, one of the squadron leaders came to congratulate me with a slap on the back.

"Sotkari, you have killed twice the amount of Lostai than the average Arandan soldier! Later, we shall share a drink to celebrate."

The adrenaline had died down, and somehow, I did not feel proud.

We suffered many casualties but pushed the Lostai back until a group retreated to their craft and took off, leaving their remaining comrades stranded. I was surprised when Commander Larmont ordered they be taken on board the Arandan carrier ship as prisoners, instead of having his soldiers shoot them at will. Once the situation stabilized, I ran to the transportal lab and found Mina entertaining the children with songs.

"Kindor, are we safe?" she asked telepathically while maintaining a calm demeanor in front of the children.

"Yes, the Lostai have retreated and those remaining have been taken into custody. The battalion cruiser will transport them to a military jail on Aranda."

She let out a long sigh.

"Have we lost many soldiers?"

"Yes, unfortunately we have. Many of the wounded were taken on board the carrier to get proper medical care, but some we have to deal with here. We are left with half of the squadron and a section of our shield system is damaged. I am going back to the infirmary to see if my healing abilities can be of help."

In the days that followed, we worked hard to get the station back to normal function while we waited for a new group of Arandan soldiers to replenish our squadron. Besides the Namson child, there were two young Sotkari females still awaiting transport. Mina's goal was to get the children back home before another potential attack from the Lostai. She first made a quick trip to Sotkar and then, according to her previous plan, accompanied the third Namson child back to his home planet.

25

MONTOR

I unravel and spread her out
A treasured scroll that requires careful study
Softly licking my fingers
In trembling anticipation
Careful to trace
The subtle curvature of each letter
Every word whispered upon my lips
A silent prayer in reverence of her form
Laid out before me

"Scroll" from *Montor's Secret Stash of Poems*

"The Chaperone say she come this morning," said Tzarst.

"Please, if she asks about me again, tell her I have not returned yet from the previous mission."

"She say she looks for her mate. Thinks may be *Zateim*. Has not seen for long time. She want show images of young son."

Thoughts of Josher brought tears to my eyes. I was grateful for my mask.

"She is mistaken. As I told you, I must keep my identity secret at all costs."

"So, face covered. She no see you. What the harm to meet her?"

"Why are you questioning me on this, Tzarst? I do not ask you for much."

"She seem kind. I not like dishonesty. I not lie. I thought we friends, but you not truthful with me. You think I simple-minded."

Deep inhales and exhales helped me to contain my impatience. For a second, I wondered if Mina might have manipulated his mind, but she would never do such a thing. I paced around, deciding what to say.

"Of course, we are friends. You are right. I should be upfront with you." I took a moment before my confession. "Yes, she is my wife. I am only trying to keep her and my son safe. If the Lostai capture us, they will have the leverage they need to force either of us to work for them."

He looked around and waved his arms in exaggerated wide circles.

"No Lostai here. Even *Zateim* need comfort of loved one. I bring her to you."

He turned around and left before I had a chance to protest. Mina had found an ally whose stubbornness matched her own. Realizing that soon she could be right in front of me, I was overcome with nervousness, like an adolescent on his first date.

I should shower and groom.

I was done in the bathroom, a towel wrapped around my waist, and on my way to the bedroom to get dressed when the door creaked.

Shermont, I wish these old doors would close automatically.

On my way over to shut it, I stopped dead in my tracks.

Mina stood in the doorway. She let the bag that was slung over her shoulder slide to the floor, took two slow steps, and then came to me in a rush.

It happened so fast that I froze. She wrapped her arms around me and pressed her face against my chest. I felt her lips, then wetness, and her body shaking. She was crying. It took all my self-control to hold back my own tears.

"Sweetness, I missed you," was all I could think to whisper as I embraced her and ran my fingers through her lustrous hair. We remained that way for several minutes.

Finally, her body stilled, and she stepped back to stare up at me. Her teary eyes reflected the daylight that streamed through the windows, making them even more brilliant. They reminded me of honey, brandy, and gemstones. I bent over and *kix* her lips. The raspy sound of a Namson chuckle interrupted us. I looked up, and Mina turned around.

"*Zateim* waste no time," said Tzarst, who had walked in the open front door, as he took in the view of me clad only in a towel. He studied my face. This was the first time I stood before him without a mask.

"Uhh, give me a moment to get dressed," I said.

"After all time here, he still not remember to lock door," he told Mina as I bolted to the bedroom. She giggled.

When I returned, the door was closed.

"*Zateim*, what can do to make time with The Chaperone more pleasant and with no worries?"

Flustered, I turned to Mina.

"Ummm, I do not know. Mina, how long were you planning to stay?"

She pulled a device out of her bag, studied the display for a second, and made a mental calculation.

"I, I think I can stay until tomorrow," she stated in a tone that sounded less than confident.

She had not thought this through, and my concern for her safe return made me irritable.

"Thank you, Tzarst. I really appreciate that. Mina and I need some time to talk in private. Afterwards, I will contact you and let you know if we need anything."

"I understand, *Zateim*."

He left, and this time I remembered to lock the door.

"Mina, tell me, do you even know what you are doing?"

I did not mean for my voice to sound so cranky and condescending, but I was worried she had taken an unnecessary risk.

"Of course I do! I have accompanied many children safely to their home worlds. I had Namson children to return and a hunch that the famous *Zateim* was my husband, so I asked Tzarst if I could meet you."

"When you delivered the children back home in the past, how soon did you need to return to your point of origin?"

Her head bowed. I had hit a nerve. Before answering, she breathed deeply and rolled her shoulders. I was forcing her to admit something she would have preferred to keep to herself. We knew each other all too well.

"Normally, I might spend no more than a few hours with the families because we have not been able to confirm what certain readings on the *hanstoric* represent. There are numbers that could mean remaining hours or magnetic field depletion or something else, but we are not sure. Based on past experience, I am assuming they refer to hours. Right now, it shows fifty, so that would be more than enough time for me to stay until tomorrow and return safely to Dit Lar."

"*Shermont!*" I could not help cursing. "Are you crazy? You just said you have not confirmed what those numbers mean. They could mean anything!"

She crossed her arms and stared up at me defiantly.

"Please, please, can you just stop drilling me? Is it too much for a wife to ask to be able to spend one night with her husband?"

"Do you know how guilty I would feel if you could not return safely...if something happened to you...what about Josher?"

My voice had softened, but I knew the deep furrow between my brows was still there.

"I have faith I will be able to return without a problem to Dit Lar. Right now, Josher is under Kindor's care, and I have given him instructions to use the transportal to take Josher somewhere safe if necessary."

"Faith? You must be joking. Mina, you are too impulsive, never thinking about the consequences. Then you wonder why I get upset."

She sat down, rubbing her temples, and took some time before speaking again.

"I should have never tried to find you. Sorry I bothered you."

Without another word she stood, picked up her bag, unlocked the door, and walked out. My heart pounded so hard it hurt, and I ran after her.

"Wait," I said.

My beautiful, stubborn wife ignored me, so I did what any proud Arandan male would do. I picked her up, brought her back inside, and lay her on my bed. To my relief, she did not protest. I went back to close the stupid old door before returning to the bedroom.

"I am not sure what you are thinking, but if I stay, I am spending the rest of the day and the night here. I did not come for sex," she said, biting her lip, "or I should say, not only for sex."

I found her candor endearing. Laughing softly to myself, I sat beside her, stroking her cheek with the back of my hand.

"Tzarst mentioned you have images of Josher to show me."

"Yes," she said, getting off the bed and pulling her tablet out of the bag.

We sat next to each other on the bed for a while scrolling through the video images. In the five lunar cycles since I had last seen him, Josher had grown quite taller. He was no longer a baby but a talkative toddler that walked and ran confidently. Some videos showed him engaged in holographic sports and martial arts games. It pleased me to see him displaying agility and strength but always with a joyful smile on his face. He looked so much like me except for the eyes and with no darkness in his expression. In some of the videos, Josher sat on Kindor's lap or they played games together.

My jaw tightened, and my expression prompted Mina to say, "We show Josher pictures of you often and remind him his *Ta Ri* is coming back soon."

Although I was sure my wife had remained loyal during my absence, Kindor was stealing my son's heart day by day. I pushed back the tears.

"That is nice," I said, pretending to be pleased.

She took my hand in both of hers.

"Tell me about what has happened with you since we last saw each other."

I told her about my escape to Fronidia, my conversation with Portars, and my adventures so far on the Namson planet. She asked many questions. One was particularly humorous.

"Should I be worried about any Namson female catching your attention?"

"I would have to first figure out which are the females. They know each other by sense of smell. Me? I do not have a clue."

We laughed, and she allowed herself to fall back on the bed, arms splayed and legs slightly separated, still dangling over the edge of the tall bed that had been custom made for my height. Her belly button peeked at me from under her blouse. Something about her positioned like that reminded me of a table set with a feast. I could not wait to taste her sweetness.

"Mina, I am sorry for being so ill-tempered before. Not too many things scare me, but the idea of something bad happening to you terrifies me."

She smiled, flirtation in her eyes. I got down on my knees and gently pulled apart the magnetic strips that held her blouse together. Pressing my face gently against her abdomen, with a deep inhale, I took in her scent, not surprised to find nothing underneath when I pulled off her pants. Sliding down, I spread her legs further and reveled in the taste of her. When I looked up, I saw she had removed her blouse.

"Sweetness, can I?"

"Please," she said, her breathing heavy.

She did not move while I stood and undressed in a rush. Sliding over her, I pushed in deep with one swift thrust and remained upright so I could take in the view of everything— her heaving breasts, undulating body, even our hips separating and reconnecting. Nothing I had experienced in any of my previous relationships could match the euphoria of making love to her. The Sotkari Ta genes we shared had something to do with that, but truly, my feelings for her ran deep.

Later, as we lay side by side, we planned what to do with our remaining time together.

"There is not much in recreation here, but every nine days, the villagers have a thanksgiving festival. It is scheduled to take place in two days, but I will ask Tzarst if there is a possibility of having it today instead. It is actually a very enjoyable activity. They put out food and drink and set tables in the plaza. Everyone eats together and participates in competitive sports and games, and later in the evening, there are musical, dramatic, and comedic performances. You would like it."

I grabbed my tablet from the side table and called Tzarst to discuss it. He said Forinza had the exact same idea and had already set the gears in motion to set it up. As I explained this to Mina, she pressed her lips against my chest and stroked my arms. Of course, I was at once hard for her again, but she protested, crossing her legs.

"No, no. This is not about sex. I just want to enjoy being close to you, the feel of your skin, your muscles," she said as one finger traced my pectorals.

"Yes," I answered, my voice deep with lust, "but Mina, the one thing leads to the other."

She inched up so our faces were level and *kix* me with such passion I almost emptied myself without even having started. She pulled away, a mischievous smile gracing her beautiful face. I regained my senses and chuckled.

"Really? Two can play this game."

I moved down and licked her nipples, slowly and with precision. They came to life in my mouth, like soldiers ready for battle.

"No," she pouted at first, but followed with, "oh, yes."

We frolicked, teasing each other until we were joined, her legs wrapped around me. After a few hours in bed, we showered together, dressed, and walked over to the plaza, where most of the villagers had already assembled. A quarter of the plaza was enclosed under a tarp with several long tables and chairs set underneath. Nearby, steamy cauldrons, pots, and skewered meat were set over stone pits. Across from the food area, stands were set up for all manner of betting games. An open field bordering the plaza hosted a spirited game of *vernit*. The acrid smell of Namson food filled the air. Soon, the sounds of loud croaking, whistles, and raspy laughing overwhelmed our ears.

Mina and I had not eaten, and our previous activities had brought on an appetite. Most of Namson cuisine did not agree with me, but I had acquired a taste for a few staples. I liked the deep-fried balls made of mashed tubers filled with ground shrimp called *lorin*. Their fish dishes were excellent, and *grem*, a dessert made of pockets of dough filled with a sweet, macerated fruit, reminded me of Arandan pies. Everyone was curious about the nature of the relationship between the *Zateim* and The Chaperone, but we did not get into many details. As usual, Mina charmed everyone I introduced her to. They all recognized her genuine warmth and sincerity.

After eating, I walked her over to a stand that offered an intoxicating beverage called *zorinto* made of fermented grain and mixed with a sour juice. The *zorinto* made me cockier than usual, if that was possible. Wanting to show off my prowess in front of Mina, I decided to participate in a round of *vernit*. The object of *vernit* was to get a heavy ball over a goal line. Team members passed the ball to each other while mounted on a domesticated beast called a *santrock*, a stocky animal with two sets of horns and thick legs. It stumbled, rather than ran, across the field. I was strong enough to hurl the ball long distances accurately, but I did not have much experience controlling my mount.

Mina sat next to Forinza giggling, and even though they did not speak the same language, I felt sure they were finding ways to make fun of me. Tzarst and I were on the same team, so when we won the match in spite of my problems with the *santrock*, we both returned to our females with an exaggerated swagger, making them giggle even more. After sharing many more glasses of *zorinto,* as dusk fell, we settled down to enjoy the live music and drama performances. Tzarst served as a translator for Forinza and Mina. Every time I glanced Mina's way, her smile warmed my soul. Later in the evening when the clouds rolled in, everyone worked together to close down the stands and put away any remaining food and drink before going home.

We arrived at my dwelling just before the thunderstorm began. Mina and I showered and tumbled into bed, both exhausted but happy. Pulling her close with my torso pressed against her back, one hand holding hers, another resting gently on her breast, I *kix* the top of her head many times before falling asleep.

The morning light sneaked through the window to awaken us. Mina turned towards me.

"Good morning, my love. Do you have a busy schedule today?" she asked.

"My schedule is you," I answered.

She got out of bed and checked the *hanstoric*.

"I will return to Dit Lar before nightfall, but I would like to spend the day with you."

She came back to bed and straddled me, leaning over to *kix* my lips.

I am so lucky to have such a sensual spouse.

"Do you want a tour of the different provinces that are under Namson control? I could introduce you to some of the other province leaders. We can go in a transport pod and be back by late afternoon. It may be helpful for the next time you bring Namson children home."

"Yes, I think I would like that."

She let her head rest on my chest and sighed.

"Montor, there are a few topics we need to talk about. I did not want to spoil our first meeting with a difficult discussion after being separated so long, but I think it is necessary."

I braced myself for whatever was on her mind.

"I have not forgotten what you told me when we were forced to leave you on that moon. You said you had manipulated my mind to make me believe I loved you, that our love was a farce. Obviously, I did not believe that, but I realized later that you actually took control of my thoughts in that moment to make me angry and willing to leave you there. This makes me wonder, how many times have you manipulated my mind?"

Grimah! This is a tricky one. How honest should I be?

"I have manipulated you three times."

She became thoughtful, pursing her lips.

"Wait...what?"

She bolted out of bed and stood naked with her hands on her hips and outrage on her face.

She has continued the Sotkari Ta physical workout routine. Her body looks good.

"I know of two times," she said, speaking each word with pause. "There was this time on the moon, and the other was when you forced me to injure you on Renna One the day you helped me escape. You needed to make it look like you were ambushed, and I did not want to hurt you. You angered me that time as well, but are you saying there was a third time?"

This next confession will be hard.

I took a deep breath.

"The first time we were intimate."

She froze. I could almost see her blink in slow motion. She hugged herself and doubled over as if in physical pain.

"No, please, no. So, are you saying our love IS a farce?"

"Wait, listen to me. It was when you were showing me how to *kix*. You were so uptight, and I was trying to get you more relaxed so Zorla could be convinced that we were on our way to making Sotkari Ta babies for him. Remember the charade we had planned. So I made you feel flirtatious, but Mina, only for a moment. I immediately stopped because I realized I was losing control. Anyway, it was too late. I had already fallen for you. I loved you from that moment on, and whatever you felt after that was real. Come back here, sweetness, please."

Bristling, she straightened up and crossed her arms.

"How dare you!"

I started to get up out of bed. She flashed a warning look,

outstretching her arm as if making sure to keep space between us.

"Stay away from me."

"It was just for a moment, Mina. It had nothing to do with everything else we have experienced."

She looked away, and for a few moments, the only sound in the room was her foot tapping the floor.

Grrrr...She will make me beg.

"Mina, please come back to bed. We love each other."

She turned to meet my eyes. Hers were frozen amber.

"How many other times have you done this to me? I want to know each and every time."

"Mina, there have been no other times. I promise you. Only those three times. Please forgive me." No one else except maybe Lasarta and Kaya could bring me down to this level of humility. "Please, Mina. I, I beg you."

Finally, she returned to bed, laying on me again, and I embraced her.

"Mina, I will never do that to you again. You can be sure our love is not a farce. It is the strongest, most honest emotion I have ever felt, and I know you love me too."

"Really? Did you read my mind just now?"

"No, of course not. Please, sweetness, can you forgive me?"

She sighed.

"OK, I forgive you, but let me be clear. I consider it a violation. I need to be able to trust you. You better not read or manipulate my mind without my permission again. Promise me."

I brought her hand to my lips.

"I promise."

Her fingers brushed my cheek. I was thankful that she believed me and we could put this doubt behind us.

"Now, I have another serious concern. Montor, how long will we live like this? I want us to have a permanent home and raise our son together. I do not think we need to wait until the war is over. Who knows when that will be? Fronidia has expelled all Lostai already and could be a safe place for us."

"Well, we both currently have important roles in this struggle against the Lostai."

"Yes, but we need to give ourselves a target date, a deadline, when we feel we have sacrificed enough of our family time. No one would think less of us for it. You were ready to settle down in Fronidia if it had not been for the Lostai coming after us. You can work on strategy in a safe environment without us having to be separated."

"But these people are counting on me now. Do you have a timeframe in mind?"

As usual, she took her time before replying, becoming thoughtful and then not directly answering my question.

"In one lunar cycle, it will be the first revolution since Josher's birthdate. According to your tradition, you are supposed to give him his first personal amulet at that time, no?"

"Hmm, I do not know." I hesitated. "That does not give a lot of time for me to leave things organized here."

She propped up on her arms, looking up at me, and her expression was deadly serious.

"Then perhaps Kindor can do it. I can ask Larmont or one of the other Arandan soldiers what is involved with that ritual."

I grabbed her shoulders, perhaps a little too roughly.

"That is not fair! You are trying to hurt me with your words."

She remained stone-faced.

"Montor, I have brought an extra *hanstoric* that I will leave with you. I will show you how to use it in case there is an emergency and you need to leave here in a hurry or for whatever." She then rolled off me and remained staring at the ceiling. A solitary tear slid down the side of her face.

Is there any request that I will not grant her?

"Mina, I am sorry. I will come to Dit Lar in time for Josher's birthday, and let us plan to move back to Fronidia as a family in five lunar cycles. These people have accomplished a lot, but I fear that if I leave before we free a few more provinces, they will not be strong enough to keep the Lostai out. All our hard work will be for nothing. In the meantime, we can visit each other. How does that sound to you?"

She turned to me, tears flowing freely now.

"I guess that is a plan."

I pulled her close, brushing the tears from her eyes with the back of my hand.

"I love you, Mina. Deeply. More than I ever thought I would or could. I do not want you to be sad. I also wish for us to have a normal life together."

She hooked her arms around my neck.

"It is going to be hard to leave you this evening, but our love will give me patience. Montor, I hope we can be together again soon."

26

KINDOR

One day and one night passed beyond Mina's expected return time. Strangely, I was not worried for her safety. No. I was enraged, consumed with a jealous anger that I did my best to conceal from Larmont, his soldiers, and, above all, Josher. The time Mina and I had shared on Dit Lar had fanned the flames of my love for her. I finished off the bottle of brandy cursing the fact that she probably was in his arms.

I need to stop clinging to a female who has not one but two husbands. I have confused my place in her life. What an idiot I am, hoping to be something significant. Instead, I am just like a faithful pet to her. It is time to see if one of the female Arandan soldiers might have me.

Security alarms awoke me from my drunken stupor. I shook it off and contacted Larmont on the viewer, communicating to him using my tablet.

"Commander, what is happening?"

"Another Lostai attack, but a much larger contingent, six battle crafts. Our shielding has been completely compromised. I already have authorized our troops to abandon the base if they can. I will not allow my soldiers to commit suicide. We will return and take Dit Lar back, but now we must retreat. Take Montor's son through the transportal at once, as Mina instructed."

"But what about Mina? She is due to arrive at any moment. The Lostai will capture her."

"A small group of us will stay as long as we can to hopefully protect her. That is all I can do. I know you care much for her, but she would want you to prioritize her son's safety."

"Yes, I know," I said.

Suddenly sober, I grabbed basic clothing and personal items, then awakened Josher. He already communicated easily using telepathy.

"Son, we are going on a trip."

"*Fa* Kindor, where? Is *Ro Ma* here?"

"We will meet her later, but now we must hurry," I said, trying to conceal any uneasiness from my expression.

We rushed to the crystalline caves, and I identified our destination on the *hanstoric* screen: Frazin, a township in Fronidia where my family once lived before we moved to Zuntar. Mina had never been there, and I had never mentioned it to her. She would have no way to guess where we had gone, and that was exactly how she wanted it. Josher would be safe.

I braced myself for whatever fantastical sensation we were supposed to feel when traveling across the star system in a flash. Instead, it was like being anesthetized without any concept of the amount of time that had passed.

We landed, if that is how one could describe it, in a park at the center of town.

"Josher, how do you feel?" I asked.

"*Fa* Kindor, that was strange."

I got on one knee to inspect him.

"Yes, but do you feel OK?"

"Yes, *Fa*."

We walked out of the park and strolled to one of the main streets to find a place where we could stay until I sorted out our next steps. The display on my tablet informed me it was morning, local time.

Frazin bordered an exotic vacation spot called Jamboran. The residents of Frazin were the waiters, maintenance workers, housekeepers, cooks, and administrative personnel that kept Jamboran running—humble, busy people who did not have time to pay attention to anything other than going to work and getting back home to rest. That suited Josher and me just fine as we needed to maintain a low profile.

I had enough funds on my remuneration chip to rent a room at a boarding house where many of the lower-income laborers lived. When I walked up to the front desk to inquire about a room, the desk clerk looked at Josher and then at me.

"Sir, is this your child?"

I used Fronidian sign language, which the clerk understood.

"No, I am his caregiver."

The desk clerk eyed me with a skeptical look.

"Where are his parents?"

"It is a long story, but I have an official authorization from his mother to travel with him—"

"Wait. Let me contact my manager so you can discuss it with her."

I shook my head impatiently and waited for the manager, a middle-aged Fronidian with wavy brown hair and bright emerald green pupils that popped against the blackness of her Fronidian eyes.

"We need to triple-check your permission for traveling with this child."

"Yes, I have it here. I was just about to show it to your clerk."

I scrolled to the screen on my tablet with the authorization

Mina had left me, which showed Mina's and Josher's genetic sequencing as proof of its authenticity.

The manager reviewed them and found the authorization to be in order.

"Sorry for the inconvenience, sir, but we have enacted new laws to crack down on local Sotkari that are helping Lostai military in all manner of illegal activity, some of which include child abductions."

My blood boiled at the thought of Sotkari collaborating with Lostai military.

"No problem, I understand."

She led us to a small room and provided us some complimentary snacks for our trouble. We settled in, but I needed to kill time as Josher was a curious child who grew bored easily. I myself wished for some distraction for my frazzled nerves. The touristy area's eateries, souvenir shops, and entertainment venues supplied plenty to explore.

"What do you think, Josher? Do you want to see what new things we can discover in this town?"

"Sure, *Fa* Kindor."

He was such an agreeable and inquisitive child, skipping along and pointing out things that caught his attention. Mina had done an excellent job as a parent so far, already having taught him the foundations of good manners and self-control. Of course, even he had his moments when he did not hesitate to bluntly speak his mind. I guess he inherited that from his father.

"No more walking. I am tired."

He was right to complain. I had lost track of time, my thoughts focused on Mina.

Is she safe? What did she find upon her return to Dit Lar?

My heart was heavy with guilt over the earlier angry thoughts I had directed towards her.

"OK, do you want something to eat?"

"Yes, yes!" he said, jumping.

I found a restaurant that catered to children, immersing customers in a holographic representation of a popular super-hero show with the meals served by droids dressed up as the main characters. Josher loved it, apparently familiar with the story, explaining to me each character's special power. I smiled thinking about how Josher would grow up to have powers similar to some of these fictional characters.

When we arrived back at the boarding house, Josher was ready for a nap. I took advantage to review the news stream for anything regarding the situation on Dit Lar. It did not take me long to find a Lostai communique confirming they had retaken the planet, but there was no information regarding prisoners. I buried my face in my hands, angered by the feeling of helpless-ness. Some people considered me a powerful being, and yet I could not think of a single thing I could do to help Mina right now. Weariness took over as I lay on the bed and fell asleep until Josher's insistent voice roused me.

"*Fa*, when is *Ro Ma* coming?"

I did my best to erase the worry from my expression.

"She is going to be away for a few more days, but we are going to have some fun together in this town."

He looked to the ceiling and pursed his lips, digesting this piece of information.

"OK. I am hungry. Is it dinner time?"

27

MINA

I surprised the Lostai soldiers with my arrival, but it only took them a couple of seconds to recover and draw their weapons. I froze and my heart sunk. My worst fear had come true.

"Do not move and raise your hands where we can see them!"

I scoped out the situation.

Hmm, ten soldiers. Using my telekinetic abilities, I could disarm a few of them but not all at the same time. I should play nice for now, follow their instructions, and perhaps incapacitate whoever is in charge later.

They cuffed me while requesting orders from their commander, who told them to keep me there. A few minutes later, I stood face to face with an old foe.

"Wow, Mina, it's been a while or should I call you The Chaperone?" he said in English.

I rushed to lock my mind so he couldn't use telepathy on me.

"Gio Napoletano, what the hell are you doing here?"

Just the sight of him caused a tremor throughout my body.

Images of us dancing came to mind followed by the memory of being cuffed to a bed while he ripped open my blouse. Montor rescued me that day. I remembered threatening to kill Gio if we ever met again.

"Well, Zorla is in command here now. He expected we'd find you here and wanted the assistance of someone you couldn't play mind games with."

"You're working for them? I thought you were done with your military duties. I once even suspected you might be aligned with the rebel group on Renna One."

"I'm aligned with whoever pays the highest price, and right now, that's Zorla."

"Where are the Arandan soldiers?"

"We have some incarcerated here. Most are dead and some escaped, but that is not any concern of yours. There is only one question you need to answer, Mina. Where are Montor and your son?"

I took a moment to say a silent prayer of thanks. The fact that he asked for my son confirmed Kindor was able to transport himself and Josher off the planet.

Gio and three soldiers took me to a holding cell with a magnetic force field that I could not manipulate and also blocked my ability to access anyone's mind outside of it. Zorla arrived soon after. I felt a sudden increase of perspiration across my body. The memories of his punishments were still fresh, even though it had been over a year since I had escaped Xixsted.

"Mina, I must admit, I am very upset with you. Not only did you abandon your duties as a Lostai soldier, but you turned Montor, my most prized assistant, against me. On top of that, you are hiding your offspring from me," Zorla said.

Bitter hatred consumed me like I had never felt before. I ran up to the edge of the cell and glared at him. The cuffs exploded off my wrists, small pieces of metal flung everywhere.

On the other side of the force field, the three guards took a step back.

"I never agreed to be a Lostai soldier! You bastards kidnapped me!"

Zorla was unfazed by my outburst. Cold, calculating, deep-set eyes stared back.

"You could have had an illustrious future in our military, and after serving your time with us, like Gio here, you would have been free to do what you pleased. Instead, you will be our prisoner forever, and we will do with you...as we please. First, I need to know where Montor and your son are."

Detesting the satisfied look on his face, I sauntered around the cell with a bit of arrogance and fake bravado.

"Unfortunately for you, I purposely have kept myself ignorant of that information, so there is no way you are finding that out from me."

This was only true about Josher, but I hoped I could convince them I was also unaware of Montor's whereabouts.

Zorla's mouth curled into a sinister smile.

"We shall see." He turned to Gio. "Use whatever means necessary to get that information from her. You requested she not be scarred for when you mate with her later, so feel free to use our infirmary to heal her injuries when you are done. Also, I want her friends from the *Barinta* to see her defeated and humiliated. I am not convinced they have told us all they know. Let us strike a little fear in their hearts."

I stopped dead in my tracks and walked towards the edge of the cell again to get closer to him.

"You have them? Where are they?" I asked.

"Yes, we captured their ship and have incarcerated them here so that you all will have a nice reunion."

Cold fear consumed me.

I might be strong enough to resist torture, but can I bear watching any of them be harmed?

Again, I considered my options. The last time I had seen Gio, his mental abilities seemed weakened from lack of practice. If that were still the case, I could have a good chance to overcome him and the three Lostai soldiers, or maybe I could try to manipulate Zorla's mind.

"Gio, I am leaving here before she tries to play her mind games with me. I have told everyone that you are the sole person in command of this base and its prisoners until I return. I should be back in ten days. Hopefully by then, we will have the information we seek," Zorla said.

Zorla left in a rush, and my struggle began.

Gio opened the force field, stepped in, and grabbed me by the shoulders.

"Mina, I don't want to hurt you. We checked your tablet and it's encrypted, so we can't get any info off it. Let's make this simple. Just tell me where Montor and his son are."

I didn't answer. With the magnetic field no longer an obstruction, I used telepathy to cause two of the Lostai soldiers to lose consciousness.

"Shit!" shouted Gio, grabbing me by the neck.

I tucked my chin, grabbed him by the wrists, and, pulling him towards me, kneed him in the groin. He doubled over. I kicked him again, and he fell.

The third soldier lunged at me. I tried to manipulate his mind, but Gio side-glanced and apparently did the same. I kicked the soldier hard in the face and chest while trying to reach his mind to force him to fight Gio. The soldier's behavior became erratic. Neither Gio nor I would get from him what we wanted. Instead, the soldier turned away from us, pressing his fingers to his temples, rocking back and forth and crying like a baby.

That was my first experience of someone being assaulted by telepathy from two different sources. As much as I hated the

Lostai and what they represented, I couldn't help feeling sorry for the soldier.

Gio rolled his eyes and sighed.

"I guess I will have to beat it out of you myself."

My sympathy was short-lived. I couldn't risk the soldier coming out of his distress, so I struck him in the head and knocked him out. Gio jumped back to his feet.

"Mina, this is your last chance," he said as we squared off.

We exchanged blows. Gio was taller and stronger, but I had faithfully maintained a daily workout regimen for over two years. He landed two hard punches to my face. A gash opened on my brow bone. Blood trickled down, and my lip was split too. Ignoring the sting and metallic taste in my mouth, I focused all my power and intercepted with a straight knee to the ribs. The dull pop satisfied me. He doubled over in pain, but before I could capitalize on my strike, he retreated to outside the cell, grabbed a vial from a side table and sprayed into my face.

I awoke in horror to find myself naked, paralyzed, and strapped to a chair.

"What have you done to me? Why don't I have clothes on?"

He cupped my chin roughly.

"We underestimated you. I didn't think I'd need the spray. You, Mina, need to be taken down a notch. Who do you and Montor think you are? You, me, Montor, and thousands of others that have been taken—we're all in the same boat, but no..."

He poked me hard on my collarbone.

"You seem to think you are better than us. You know how many hostages Montor beat into submission, including me? You think I liked it? He taught me how to be a soldier for the

Lostai. Now, all of a sudden, he's a noble rebel. Honestly, it pisses the hell outta me!"

"I don't presume to be anything other than someone who refuses to be used by the Lostai and their agenda. I don't excuse whatever Montor did in the past, but everyone can make a choice to change. So can you."

"Spare me. I'm long past that point," he replied, pushing his palm against my face.

He lost all semblance of agitation, adopted a calm expression, and turned to grab a syringe.

"Mina, I'm done wasting time." He flicked the syringe with his finger. "A shot of this and you'll be spilling all your secrets."

My mental energy was running low, but I was able to sever the straps. That didn't gain me much since I was physically incapacitated. During our fight, adrenaline had kept pain to a minimum, but now throbbing and puffiness assaulted my face.

I took a deep breath to get centered as Gio injected the truth serum into my arm and interrogated me again.

Mina, this is what you've trained for.

Closing my eyes, I entered through prayer into a trance, my thoughts focused on repelling the effects of the drug. The proximity of Gio's face to mine, his breath, and his loud shouting faded, his voice now a faraway echo.

The serum was ineffective. I didn't give up Montor's location, and I had no idea where Kindor had taken Josher. Once he realized the serum was not working on me, he used a *zirem* on my feet, legs, back, and stomach. This brought back memories of the times Zorla punished me with that same electric rod. I didn't want to cry, but the agony became too much. Gio hovered the *zirem* near my breasts, his eyes lecherous.

"These are too pretty to mess with," he said.

My body trembled as the electric burns caused waves of hot pain, and I vomited. I could almost taste my seared skin, and the foul odor of puke made the nausea even worse. Gio lost his calm demeanor and punched me in the face and abdomen I don't know how many times while I sat limp and defenseless.

"Mina, I don't want to keep hurting you. Where the hell is Montor and your son!" His voice grew high-pitched and frantic.

I said nothing. The bleeding became much worse, warm and pasty against my skin. The taste of vomit and blood converged into a disgusting mix. Before I passed out, he dragged me to another area. Someone gasped as he hurled me to the floor. He bent over, grabbed a fistful of my hair, and lifted my head from the ground, twisting my neck to force me to look sideways. Both my eyes were swollen almost shut, but I was able to descry across from me Lasarta, Foxor, Lorret, Damari, and Sortomor in a holding cell secured by a force field and two Lostai soldiers. There were no mechanical parts for me to manipulate that could help release them. The expressions on their faces confirmed to me what my aching, naked body already knew. I was in pretty bad shape.

"Mina!" one of them cried out.

Gio stomped on one of my hands with his heavy boots. The crunch shot agonizing pain up my arm. I opened my mouth to scream, but no sound came out. Gio spoke in Lostai so everyone could understand. Uncontrollable tremors rocked my body.

"Shut up! Anyone as much as whispers and I will punish her again."

I heard soft whimpering, and he kicked me in the side.

"Shhh." someone else said, and he stomped my other hand. Finally, he got the silence he wanted.

"This filthy whore still has not given us the information we need. You see what I have done to her. I will do the same to each and every one of you until someone tells me where Montor and his son are."

I wondered if Gio knew Damari had embedded Sotkari Ta genes and the same telepathic and telekinetic abilities he and I had He had never met Damari before but knew, being from Earth, that he must be a victim of abduction. The Lostai took people either for their Sotkari Ta genes or as slave labor. I communicated to Damari telepathically.

"Lock your mind, Damari. This man, Gio, is Sotkari Ta."

"Bwoy, Mina. Me really sorry fi see you like dis. Wha me fi do?" answered Damari, his Jamaican accent in my mind, even heavier than usual.

"Yes, stay calm for now and wait for my input. I'm going to try to negotiate something with him. We need to get you guys away from here. I'm worried he will try to force me to give out information by torturing any or all of you. Also, he can manipulate their minds to get them to reveal United Rebel Front confidential information."

I summoned up enough strength to ignore my pain and turned my attention to speak to Gio in English.

"Gio, can I talk to you?"

"Go ahead."

"Gio, Montor has been missing for several months now. About three months ago, we learned he had stopped in Fronidia, but that's all we know. He is purposely staying away from his family and friends to keep the Lostai away from us. I left instructions that if the Lostai retook this planet, my son was to be transported to another location, and I refused to know where. I swear to you, these people have no additional information. You are wasting your time and energy, so I'd like to propose something to you."

"Yeah, I'm listening."

"I want to negotiate with you for their release and safe return to Aranda using the transportal. You once wanted me. Are you still interested?"

A cruel smile crept from his eyes to his lips as he assessed my broken body.

"Mina, you're not looking too good to me anymore, but

later, I plan to have my way with you anyway, so not much negotiating needed on my part."

"I assumed as much, but if you agree to my terms, I won't resist and can use my energy to make it more pleasurable for you. For each person you allow to return to Aranda using the transportal, I will sleep with you one night and make it worth your while. Damari will accompany each person and bring back the *hanstoric* so the next person can use it.

He narrowed his eyes.

"Why him?"

"No reason, other than he is the youngest."

"Liar. He is Sotkari Ta, isn't he?"

My heart skipped a beat.

"Yes, but not trained at all," I lied.

"What do you think will happen when Zorla comes back to find missing prisoners?" asked Gio.

"We can manipulate his mind and make him forget they were even here," I answered.

Taking only a few minutes to ponder the proposal, he gestured to the guards.

"Take her to the infirmary. Have them patch her up for me."

As he helped me up, I spoke telepathically to Damari.

"I've convinced Gio to let the prisoners use the transportal to travel back to Aranda. I told him each person will go one at a time and that you will accompany each prisoner and bring back the *hanstoric* here for the next person to use. Instead, when Gio and I come to send the first person, we need to jump into action. I will render the two soldiers unconscious, and I need you to take their weapons, keep one, and give the other to Foxor or Sortomor. Then we will force Gio to give us the *hanstoric*, and I will transport you all back to Aranda at once. I think if all of you stand close to each other, you can be transported together."

He was very upset, eyes glistening.

"Mina, me ready fi dead right yah so wid you. Wah a go happen to you after we gone?"

"Well, I'm hoping the United Rebel Front will come back to retake this planet and free me."

"Then me a go stay wid you until the end."

The resolve in his expression was unquestionable as he wiped the tears from his face, so I didn't bother to argue.

"OK, Damari."

Later in the day, after my injuries were healed and erased, Gio allowed me to go to my quarters to bathe, put on nice clothes, and make myself up. As I got ready, I prayed and prepared myself mentally for what would come next.

When I was ready, he came by to escort me to the holding area. He raked me with his lascivious eyes.

"The Chaperone is looking exceptionally gorgeous tonight," he said with an approving look.

He also dressed up.

It's a shame he's so evil.

With his shiny dark hair, hooded eyes, creamy white skin, and beautifully shaped mouth, he was very handsome, representing well his Italian background. He explained to the prisoners the deal we had struck. Of course, they all shouted out to me, telling me not to do it.

"Silence! Only I will address my whore, and she better make this fun for me, or I might decide to take one of you instead. Male or female, Either is fine for me," Gio said as he eyed Damari's strong build and smooth dark skin.

I worried I might have put Damari in danger by admitting to Gio that he was Sotkari Ta. Gio was after the potent sensations that sex between Sotkari Ta provided. I glanced back to Damari.

"Make sure everyone is clear on the plan," I communicated telepathically to him.

I got close to Gio, looked up into his eyes with as smoldering an expression as I could muster, and gave his arm a squeeze.

"You know, Gio, the truth is you're an attractive man. I'm ready to make this a memorable experience for you, but I'm concerned about Lasarta. She's very sensitive, and I'm afraid how all this can affect her mental state. Please get the *hanstoric* and let Damari take her through the transportal now. You'll still have plenty of prisoners to hold me accountable with. I'll be much more compliant if you allow me this one request."

Placing his hand behind my neck, he lowered to give me a lusty kiss. Inside, I gagged with disgust but maintained composure and tried my best to transmit sexual energy. He ran his fingers up through my hair and pressed his body against mine.

"Hmmm, this feels even better than I expected. I think I might keep you forever," he said in a husky voice. "OK, I'll allow it."

I used my mental strength to combat the feelings his words and tone conjured up. The idea of being in bed with Gio both repulsed and horrified me.

Steady, Mina, steady.

He made a call and requested someone to bring him the *hanstoric*. While we waited for the soldier to bring the device, I transmitted a message telepathically to Damari.

"Be ready. It's happening now."

The soldier arrived with the *hanstoric*, and Gio handed it to me while he addressed the group in the cell.

"Mina is going to be a nice girl for me, so the older female gets to leave first."

Meanwhile, I scrolled through the screens, getting the destination set so that it would only take a quick tap to activate it when the time came. Gio ran his hand down my back and gave my butt a good squeeze.

I wish I could strangle him, kill him with my bare hands.

He signaled to the Lostai security guards to let down the

force field. I gave Damari the faintest of nods and closed my eyes. The security guards fell to the ground. Foxor and Damari grabbed their weapons and pointed them at Gio.

"You bitch!" Gio shouted in English.

"Everyone gather here. Let's do this quick," I said.

"No, Mina. Damari, take the females and go. Sortomor and I will stay. We are not leaving you alone," said Foxor.

I know Foxor meant well, but throwing a wrench into our plan was not helpful. Gio could manipulate any one of them except Damari. The thought had not quite crossed my mind when Foxor stopped pointing the weapon at Gio and aimed it at Lasarta. Everyone froze until Lasarta shouted something to Foxor in Arandan. He ignored her and appeared as if in a trance. Keeping the weapon aimed at her, he spoke in Lostai in a monotone voice.

"No one move or I shoot her."

Gio grabbed me by the arm.

"OK, Mina, there's going to be a minor change in your plans. If you don't want me to make this stupid Arandan kill his wife, you are going to program Renna One as the destination. Here is the exact location code I want you to punch in." he said, showing me his tablet. "You and I are taking a little trip. Hurry, I have no qualms in making this guy kill his wife and friends."

The security guards regained consciousness, I assumed also through Gio's manipulation. I knocked one out again.

Damari, distraught, didn't know where to point his weapon.

Foxor continued to speak orders.

"Damari, drop your weapon."

Foxor pressed the weapon hard against Lasarta's chest. Damari had no choice but to obey. I used telekinesis to hurl the weapon out of Foxor's hands and into mine, but he grabbed Lasarta by the neck and started to choke her. Once again, Gio revived the guard I had put down. One guard grabbed Lorret and the other the weapon Damari had dropped. Lasarta gasped for breath. I feared for her life and dropped the weapon. It occurred to me that if I left with Gio, the *Barinta* crew would less likely be tortured, at least until Zorla returned.

God, I hope the United Rebel Front is already planning to retake the planet.

"OK, Gio, stop this. I'll go with you to Renna One."

"Good choice, Mina."

Foxor let go of Lasarta, and she fell to the ground but after coughing a bit, seemed to be OK. Poor Foxor looked so confused.

"Put everyone back in the holding cell," Gio ordered the soldiers. "I am taking the whore with me to look for her son. I'll be in contact shortly to give you further instructions."

They did as he said, and with a smug look on his face, he communicated to me telepathically.

"These assholes will never hear from me again. To give myself some time to avoid dealing with Zorla, I have manipulated their minds so they will not call him for a few days. I couldn't care less about Montor and your son. I already received half of Zorla's payment. You're mine now, honey."

28

MONTOR

Nothing can pacify
The anger
The rage
But I will make them pay

"Debt" from *Montor's Secret Stash of Poems*

The day after Mina left, Portars contacted me with an urgent message. He broke the news that the Lostai had retaken Dit Lar. The sensation of a heavy block falling on my chest sunk me into my chair. After the initial shock, my brain and voice produced robotic, rapid-fire questions, the first, of course, being, "Mina and my son? Are they safe?"

"We know for sure Kindor was able to leave with your son before the Lostai took over. Mina had left him strict instructions about this. His location is unknown but most probably he took your son to a safe place."

I exhaled a loud breath of relief.

"And Mina?"

His eyes shifted downward. Even before he shook his head, I knew the news was grim.

"Commander Larmont and a few soldiers waited so long for her, they ended up being captured by the Lostai. Our understanding is that she arrived at Dit Lar after the Lostai took control of the planet, but we do not have other concrete information."

He let a moment go by, allowing me to digest the implications of his words before continuing.

"Unfortunately, there is more bad news. The *Barinta* was also captured, and our understanding is that the Lostai are holding the crew on Dit Lar."

I jumped out of the chair as if someone were controlling my movements by remote control.

"I have a *hanstoric* Mina left with me. I am going there right now."

"Montor, wait. What can you accomplish alone? That would only make matters worse. Of course, we will retake Dit Lar and rescue the prisoners, but we need to regroup and carefully plan how we will retaliate. How strong are the Namson forces?"

"We have secured several provinces, and the shields that protect them are holding well, but I had hoped to assist them in gaining control of several more." I shook my head. "That will need to wait. I need to get to Dit Lar. My wife and foster parents are in danger. Zorla will surely try to get information on my whereabouts from them."

A jumble of rage and fear consumed me.

"Use the *hanstoric* to transport to Aranda so we can coordinate sending more aid to the Namson and you can lead the mission to retake Dit Lar."

"Yes, sir."

I saluted, then ended the transmission in haste, no longer

able to control the need to break things. What I could not destroy with my bare hands, I flung across the rooms using telekinetic powers. While in the midst of this mental breakdown, someone knocked on the door. I ignored it. The knocker insisted. Gritting my teeth, I marched over there with the idea of ripping apart that person too. I opened the stupid door with such force, it slammed against the wall and closed again. My chest heaved with anger. The door creaked opened again, and Tzarst peeked in.

"*Zateim*?"

"What do you want?"

"Is all right?"

In that moment of anger, I grabbed my friend by the neck and lifted him a full arm's length off the ground. The way his fingers moved made him appear like an old-fashioned puppet.

"*Zateim*, I not want hurt you, but this upsetting me," he said, words interspersed with choking noises.

A hilarious joke, but it served its purpose. We both knew I could destroy him in a minute. I dropped him to the ground, overcome with shame.

"I am so sorry, Tzarst."

He stroked his neck.

"Why so upset?"

"The Lostai have retaken Dit Lar. My previous crew, including my foster parents, are captured. I do not know where my wife is. If they have her..."

"Calm down, *Zateim*."

"Easy for you to say. Your spouse is not in the hands of the Lostai probably being tortured for information."

His spindly fingers reached up to touch my shoulder.

"I know how *Zateim* feel. Remember, I in Lostai military camp long time wondering if family slaughtered."

"She wanted us to be a normal family. We made plans to meet again."

My voice trailed off, and I covered my mouth. I did not want him to see my face crumpled in grief.

"She seemed with quiet strength. You rescue her. Tell me, how can help?"

I ask him inside and poured a glass of his favorite wine before slumping in a chair. He mentioned nothing of the damaged furniture or the shattered bottles, glasses, and plates. I let him know I would be leaving immediately to Aranda to plan a rescue but also secure additional resources for the Namson guerillas.

"We need to continue to take control of more provinces here. The more the Lostai are forced to engage rebel forces in various locations, the thinner their resources will be spread. I need someone to take over for me here. I know of no better person than you for this role, but I understand if you would rather recommend someone else. You have already lost too much time away from your family."

"Will consult with Forinza."

In the end, they struck a deal. Forinza agreed for Tzarst to take on the leadership role until he could identify and groom someone else. She was clear that he was to be back home in no more than three lunar cycles. The next day, I was in Penstarox.

I guess my reputation for having a bad disposition is why everyone either avoided me or kept their greetings brief and their conversation to the point. Commander Portars was the only one brave enough to address my grief. He knew I valued his friendship and respected him as my commanding officer.

"Montor, how are you doing?"

"Sir, what do you expect me to say? I am frustrated that we cannot immediately move to retake Dit Lar. Every hour that goes by is an hour that my family is at the mercy of the Lostai."

"I know you must be torn up inside, but you need to channel that pain into focus. We need to carefully put together our plan of attack so there is no chance of failure."

His words were helpful and steadied me for the task. The next few days, I pored over intelligence reports, coordinated with the rebel units on Sotkar and Namson, and selected the soldiers and crafts that I would lead into battle. I made sure to rest well, eat properly, and waste no time on social activities, continuing my workouts, physically and mentally, exercising harder than ever. If it came down to hand-to-hand combat, someone was going to feel my wrath. Meditation helped keep me focused.

My clarity suffered a setback when the Lostai released their official reports to sector-wide public broadcasting, bragging about their retaking of Dit Lar. I saw images of Mina naked, being dragged across the floor, her face swollen and bloody, *zirem* burns on her body; Gio Napoletano calling her a whore and stomping her hands with heavy boots; the *Barinta* crew in a jail cell, Lasarta whimpering. My gut ripped apart. I got into a physical altercation with another Arandan soldier just so I could punch someone. Commander Portars came to my rescue again, separating us himself. He ordered me to his office and gestured to the chair.

"Montor, sit and calm down. You need to get your focus back. Normally, we would never have had access to view this. These images were purposely leaked on our news stream. It is obvious your old commander Zorla is taunting you. He wants you broken down emotionally so that you will make mistakes."

He leaned over the desk and stared down at me with narrowed eyes, his words firm.

"Do not fall into his trap. Continue your careful planning. Soon, we will be ready to rescue them. We will make them pay."

I turned away to hide my tears, but it was useless. He could hear the tremor in my voice.

"Sir, I only ask you not to force me to take prisoners. Zorla and Gio cannot live through this."

"You can take your revenge with those two who were directly involved in touching your wife, but the other soldiers must be treated fairly. If we hope to gain more allies, we need to show we are better than the Lostai."

I took his words to heart and refocused on planning our attack. Zorla miscalculated when he released those videos of Mina. Images of the beloved Chaperone being brutally beaten created widespread outrage across the sector. The planet Tormix joined the United Rebel Front. Mina had returned hostages there. On Aranda and Sotkar, people joined the military in droves, many specifically requesting to be assigned to the mission of retaking Dit Lar. Fronidia remained neutral but expelled all Lostai from their planet and enacted stricter laws to capture any of their citizens that might be collaborating with the Lostai military.

Each agonizing day that went by, I thought of new ways of killing Gio and Zorla. After securing the personnel and squadrons to staff ten battalion cruisers, I encountered a problem. Intelligence reports showed that the Lostai had upgraded the shields around Dit Lar. It would be a waste of time to go there with our current weapons system. Our science team worked day and night to understand what changes were needed to allow our photon blasts to penetrate their shields. I walked over to their lab one afternoon to check on their progress.

"How long to complete the modifications?" I asked the head of the science department.

"Well, we still have not even figured out what changes they made to their system. I estimate at least two lunar cycles."

I grabbed him by the neck and squeezed hard.

"My wife will be dead by then!"

He could barely speak. Between gasps, he said, "I am... sorry...but...but the Lostai are...are...being much more careful in guarding their technology."

I let him go and told him to get out of my sight. Surely, he was on his way to lodge a formal complaint with Commander Portars about my behavior. In the meantime, I needed to think of a way to get to Dit Lar. I walked back to my office and paced like a trapped animal until I noticed the *hanstoric* on my desk. An idea came to mind. I contacted Kaonto, the leader of the Sotkari insurgency.

"Montor, it is wonderful to talk to you. It has been so long. At the same time, my heart is heavy. I saw the video the Lostai military leaked to all the news streams."

I could only imagine the expression on my face. He hurried on.

"But what can I do for you?"

"Kaonto, I have put together an armada of ten battalion cruisers ready to go at my command, but we do not currently have the technology to get through the Lostai upgraded shields. I have the *hanstoric* Mina left with me. When we arrive to orbit Dit Lar, I intend to transport myself to the crystalline cave. I have heard Mina could transport two people with her at once, so I would request your two strongest, bravest, best-trained Sotkari Ta soldiers that are already here to accompany me. We will have to turn off the system from the inside."

"Montor, the Lostai have hundreds of soldiers stationed there. I do not have a problem assigning two of our best soldiers to go with you, but I cannot see how you expect to be successful."

"We will go in heavily armed. We will catch them by surprise." I stepped up to the screen, my eyes locked on his, as if he were with me in the room. "Kaonto, I need to get my wife, my foster parents, and my friends out of there. I cannot wait any longer. What would you do?"

He stared back at me from the screen, his jaw clenched.

"Exactly the same. OK, let me review the roster of Sotkari Ta soldiers that are part of your fleet, and I will find the two best and have them report to you by end of today."

I crossed my arms over my chest and bowed, the Arandan military salute.

"Kaonto, thank you. I know we will be successful."

"May the Farthest Light guide you."

At the end of the day, the two soldiers he selected came by my office. Their names were Kristom and Komar. I debriefed them of my plan. The next morning, I sent communication to the nine other battalion captains that we would head out by midday. The most direct flight plan at top speeds would get us to Dit Lar in ten days.

Far before we approached Dit Lar's atmosphere, we used our long-range weapons to target the Lostai security ships orbiting the planet. We found they had also improved their sensors and could detect us farther out than before. They returned fire, but our excellent navigation system engineers and helmsmen evaded them. By the time we reached just outside the atmosphere, we had taken out three of the six Lostai security ships. Knowing the Lostai likely already had called for backup, we needed to move quickly. While our cruisers continued to engage the remaining Lostai security ships, I used the *hanstoric* to transport Kristom, Komar, and myself to the crystalline caves.

The jump using the *hanstoric* felt like I had dozed off and then been brusquely roused. We arrived deep in the cave and found no one in that area. The cave contained several passages.

As I walked farther down one of the branches, I saw some holding cells guarded by two Lostai. It was quick business for me to reach their minds, cause them to release the force fields and render them unconscious. We rushed to see Lasarta, Foxor, Sortomor, Damari, and Lorret tumble out of the holding area. Mina was not with them.

I brought my finger to my mouth, signaling that they remain quiet and follow me to the area where we first arrived. Even after clarifying we did not have time for explanations, Foxor insisted on talking to me, sobbing between his words. I had never seen him this way.

"Montor, I am so sorry. It is my fault he took her."

Shermont! The situation is much worse than I expected.

"She told us to leave with the *hanstoric,* but we did not want to leave her. He took control of my mind. I almost killed Lasarta."

I covered my eyes so no one could see my tears.

"Enough! We do not have time for this now."

I had never raised my voice to Foxor before, but I could not allow myself to be distracted by anguish and rage. I handed the *hanstoric* to Kristom.

"Take Lasarta and Foxor back to the ship. Come back immediately so we can also transport Lorret. Damari and Sortomor, you stay here with me. We need to figure out how to shut down the shields, and I could use all the help I can get."

While Kristom transported Lasarta, Foxor, and later Lorret, I asked Damari and Sortomor about the layout of the military offices. They showed me which passages led to other prison cells where Commander Larmont and the last soldiers who had waited for Mina were being held. We rendered unconscious any Lostai guards we encountered along the way and freed Commander Larmont and five other Arandan soldiers, arming them with the weapons taken from the Lostai guards.

"Where is the operations base?" I asked Commander Larmont.

He gestured towards another passage.

"At the end of this tunnel, the cave opens into an enormous room, but there will be hundreds of soldiers around that area and outside the cave entrance. They have also set up camp on several different points of the planet."

"That is not a problem. We just need to manipulate a few soldiers from afar to do what we want. Once the shield is down, we will bring on our full attack. We have ten battalion cruisers in orbit, sir."

We continued down the tunnel, and I saw from afar the light coming from the large room Commander Larmont had described.

"Where are the shield and weapon controls?"

"Towards the far left."

The tunnel continued dark and narrow until we reached the entrance to the large room. I took the two Sotkari Ta and Damari with me and asked Commander Larmont, his soldiers, and Sortomor to cover us if we were detected. Scanning the area Commander Larmont had mentioned, the controls at the far left came into view. I focused my attention on the three Lostai that appeared to be manning them, planting in their mind the command to bring down the shields and stop any defensive action.

I enjoyed the moment of confusion and then shouting, pushing, and shoving that ensued amongst the Lostai soldiers as they tried to figure out why their tactical officers had turned off their defensive systems. Once my ship captains confirmed to me that the shields were down, I gave the order to attack.

We continued to render unconscious as many Lostai soldiers as possible, but finally others realized we were in the tunnel and turned towards us. Commander Larmont and the others joined us as we fired our weapons against them. The roar of several ships landing outside reverberated throughout the cave.

We made our way outside of the cave entrance. United Rebel Front soldiers poured out of our ships. Laser fire and photon blasts lit up the entire area.

"Damari, cover me. I need to find Zorla."

Damari and I went back inside to the operations base, scanned for Lostai dressed in commanding officer uniforms, only identifying a few lieutenants. With weapons in both hands, I shot at will, creating a path towards the closest one. I grabbed him and pulled him to a corner. He looked at me with disgust.

"I know you. You are the traitor."

I punched him hard. Dark blood spurted from his nose.

"Where is Zorla?"

"I am not answering."

I manipulated his mind, forcing him to reply.

"Zorla returned to Losta some time ago, leaving the Earthian, Gio Napoletano, in charge. He was concerned the female Earthian could manipulate his mind. Then Gio took the female with him and has not communicated back to us. Zorla has been giving orders remotely from Losta."

I punched him again, knocking him out.

"It figures. That coward," I muttered under my breath.

The surrounding pandemonium was minor compared to the confusion in my mind.

Where could Gio have taken Mina? What can I do now?

"Montor, you back should to ship," Damari said. Sometimes, it was so hard to understand his broken Lostai.

I was about to take my frustration out on him for attempting to give me orders.

He is right, though. I should probably talk to Foxor and Lasarta. Maybe Gio mentioned something that could be a clue of where he went.

The ship they were on was still in orbit, so I needed to find Kristom, who still had the *hanstoric* with him. Damari and I worked our way outside of the cave, again.

A blast knocked both of us off our feet. I was slammed hard against a pile of large boulders. My legs felt like ice for a millisecond, and then I did not feel them at all. Dazed, I tried to stand, but my legs did not respond. Someone was dragging me away. I looked over my shoulder and saw Damari exerting a lot of effort to pull my much larger body out of danger. Kristom approached us.

"Kristom, I think I am paralyzed."

He touched my legs, reached around to my back, concentrated for a few seconds, and shook his head, tight-lipped.

"I will transport you to your ship. This is a serious injury."

"*Shermont!*" I closed my eyes and cursed my luck.

29

KINDOR

My heart broke each time Josher asked for his mother. They had never been separated for more than a day or two. He probably also sensed my anxiety. Finally, after ten days, I decided to take him to stay with my mother, my niece, and my niece's husband. I intended to go to the Fronidian capital to contact the United Rebel Front in case they had information on Mina's status. Josher had spent the first few months of his life with my family. My niece, Karrina, grew to love him and would be happy for the opportunity to spend time with him.

I found my family doing well when I arrived at their home. My niece's husband, Tadium, a good person from a wealthy and powerful Fronidian family, deeply loved her. Their home and neighborhood reflected their high-income status. I was pleased to hear they had just learned she was pregnant for the first time. My mother kept busy by running a morning meal shop nearby. It was much smaller than the restaurant we had owned in Zuntar, where Mina had worked with us for six lunar cycles. My mother had no need to work, but she detested being idle.

Karrina was overjoyed but surprised to see how much

Josher had grown. He did not remember her as he was only four lunar cycles old when I left with Mina to look for his father.

"*Sa veranttay*, how handsome you've become," she greeted him in Fronidian, a language he did not understand, so I translated for him.

I explained that he understood basic Sotkari, so before long she was feeding him treats and having a conversation about his favorite games and foods. My mother, as usual, was reserved but, I knew, happy to see me. Although we called each other often, it had been seven lunar cycles since we had seen each other, when I left Zuntar with Mina and Josher. Back then, it had upset her that I had fallen in love with Mina and followed her in joining the *Barinta* crew. Later, she was filled with pride once she learned we had played a pivotal role in the Sotkari uprising against the Lostai. Now, she was sincerely worried for Mina's safety.

Each day that passed without knowing about Mina was agony. I waited some days before heading to the capital city of Fro Gantar to be sure Josher was settled in and would not be upset by my absence. Mina and I had been the only two constants in his life since he was born. Fortunately, he sensed Karrina's genuine affection and soon enough became her shadow as she went about her daily chores and errands. Tadium enjoyed seeing Karrina's motherly instincts blossom while anticipating the birth of their child. He let me borrow a trans-planetary shuttle and lent me some funds for my trip.

When I arrived to Fro Gantar, I checked into a modest hotel and promptly reviewed all the news feeds. My nerves frayed as I cycled through the latest updates from each planet in the sector. Finally, on the Arandan channel a military officer discussed the latest skirmishes with the Lostai. He confirmed that the United Rebel Front had regained control of Dit Lar. My heart beat like a rapid-fire weapon as I wondered whether Mina was safe.

My next stop was the Arandan embassy. As a previous member of the *Barinta*, I had a certain amount of clout with the United Rebel Front, so I expected no trouble in getting official information on Mina's status. As I walked into the receiving area, someone shouted out my name. I turned and saw Colora. She ran over to me, and we embraced, a custom not used in either of our cultures, but curiously, something we had both learned from Mina. I hid my anxiety behind a fake smile while I communicated to her in Fronidian sign language.

"Colora, I am so pleased to see you. How are you doing?"

"You must not know what has happened," she said, avoiding my eyes.

I masked my fear.

"Are you referring to Dit Lar?"

Our conversation turned choppy at first. We were both wary of the news we were about to share.

"Do you have Josher?"

"Yes, he is safe."

Anyone could be used by the Lostai, so I did not specify anything else about his location.

"The United Rebel Front is interested in researching whether the *hanstorics* can be recharged here. Sortomor dropped me off here to request permission from the Fronidian government before they continued to Renna One. Soon after, the Lostai captured the *Barinta* crew and took them to Dit Lar. Mina was on Dit Lar when the Lostai took over, but someone took her away. We have been able to intercept Lostai military communications."

"Is the person who took Mina a friend? Does he work with the United Rebel Front?"

"No...no..."

She began to cry and hesitated. I wanted to shake her by the shoulders.

"Please, Colora, tell me what happened."

She wiped the tears away and with an exhale regained composure.

"Zorla had left this person in charge of interrogating Mina and the *Barinta* crew. The leaked Lostai video shows images of Mina being brutally beaten..."

"What!"

A dark anguish like nothing I had ever experienced before engulfed my soul.

"I think the purpose was to taunt Montor to lure him out of wherever he was. Sure enough, Montor arrived with an armada to retake Dit Lar. They were successful. Dit Lar is back under the control of the United Rebel Front."

I exhaled.

Mina was rescued, then?

"So, that is a good thing. What happened with Mina?"

"When Montor and his armada arrived, Mina had already been taken. Montor has been seriously injured and is recovering in Aranda."

Did she say taken?

"But why did this person take Mina?"

"I am not sure. I think he had met her before. The Lostai are now looking for him too as he was not authorized to take her off Dit Lar." She buried her face in her hands. "Kindor, I wish I had not seen the video of him hurting her. It was terrible."

My angst turned to fury as I focused on one thing.

"What else do you know about him?"

"He is an Earthian Sotkari Ta that served under Montor's command for many revolutions. His name is Gio Napoletano."

"Colora, I will not rest until I find her."

Colora nodded while wiping away new tears.

"I will ask Portars to give me the pass codes that will allow you access to the classified information we have about Montor's service with the Lostai. There you will likely find information on Gio. Also, he has businesses and properties on Renna One that should be of public record."

"Thank you, Colora."

She embraced me again. Her voice trembled as she said, "I hope you can find her, Kindor."

"I will."

I contacted Karrina and explained that I would be away for a while. Josher was safe with her and Tadium since the Lostai were no longer welcomed on Fronidia. When I returned to my hotel room, I allowed myself some time to grieve. I cursed Montor for having motivated Mina to extend her stay on the Namson planet. Had she immediately returned after delivering the rescued hostages, she would have escaped Dit Lar with me and her son. Afraid it would affect my focus and decision-making, I decided not to view the images Colora had mentioned. What she had described to me was bad enough. After meditation, I pored over all the records and history I had gathered on Gio Napoletano.

Gio was kidnapped from Earth as a teenager and taken to Xixsted, where he was assigned to Montor's squadron. He had embedded Sotkari Ta genes, similar to Montor and Mina. Montor was not much older than he but, having been raised on the military station and mentored by a Sotkari Ta elder, was already a powerful and respected Lostai squadron leader by the time Gio arrived to Xixsted. Instead of resisting his captors, Gio embraced his new life as a Lostai soldier and served out the required fifteen-revolution tenure. He then took his savings and invested in precious metal and jewelry businesses, becoming quite successful, albeit through some shady dealings with the criminal underworld.

Gio also seemed willing to sell his services to whoever might be in need of someone with telepathic, telekinetic, and mind control abilities. He apparently was not partial to any particular group, sometimes working for the Lostai, sometimes for the insurgency or other random parties. His last known primary residence was on Renna One, so I designated that to be my first stop in my quest to find him. I had the *hanstoric* with me. The figures on the display had not changed. It appeared I would have enough charge for one jump. I left to Renna One in Tadium's shuttle with the idea of using the *hanstoric* to bring Mina quickly back to Fronidia. The trip to Renna One took fifteen days.

I arrived in the evening and programmed Tadium's shuttle to return to Fronidia on autopilot to ensure the Lostai would not find it anywhere on Renna One. After finding a place to stay near a jewelry factory owned by Gio Napoletano, I placed an audio call to my niece and talked to Josher. We cannot communicate telepathically over a call, so I answered him by typing in my tablet.

"*Fa* Kindor, *Fa* Tadium is showing me how fight *vatimex*," Josher said, referring to a Fronidian martial art form.

"That sounds like fun."

"When are you coming back? I miss *Ro Ma*."

"Soon, Josher. I will come back soon with your mother."

That night, I did not sleep well.

A small room.

Mina's voice crying out in agony.

When I arrive, blood everywhere.

I try to rouse her, but she does not wake.

She is gone.

The nightmares haunted me until dawn.

With no clues of where to begin my search for Gio Napoletano, I decided my first stop should be the jewelry factory that he owned. Renna One was home to people from many planets but under Lostai rule, and everyone spoke that language. I could be at risk there. To avoid drawing the attention of Lostai patrol, I gathered my hair in a high bun, the style typically adopted by the traitorous Sotkari Ta that were allied with the Lostai. I pretended to be looking for work and asked for the Hiring Manager.

"Unfortunately, you need an appointment, sir," said the Hiring Manager's assistant.

"OK, no problem. When can I return?" I replied using my tablet.

She checked his agenda and scheduled an appointment for the next day. I walked around the facility with my tablet, asking the supervisors and employees random questions, acting like I was getting familiarized with the work environment.

"What is it like to work here? Is the boss fair?"

A young Rennan looked up from his workstation.

"The pay is good. The owner is an Earthian, but he hardly ever comes around here."

"Really? I thought he lived here on Renna One."

"Yes, but he does not mix with the lower class. He likes to go to fancy places like Zamandi's Room. I work there sometimes as a bartender in the evenings."

"I am new in the area. I could use some socializing."

"You should go there. You will find all kinds of interesting people, but it is expensive. If you see me there, I can introduce you to some of the regulars."

"Thanks for the tip."

I secured a job in the equipment repair area of the jewelry factory to cover the cost of the expensive clothes that were appropriate for attending a place like Zamandi's Room. On my third visit there, I ran into my Rennan acquaintance from the factory. His name was Lomo, and I found him tending one of the bars. I told him I owned a small lot of land in Fronidia that had a rare mineral mine and was interested in approaching Gio with a business proposition.

"It is odd, but it has been more than one lunar cycle since I have seen Gio here, but I can introduce you to a good friend of his."

I could not afford to go to Zamandi's Room every night, but I had dinner and drinks there at least three times that week. Sure enough, on the third night Lomo called an Earthian male over to where I was sitting.

"Tony, this is the person we talked about. He is looking for Gio."

This male was Sotkari Ta. His light appeared in my mind in an instant. I quickly blocked my thoughts. Cocking his head ever so slightly, he did the same while speaking out loud in Lostai.

"Pleased to meet you."

We grasped wrists in the typical Sotkari Ta salutation. As we had blocked each other, I used my tablet to communicate.

"Greetings. My name is Kindor Grahmon. Nice to meet you, too. I have a business proposition for Gio Napoletano. Can you put me in contact with him? Also, do you happen to know Lostai sign language? It feels more natural for me to communicate that way rather than using the tablet."

Tony offered to buy me a drink, and I accepted. He was my height, fair-skinned with a muscular build, blond and blue-eyed, and got right to the point.

"My name is Tony Springer. We are both Sotkari Ta. I think it would be easier for us to communicate telepathically. I will unblock and promise not to violate your mind if you do the same."

I needed to gain this person's trust, so I agreed but not before making a point to keep Mina out of my thoughts. I did my best to focus on our immediate conversation.

"Lomo tells me Gio normally comes here often, but he has not seen him in over a lunar cycle."

Tony took a slow sip of his drink.

"Umm...yes, that is true. He seems to be away—on business."

"Oh, so he is not on Renna One?"

"I do not know."

Tony averted his eyes and flicked some imaginary thing from his cheek. I did not need to read his mind to know he was hiding something.

"Is it true you are close friends? Do you know when he will be back?"

"I am not sure, but he usually is not away for long."

"OK. Well, I will be here on Renna One for a while. If you talk to him, let him know I would like to meet him," I said, looking around. "I like this place. I expect we will run into each other again."

He raised his glass.

"Let us toast to that."

When I returned to the hotel, I researched any public information available on Tony Springer. He also served in the Lostai military but not in the same squadron as Montor and Gio. He did not own any businesses but did freelance security work for small corporations and had worked for Gio.

The following week, I continued to visit Zamandi's room and ran into Tony again. I did not ask about Gio but tried to be friendly. By the third time, he noted I had been eating alone and suggested that we have our evening meals together. It did not take long for me to realize he was flirting with me. Also, he drank intoxicating beverages heavily. I decided to use both to my advantage.

We shared meals in three different restaurants in the Zamandi's Room complex but had not visited the lounge or dance areas. The fourth night we had dinner together, I asked him to show me around, launching a long night of drinking, dancing, and talking. I pretended to match him drinking but got rid of my glasses after one sip. By the early morning hours, he was quite drunk, and his secrets slipped out. As we sat in an intimate corner of one of the lounges, being under the effect of alcohol drove him to speak out loud instead of using telepathy.

"You know, Gio and I, we have been more than friends," his speech was slurred, "but he does not appreciate me."

"I know how that feels—to love someone who does not love me in the same way," I said.

"I have done a lot of favors for him, go—gone along with ple—plenty of things that make me feel terrible and could get me into trouble. I do these...these...these things out of love, but I have come to realize he is a troubled person." He banged his fist on the table and shook his head. "He is not going to change and is not worth the misery I am feeling."

"Yes, at some point we have to face reality. You should not be made to feel guilty for the bad things that he does."

I stared into Tony's eyes and did something I had done only once before—at Montor's request and only to help get the *Barinta* crew out of danger. I went against my word and principles and manipulated his mind.

"I know, I know. I cannot sleep because...Kindor...Kindor... because he is hurting someone in a bad way..." Tears welled in his eyes. "I am not that kind of person."

I felt the knot in my throat but steadied myself.

"You need to get that off your chest. Trust me."

He stopped shaking his head and met my eyes. Jutting out his chin, Tony said, "He is holding hostage a Sotkari Ta Earthian female. He is obsessed with her and is full of rage because she will not give herself to him the way he wants."

My heart painfully pounded in my chest. I looked away so he could not see how upset I was.

"He beats her, has a physician heal her wounds, and hurts

her again. He leaves her locked up alone for days with barely any food. I am not sure if he has taken her by force, but he wants to manipulate her into believing he is her husband so that she can give herself freely. She fights and blocks him continuously, day and night. He cannot access her mind and enjoy her fully."

My heart broke as I envisioned the female whom I loved going through such an ordeal. I could no longer conceal my horror.

"As if the physical and emotional abuse are not bad enough, Sotkari Ta are not meant to be in a constant blocking mode. It is only to be used as an occasional defense. This will break down her mental stability." I grabbed his arm and looked him straight in the eyes to make sure he understood the seriousness of the matter.

"Yes, yes, I know. I think she is losing her mind because she has no time to rest. He told me she blocks him even at night, at all hours. It only angers him more." He covered his face with his hands. "I do not think she can hold on much longer. She has begun to lose her memory."

A gasp escaped me, and an angry heat flushed through my body. I did not want him to realize I knew Mina and was emotionally invested in the situation. Standing and walking around helped me get my breathing under control. I sat again and grabbed both of his hands.

"Tony, look at me. We need to rescue her. You know it is the right thing to do. Then you can be at peace."

30

MONTOR

Incarcerated
No locked doors or windows
Just sad without you

"Incarcerated" from *Montor's Secret Stash of Poems*

Despite heavy eyelids, an urgency to wake up forced my eyes open. I found myself in a bed in a private medical room. Lasarta and a physician spoke in hushed tones. The first thing I did was wiggle my toes and exhale a sigh of relief.

"Where am I? How long have I been here?" My voice sounded dry, as if it had been a long while since I had uttered a word.

Lasarta's brow furrowed, and she looked at the physician.

"This is the infirmary in Penstarox. In addition to taking care of a punctured lung, several broken ribs, swelling on your brain, and a broken arm, you required a series of very complicated procedures to repair your spinal column and spinal cord. You were not being cooperative at first, so we induced a coma. You have been out for about one lunar cycle," said the physician.

"What!" I roared, slamming my hands against the mattress.

Lasarta practically jumped out of her shoes.

I growled as a sharp pain pierced my lower back.

"I suggest you avoid any brusque movements. You are still recovering from your surgeries. In one more week, I think you will be ready to start rehabilitation," said the physician.

"Has Mina been found?" I asked.

Lasarta's heavy hand on my shoulder foreshadowed her reply.

"No, Montor. Colora notified us that she ran into Kindor in Fronidia soon after the Dit Lar battle. He told her he was going to look for Mina, but we have not heard anything," she said.

I had never felt so defeated.

"Kindor," I muttered. "Always ready to take my place. I should be the one to rescue her. What about Josher?"

"He told her Josher is safe but did not give her any information where he was."

"He probably took Josher to his family. I suppose he is safer with them in Fronidia," I admitted. "Has the United Rebel Front sent out a squadron to search for Mina?"

"I am not sure. Perhaps you should talk to Commander Portars about it, but the fighting with the Lostai has increased in our area. Our resources are strained. Even here in Aranda, we have had to refortify our shields and secure our planetary border."

I looked at the physician.

"How long will the rehabilitation take? I need to be out of this stupid infirmary as soon as possible."

"You are a very strong patient. I think in another lunar cycle you will be ready to leave the infirmary," answered the physician.

"*Shermont!* Another lunar cycle!"

"Calm down, Montor. Getting angry will only make matters worse. I will cook meals for you that will help you regain your strength," Lasarta said.

I wanted to say a million more curse words, but out of respect for her, I just nodded.

Instead of one week, I started rehabilitation in two days. Poor Lasarta ran back and forth from the kitchen area to my room to feed me homemade meals and snacks several times a day. She brought flowers and set up the communication system to play upbeat modern Arandan music. I usually changed it to the sad folk music that I preferred. My friends—Commander Portars, Damari, Kristom, Komar, Lorret—trickled in to visit me.

Even in the best of times, I had been prone to bouts of crankiness. Now, I was always in a foul mood, outright rude and disrespectful with everyone except Lasarta. I even gave Commander Portars a hard time for not doing more to help find Mina. They stopped coming by. Being alone allowed me to focus on my rehabilitation, anyway. I was almost back to my pre-injury strength when Kaonto and Colora traveled to Aranda to see me. Considering they had made a long trip, I behaved civilly with them.

"Montor, it is good to see you, especially on your feet," Kaonto said.

"Thank you. It has been frustrating to be stuck in here."

"It is just a matter of time till you get back to your previous form."

"Well, you have a brand-new back, so I expect you are now

even better than before," said Colora with a wink, a joke that only she and I could understand.

Her mischief brought an unexpected smile to my face.

"Colora, you never change." I became serious again. "Any chance Kindor has been in touch with you?"

She became serious too and shook her head. As we walked towards the dining area, I ran into Sortomor, who had not come to see me.

"Montor, good to see you are recovering," Sortomor said, not meeting my eyes and attempting to walk past me without stopping. I blocked his way.

"Kaonto, Colora, go ahead and save me a seat. I have some unfinished business to discuss here."

As they continued down the hall, I turned my attention to Sortomor.

"Spare me your hypocrisy. I never got to talk to you about how you treated my wife while she was on the *Barinta*."

He rolled his eyes.

"I have no idea what you are referring to."

I grabbed him by the collar and slammed him against the wall. It felt good. He was stunned.

"You know very well what I am referring to. You threw her off MY ship."

"Montor, relax. She was disrespectful. You would not have tolerated it, either."

I kneed him hard in the abdomen. He doubled over.

"She was a distressed wife, not a soldier!"

He straightened up.

"I hear her Sotkari shadow has gone to look for her. I am sure he will take good care of her," he said with a smirk.

I punched him three times rapid-fire in the middle of his face with the full force of my rage and felt his nose crunch. Dazed, he attempted to defend himself, but my attack was too quick, too accurate. Blood covered my knuckles. I slammed him against the wall again, getting ready to land another punch.

The sound of running feet prompted me to glance over my shoulder. Colora and Kaonto returned. Soldiers approached, too. I wanted to take out all my anger and frustration on Sortomor and beat him to a pulp. Kaonto pulled me away.

"Come, Montor, let us go eat. You have already made your point."

"Let go of me!"

I pushed him so hard he fell on his butt.

A voice I had not heard in a while left me petrified.

"Montor! Stop it right now!"

The voice belonged to Foxor, who had not come by to visit me, either. I had not spoken to him since we rescued the *Barinta* crew on Dit Lar.

"Come with me. Now!" he ordered. His stern tone made me feel like a small child.

I forgot about everyone around us and followed him as we walked into one of the holographic rooms. He set it up to simulate an Arandan shoreline with a few lounge chairs on a tranquil beach. We sat and neither of us spoke for a while. His fingers tapped the armrests.

"You have not come to see me," I said, cracking my bloody knuckles.

"I have not been in a good way, Montor. I am sure Lasarta has not wanted to concern you…"

I turned to him.

"What do you mean?"

"I am angry, too, with myself. I have tried to drown my feelings with intoxicating beverages and drugs. I have not been pleasant to deal with. Lasarta and I have argued. We are not sleeping together. It is my fault. Everything is my fault."

"That is incorrect."

"If we had followed Mina's plan, that evil person would not

have had access to the *hanstoric* to take her away. She would have been in Dit Lar when you arrived. He used me, and I assisted him..."

He buried his face in his hands, and his body shook. I placed a hand on his shoulder.

"You must stop blaming yourself. I understand why you did not want to leave like a coward."

I stared up at the fake sky.

"Foxor, the truth is, if I had done some things differently, perhaps none of this would have happened. We spent some time together when she came to the Namson planet. Perhaps if she had left sooner, they would not have captured her. That female is so stubborn."

I stopped a moment to wipe a tear away before it made it down my cheek.

"She was sad that we were separated. She wanted me to come back with her."

"Montor, she was so brave, so steadfast. She knew where you were and did not give any information on your location, even after all he did to her." He took a deep, pained breath and closed his eyes. "She made an unspeakable sacrifice for you, for us, for the rebel movement."

I stood and paced around to try and shake off wanting to bawl like a baby.

"I cannot even think of it."

He stood and placed both hands on my shoulders, eyes glistening as they looked into mine.

"Montor, I am going to give you the same advice Lasarta gave me. I admit I have not been following it, but going forward, I will. I cannot preach to you unless I apply it to myself. We must stop beating ourselves up and alienating our loved ones. They care for Mina, too. They are suffering, too. Concentrate on your recovery so you can be in the best shape to go find her."

Foxor's words centered me. In the weeks that followed, I avoided petty fights and complaints, focusing my energy on recovering my strength as quickly as possible. I saved my anger and frustration for the person who really deserved it.

Gio, I am coming for you.

31

KINDOR

Tony was in no shape to pilot himself back home. I brought him to my hotel room and let him sleep in the bed while I rested on a chair. He woke up in the morning with a bad hangover.

"I think I can help with the headache."

I had him sit in the chair while I stood behind him massaging his temples, scalp, and shoulders.

"That feels great. Thank you."

He looked around and realized he was in my room.

"I cannot remember everything from last night. Did we?"

"Umm, no. I just felt you should not go home alone."

"Oh, good. I would have wanted to remember. Well, you know, us both being Sotkari Ta and all."

"Right. We did talk about Mina, though."

He jumped out of his chair and turned to me, his eyes wide.

"How do you know her name?"

"Tony, I have a confession to make. Mina is a close friend of mine, and I am here in Renna One to rescue her from Gio."

His shoulders dropped.

"And here I thought you liked me."

"I do like you but not in that way. I think we both agree we cannot sit around and let Gio continue to hurt Mina, right? The guilt is killing you."

He ran his fingers through his hair.

"Yes, but the Lostai are looking for them too. They already interrogated me. I could be in big trouble if they find out I lied to them. Honestly, I do not want to be anywhere near Mina now."

I shuddered at the thought that the Lostai might reach Mina before I could.

"OK, I have a device that allows me to transport myself and Mina off this planet in an instant. I just need you to tell me where he has her."

He paced the room and stared out a window.

"I do not know. Gio would never forgive me if I did that."

"Tony, Mina does not deserve what Gio is doing to her. She is a good person, a mother. Her child needs her." I grabbed his arm. "Will you be able to live with knowing that your silence might deprive a child of their mother?"

He turned around, a pained look on his face.

"OK, but he cannot know it was me."

"Of course not."

He showed me an image of Gio on his tablet, gave me the location codes for where he was holding Mina, and explained other details.

"Gio has Mina behind a force field and usually goes out midday to run errands."

I understood then why it had been hard to locate him. He had her hidden in the monastery of a strange religious cult. The monks wore face coverings. Gio must have transported himself and Mina directly into the monastery and now disguised himself to get in and out of there undetected.

Before Tony left, he grasped my hand in an Earthian handshake.

"Thank you for listening to me spill my guts out and helping me with the hangover. Maybe once you get Mina to safety, you can come back around here, and we can spend some more time together."

I hated to disappoint his hopeful eyes. He was a good person who deserved to be loved sincerely.

"Tony, I truly appreciate your help. I will let Mina know we owe her rescue to you, but honestly, I do not think I will be back here. I hope all goes well with you. Remember, do not sell yourself short. Anyone would be lucky to have you as a partner."

"It is hard when you love the wrong person," he said.

I nodded.

"Believe me, I know."

With the *hanstoric* in my travel bag, I headed to a transport pod rental and replicator station, reproduced a large, hooded cloak and mask, and put them on. I set up the *hanstoric* with Karrina's home location in Fronidia, so it would be a matter of just tapping the screen at the right moment.

The monastery was only a half hour away. I parked nearby and observed the surrounding area. The large, cylindrical building had no windows. Several people wearing dark hooded cloaks were walking in, out, and around the building. I strolled over to the entrance and found someone behind a desk in the lobby.

"Name please," he asked without looking up.

I accessed his mind, and he let me in. There were no stairways. Doors and miniscule light bulbs lined the dark hallways. The floor ramped and spiraled upwards in a circular pattern.

So many rooms. How am I going to find Mina?

I walked up the hallway and focused, scanning the area hoping a Sotkari Ta light would appear in my mind. By the time I reached the fourth and final level, my heart exploded in my chest. After sensing nothing that indicated Mina was in the area, I walked all the way back down to the lobby and manipulated the receptionist's mind again. Each time, it got easier to forget my scruples.

"I do not know why I am telling you this, but there are rooms in the basement below. The entrance is at the back of the building. Here is the access code."

"Thank you."

I ran to the back of the building and found the entrance to the basement. Two flights of stairs led down to an area with machinery and equipment. I concentrated, and Mina's light appeared in my mind. Catching my breath, I took slow, careful steps to inspect the area. Nothing that looked like a room came into view. It occurred to me Gio might have camouflaged the area with holographic images.

I am going to have to wait for him to come.

The hours crept by. I had no choice but to do nothing other than sit with the *hanstoric* ready in my hand. Finally, I heard footsteps and hid behind some cabinets. Someone walked in and took off their cloak and mask. I recognized him as Gio. His mind was blocked.

Hatred for this Earthian filled my soul, and a part of me wanted to stop his heart from beating, but I could not go that far. I watched as he walked straight to an area of electronic panels. He had a handheld device, and when he flicked his fingers across the display, as I suspected, everything changed.

A room appeared with transparent walls, most likely the force fields. My heart broke at the sight of Mina sitting on a bed, her head hung low, hair disheveled. She noticed he had arrived and looked up.

I must be quick.

He tapped the display and deactivated the force field.

I lunged and kicked him hard in the back. He fell forward near her bare feet, and Mina took one second to look at me, no light of recognition in her eyes. The next second, she looked down at him, stomping his head and face with the heel of her foot, leaving him dazed. I took advantage to grab her hand and pull her with me back towards the stairway. She did not struggle, and when there was sufficient distance between us and Gio, I tapped the *hanstoric* screen.

My eyes opened to the darkness of night. We stood on Karrina's front porch. Mina yanked her hand out of mine and took a few steps back. She looked around, a bewildered expression on her face. Eyeing me with suspicion, she said something in a language I did not understand.

Her mind was blocked, so I could only communicate by sign language. "Mina, do you not recognize me?"

She had not forgotten Sotkari sign language because she answered out loud in basic Sotkari.

"Should I? Ohhhh..." She pressed her fingertips against her temples. "My head hurts so much."

"Mina, you need to rest your mind. I am a friend you can trust. I will not violate you in any way."

I pressed the buzzer, and Karrina opened the door.

"Mina! I am so glad to see you are safe," said Karrina. "I was just about to put Josher to bed. He will be so happy that you can tuck him in yourself."

Mina furrowed her brow and scowled. Karrina looked at me, confused.

"I think she is experiencing memory loss," I said.

"Oh! Well, no worries. Even if you do not remember me, be assured that we are good friends. Please come in."

Mina hesitated. I took her hand and transferred friendship energy.

"No one will hurt you here."

Mina looked at the ground but took small steps inside.

"*Ro Ma! Ro Ma!*" Josher ran up to Mina and wrapped his arms around her hips.

She looked at me and back at Karrina.

"He is calling me mother. Why? I do not know this child," she shouted now in Arandan, her hands shaking.

Apparently, the loss of memory had not affected her language skills. I swept Josher up in my arms and communicated to him telepathically.

"Hey there, your mother is not feeling well. I will put you to bed."

When I came back, I found Karrina preparing a meal in the kitchen.

"The situation with Josher made Mina very upset. She started to cry. I did my best to calm her down and gave her a sedative. She is showering, and I gave her one of my sleeping blouses and a change of clothes for tomorrow. She is disoriented, but at least she does not appear physically injured," explained Karrina.

"The Earthian that held her hostage injured and healed her over and over. I think she has been abused in the worst way. We need to find a physician who is familiar with Sotkari Ta brain waves, neurology, and psychology. Mina has suffered severe mental trauma and has been blocking her mind without proper rest times."

Karrina's alarmed expression reflected exactly how I felt.

"OK, I will do some research tonight and also ask Tadium. We will bring someone in to see her as soon as possible."

"Karrina, we need to be discreet. I do not want the Lostai to have any idea Mina is here. Once she is checked by the physician, I intend to take her and Josher somewhere far away where she can heal without any worries."

Karrina tilted her head and studied my face. It made me turn away for a moment.

"Is she not married? What about her husband? Are you not going to let him know you found her?"

"He was badly injured in a battle with the Lostai and is recovering in Aranda. I am concerned that the Lostai may be monitoring him. I will not chance Mina being endangered again."

Karrina bit her lip as she served me food but said nothing more.

The next day, Mother was up early to prepare the morning meal and hot sweet tea.

"Karrina has said you intend to take Mina with you somewhere. Be careful, son. I fear this female has confused your way yet again. Is she not married?"

I tried to hide my irritation.

Has everyone decided to ask me the same question?

"Yes, Mother, but right now, she and Josher need protection."

"Good morning."

My heart skipped a beat at the sound of Mina's voice in my mind. Her telepathic abilities were still sound. Also, she had unblocked her mind.

"Good morning, Mina. I hope you rested well," I said.

"Not well, but better than in a long time. Thank you. Really, thank you for getting me away from that bastard."

Mother extended her arm and grabbed Mina's wrist.

"Mina, my name is Kora. I am Kindor's mother. We have met before, but I understand you have been through a terrible ordeal and have trouble remembering."

Mina covered her face with her hands. Her eyes teary when she removed them.

"This is too painful. I am trying hard to remember, but nothing comes. The only person I seem to know is Gio, the evil person who hurt me."

"Mina, relax," I tried to assure her. "Try not to stress yourself. Do not try to remember anything. Just focus on the present for now. Sit with me. Mother has prepared a wonderful fruit and nut bread."

Karrina found a Sotkari Ta physician descended from a family that had migrated to Fronidia when the Lostai invaded Sotkar. He examined Mina and told us what I already had imagined.

"The combination of keeping her mind blocked for extended periods of time without proper rest and the traumatic events she has lived through has caused her memory loss. Her mind is self-protecting."

"It is interesting she can remember languages and sign language," I mentioned.

"Yes, her amnesia does not affect her procedural memory, or in other words, the things that a person learns over time. It is the memory of past experiences and relationships that are being impacted. For example, such patients will remember how to do tasks but not recall events, people, or places."

While the physician spoke, Mina punched her forehead.

"It is not only the memory loss. There is physical pain. I feel like my skull is cracking open."

"Mina, you need to focus on the present time," the physician asserted gently. "I believe your memories will return, but you need to give yourself time to heal and feel psychologically safe. You must not ask questions about your past. No one should inform you of what you cannot remember because that will result in more stress. You need to wait until your memories happen naturally and organically."

In that moment, I asked forgiveness from the Farthest Light. The physician's orders could not have pleased me more. I did not want Mina focusing on her past.

Mother gave me a death stare and left the room. She knew me too well.

32

KINDOR

During the first few days after we arrived at Karrina's house, Mina did not speak much with anyone other than Josher. She retained no memory of anything before arriving to Renna One with Gio, but Josher's behavior convinced her he was her son. I secretly told Josher not to mention his father or things that had happened before, explaining that it would upset his mother. After all this time without seeing Montor, he really had not been bringing him up much, anyway.

On the fourth day after our arrival, Karrina took Mina shopping to buy clothing and toiletries. They returned with prepared food from a popular eatery and promptly served it at the dining table. Tadium was working late, so we all sat together to have the evening meal, communicating telepathically in conference mode.

"The person who gave me Mina's location said the Lostai are looking for her. They interrogated him because he is a good friend of the person who took Mina," I said.

Mina, who had been distracted until then, asked, "What is that person's name? He saved my life."

I thought I saved your life.

"His name is Tony."

She covered her eyes and grimaced.

"Mina, are you ok?"

"I was trying to remember if I knew him, but it feels like someone is cracking my head open with a hammer."

"Remember, the doctor said you need to avoid trying to recall memories and give yourself time to heal," I said.

I saw through the corner of my eye Mother shooting me one of her looks, but I ignored it and continued.

"I think the right thing to do is for Mina, Josher, and I to relocate to a remote area here on Fronidia. We will stay hidden to give Mina a quiet place to feel safe and recover."

I worried Mina might resist the idea. Instead, she said, "Gio is still alive. He might be searching for me. It sounds like a good idea. Excuse me, I am going to lie down."

After she retired, Mother took control of the conversation.

"What are you thinking, Kindor? This female has a husband, the father of her son. What you need to do is contact him so he can take charge of his family. When are you going to get on with your life? You are not a young man anymore."

"Her husband was injured. I do not know if he has recovered."

Mother slammed her palm on the table. Karrina almost fell from her seat.

"Of course you do not know! You purposely have not reached out to let him or any of Mina's friends know you found her."

"Really, Kindor, her friends and husband should know she is safe," said Karrina, taking my mother's side, for a change.

"I am afraid the Lostai might intercept our communications. Mina has been tortured. I will not risk them finding her. Even she agreed it was a good idea."

"Mina is not in a position to make decisions for herself and her child. Her mind is not right," replied Mother.

"Unless she refuses, I am going along with my plan. I am not telling any of you where we are going, and if any of her friends or her husband contacts you, do not tell them she was here. That would only attract the attention of the people who are looking for her," I insisted.

Mother shoved away her unfinished dinner and left the table.

I took a deep breath.

"I guess it is dinner for two tonight," I said to Karrina.

I tried to change the subject, but Karrina was strangely taciturn. She finished her meal, quietly cleaned up, and excused herself to her room.

I researched the places on Fronidia where I believed Mina and I could remain inconspicuous and found a small mining town called Wayont. It just happened they were recruiting people with my experience in robotics and computer repair. The electromagnetic properties of the mines there would camouflage our Sotkari Ta brain waves. It was the perfect place. In addition, I was curious to learn whether those same properties might recharge the *hanstoric*.

It took me another two days to get the logistics organized. Karrina was sad to say goodbye to Josher and wished us luck. Mother maintained the same disapproving expression but sent us off with a blessing. Wayont was not accessible by air due to the powerful storms that affected the area, another factor making it the perfect hiding place. We traveled there in an amphibious vehicle similar to the one I owned when I lived in Zuntar.

Just before getting into the vehicle, Mina suffered another

debilitating headache. I wondered if seeing a vehicle similar to the one we traveled in when I first met her was triggering a memory, but she said it was only pain. During the trip Mina tended to Josher's needs and was polite with me but remained distanced. I slept in the reclining driver's seat, and Mina slept in the berth in the back, with Josher next to her in his crib—or at least we tried to sleep. It did not take long to understand why, even after spending a few days in the comfort of Karrina's home, Mina still looked so worn out and tired. She was having horrible nightmares, screaming and crying in her sleep. Of course, this was upsetting for Josher. The first night when this happened, I reached out to hold Mina's hand, and she pulled away.

"Do not put one finger on me," she shouted, her eyes wild with fear.

"Mina, I am not going to hurt you. How can I help? What can I do?"

"Nothing...nothing...no one can help me," she said and started to cry.

"OK, OK, at least I will sit with you here for a while so you can feel secure."

After that, she settled down a bit, and we all got a few hours of sleep. The same scene repeated itself almost every night.

The ten-day route took us over rugged terrain and two large bodies of water. After an exhausting ten days, we arrived in the early morning to Wayont. Despite being so remote, technological advances and modern amenities kept Wayont's mining community and supervisory personnel comfortable and connected with the outside world. The twenty housing units each consisted of ten floors, eight apartments per floor. In addition to the housing units, the area contained a government building and a large commercial complex with restaurants, recreational holographic rooms, taverns, stores, and reproduction stations. Each apartment came equipped with a sector-class communication system, holographic entertainment, and a reproduction station. Our second-floor apartment consisted of three bedrooms, a traditional refrigeration and food preparation area, a resting room, and a dining room. We also had a balcony with a view of the mountains. Once settled in, Josher became excited about his new surroundings.

"*Ro Ma*, let us explore."

Mina looked at me. I liked how she leaned on me for advice.

"Yes, I am hungry. Let us go to the commercial center," I said.

Most of the people at the commercial center were Fronidian. Josher chose a restaurant that served the meat pies he liked. We sat in a private holographic room that simulated a popular children's show. Mina studied her son as he gobbled his food and giggled at the antics of the holographic characters.

"Mina, you barely have eaten anything. Are you feeling OK?"

She bit her lip, a sad look on her face.

"It aggravates me that I do not remember important events such as his birth or first steps," she said.

I took her hand in mine. This time, she allowed it.

"I can imagine how tough that is, but the doctor said you have not lost your memories forever. He expects you to recover."

Her eyes met mine.

"I suppose you are someone important in my life if you traveled so far to rescue me and now bring me to this place to keep me safe. I notice you and Josher have a strong bond."

She was fishing for answers.

"You know I will not comment on that. The doctor said you are in a delicate mental and emotional state and that we should not talk about your past. All you need to know is that I will be by your side as long as you want me to be."

"Thank you, Kindor."

Mina took a few more bites as we watched the remainder of the simulation.

Within a few days, Mina, Josher, and I settled into a routine. Each morning, all three of us did physical and mental Sotkari Ta exercises as well as meditation. Mina prepared the morning meal for us, and then I left to work. Josher was at a developmental stage appropriate to begin receiving instruction. Mina spent part of her day teaching Josher early-stage reading, science, and mathematics. I remembered it was always important to Mina that Josher have a strong sense of identity and understanding of his racial background, so I showed her how to access historical information about the sector and the Arandan race. It made sense that this would bring up questions for Mina about Josher's ancestry, but we avoided the topic. When I arrived from work, Mina had the evening meal ready for us. Afterwards, we settled down to watch newscasts and entertainment programs or played holographic games with Josher. On my rest days, we explored the town's different eateries and shops.

As the days passed, Mina started to come out of her shell, and things went smoothly until bedtime. Almost every night, Mina's bloodcurdling cries and hysterics woke us. At first, sedatives helped, but we could not keep her on those medications forever. It began to take a toll on me, and I found myself feeling groggy at work by midday. I was also concerned about how this might affect Josher's emotional state.

One night, I decided to try a different approach. As usual, I found her in a fetal position, her whole body shaking. I sat on the edge of her bed and asked, "Mina, have I earned your trust?"

She hesitated for a long while before sitting up and looking at me.

"I guess so."

"OK, I think I can help you relax, but you need to let me touch you. I promise to stop the moment you tell me to."

"What exactly do you have in mind?" she said with a scowl.

"Nothing bad, I promise. I can use my hands to transfer healing energy. Will you let me try?"

It broke my heart to see her so afraid. Her eyes filled again with tears, lips trembling as she nodded.

"OK, lie down and close your eyes," I said.

With my mind focused on feelings of security, warmth, and bonding, I massaged the palms of her hand, her arms, shoulders, neck, and scalp. I felt her body releasing the tension.

"Oh, Kindor, thank you. This is so soothing."

I finalized by applying soft pressure on her cheekbones, brow bones, and forehead. She fell asleep, and I remained a few minutes, contemplating her face and her curly hair splayed across the pillow. My heart swelled with passion.

She is so beautiful.

From then on, when Mina settled in her bed at night, I used my hands and energy to help her relax. It worked. In time, the nightmares dwindled. Unfortunately, the more Mina relaxed, the more wound up I became.

33

MONTOR

Countless steps
Pacing back and forth
A mystery
A heartache
Where is she?

"Mystery" from *Montor's Secret Stash of Poems*

L asarta prepared my favorite meal and dessert to celebrate the occasion. I was finally discharged from the infirmary. She decorated a conference room, piped in lively Arandan music, and invited my friends, my physician, and the medical staff to join us.

"Montor, you are in fine shape. I have not had a patient before as dedicated to their rehabilitation as you," said the physician.

"Not much else for me to do around here. Thank you for doing such a good job with my spinal surgeries."

Colora took me by the hand and led me to the center of the room.

"Let us see if you remember how to dance," she said.

I went along with her, trying to avoid souring everyone's mood, but it only brought me memories of Mina. My soul stewed as time passed with no news of Kindor, Gio, or Mina. I would have loved to at least talk to Josher but decided not to contact Kindor's family in case the Lostai had a way to intercept our communication systems. Although Gio could be anywhere in the sector, he had several businesses and many contacts on Renna One. If he were hiding from the Lostai, he would want to be somewhere he was very familiar with. I resolved to start my search there.

The *Barinta* had been repaired, and I asked Damari, Kristom, and Komar to accompany me. It was a large ship for only the four of us but with a superb sensor, shields, and weapons array while still appearing to be a recreational craft. I changed its identification codes, some aspects of the outer hull, and its insignia to confuse any Lostai who were already familiar with it.

The song was over, and I returned to raise a toast.

"To dancing again with my beautiful and brave wife, The Chaperone."

Everyone cheered, but they could not hide the sadness in their eyes. Plenty of them had already lost hope of ever seeing Mina again. It had been two lunar cycles since that bastard Gio took her. I convinced myself that I would find her safe and sound because believing anything else would be my death sentence. During my recovery, Kristom and Komar traveled to Dit Lar to recharge the *hanstoric* that Mina had given me so we could have it with us on our trip, ready to use if necessary. While our little party wrapped up, Foxor approached me.

"Montor, I would like to go with you. I feel the least I can do is help to rescue Mina."

My reply required finesse, a quality I did not possess. I did not want to insult my proud foster father, but truthfully anyone not a Sotkari Ta could be a liability. Gio had already used him that way.

"I understand, but you need to take care of Lasarta. You know the Lostai are now threatening to reclaim Aranda for their empire. You are familiar with our planet and would be more of an asset here if they attempt to invade us."

He nodded his head, sucking his teeth.

"A diplomatic way of saying you do not want me causing problems on your rescue mission."

I looked down.

"Foxor, that is not what I said."

"That is fine, son. I will try to be of some use here. I cannot wait to see you bring Mina back here on your arm."

The next morning, I left for Renna One with my skeleton crew. The route took us fifteen days. Colora's Members Only establishment was still in operation, managed by a Fronidian who had been Jortan's business partner. It was a discreet place, and we booked two rooms there. Although Renna One was still under the Lostai Empire, official military presence and skirmishes were kept to a minimum to avoid scaring off the vacationers and businesspeople who spent large sums there. Many Lostai soldiers enjoyed Renna One's restaurants and bars for recreation, and as a well-known deserter, I could not go places where I might be recognized. I sent Kristom, Komar, and Damari to frequent the bars and restaurants Gio used to go to while I visited his factories, where I was less likely to run into Lostai military.

Each evening, we met over dinner at Members Only and compared notes on what we had learned. A bartender at Zamandi's Room told Komar that Gio had not been around in about two lunar cycles. His old friend, Tony, had also vanished.

Weeks went by before we received some worthwhile information. A part-time bartender who had not worked in Zamandi's Room for some time was back.

"The bartender's name is Lomo. I asked him about Gio's friend Tony. He said a Sotkari named Kindor was looking for Gio, so he introduced him to Tony, and they became friends," said Kristom.

"Friends?" I asked with a smirk.

"Yes, they ate together several evenings for a few weeks, and one evening, they danced until the early morning hours. Ever since that evening, Tony has not been back."

I could not stop myself from laughing out loud at the thought of stuffy Kindor trying to be social with Tony, who was a well-known flirt. Once I got over the humor of it, I became serious.

"I wonder, is it a coincidence that Tony disappears after Kindor arrives?" I said.

"It could be that Kindor has convinced Tony to take him where Mina is," said Kristom.

"But if that were the case, why would Kindor not contact you with whatever information he has about your wife's location?" said Komar.

Kristom must have detected the irritation in my expression and tried to be diplomatic.

"Maybe we have not heard from him because Mina's location is far away, and he has not arrived yet."

"Too much time has gone by. Too many unanswered questions. It has been three lunar cycles since Gio took Mina. What if he took her to Zorla in Losta?" Heat flushed throughout my body at the thought of it.

The next few evenings, I meditated more than usual. It helped me focus on all the details I had learned about Gio over the many revolutions we had known each other. I recalled he used aliases for some of his illegal ventures. Using these aliases and public information systems to complement my own knowledge of Gio's history, we made a wider list of his businesses, properties, acquaintances, and preferences. I sent Damari, Kristom, and Komar to visit these locations and people.

During this time, my friends excused my bad temper. My rage grew day by day. Meditation was the only thing that kept me from going crazy as another lunar cycle went by until we hit on some promising information. It led us to a dwelling registered under one of the aliases in a low-income residential neighborhood. My three-man crew staked out the area and observed who came in and out of the house. Sure enough, I received a transmission from Damari during early morning hours saying that they had seen someone fitting Gio's description arrive.

"Did he come home alone?" I asked.

"Yes."

I took weapons with me in case I ran into trouble with local law enforcement, but I intended to kill Gio with my bare hands. Every muscle, every nerve ending anticipated the moment I could make him pay. I was a predator, and he was my prey. In an hour, I met up with my crew just outside of the modest home.

"OK, you can leave now," I said.

"Montor, with respect, we behind go bushes back there and wait you for, in case back up you need," said Damari.

I know they meant well, but anger boiled inside of me.

"Listen to me. I do not want any of you to go in there after me. I have been waiting a long time to have this chat with Gio. Do not spoil it for me."

"Understood, sir. Witnessed I what he do to Mina. We not you interrupt, although I wish kill could him myself."

Damari impressed me more each day with his loyalty and maturity. And to think I beat him to a pulp when he first arrived at Xixsted.

I walked up to the door and requested entry. Gio would be

able to see who was at the door before allowing me to enter, but I would be ready if the bastard tried to escape through a back exit. The precaution was unnecessary because the door opened.

"Montor! Wow, it has been a long time, old friend. What brings you here so late?"

He pretended not to be affected by my visit, but his pale face flushed. I was ready to tear the filthy piece of crap apart, but I needed to get information on Mina first.

"Gio, I know you took Mina with you from Dit Lar. Where is my wife?"

His lips pressed into a tight line.

"Oh, *Grimah*. I did not realize you married her," he whispered, after which he muttered something under his breath that sounded like, "*Ahm a ded man.*"

He extended his arm, gesturing for me to enter.

"Come in. Let me offer you some good Arandan brandy I have been saving for exactly such an occasion. Here, have a seat."

I had been his commanding officer for fifteen revolutions. Ever since he was released from the Lostai military, he had treated me with a fake, exaggerated friendliness. Tonight was no different.

OK, I am willing to play along for just a bit more, you lowly germ.

He poured us each a glass of brandy, staring at his before he took a sip.

"Her eyes are the same color, right?" he said.

I drank the whole glassful in one gulp.

"Enough games, Gio. Where is she?" With each word, it became harder for me to maintain control.

He rubbed his fist across his mouth.

"A Sotkari came to rescue her. I am sure stupid Tony gave him the location of my hiding place. He was the only one who knew it. He is lucky I have not been able to find him, or I would have killed him already."

Tony's conscience must really have been bothering him if he went against Gio. They had a long history and were more than just friends.

"Did he say his name? Where he was taking her?" I asked.

Gio shrugged in a careless and defeated manner. I already imagined my hands wringing his neck.

"He did not say anything. I do not know. He surprised me. It was all very quick," he said and took another sip. "You know, Montor, I thought she was just part of your mission to procreate Sotkari Ta babies and that perhaps she grew into a diversion for you. I did not know you had married her—and why did you join the rebellion? It is all so strange to me. You never seemed to care about anything or anyone other than yourself. It was a lesson you taught me well."

There was no need to wait any longer. I stood, and so did he.

"Gio, what did you do with Mina all this time? I saw a video. You were brutal. What would you do if someone did that to your wife?"

"I have never been married. Maybe back on Earth, I could have had a family if the Lostai had not taken me. Things did not turn out how I wanted..."

He seemed to be talking to himself now.

"She fought me hard, both physically and mentally. To think I took that risk and stole her away, only to have her lie there like a mannequin, unresponsive and cold. Her mind is powerful. She never let me in."

He tilted his head and looked at the amulets that hung from the cord around my neck. "I punished her for it, but I let her keep the little trinkets you gifted her. You should be forever in my debt. I was the one who helped Zorla kidnap her from Earth."

My mind went blank. Only the desire to inflict pain remained. I thought I would shout loud curse words. I thought I would roar. Instead, a silent fury guided my fists. He fought back, but clearly he had not been keeping up with his work-outs. When my arms tired, I used my legs. He was in bad shape on the ground, no longer defending himself, his face bloody and swollen. I carried a *zirem* with me, the same weapon Zorla had used on Mina's back on Xixsted. I put it on the highest setting and started with his chest. It burned through his shirt and seared his skin.

So satisfying.

He tried to be stoic and did not complain. I used it on his arms and on his once-handsome face. Next, I dragged it up each leg and his crotch. Finally, he screamed.

"You know you are not living through this. You put your filthy hands on my beautiful wife," I said, my voice flat.

I used my telekinetic powers to separate the bones in his arms and legs. Exhausted, I was satisfied with his cries of pain.

Time to end this.

I strangled him, his own blood smeared on his neck, staring into his eyes until he took his last breath. My own breath came in dragged gasps. Staring at my bloody fists, I shook my head.

I am so tired. Where is Mina?

I sat and served myself another glass of brandy but sipped it slowly. Then I had another and another. Damari, Komar, and Kristom said nothing when I stumbled out of Gio's house holding the bottle of brandy in my bloody hand. I thrusted it into Damari's chest.

"Here, take a swig. As you can see, I have had enough."

At first, they declined but I shouted with anger, "Did you not hear me? Have some! Let us cheer to that bastard's last breath."

They looked at each other in silence and nodded to me. After the bottle was empty, we returned to Members Only. I washed up, composed myself, and contacted Commander Portars.

"Montor, what happened?"

"We found Gio. Sir, I killed him."

"And Mina?"

"She was not with him. We know Kindor was here associating with one of Gio's old friends, and Gio did say a Sotkari came to rescue Mina. He did not know the Sotkari's name or where he took her."

"Probably it was Kindor who rescued Mina from Gio."

I paced around my room, punching my open hand, my voice thundering with the thought that had been pestering me.

"Then why has he not contacted us! What if it was not Kindor, but instead a Sotkari Ta working with Zorla! *Shermont*, Portars, I am losing my mind. I need to find my wife!"

"Calm down, Montor."

"I am going to contact Kindor's family. Kindor took Josher there. Maybe it is just a matter of timing, and she is there now."

"We have just set up a communication frequency the Lostai will unlikely be able to access. I'll send you the details. Let me know what you find out. At that time, I will update you about a situation I fear might be brewing in Sotkar."

We took a transport pod to the satellite docking station where the *Barinta* was parked. On the ship, I accessed the personnel and communication records to get the contact codes for Kindor's family. Using the large viewer in the captain's office, I put through the call. For some reason, it took a few tries to get connected. When the transmission finally went through, I saw on the screen an attractive young Sotkari female I assumed was Kindor's niece. His family had never met me before, so I started off by introducing myself.

"Hello, my name is Montor. I am Mina's husband, Josher's father."

"Greetings, I am Karrina, Kindor's niece."

"It is nice to meet you. Kindor and Mina have spoken to me about you. I am contacting you in the hopes you can give me news of Mina and Josher. I learned that Kindor took Josher to be with you and went to search for Mina. I am in Renna One and found here the person who was holding her hostage. He told me a Sotkari rescued her. Is she there?"

"Umm...no, she is...they are not here," she replied in a tremulous voice.

My years of experience in the military made it easy for me to spot when someone was hiding information during an interrogation.

"Where are they? Kindor has not returned?"

"Well, yes, but—"

"Karrina, I do not mean to be rude, but I am distraught about what has happened to my wife. I need straight answers. Also, I would like to see my son."

"He, he is not here."

Suddenly, an older Sotkari female who looked very much like Kindor stepped into the screen's view and cut Karrina off. She used Lostai sign language as we could not establish a telepathic connection across this distance.

"Montor, I am Kora, Kindor's mother. I apologize. My granddaughter is flustered because Kindor is worried about the Lostai intercepting our communication system. He asked us not to comment to anyone about Mina, but the truth is Kindor found her. He came here to get Josher, and they left to an undisclosed location."

What is that Sotkari up to now?

Impatience crept into my voice.

"Undisclosed? He has not contacted me or anyone of our crew to give us the good news that he rescued Mina. Why? What is he thinking?"

She took a deep breath.

"He heard you were injured and, like I mentioned, is

concerned that the person who took Mina or the Lostai could find her. He said he wants to keep her in a safe place to heal."

I lost all civility. My temples throbbed with anger.

"Look at me. Do I look injured to you?" I brought my hands into view and clenched them into fists. "I just finished killing the person who took Mina with my bare hands and—wait, did you say Mina needs to heal? What is wrong with her?"

Karrina covered her mouth and looked at her grandmother, her face a picture of worry. Kora, however, remained unfazed.

"Mina is physically well, but the trauma of her ordeal has left her with memory loss. She did not even recognize Josher. A doctor evaluated her and said she should be able to recover her memory after she has had time to heal."

I could not stop myself from using the same menacing tone as when I faced an enemy.

"Listen very carefully. I am going to Fronidia to find Mina. If Kindor contacts you, tell him he had better get back to me with the location of my wife and son immediately. I owe Kindor a lot, but I think his behavior is highly irregular, and my patience has limits."

Karrina's eyes opened wider, and Kora nodded with a grim look on her face.

"Yes, Montor. I can imagine how you feel. If he contacts us, we will relay the message."

34

MONTOR

A child of the dark
Became an angry adult
She brought me to light

"Dark and Light" from *Montor's Secret Stash of Poems*

The next morning, Damari, Kristom, Komar, and I left Renna One, expecting to arrive in Fronidia in fifteen days, but Commander Portars had other plans. As soon as we cleared the Rennan atmosphere, I received a transmission.

"Montor, did you speak with Kindor's family?"

"Yes."

"And?"

I had hoped to avoid this conversation.

"It was Kindor who rescued Mina."

"Well, that is wonderful news. Where does he have her?"

I could not hide the growl of frustration in my voice.

"Kindor has taken Josher and Mina to an undisclosed location in Fronidia."

"That is fine. You do not need to tell me where they are."

I could not even raise my eyes to the screen.

"I do not know where he took them."

"What?"

"He did not tell his family where he went."

"And Mina agreed to this? She has not contacted you?"

"Kindor's mother told me Mina has suffered some kind of mental breakdown and has lost her memory. She did not even recognize Josher."

Portars shook his head as if embarrassed for me.

"What a strange situation you find yourself in, Montor."

I slammed my fists on the console.

"Well, I am going to remedy it soon enough. The *Barinta* is on its way to Fronidia."

"Unfortunately, I need to divert your attention to a major problem that is occurring on Sotkar. As you know, the Lostai have maintained control of the southwestern continent. With the help of their Fronidian Sotkari Ta allies, they have released a pathogen that is causing a pandemic on Sotkar. I believe they have infiltrated Kaonto's inner circle. Kaonto and all his lieutenants have fallen gravely ill."

"Sir, with all due respect, what can we four on the *Barinta* do about this? We are more than a lunar cycle away from Sotkar. I need to get to Fronidia as soon as possible. There must be another United Rebel Front ship nearby."

Portars looked at me in the stern way that only a commanding officer can.

"Montor, you are our Strategic and Liaison Officer. I will not tell you how we need to address this issue. That is your job."

His words and expression flipped me back into military mode.

"Yes, sir. Sorry, you are correct. Send me the information

you have, and I will get back to you with an action plan within the hour."

"Good." After he saluted, his expression softened. "Montor, I know you are anxious to reunite with your family. Once you have a strategy in place, go ahead and look for them. In the meantime, at least you know they are in the safest place possible in the sector and accompanied by someone who can protect them."

True, and that someone is in love with my wife, who happens to not remember me.

One hour later, I was talking to Commander Portars again.

"Sir, I see from the data you sent me that Arandans appear to be immune to the virus. I have a charged *hanstoric*, the one Mina left with me when we met on the Namson planet. I will transport myself directly to Kaonto's office on Marimbo Tu. There are some Arandan officers there who had been helping Kaonto with training. We will take charge of the situation. The closest Arandan ship is ten days away. There are five hundred Arandan soldiers on board. I have rerouted them to Sotkar and given orders for all Sotkari citizens who are not essential personnel to be quarantined for ten days. Damari, Kristom, and Komar will also take the *Barinta* to Sotkar and remain in orbit until we have secured the appropriate antiviral."

"OK, keep me updated and stay safe, and Montor, once things are under control, go ahead to Fronidia."

"Yes, thank you, sir."

I arrived at Sotkar to find pandemonium. The contagious illness attacked the nervous system, causing paralysis in different parts of the body. Some recovered after a few weeks, some suffered permanent paralysis, and some died once the paralysis reached critical organs. Hospitals were at full capacity.

More and more people were falling sick. Important utilities and functions were not being properly attended to for lack of personnel.

Even more problematic than the spread of the disease itself was the fact that some portions of the population were now lacking in basic necessities. Technically, this should have been an impossibility. At least two centuries before, the Sotkari had implemented a public policy eliminating the need for currency by ensuring every single family equal access to the charged energy cells that fueled reproducers. When a cell depleted its charge, you simply exchanged it at the distribution center for a newly charged one. Unscrupulous and desperate people who were worried that visits to the distribution centers would expose them to the disease had come up with ways to cheat the system and hoard extra cells, creating a shortage. Now, the elderly, orphans, those with less guile, and the sick who were without these charged energy cells had no way to replicate their essential needs. Violence erupted as people fought over food and medicine.

I thought these were a wise and spiritual people.

In Kaonto's office, I debriefed the Arandan soldiers. The highest-ranking officer introduced himself as Carso.

"Pleased to meet you, Sergeant Carso. Explain to me how Kaonto contracted the disease."

"Yes, sir. This is an airborne illness. We are on a very isolated island. The disease broke out first in the northern continent. Traffic to this island has always been kept to a minimum, but when people started becoming ill on the mainland, Kaonto stopped all traffic to this island to protect his family. He had everyone here tested. Everyone was negative, so it makes no sense that he and his lieutenants later fell ill—all except one," Carso said.

What kind of scum betrays their own people?

"Where is that person? What is their name?"

"He left the island when Kaonto fell ill. I do not know where he is. His name is Krimal Verlox."

"OK, I will track him down later. It is obvious the Lostai intend to take advantage of this confusion to try to retake Sotkar. Have they been able to make any incursions outside of the southwestern continent?"

"So far, they have not. The shields around the rest of Sotkar are holding."

"OK, so our priority is to maintain those shields functioning at maximum efficiency."

"Yes, sir. That is why I sent some of my officers to each of the fifteen shield grid stations."

"Good job. Next, what do you know about the diagnostic, vaccination, and medicine supplies?"

"Yesterday, the scientists finally synthesized a vaccine and an antiviral. We have a supply here in Sotkar but nowhere near enough. Sir, fifty thousand have died, and this started just ten days ago. The assistant health administrator estimates there are already over one million infected, and the rate is increasing."

Carso and I shared a moment of silence as the gravity of the situation became clear to me.

"OK, send me the composition of these medicines. I will ask Commander Portars to contact the Fronidian central government. I am sure they can help with this. I need a list of the provinces lacking in leadership. From those whose chain of command is still in place, I want a list of households without a charged energy cell and any areas at extreme risk for lack of food and other supplies. There is an Arandan ship on its way here with five hundred soldiers, but they are ten days away. We need to identify healthy people who can fill key vacant positions and vaccinate them immediately. I also need to know if there are any weaknesses in our communication systems. Does anything urgent come to mind that I have not addressed?"

"No, sir."

"I would like to see Kaonto if possible. Can he have visitors? Is he able to speak?"

"Yes, he is in the infirmary here with his wife and son. They are infected also. Come with me."

My chest tightened as the mention of Kaonto's family brought to mind my own.

Where does that sneaky Kindor have my wife and son?

I pushed the question to the back of my mind as I followed Carso. I found Kaonto in a wheelchair. His wife was on a cot next to his, and his son was playing an electronic game.

"Montor, I am glad to see you. Sorry I cannot stand up to greet you properly."

"No worries. Kaonto, I am so sorry this has happened, but rest assured, I will do my best to get things under control. What have the doctors said about you and your family's prognosis?"

"My son and I are responding well to the medication. As you can see, he does not even appear to be sick anymore, but the fingers of his right hand are still without movement. I can now move my arms, but we do not know yet if I will ever get up from this chair. My wife, though..."

He turned away as his voice trailed off. I looked towards her bed. She appeared to be in a coma—eyes shut, immobile. I placed my hand on his shoulder, but I did not know what to say. He took a moment to compose himself.

"I still have hope, but I just do not know."

"Kaonto, what of this Krimal Verlox?"

"Once we all got sick here on the island, he left without a trace. I am sure now that the Lostai have been planning this for a while because he has been the assistant to one of my lieutenants for several lunar cycles now. I fear the Lostai have other Fronidian Sotkari Ta planted in our population and military. Krimal probably was vaccinated and then released the pathogen here."

These must be the lowly Sotkari scum who are causing fights, shortages, and chaos.

"Give me a list of the provincial leaders in whom you have full faith, those you have known since before the revolution. I will put out a notice to them and my Arandan officers to be on the lookout for unusual behavior that might help us identify any Lostai sympathizers. The shield system is holding, and there is a crew of five hundred Arandan soldiers on their way here. I will have Commander Portars request medical supplies from the Fronidians. We will not allow the Lostai to take Sotkar again. I promise you that."

"Thank you, Montor. Oh, I almost forgot, what about Mina? Do you have any news?"

"Umm, Kindor rescued her. She and Josher are with him on Fronidia."

"That is wonderful news. I am so glad to hear it."

"Right." I could not suppress the strain in my voice.

He cocked his head, studying my face with a confused expression but thankfully, wisely, kept his thoughts to himself.

"Montor, there is something else of concern I need to share with you."

Shermont! More bad news?

"You need to check on Kaya. Last I heard from her, she took into her home some children whose parents had died without considering they might be infected. She exposed herself, and I do not know what her current status is."

The air shot out of me.

"OK. I will go to see her right away."

On my way to visit Kaya, I contacted Commander Portars to update him on the steps taken so far and what help I needed from him. I arrived at Kaya's house in the late afternoon. At the door, a young boy greeted me. His light in my mind confirmed he was Sotkari Ta, so I addressed him telepathically.

"Hello there. I am here to see Kaya. Is she home?"

"And who are you, sir?"

"I am her foster son, and she will surely be upset that you have me waiting out here so long."

The boy looked me up and down.

"You look nothing like her, sir."

My patience reached its limit, and I brushed past him into the house. Inside, I saw at least ten more children varying in age from toddlers to teenagers. One was on the sofa motionless like Kaonto's wife. A sick feeling crept into my stomach, and I rushed to the bedrooms. In the first, I found another child in bed. In the second, I found Kaya. She extended her arm but did not make a move to get out of bed. I knelt on the floor, leaned over, and rested my face against her chest in a way I had not done since I was a child.

Finally, I looked up and asked, "Kaya, what has happened here?"

"Montor, how are you? I am so happy to see you, son. I have been so worried for you and your family. First, no one knew where you were. Now, it is Mina who is lost."

"No, she has been found."

"Wonderful! My prayers to the Farthest Light have been answered! Where is she?"

How many times will I have to repeat the same stupid story?

"Kindor rescued her. She and Josher are with him on Fronidia."

"Oh, that is good."

"Ah, yes, but Kaya, are you sick? Who are all these children?"

She explained to me that the children came from three households that lived nearby. After the parents fell ill and died, some evil people looted their homes, taking the reproducers and energy cells and leaving the children to fend for themselves.

"I do not know what is happening here, Montor. These

people behaved as ruthlessly as a Lostai general. They stole the reproducers and justified it by saying that the children were probably already infected and about to die anyway."

She shook her head, a sad expression in her eyes, before she continued.

"Can you imagine? How heartless! This area is so remote. There was nowhere else for them to turn. The oldest girl came to me seeking help. How could I turn my back on them? I have lived long enough."

"I think Lostai sympathizers have infiltrated Sotkar and are purposely causing havoc here. The Lostai have released this pathogen in an attempt to retake Sotkar, but do not worry, I have taken charge of the situation, and I will not allow that to happen," I said.

She clasped my hand, and my heart swelled as I sensed her maternal energy.

"I am so proud of you, son."

"It is my duty." I closed my eyes and braced myself before asking my next question. "Kaya, since when have you been like this? Are you getting any medication?"

"No, the paralysis in my legs happened so fast. I called for a doctor, but no one has come. I sent the oldest girl to the government offices where they are distributing the medicines, and she was able to get some. We gave it to the younger children who are showing symptoms."

Shermont! Why does she have to be so selfless?

I got up from my knees to sit on the edge of the bed, leaned over, and pressed my forehead against hers for a moment.

"I will have a doctor come here to examine you and the children. The hospitals are already at capacity. Otherwise, I would take you to one myself."

She stared into my eyes, their expression strong in contrast to how frail her body felt.

"Son, it makes me so happy to see how you defeated all the

hate and evil the Lostai tried to instill in you. You gave up an easy life to stand up for what is right. I hope you make time soon to be happy with your family. Please, tell Mina I am so thankful she brought out the best qualities in you and—"

"I am not a messenger," I said too roughly. Embarrassed that my eyes were hot and wet, I covered them. "You will be better soon and can tell Mina whatever you want when you see her again."

I rushed out of there with a heavy heart.

Carso helped me find a doctor who came to attend to Kaya and the children. When I returned to visit in a few days, she was in much worse condition, no longer able to move her arms and breathing with great difficulty.

It crushed me to see her physically broken when her mental abilities were still so strong. Transferring healing energy was of no use. Her sickness had progressed beyond that kind of repair. Stroking her cheeks and holding her hands, I recalled how her love and care had been rays of sunshine in my otherwise bleak childhood on Xixsted. I had not embraced Kaya since before puberty. Neither of our cultures used that form of affection between adults who are not couples, but I feared she was down to her last minutes. Feeling like a child again prompted me to gather her in my arms.

"Montor, do not feel sad. I have lived a long life. I lost my biological son and gained a new son in you. Now, I will become light because I have fulfilled my purpose. Every time you meditate and reach for the Farthest Light, we will be in contact. I have faith that you will be happy with your son and Mina. You did not let me finish the other day. Please tell her I am grateful that the bond you two share helped you find your path to an honorable life."

Her breathing became more and more shallow, and I maintained our embrace so she could not see my tears. She took her last breath in my arms. A piece of my soul left with her.

Within one lunar cycle, the situation on Sotkar was much improved but not before another one hundred fifty thousand died and four million were infected. Kaonto regained the use of his legs but with a limp. His wife, unfortunately, never recovered. We captured and incarcerated several filthy Lostai allies, but I was sure there were several of the bastards still out there.

I prepared what I thought would be my final report to Commander Portars before heading to Fronidia when I received bad news. A portion of the shield separating the Lostai-controlled southwestern continent and the rest of Sotkar was compromised. The atmospheric shields were still holding, but the rupture near the surface allowed Lostai troops to enter by land and sea into what we were now calling Liberated Sotkar. They had sent tens of thousands of combat pods flying low over the sea into the west-equatorial continent.

Kaonto asked me to help lead a contingent to face the incoming Lostai threat while he addressed the ruptured shield. Damari, Kristom, and Komar landed the *Barinta* and joined me. We traveled to the battle area in a shuttle outfitted with a full weapons array. On such short notice and after suffering losses due to the disease, I mobilized a scant ten thousand troops on the shoreline with surface-to-air torpedoes. We arrived in time to see the first flashes of Lostai thermo-blasters rain on the beach.

"Sir, they outnumber us five to one. We should retreat and regroup," said Komar.

"No! A lot of blood has been shed to take back Sotkar from the Lostai. I will not concede them one inch of Liberated Sotkari territory," I replied, looking each one of them in the eyes.

"Yes, sir," they acknowledged in unison.

"Komar, contact Kaonto—immediately."

He connected me on the main viewer.

"Montor, we still are working on repairing the shield. What is happening there?"

"Kaonto, we are outnumbered. I have an idea, but I need to know first whether any Lostai ships are approaching Sotkari atmosphere."

"Give me a minute. Yes, there is one that appears to be heading here. It is two days out, though."

"*Shermont!* I will need to mobilize some of our space fleet to engage them. OK, I want you to deactivate a small section of our shields above the combat area."

"Have you lost your mind? I cannot do that."

"Trust me. Do it now."

The clench in his jaw indicated his concern, but he agreed.

"OK, I will send the message to our shield stations. In five minutes, it should be done, but as soon as you do whatever it is you have in mind, contact me immediately so I can reactivate."

"Yes. Montor out."

As soon as he signed off, I contacted Commander Portars and explained the situation. I requested that he send the nearest United Rebel Front crafts regardless of size or power to engage the approaching Lostai ship and keep it busy.

"Komar, when we get the signal that the shields are down, I want you to take us just outside the atmosphere. These Lostai combat pods are not made for space travel. They cannot follow or target us at that altitude. I want it to be quick. The sudden shift in environmental controls on this small shuttle will be uncomfortable, but we can handle it."

Komar received the signal, and we all braced for the sudden gravitational change. It felt like someone had piled heavy weights on our chests and then lifted them in an instant the moment we cleared the atmosphere.

"OK, we are out of their reach, sir," said Kristom, his grey skin paling from slate to the color of fog.

"Perfect. Target their combat pods and pick them off as fast as you can."

"OK, sir, but we will have to keep this up continuously for hours to make a dent in their forces."

"Exactly. With this being the only area where the shield is down, we will be an easy target for the Lostai ship that is on its way here, so we need to make good use of our time. When you get tired, one of us will replace you. We must continue firing on them nonstop for the next two days to give our ground troops a fighting chance."

We took turns, two of us resting while the other two piloted and manned the weapons system. In the meantime, a battle ensued between the approaching Lostai ship and three smaller United Rebel Front crafts. This gained us an extra day, allowing us to take down ten thousand Lostai combat pods.

"Sir, a call is coming in from the United Rebel Front."

"Yes, put it through."

"Captain, I am sorry. We were forced to retreat. The Lostai destroyed our two other companion crafts. Be aware. They will arrive to Sotkari atmosphere any minute now."

My blood boiled at the thought of the two United Rebel Front crafts that were lost.

"No need to apologize. You gained us an extra day. Be safe."

As soon as the communication terminated, Kristom picked up the Lostai ship on our sensors.

"Sir, they are here. Should I advise Kaonto to reactivate the shields?"

"Hold on. I want to get a few more of these Lostai bastards. Give me the weapons control!"

"But sir—"

"Are you questioning my orders?"

"No, sir."

In those few seconds, I picked off twenty more Lostai combat pods.

"Sir, our sensors show they are powering up their weapons array!"

"OK, Kristom, send Kaonto the message. Komar, take us down at a severe angle. Cut the descent time in half! Strap in. It is going to be a rough landing both on our stomachs and on the shuttle."

The shield was sealed with only seconds to spare before the Lostai ship released the photon blast. Although the shields protected us from damage, the reverberation knocked our shuttle off its landing pattern, causing us to free-fall to the surface. It tossed us around the main cabin, but I gathered my bearings and flipped to manual navigation. Strapping in, I took control of our descent.

"Quit dancing around and get strapped in!" I shouted to my bewildered crewmates.

Of the three of them, Damari was the one who best maintained his composure. Interesting, considering his people had not yet mastered space travel. He helped the others regain their balance, strapped them in, and told them to brace for a rough landing.

Earthians are full of surprises.

I contacted Kaonto to inform him of our status. He gave me the good news that the compromised surface shield was repaired, stopping the steady flow of Lostai combat pods into Liberated Sotkari airspace. We still had to contend with the ones that had already made it through. Our surface-to-air torpedoes proved to be very efficient, and the Lostai decided to land the pods for a ground battle.

I targeted an isolated strip of shoreline for our crash landing. The fine, moist sand acted as a cushion, and miraculously the shuttle did not break apart. We emerged from the shuttle, dazed but not injured other than a few cuts and bruises. I called in our location, and someone came to take us to the battlefield.

The ground battle commander informed me two of his lieutenants had been killed, so I asked him for my orders. The
battle lasted seven days, but we finally defeated the Lostai
forces. Local news journalists interviewed the commander, his
lieutenants, and me, calling us out as heroes. I remained on
Sotkar another three weeks to help coordinate interrogation of
the Lostai prisoners and analyze the intelligence we gathered.
After sending the data to Kaonto and Commander Portars, I
requested permission to leave Sotkar.

"Commander Portars, I would like to take the *Barinta* with
Damari, Komar, and Kristom with me to Fronidia, so they can
help me with my search."

He clucked and shook his head like a grandfather disci-
plining a child.

"I must decline that request. You are going to Fronidia on a
personal matter. Quite frankly, I would think you would want
the least amount of people aware of the reason for your trip. A
husband looking for his wife who is living with another male is
not exactly official business or something a proud Arandan
male should be advertising." My hands balled into fists as he
continued, "You may go alone on a civilian shuttlecraft."

Had it not been for the extreme respect I held for
Commander Portars, I would have reminded him using offensive language and a loud voice how much Mina, I...our family
had sacrificed for the United Rebel Front. Instead, I swallowed
my frustration until the communication ended and punched
the console.

35

MINA

Wayont turned out to be a pleasant place to heal from the demons that tormented me. I had no memories of my life prior to what I had lived at the hands of that evil person, Gio, and the time since Kindor rescued me. My body offered clues of my past: ugly scars on my back I already had by the time Gio took me, a tattoo of red characters on my arm, a bracelet I couldn't take off, and an amulet on a cord I wore around my neck. In the beginning, I focused on these images to try to remember something other than my time with Gio, but the headaches were unbearable.

I didn't know what to make of Kindor. Not only did he rescue me, but he had made a point to hide me from Gio and anyone else who could hurt me. He was gentle and patient. In the beginning, I didn't even want to talk to him, but he earned my trust. The relaxing massages he gave me helped prevent the nightmares where I relived the torture Gio had inflicted. Still, a significant mystery hung over us.

What types of feelings does Kindor have for me?

Josher called him Uncle, but if we were siblings, we must have come from a bi-racial family. I spoke languages he only

knew a few words of, and vice versa. He could very well have
been my husband or lover. Although our relationship remained
platonic, I sensed a strong bond united us beyond the gratitude
I owed him. Of course, he told me nothing, but there was so
much emotion in his eyes and tenderness in his touch.

Josher was another mystery. He called me Mother in a
language I barely understood. He looked nothing like either
Kindor or me. Despite how much they loved each other, I didn't
think Josher was Kindor's son. Otherwise, he would have called
him Father. More likely, he was my son from a previous relationship.

*Why isn't Josher's father here with us? Is he dead? Did we
separate?*

Although very young, I suspected Josher knew his father.
Based on the doctor's orders, Kindor forbade Josher to speak to
me of the past, and being a very judicious child, he had not let
anything slip.

Our apartment was on the second floor of a ten-story building. We became friendly with some of our neighbors. Kindor
introduced me as his wife and Josher as his stepson. He said it
would avoid us having to explain too much about my situation.
It made sense to me, so I went along with it. A young couple,
Vadira and Hoolon, with a son about Josher's size lived in the
apartment across from ours. I babysat and taught their child,
named Gramita, basic preschool instruction with Josher to earn
some extra income and help Kindor with our expenses. Their
family name was Molora. Next to them lived a middle-aged
couple. The neighbor in the apartment right next to ours was a
single guy who sometimes gave me the creeps but in general
kept to himself.

One evening while we were having dinner with the Moloras
at a seafood restaurant, Vadira asked me about an upcoming
holiday party sponsored by the mining company.

"Are you and Kindor coming?"

"I am not sure. It is an adult event, and we do not like to leave Josher with anyone."

"I know what you mean. We are very careful with Gramita, too. Still, a couple needs some adult fun time alone."

She winked with a mischievous smile. Something about her flirty personality made me feel as though I had met her long ago. Of course, a twinge of a headache accompanied the thought. I brushed it away as she continued.

"I am going to ask Hoolon to convince Kindor. Our neighbors, that older couple, the Nortras, will be taking care of Gramita. I am sure they can take care of Josher as well."

Vadira's eyes lit up with excitement as she started describing the dress and jewelry she planned to wear. The owners of the mining company hosted this party every year to celebrate a local holiday. Vadira explained they could not go last year because Gramita was sick.

"This year for sure I will not miss it. They are bringing two popular live bands. The owners and high-level management will be there. It is not just a holographic event. Everything will be real, very fancy. Even some local celebrities and politicians will attend. We have three lunar cycles to plan for it. It will be the perfect date night for Hoolon and me. Mina, I really hope you and Kindor come with us," she said.

My mind wandered as she went on. If she only knew that Kindor and I were a farce and not a couple at all.

How long will I live in this limbo?

We finished dinner and went home, and I put Josher to bed.

"Would you like to join me for a drink?" Kindor asked.

I nodded. After pouring us each a glass of brandy, he invited me to sit by him as he activated the viewer, accessing the Sector newsfeed. I relaxed into the sofa as news of a skirmish on Sotkar between the Sotkari and the Lostai flashed across the screen. Kindor's brow furrowed as the reporter was about to interview one of the military leaders involved. Without a word, he switched it off and stood, pacing with his hand over his mouth.

How rude!

"Why did you turn it off? I was watching that. Are you not interested in news of your planet?"

"Sorry, it upsets me that we have not been able to get the Lostai completely off Sotkar already." His thoughts entered my mind with a hint of frustration. "I should be there doing my part."

Embarrassed, I theorized there were other places he wanted to be instead of here babysitting me. I stood and looked up at him. The idea that Gio might be out there somewhere looking for me was terrifying, but I couldn't expect Kindor to be my bodyguard forever.

"Kindor, I plan to expand my teaching business by offering traditional cooking classes remotely using the viewer and our communications equipment. It seems I am good at it, and not very many people here know how to cook without reproducers. There is a nostalgic trend here in Fronidia that I can take advantage of. With my earnings, I can afford to move into a small apartment on my own. Josher and I do not need much. You do not have to stay stuck here with us. Do what you need to do."

He placed his hands on my shoulders.

"Mina, there is no place I would rather be than here. I consider it a blessing every hour, every minute, that I share with you and Josher."

An adrenaline rush made me suck in my stomach and catch my breath. The space between us narrowed, and I felt lost in those smoldering blue eyes.

"Kindor, do you want to *kiss* me?"

I think I might want him to.

"*Kich* you? Ah, yes, I know what you mean. No, we Sotkari have other ways."

His hand moved up to my neck, and he traced my lips with his thumb. I felt weak in the knees and imagined his fingers touching me in other places.

What happens now?

His lips became a fine line. He shook his head and stepped back.

He wants me. What's stopping him?

Running his fingers through his hair, he said, "I am tired, Mina...going to bed."

He rushed to his room, and I finished my glass of brandy alone.

I guess no massage tonight.

Vadira contacted me on my tablet. I saw on the display the excitement in her eyes.

"Have you heard the good news? In two lunar cycles, we are going to be dancing the night away with our husbands in the company of the rich and famous," she said in a jubilant voice, twirling her hands with a dramatic flair.

"Yes, Kindor told me."

It surprised me that Kindor agreed to go to a party attended by people coming in from other towns and cities. Besides the occasional outing to the commercial complex, he preferred we keep a low profile, not even contacting his family for fear that someone could trace the communication. I agreed with his precautions. The fear that I might run into Gio one day was forever looming. I also had this gnawing feeling that Josher needed to be hidden also, and leaving him with a caregiver worried me.

"We need to ask our husbands to watch over the boys while we go shopping."

"I was thinking of having Kindor come along so he can give me his opinion."

"No, no. Are you crazy? We have to surprise them that night, like we did on our weddings."

I laughed to myself.

My wedding? Have I ever even been married?

She picked me up within an hour, and we visited stores and reproduction stations at the commercial center. At first, I wasn't so enthusiastic, but I soon got caught up in the whole thing— that is, until an image of a Fronidian female helping me try on a white dress, her facial features blurred, flashed in my mind, followed by a terrible headache.

"Mina! What is wrong?"

I doubled over in pain. Vadira helped me to a chair.

"I am sorry. I get terrible headaches sometimes. You know, Vadira, I almost feel like we have been shopping together before."

She waved me off, assuring me this was the first time we had ever shopped together.

After a few minutes, the pain subsided, and we continued trying on clothes and shoes. She helped me pick out a midriff blouse and long skirt set she said was the same color as my eyes. The skirt hugged my body and had a deep slit in the front that showed off the full length of my left leg. I selected a pair of ornamented flat sandals to go with my outfit. We purchased jewelry and made an appointment at a salon for the afternoon before the party.

After I returned home and the Moloras left, Kindor asked me how the shopping trip went. I started to show him the cost of what I bought, but he shook his head.

"I am not worried about that. You earned that income. Besides, you deserve something nice."

Things had been a little strained between us since the evening when I asked Kindor if he wanted to kiss me. Our conversations were mundane. Troubled and sad most of the time, he continued my evening massages but otherwise kept his distance. Despite all my concerns, I was now looking forward to the party, hoping it would help ease the tension.

"Thank you. The shopping went fine. Vadira helped me decide what was adequate for this type of activity, as I do not have a clue. I would just as easily have gone with you, but she was adamant this was a female outing."

"I probably would not have been much help. She seems to be very stylish. I am sure she did not steer you wrong. Tomorrow, I will be home a little later than usual as Hoolon and I are going to do a little shopping of our own," he said with a sheepish grin.

"It warms my heart to see you smile. You have been tense lately. I feel it is my fault. I made you feel uncomfortable, and I am so sorry for that."

He took a step closer.

"No, Mina. It is not you...it is me."

I reached up and caressed his cheek. Any time we touched casually, and especially with his massages, I felt like he was attracted to me. Now, I sensed a tortured soul, torn and ambivalent.

Maybe he hesitates because of what I went through with Gio.

As horrifying as that experience had been, I didn't want it to rule the rest of my life.

"Kindor, there is some bond between us you seem to struggle with. Certain things about my past I deserve to know. I do not care what any doctor says. I need to discover what it is. Do not do anything. Just let me..."

I coaxed his head down and leaned in to press my lips against his. He didn't kiss me back but inhaled deeply instead and shuddered with the exhale. I was sure he didn't dislike it, but as he had mentioned before, kissing wasn't his thing. Instead, he traced a line with his finger from my forehead, over my nose and lips, and down my cleavage to the fabric of my blouse.

"Go ahead. Unfasten the buttons," I whispered, flushed and excited.

He toyed with the button, but when his fingers brushed against the amulet that hung from the cord around my neck, he stepped back.

"Mina, I should not take this any further, but I promise to smile more. Trust me, you and Josher make me very happy. Do not feel responsible for my mood swings."

"It is not just about whether you are moody or not. I want to know about our history. This situation I am in feels odd. Are we only friends, or is there something more?"

He averted his eyes.

"This is all very confusing for the both of us. You need to heal. Maybe one day, but not today."

Two months went by quick, and the big party day arrived. Kindor tried his best to hide whatever troubled him, but I knew it still simmered beneath the surface of his fake smiles. Vadira insisted we take our clothing and accessories to the salon so our husbands wouldn't see us until we were completely transformed.

"We cannot spoil the magic," she said.

Vadira had her hair straightened and dyed a bright magenta. She also changed the color of her pupils to a shade lighter than her hair. The top of her dress consisted of two wide strips of black material attached to a thick waistband that went from the lower back, over her shoulders, barely covering her small breasts, and down over her abdomen. A lot of her pale Fronidian skin was on display. The bottom portion of the dress ballooned out and reached her ankles. Shiny fibers the color of her hair were woven throughout the black material.

I had my hair washed, trimmed, and conditioned but nothing else. The curls fell freely to my shoulders. I originally had my short blouse fastened to the collarbone, but Vadira insisted it appeared too modest. She unbuttoned it, offering a generous view of my cleavage. My only accessories were thick hoop earrings made from an amber-colored stone. I looked at myself in the reverse viewer. The golden-orange lipstick and eyeshadow completed the look.

I didn't tell anyone, but I experienced mini headaches throughout the whole process and did my best to ignore the images of me in a white dress that flashed sporadically in my mind.

I finished first, and when Vadira stepped into the waiting room, she twirled around and asked, "Mina, what do you think?"

"Vadira, you look spectacular!"

A minute later, Kindor and Hoolon arrived.

Hoolon rushed to Vadira with a wide smile. He whispered something in her ear, and she giggled while he slipped his hand under the straps to fondle her breasts. She countered by giving his butt a good squeeze. I pretended not to look, but her flirty behavior, once again, reminded me of someone. When I tried to think of who, I felt like a vise was tightening around my head.

Kindor's reaction was the opposite of Hoolon's. He stopped in his tracks.

Vadira shook her head as she said, "These Sotkari are so dry. Well, Kindor, what do you think of Mina's look?"

"I have no words. She is beautiful," he signed.

I smiled and checked him out. His hair was pulled up in a bun, emphasizing his chiseled features and striking eyes. He wore slim white pants and a long dark jacket that accentuated his athletic build, but the bright ultramarine shirt was what captured my attention. The color matched his eyes exactly.

There's no doubt. The guy is handsome.

He took me by the hand, and we piled into the transport pod. The mining company set up the party in two chambers of a large crystalline cave. We arrived and were ushered into the first chamber. One of the owners gave a speech and introduced the special guests. Afterwards, the owners, management, politicians, and celebrities mingled with the crowd while everyone was served drinks and snacks.

I was about to try a snack when Kindor warned, "I would be careful with those. They are hallucinogenic."

I threw it away.

"I want to be able to remember this evening," I said with a nervous laugh.

About an hour later, we were invited to move into the next chamber. Tables were set in circles around a center stage and dance floor. The crystalline stones reflected the emerald green lighting illuminating the area. Green and beige settings with bright yellow centerpieces adorned the tables. Vadira became ecstatic once she realized we were assigned a table next to the town mayor with a clear route to the dance floor. The menu contained four dinner plans. We decided to each pick a different one so we could share and try everything. Waiters served us elegant dishes and kept a steady flow of intoxicating beverages coming.

The first band was composed of thirteen members. The instruments didn't look familiar, but I had heard similar music on the local telecasts. Vadira and Hoolon ate fast and wasted no time between servings to run to the dance floor. Kindor and I made fun of their haste and enthusiasm. In contrast, we took time to savor our lavish meal.

"Mmm, Kindor, try this," I said, pointing to something the Fronidians called *jouter* served in what looked like miniature crockpots. Everyone got their own little pot. On the bottom were vegetables and grains. On the top, pieces of fish.

He tasted it and then poked some sort of meat ball with his utensil and fed it to me.

"Very good," I said.

Our glasses were filled again. We cheered and laughed while continuing to sample each other's food until the very last dessert item. I was happy to see Kindor genuinely enjoying himself. The first band collected their instruments and made way for the second band as they set up to play for the rest of the evening.

We each had several rounds of drinks, and Kindor was looser than I had ever seen him. We both looked at Vadira and Hoolon's spots. Their chairs were empty. We hadn't seen them in a while.

"Oh, I am stuffed," I said.

"Mina, we need to move our bodies a bit after all this food," Kindor said, his voice in my mind playful in a way I had never heard before.

"Oh, no. I...I do not know how to dance to that music."

"Oh yes, you do. I showed—" He stopped himself before completing the thought, but it was clear. We had danced before. I didn't try to remember, to avoid bringing on one of those debilitating headaches, but this notion motivated me to go with him to the dance floor.

"Mina, it is three steps to the front, three steps back, then a quick double step," Kindor said.

"Oww!"

"Mina, are you OK?"

I waved it off, but it was a jab in my brain, another painful déjà vu moment. I couldn't help but feel like he had said these exact words to me before.

By following his instructions, we were soon moving in sync. He twirled me around, and I improvised a few moves. His genuine smile made me confident that I wasn't doing something ridiculous. Several songs later, we were ready to head back to the table to rest, but the band shifted to a slower tempo, and he decided to stay. He spread his legs and pulled me close. I noticed all the other males did the same.

"How does this one go?" I asked him.

"In this dance, the males do all the work," he answered, "but our bodies must remain connected the whole time."

The music sounded like a heartbeat with electronic sounds in the background. He swayed me forwards, backwards, and in a circular motion, his hands on the small of my back guiding me. My cropped blouse allowed his hands to touch my bare skin. The result was something very intimate as his pelvic area pressed against mine. The thumping in his chest was almost as loud as the music.

I don't care about his customs. I don't care if it's appropriate. I want to kiss him.

Reaching my hands up around his neck, I pressed my lips against his. This time, he responded, parting his lips slightly, his tongue barely meeting mine. He gave my waist a little squeeze. The unfamiliar shock that flowed through me caused my hands to flail away from his neck like I'd been electrocuted. I looked up at him and saw he was equally discombobulated. It took a few minutes for us to get back into the dance routine. The band moved back to an up-tempo rhythm. I couldn't decide whether or not I was grateful that we were dancing separately again. Despite the initial jolt, I ached for him to put his hands on my bare skin again. After the song was over, he led me back to the table, trying to avoid any awkwardness by joking about Vadira and Hoolon.

"I wonder what those two are up to. They were not on the dance floor."

As if on cue, they reappeared looking a bit disheveled.

Elbowing me, Vadira whispered, "Hoolon could not wait till we got home."

She giggled too loud. I was sure she was quite intoxicated and laughed with her, wondering where they went to do the deed. Hoolon ordered another round, after which it was clear Vadira shouldn't have any more. We all left together and picked up our respective sons from the caregiver.

"Do you want one last drink before we call it a night?" Kindor asked as we walked into our apartment.

"Sure," I replied, carrying Josher to his room. "I will be right back after I put Josher to bed."

I laid Josher down, taking off his shoes and foot coverings, but I didn't bother taking off his clothes to avoid waking him. The weather was a little warm, so I covered him with only a light sheet and kissed his forehead before quietly leaving the room. Kindor stood on the dimly lit balcony with a glass in each hand. I walked over and took one.

"Here is to a wonderful evening. Thank you, Kindor."

"I am the one who should be thankful to have had such a beautiful female by my side."

I sipped and smiled, taking in the view of the mountains, the royal blue night sky bright against the dark rocky ledge. Being alone with him made my heart beat faster.

"I never suspected you would be such a wonderful dancer, but now my feet are little sore," I said, sitting on the sofa and placing my glass on the side table.

I slipped off the sandals to rub my feet. Kindor sat and set his glass down also.

"Lie down and let me help with that."

I didn't hesitate. His hands worked wonders, and I hadn't forgotten how they felt on my skin. In all honesty, I was only slightly less drunk than Vadira. I lay back and placed my feet in his lap. He took one of my feet in his hands and slid his thumbs between my toes and then down the sole.

It feels so good.

His eyes remained fixed on my feet as he continued to massage them, but when I moaned, he looked up, taking in the view of my leg and thigh exposed by the slit in my skirt. Leaning over, he slid his hand all the way up and under the skirt fabric until he reached my underwear. Only then did he look me in the eyes. Despite the longing in his expression, he didn't transmit anything, so I spoke for the both of us.

"I want you, too."

He leaned in further. I ran my hands through his hair, getting rid of the band that kept it in a bun, and pressed his head against my exposed tummy. His breathing sped up, and he reached up to unfasten my blouse. Stretched over me completely now, he hovered above me with his lips less than an inch from mine.

"Do you want to *kich* me again, Mina? I am afraid I will not be much good at it."

Breathless, all I could think to say was, "That is OK."

As I kissed him, he guided my arms out the sleeves of the blouse and tossed it aside. I was not wearing a bra. He caressed my breasts in circular motions with his fingertips, and my hips began to move. Turning his attention to the skirt, he groped, looking for how to take it off.

"Not fair," I whispered. "You have all your clothes on."

He smiled, sat up, and took off his jacket.

"Mina, do you wish to go inside?"

The sofa was wider than a twin bed and comfortable enough.

"I think I would like to stay here. The night is warm, and I like the smell of the air."

"And I like the smell of you." His voice in my mind was husky with desire.

I sat up and unbuttoned his shirt. His lean, athletic build turned me on even more. Following his lead, I caressed his chest and abdomen using my fingers the same way he had done on me.

"Mina, I cannot control myself anymore. I have waited so long."

I took off his shirt and unfastened his pants. We both stood and finished undressing each other. He grabbed me and lifted me up easily while I wrapped my legs around his hips. We lay on the sofa, him on top of me. He propped himself on his elbows to gaze into my eyes.

"Mina, are you sure about this? You can still change your mind."

His erection poked my thigh.

What is he talking about now? Can't he feel how wet I am?

"Not changing my mind. I am so ready."

He adjusted his position and pushed all the way in, fast and deep. For the first time ever, I heard a sound coming from his throat, a groan that started out deep but turned high-pitched. It lasted only a few seconds before I heard his voice in my mind again.

"Mina, I love you so much."

We came together with an urgency. My hips rose to meet his, and he pinned me down hard with each thrust. I prayed the neighbors couldn't hear my moans and the rest of the noises we made. Orgasmic pops titillated me before my body clenched into the final one that rocked me from head to toe. He groaned a second time, and we finished so breathless I worried we might die then and there. Once his breathing returned to normal, he carried me inside to his bedroom. I fell asleep with my cheek against his chest, his hands in my hair and our legs entwined.

Later in the night, a vision rattled me, and I awoke with a jolt, my hands slamming the mattress.

"What is it, Mina? Did you have a bad dream?"

"No, not a dream. It was more like a vision."

"A memory?" Kindor asked.

"I do not know. It is the strangest thing. Just a pair of yellow feline eyes. They looked so sad and angry, but I could not see the face. I am sorry I woke you. Go back to sleep. I am fine."

Kindor didn't reply. All I sensed from him was a cold ache.

36

MONTOR

I entrust my brain
To never forget
The sexy curve
Of her hips

"Sexy Curves" from *Montor's Secret Stash of Poems*

My first stop in Fronidia was the population registrar's office. I requested a search for Mina Ventamu, but she did not appear in the Fronidian database. Gritting my teeth, I asked that they search for Mina Grahmon.

"Sir, we cannot give you information on a person who is not of your immediate family. You know we have strict privacy rules here."

I tried to contain my impatience. When Mina and I were married, we updated Josher's Fronidian birth records to include me as his biological father and with my last name. I had no doubt he was in the database.

"What about Josher Ventamu?"

"Josher Ventamu was born in Rondarium and lived in Zuntar the first months of his life, but we have no sure information of his current whereabouts."

I clenched my fists but thanked her and moved on. The strict Fronidian privacy regulations prevented me from tracking Kindor's spending or communication trail. I did not have connections in any Fronidian governmental agency that could provide me special clearance.

Next, I paid Kindor's family a visit, arriving in a very bad mood. Kindor's niece invited me to come in but looked at me as if I were a monster.

"Sir, Mina and Josher are not here," she said, a tremor in her voice.

"I can see that for myself, but you must know where they are."

"No, sir. We have absolutely no idea where Kindor took them."

"I do not believe a word you are telling me. It has been several lunar cycles since they left. Kindor must have been in contact since then. I am not leaving here until you tell me the truth. You know, through my military connections, I can get your communication records."

I hoped she would believe my bluff and made a point to intimidate. My hands were on my waist, my voice was angry, and I glared down at her.

A voice in my mind, firm and confident, distracted me.

"Sir Montor, I will not allow you to harass my grand-daughter in her own house, and I am sure her husband will not stand for it either. He will arrive from work any minute."

I turned and saw Kindor's mother enter the room.

No doubt she is a pureblood Sotkari Ta.

She reminded me of Kaya, proud and strong, taking me down a notch with her attitude.

"All right, I believe you, but you must understand. I am desperate for news of my wife and child. Are you sure you do not have any information that could help me find them?"

Kindor's niece shook her head, but his mother communicated again.

"Montor, honestly, if I knew where they were, I would tell you without hesitation. I never approved of Kindor taking them under his responsibility. She is a married female. Her husband should be taking care of her, not my son. For how long is he going to do your job?"

Clearly, this female is not intimidated or impressed with me at all.

I rolled my shoulders back to ease the tension and mask how uncomfortable I felt. If she had been a male, that last comment would have earned her a swift punch to the jaw.

"OK, understood. I will be on my way. Here are my contact codes. If by any chance you hear from them, please ask that they call me. I will remain here in Fronidia until I find them. Thank you and have a good evening."

As I left their neighborhood, I tried to put myself in Kindor's mindset. If he really were concerned that the Lostai might find a covert way to capture Mina here in Fronidia, he would have probably looked for a mountainous area not easily accessible by air with the electromagnetic properties that hindered Lostai sensors. I compiled a list of communities that matched these parameters and knew that Zuntar, the village where Mina had once lived with Kindor's family, was such a place. I arrived there late at night and found lodging.

The next morning, I strolled around the streets of Zuntar, a quaint town whose residents were mainly plantation workers. I walked into a restaurant and ordered muffins and hot sweet tea, explaining to the chatty, middle-aged waiter that I was looking to reconnect with old friends. He recognized the images I showed him of Kindor and Mina.

"Oh, yes, I know these people. He was the owner of this place before my boss bought it from his mother. She worked for them preparing food here and rented a room in their house."

"Have you seen them around here lately?"

"No. They left, and we never heard from them again. Rumor has it they ran off together because his mother disapproved of their relationship. Then his mother sold the place when her granddaughter married the plantation owner's son."

That conversation only served to make me crankier. I decided not to waste any more time in Zuntar and to move on to the other communities on my list. Some of them were not accessible by air, so I stopped at a larger city first to rent an amphibious vehicle that could travel over all types of terrain and bodies of water. This slowed my travel time, but I had no other choice.

I visited seven towns in two lunar cycles. Every day, I woke up crankier than the day before. No one recognized the images of Kindor, Mina, or Josher.

Shermont! I am not even sure if I am targeting the right places. Kindor might have decided hiding in a big city would be easier.

I arrived at night to a mining town named Wayont. The town was split in four self-contained areas: the actual mines and the residential, commercial, and government complexes. One of the buildings provided temporary lodging for visitors. The commercial complex seemed like the best place to start looking around and mingling with people.

I stopped in an eatery where quick meals were served and waited in the queue to place my order. Only Fronidians made up the clientele. Similar to the other towns I had visited, Mina would not have blended in here. The young female standing behind me, flirtatious like most Fronidians, wasted no time flashing me a smile.

"Hello there. Are you new in town? I have not seen you here before, and this is the one place I come for my morning meal. I think I would have noticed someone as big as you."

I chuckled, and she ran her hand over her hips in a coquettish manner.

"Yes, I am just visiting. My name is Montor."

"What brings you to our little town, Big Montor?"

"A business venture, but also I am looking for some friends I have lost contact with whom I believe are living here now."

They called my name, and I moved up to get my food.

"Maybe I can sit with you and show you their images, in case you have seen them around."

She thought I was flirting with her and slid her tongue to the corner of her lip.

"An excellent idea, Big Montor."

We sat and I showed her images of Mina, Josher, and Kindor. She studied them for a moment but did not recognize them. I devoured my meal and lost interest in whatever it was she said to me. Before we parted ways, she gave me her contact codes with a wink.

It took me the whole day to stroll through what I estimated to be only a quarter of the extensive commercial complex. I stopped in shops and pretended to be looking for different items, asking the attendants for advice and then showing the images on my tablet. In the evening, I made a point to eat at an establishment that catered to families with children, but by the end of the day, I had made no progress in my search.

This situation is stupid and unacceptable. Kindor will have to answer for this.

In the days that followed, I continued exploring the commercial complex, but still no one recognized Mina or

Kindor. By the third day, I was ready to leave Wayont but decided to stay one more day to tour the taverns and bars at night, making conversation with the bartenders and other patrons. I had to fend off several females and some males who flirted with me. Trying to explore as many spots as possible, time escaped me. Already late in the evening, it being a work-day, all the hardworking, proper people had gone home. I was left to interface with drunkards and other undesirables.

I noticed one middle-aged male had been ogling the females from afar. He made no move to approach or talk to them. He just watched them. It occurred to me that this kind of deviant might be very observant. I introduced myself and showed him the images.

"Oh, I know them. This couple lives next to me."

My heart almost stopped.

"Did you say couple? No, they are not a couple."

He laughed in a lascivious manner and nodded for emphasis.

"Trust me, they are. I have seen them more than once out on the balcony."

Anger almost as ferocious as when I killed Gio flared up. I grabbed him by the shirt and pulled him close.

"Hey, hey, what is wrong with you?" he said, alarmed.

"What. Do. You. Mean...you have seen them?" I managed to ask through gritted teeth.

"Seems you are very interested," he said, meeting my eyes. "Better let go if you want to hear what I know."

I tossed him back into his seat.

"She looks like no one I have ever seen...literally from another world...caught my attention right away. I keep track of their, well, really her comings and goings. When they started to use the balcony for—"

"For what!" I shouted, and the bartender gave me a look.

"Is everything OK over there?" the bartender asked.

"Yes, yes, sorry. Everything is fine."

I glared back at the deviant and gestured for him to continue.

"They make love on the sofa on the balcony. She must have a preference for doing it out there because I have seen them through my balcony often. Hey, do not be mad at me. You asked."

Somehow, I stopped myself from hurling him across the bar.

"Give me the exact location code."

"Listen, I do not want trouble. Promise not to say I stalk her. I have kept my distance. She has never noticed—"

"Tell me now!" I roared.

"Sir, I am going to have to ask you to leave," interjected the bartender, walking over.

"Yes, fine. We are both leaving." I turned to the deviant and said under my breath, "If you do not step out with me now and give me the location codes, I am going to stalk you and break you in half. I am dead serious."

"Yes, yes. I was leaving anyway."

Once outside, he gave me the information.

"Are you going over there now?" I asked.

"Ah, no. I think I will get a drink at another bar. You have ruined my mood."

I thought about kicking him in the face but continued out of the complex instead. The adrenaline had my body in focused battle mode. Long, quick strides got me to the residential area in an hour, as opposed to the two hours it took me to walk that same distance that morning. In contrast, my emotions were all over the place. Ready to inflict physical punishment, but so sad too. My body shook all over.

Kindor, you traitorous piece of crap, my debt to you is cancelled. I can kill you now with no remorse.

37

KINDOR

I *kich* Mina's forehead, then her lips, then her neck and continued downward. She taught me to use my lips and tongue to pleasure her. I showed her the power of massage and sense of touch. Never before had I allowed myself to imagine this kind of intimacy with her. I was making up for all the time it had been out of my reach.

My mother would have said I had completely lost my way, and she would have been correct. I prayed for forgiveness every day for taking another male's wife. I should have told Mina from the beginning that we were just friends. By the time we became lovers, it was too late. I could not stop myself or turn back. She had visions of Montor's yellow eyes every so often. My love for her obscured my rational thinking and helped me push those thoughts aside, but I knew deep down in my heart our relationship was on borrowed time.

Her husband is out there being a war hero, but he could show up at any moment. Or when I least expect it, she might regain her memory.

After we made love, she cuddled up to me, and I ran my fingers through her gorgeous hair. She wore me out every time and I fell asleep quickly, but sometimes, her movements awakened me. Her sleep appeared to be getting more restless by the day.

A few hours before sunrise, the door buzzed. We both awoke with a start.

Who could it be at this hour?

A knot grew in my throat.

"Mina, stay here while I check who it is."

I opened the door. My worst nightmare walked in. One look at his wild eyes and it was clear he somehow knew I had taken what did not belong to me. He extended his arm, and we grabbed each other's wrists in the traditional Sotkari salutation.

I suppose we might as well be civil before we try to kill each other.

He spoke out loud in an eerily calm voice, looking around to check the room entrances and floorplan. He was ascertaining the number of bedrooms in the apartment.

"Kindor, my wife and son...they are here, correct?"

"Yes, they are sleeping."

He nodded, pursing his lips.

"I am going to ask you this question because I do not want to act on an assumption. I am sure that being an honorable," he rolled his eyes, "Sotkari Ta, you will answer me truthfully. Are you sleeping with my wife?"

Although his voice and diction were measured, I sensed his fury. I worried that, in his rage, he might hurt her. Words tumbled out of my mind without much thought.

"Montor, do not be angry with her. I am the one to blame. She has lost her memory and I seduced her—"

"What are you talking about? You did not seduce me. If anything, I seduced you, but who is this person questioning us and intruding at this hour?"

In my haste, I had communicated in conference mode, and

she had received my thoughts. Our necks almost snapped off as we turned to look at her.

"Mina," he gasped.

Her jaw dropped. She pressed the palms of her hands against her forehead.

"Mina, are you OK?" I said and started towards her, but Montor obstructed my way.

"Do not even dare put a hand on her," he growled.

"I am fine," she said out loud, waving me off and staring up at Montor. A hand went to her heart. "Oh, these are the eyes that have been haunting my dreams."

Montor's expression softened, but at the same time, he glanced at me and blocked his mind.

"My name is Montor. I am your husband," he said out loud. "I am Josher's father."

She doubled over in pain. I took another step towards her, but he used his telekinetic power to toss me across the room. I slammed hard against a wall. Framed art fell to the floor in a crash.

"Stop it!" Her jaw clenched, and she glared at him. "You will wake up Josher. It is clear you are his father. The resemblance is uncanny, but how do I know what kind of person you are or that we are really married? Why have you arrived now like a burglar? Where have you been?"

Afraid he might say something that could seriously harm her mental state, my hands and fingers moved quickly to communicate in sign language since his mind was blocked.

"Montor, listen to me. The doctor said she needs to heal from her neurological and emotional trauma. He advised that we not tell her anything about her past."

"How convenient for you," he answered, looking at me with contempt.

"Tell me, Montor, why should you I believe you?" she insisted.

"You have a red marking on your arm. It is my name in ancient Arandan script." He rolled up his sleeve to expose his bicep.

She caught her breath.

"And that is my name in my own handwriting," she said.

"Yes, we were branded during our wedding ceremony, and that bracelet...I gave it to you when I proposed. It is locked and cannot be removed. The key was melted during our wedding also."

"I have often wondered about that," she said under her breath, suddenly pensive. "Go on."

"You will also notice the amulet you wear around your neck is similar to mine."

She cried out in pain, rubbing her temples. Montor's attention turned to me again. He did his best to control his anger and spoke through gritted teeth to keep his voice down.

"Kindor, you pretend to be so noble, and yet you took advantage of my wife's memory loss for your own selfish desires. For that, I am going to kill you with my bare hands like I did Gio."

"You killed Gio?" she interrupted.

"Yes, I did. And I enjoyed putting him through pain before it was done," he answered, glaring at me.

To my surprise, she rushed to embrace him. He was equally caught off guard and remained stiff. Trembling, she began to cry.

"Thank you, thank you, thank you so much. I no longer need to worry about him coming to get me anymore."

I have lost her for sure. I should have killed Gio myself when I had the chance. Montor, ever the unscrupulous hero.

"Mina, I have come to bring you and Josher back with me. We are a family."

She let go and moved away from him.

"I do not even know you."

She turned to me. The conflict in her watery eyes broke my heart.

"Why? Why did you not tell me? This was one of those things you should have been open about. I cannot forgive you for this. I was not meant to be an unfaithful wife."

Montor and I shared a knowing look.

Mina was an unfaithful wife long before she slept with me.

"Wait, wait," she said. "Kindor, how was my marriage to Montor? Was it a caring relationship? Was he good to me? Did we love each other?"

Both pairs of expectant eyes were on me now. I could have lied and made things hard for him, but I did not want to mislead her like that. I almost heard my mother's disapproving voice in my mind saying, "A little late, son."

"Mina, I was at your wedding. You and Montor loved each other very much. He has always treated you well."

She walked over to me and pointed her finger at my face, her body shaking with outrage as she pronounced each word slowly.

"You mean to say you were at my wedding, and you still allowed me to..." She could not finish the sentence and instead buried her face in her hands. I never in my life had felt so low.

"*Ta Ri?*"

Their voices had awakened Josher. He was out of bed and in the middle of the room with us. He looked at Montor, and once his memory solidified what he suspected, he ran to him.

"*Ta Ri!*"

Montor swept him up in his arms, and even I was moved. He had not seen his son in over one revolution. Pangs of guilt bombarded my brain.

I have behaved like a selfish villain, keeping Josher away from his father.

After a long embrace, Montor set him on the ground and

went down on one knee. Caressing Josher's cheek, he asked, "How have you been, son?"

"Good. Where were you, *Ta Ri*?"

"Fighting some bad people, but I am here to take you back home with me now. Please, go to your room while I finish talking to your mother and Kindor."

"OK."

Josher, ever the obedient child, returned to his room. Montor's eyes glistened as he turned his attention to me again.

"Kindor, you know there are some things that an Arandan male cannot forgive. That means one of us is not living to see the sun rise. Mina, get your and Josher's basic supplies packed and wait for me at the entrance of the building. Kindor and I have some issues to take care of."

"Oh no, you are not! You will not fight over me."

"Yes, we will. I am going to punish him for touching my wife, and I am going to love every minute of it."

My feelings of regret were quickly erased by male aggression. I had enough of his threats.

"Montor, as usual, you are overconfident. I can defend myself quite well."

He lunged at me. and I used my powers to stop him dead in his tracks. He tossed me across the room again. I was slower to get up this time.

"Let us fight with our fists, not with all this cowardly nonsense," he shouted.

Mina shoved him hard in the chest, knocking him back a step. His shock at her irreverence towards him was almost comical. He had forgotten how tough she could be.

"Be quiet, you idiot. I said stop it! Montor, your son loves Kindor. If you kill him, Josher will never forgive you for it, and if something happens to you, he will not grow to enjoy his father's company. I will not allow it."

Montor shook his head, panting like an animal, his eyes wilder by the minute.

"Kindor, come outside. Let us settle this. I have the right to defend my honor."

My brain was on fire. No longer thinking straight, I wanted to fight him too.

Yes, maybe I should kill him. Mina loves me now. Why should she have to leave me?

Montor and I glared at each other while Mina stood in front of the door crossing her arms and obstructing our way, her expression resolute.

"I will not let you two destroy each other. You will have to fight over my dead body and in front of Josher. I am sure he will come out again any moment after all this commotion."

I had not met a more stubborn female. She did not budge, and we were forced to back down.

"Kindor, you are a cowardly piece of crap. Today, you hide behind my wife's kindness, but we will meet another day and discuss this situation again."

Mina's intervention gave me a moment to come to my senses, too.

He is so smug. I could stop his heartbeat in an instant, but I cannot deprive Josher of his father. He would never forgive me for that.

Now that the threat of Montor and me tearing each other apart had subsided, Mina was overwhelmed with the situation she found herself in.

"Montor, I do not know what to do. I agree with you that what Kindor has done is unforgivable. If he would have told me I was married, things would never have gone down this path, but still, you are a stranger to me. How can I just go with you and pretend like nothing has happened? Why did you not rescue me?"

"Mina, it is a long story that I can explain later, but do not think for a minute that I did not try to rescue you. We are a family and should be together. I do not expect us to be like a regular married couple if you do not remember me. I would not do that to you. That is just as bad as what Gio and this bastard did to you. You will have your own room, but you cannot expect me to just let you and Josher stay here."

His comment about my behavior stirred up guilty feelings again.

"No, no, of course not." Mina looked in my direction with disappointment and sadness in her eyes. "Kindor, if we were truly friends, then this is a betrayal of the worst kind." She rubbed the area of her arm where Montor's name was inked on her skin. "Montor, I will go with you, but wait for me downstairs while I gather Josher and my things. Give me an hour or so."

"So he can put his hands on you yet again? No!"

"I promise that will not happen."

"Mina, for your and Josher's sake, I have controlled my anger and frustration. If you are not downstairs in an hour, I am coming back up and will not be responsible for my actions."

He left, and Mina ran to her room to organize her things, after which she packed a bag for Josher. I did not move from the foyer the whole time. She asked Josher to remain in his room while she spoke to me with three travel bags by her side. With red, swollen eyes, she swallowed hard before she spoke.

"Kindor, I do not know what to say. I thought I loved you, but now I am so disappointed. I feel so deceived, so violated, again. How can I forgive you for that?"

"I thought I was doing what was best for you."

She raised her voice, chest heaving, her face flushed with emotion.

"In the same way I dealt with the fact that Josher was my son even though I did not remember him, you should have told me about my husband. You have no excuse!"

"Yes, you are right, Mina. I should have told you. I have loved you deeply for a very long time. Obviously, I lost perspective."

"I cannot believe my mind has played this cruel trick on me." Crying again, she raised her hands, looking defeated as tears streamed down her cheeks. "I need to go now. Umm, I promised him we would not touch each other."

"Yes, I know."

"But he did not say anything about Josher." She wiped the tears from her face, called Josher out, and got on her knees to speak to him. "Son, we are going with your father now. He is really looking forward to spending time with us."

"That is great!" Josher said and turned towards me. "Is *Fa* Kindor coming with us?"

My heart ripped apart.

"No, he cannot come with us." She looked up to me. "Maybe later, but we will have to say goodbye for now."

Josher ran over to me, and I gathered him up. His little arms held me tight. "*Fa* Kindor, goodbye. Love you."

He said it as if we would see each other tomorrow or the next day.

"I love you too, son." I avoided looking at him so he would not see my tears and put him down, patting his backside. "OK, time to go."

Mina gave Josher the smaller wheeled bag, and she picked up the other two. As she bit those lips that she taught me to *kich,* we both held back tears for Josher's sake. She transmitted her final thought telepathically in Lostai so Josher could not understand.

"Maybe when Montor has calmed down, I can send you news on Josher from time to time. I know he will miss you, and so will I. Thank you for rescuing me from Gio."

"Goodbye, Mina."

38

MINA

Josher and I followed Montor to where his vehicle was parked. It was similar to the one Kindor used to bring us from his family's home to Wayont. I put Josher to sleep in the berth in the back and sat in the passenger seat next to Montor. He drove in silence for at least a half hour before he turned to me.

"How long have you and Kindor been lovers?"

"I do not think we need to—"

He cut me off and raised his voice.

"How long? I want to know!"

His seething tone rattled me. My hands trembled.

"About one lunar cycle."

"So, do you love him?"

"Montor, I—"

"Do. You. Love. Him?"

Fingertips pressed into my eyes, I took a deep breath.

"I thought I did, but now, with all you have told me, I realize that nothing in my life is real right now. I am so sorry, Montor. So sorry. I know how you must feel."

"This is my fault."

I dared to put my hand on his shoulder. He winced as if it were painful. I pulled it back.

"Your fault? No."

"Yes, my fault. I stayed away from you for too long. You cannot understand now, but I thought it was the best way to keep you and Josher safe." He pressed his forehead in the palm of his hand. "It was the worst thing I could have done. It allowed Kindor to somehow think he had rights to you and led him to behave just as immorally as Gio did."

"I do not think it is fair to compare Kindor to Gio."

He looked at me with eyes that had gone almost completely dark, very little yellow visible.

"You will not defend him in front of me! He deserved to die tonight. You took that right away from me. I could become the laughingstock of my community. You will not speak of this situation with anyone."

"Of course not. I just wanted to say it was my fault too. I thought I sensed an attraction between us, and I acted on it."

"Mina, what you were sensing was Kindor's feelings for you, but he knows all you ever felt for him was friendship. He should have told you that right from the beginning and that you were married. You had just gone through a horrifying experience, had lost your memory, and were in a vulnerable state."

He looked at me again, still breathing heavy, but his pupils had returned to normal.

"Better yet, he should have notified me the minute he found you, and if he were concerned about contacting me, there are a number of trustworthy people he could have informed. He did not contact anyone with the specific intention of keeping you to himself. How is that any different from what Gio did?"

"Well, he did not hurt me."

He wasn't listening to me.

"And although we were never the best of friends because I

knew he pined for you, I thought at least we had reached some mutual respect and trust." His voice deepened. "He betrayed me too."

I held my head, feeling miserable, my eyes hot and blurry. A sharp pain punctured my throat and chest.

"Yes, you are right, he deceived me. He should not have stained our friendship that way."

After a prolonged silence, I dared to ask, "Where are we going? Are we leaving the planet?"

"No, Fronidia is the safest place for us. I have a home in the Arandan enclave, a community of Arandan immigrants here in Fronidia."

I reclined in my seat to get some rest. He drove to a city where we traded in the vehicle for a transport pod. After a two-hour flight, we arrived at his house, a medium-sized home, not very fancy but equipped with typical Fronidian advanced technology. He showed me which room would be Josher's.

"Give me a few minutes, and I will reproduce a bed appropriate for him."

After Josher's bed was in place, I stored his few clothing and accessory items, tucked him in, and then followed Montor out of the room.

"So, which is my room?" I asked, hugging myself.

He showed me to a second guest room. I had hoped I wouldn't cry again, but my emotions were getting the best of me.

"I hate this just sitting around and waiting for my memory to magically return. It has been several lunar cycles now. I cannot continue with my life on hold."

His brow furrowed as he tossed some idea around in his mind.

"OK, I am no doctor, but I have a suggestion. I found your tablet when I helped retake Dit Lar. You do not know what I am referring to, but anyway, I have your tablet. You may have been keeping a journal. There are probably images there. You could look through them little by little each day. We can talk about any questions you have."

"I like the idea of reading the journal, but I do not want to see any images. It might cause confusion about whether I am really remembering things or just recalling the images on the tablet. Please put a lock on the images for now."

"OK, and I will ask my foster parents to relocate to this community. They care for you very much. You forged a close bond with my foster mother. Perhaps there are things you will read that you prefer to discuss with a female or not with me."

I was surprised by how gently he stroked my cheek with the back of his hand and kissed my forehead.

"Do not worry, Mina. We will get through this."

I waited a week before looking at the tablet. The first entry was several passages long and seemed to cover more than a year's worth of history. Shorter daily entries followed. As I processed the words, my chest tightened, and I got dizzy. My breathing became labored. I read a story of a woman torn from her family and taken galaxies away from her home planet. This woman had a husband and three children. The Lostai forced her to train as a soldier, and she was subjected to brutal punishments.

This is not just any woman. This is me.

Montor found me on the floor and gathered me up in his arms.

"Mina, Mina! What happened?"

Violent tremors rocked my body while Montor carried me to my room and laid me on the bed. I sobbed uncontrollably. Distraught, he caressed my hair and cheeks.

"Mina, how can I help you?"

Somehow, I sat up and grabbed him by the shoulders. An unnatural energy strengthened me.

"Did, did you know?" I shouted, shaking him. "Tell me!"

"What, Mina, what?"

"The Lostai kidnapped me. I have another husband and three children...that is what!"

I felt his body go limp, like he'd been shot with a gun or stabbed.

"Yes, Mina, I know."

"Explain to me, then, why I am married to you if I have a family back on my home planet."

"Mina, it is a long story."

"Do you know them? What they look like?"

My head felt like someone had hit me with a club.

"No, Mina. We met more than a revolution after the Lostai took you, but you need to relax. I am sure all the answers to your questions are in your journal. I will make you a tea with a sedative so you can rest."

Still wailing when he returned with the tea, he held my hand until I fell asleep. The next morning, I stayed in bed all day. Montor brought me food, but I had no appetite. I remained in bed for several days with vomiting, splitting headaches, lethargy, and blurred vision. Montor tried his best to keep me hydrated and fed, but he finally brought in a Sotkari Ta doctor named Kimara to examine me.

After guiding me through meditation that eliminated the headaches, tension, and weariness, Doctor Kimara explained that every time I attempted to recover a lost memory, I was bruising my psyche.

"Mina, you need to be patient and give yourself time to heal. Reading your journal will be traumatic for you, but I understand that not knowing anything of your past can be equally disturbing. If you decide to continue reading the journal, approach it as if it were a history book, where you are learning facts without inserting yourself as the protagonist of what is happening. Meditate before each reading to help avoid trying to recall those events. I like Montor's idea of discussing your feelings after you read a passage to help you deal with the emotional aspect of your trauma."

"Thank you, doctor. I will do my best to follow your instructions, but I am getting frustrated. Tell me the truth. Do you think I will ever recover my memories?"

Smiling, she nodded.

"I am confident you will regain your memory. You do not have a physical injury. It is a psychological issue. It is just tricky how it will happen. Whether it will come back in phases or all at once and if one event will trigger it or if it is just a matter of time are all unknowns. I will come see you once every lunar cycle to check how you are doing."

Montor's foster parents arrived a few days later. They rented a house nearby. One day, Montor let me know they'd be joining us for dinner. He brought home fresh poultry, and I felt well enough to prepare a nice meal. As soon as they arrived, Montor's foster mother, Lasarta, started to cry. Her husband, Foxor, covered his mouth and turned away, apparently equally affected.

"Mina, I have prayed so much for this moment. Montor has explained your situation. I want you to know Foxor and I care about you very much, regardless of whether you remember us or not."

With the back of each hand, she stroked both my cheeks, and although I couldn't remember her, I was sure her feelings were sincere. Montor served wine, and we sat to eat. Foxor had seconds. Montor was clearly proud of the meal I prepared as his foster parents complimented the taste and presentation of the food. I didn't make dessert because Montor told me his foster father would take care of that. Lasarta helped me clean up, and Foxor served jelly-filled pastries that were to die for.

After dinner, the men went to the balcony to indulge in smoking something I wasn't familiar with. Lasarta and I enjoyed another glass of wine and remained sitting in the living room area.

"Mina, Montor mentioned you were not feeling well a few days ago."

"Yes, I have started reading my journal. I learned about my family on Earth. It was very upsetting..." My voice cracked, and I had to clear my throat before continuing. "Then I tried to recall what they look like. The doctor said I should not do that, but she does think reading the journal could be beneficial."

"Mina, you and I used to cook a lot together, and Montor enjoys spending time with Foxor. If it is OK with you, I can come each day to help you prepare the food as well as lend an ear if you need it. We can have the evening meal together as a family."

"I would like that. Montor has told me he needs to start visiting the capital city for his work, so you can keep me company."

"Yes, we can do groceries together, and this will also give me time with Josher. I cannot believe how much he has grown."

We continued to chitchat. I noticed she was careful not to talk about the past or anything too deep. In about an hour, Foxor and Montor returned inside. Foxor said it was time for them to get back home. After they left, Montor and I meditated. I told him about Lasarta's suggestion, and he was all for it.

"Mina, you prepared an excellent meal. Thank you."

"I am going to have another glass of wine. Do you want one?"

He accepted, and we sat on the front porch. Although this was a residential area, there was a small park across the street, a few eateries up the block, and a bakery near the park entrance. People still walked the streets. The ambiance was so different from where Kindor and I had lived. I tried not to think of him or imagine what he was going through. Those thoughts caused me sometimes to be furious and other times depressed. I missed him, but I couldn't forgive what he did. Getting acclimated to my new environment helped keep my mind occupied.

"Have you read any more of your journal?" Montor asked.

"To be honest, I am afraid to." A thought occurred to me. "Can I go get it now and read while you are here with me?"

"I would think you would want your privacy, but if you feel comfortable with it, sure."

I got my tablet and activated it. He sat next to me and took my hand. It was in English, so I translated to him as I went along robotically without giving much thought to the words. I read a passage about someone named Kaya whom the Lostai had forced into training Sotkari Ta hostages. I absorbed the information without trying to remember what she looked like. He reacted to different sentences with frowns, chuckles, and sighs. A hint of sadness seemed to taint even his laughter, but I tried not to think about the possible reason behind it.

As I continued reading, I understood the relationship she had with Montor and the role they both played in my escape from the Lostai. In those passages, I also talked about the beginning of my relationship with Montor. I described feeling an intense physical attraction just from touching his hand or any kind of skin contact. Kindor had briefly explained to me how this energy transfer worked between Sotkari Ta. From reading the journal, I learned Montor and I both had these Sotkari Ta genes. I wondered why I wasn't feeling these same sensations as he held my hand. Instead, I sensed friendship and caring.

He must be purposely controlling his sexual energy.

"Where is Kaya now?" I asked.

He frowned and looked down to our hands.

"Unfortunately, she passed away. She contracted the illness that recently ravaged Sotkar."

"Oh yes, I saw that in the newscasts. It was reported that Lostai allies released the virus."

"Yes. You know, one of her final thoughts was of you. She wanted to thank you. She said you brought out the best in me. She cared for you very much."

A wave of sadness came over me, and I felt the need of a hug, but I didn't even dare suggest it. I imagined the wound of my infidelity was still too raw for Montor. Although some entries evoked potent emotions, reading my own words out loud brought a certain comfort, and I continued on. I reached the part that described my time on Renna One. Montor squeezed my hand tighter when I described my growing feelings for him and the dilemma of having to leave to Fronidia without him. I was caught off guard when Gio's name appeared in the text, like I'd been sucker-punched. The tablet dropped from my hands, and I ran to the restroom to vomit. Montor ran after me and held my hair back while I puked.

When I was done vomiting everything, down to the last sip of wine, he helped me up, and I rinsed out my mouth.

"Here, let me help you to your room."

"No!"

"What?"

"I want to go back to the porch and continue reading. Please, can you stay with me some more?"

"Sure, but Mina, it seems like you have had enough for now."

"No, if I stop now, I will never be able to pick up that tablet ever again. Please." I was about to cry, but I held it back. "Please, please help me. I do not want his name to be the last thing I read from my journal."

He pressed his lips together and pulled me into an embrace. My body trembled. I couldn't control it.

"Please, please, please."

"OK, Mina, yes. Calm down. We will go back to the porch and keep reading."

We sat back down, and I picked up my tablet. He put his arm around my shoulder and pulled me close. I summoned my will power and called up the entry where I left off. I read about my first encounter with Gio, then later, about the second, which was a lot less pleasant.

"So, Gio tried to rape me once before. You saved me that time." My voice sounded robotic as I forced myself to detach from what I had just read.

He looked away and cracked his knuckles.

"Mina, I am so sorry I was not there to protect you this time. I will never forgive myself for that."

He wiped his eyes before turning back to me.

"I will never separate myself from you again. Ever. I promise."

I continued reading entries that took me to the point where I left Renna One alone in a shuttle to Fronidia. That section was also emotional, and I decided I had read enough for one day. He escorted me to my room and caressed my cheek before leaving.

Lasarta proved to be excellent company. With her help, I read through my entire journal. Another difficult section had to do with how I met Kindor, the time I spent with his family, and our relationship. My entries confirmed that Kindor and I had a strong bond of friendship, but I was not in love with him, and he knew it. Devastated by this betrayal of trust, I almost destroyed the tablet when I reached that part. It was so hard to reconcile his kindness and apparent loyalty with this type of behavior. I would have loved discussing with Lasarta my conflicted feelings for him, but out of respect to Montor, I didn't disclose to her what happened between us.

She didn't have telepathic abilities, but sometimes I wondered whether she could read my mind. When we were done with that section, she patted my hand and said, "Kindor is a special friend, but there will always be awkwardness because of his feelings. I think it is best that there be distance between you at this time."

I had recorded my last journal entry right before I returned to Dit Lar after a joyful reunion with Montor on the Namson planet. I couldn't remember what happened on Dit Lar. My latest memories were finding myself in a room with Gio and knowing that something wasn't right about him. It was so frustrating that the one thing I wished I could forget was the only thing I remembered.

As months went by, I got used to my new routine. I updated my journal with what I remembered from my terrifying ordeal with Gio, what happened with Kindor, and up to the present time.

During workdays, Montor, Josher, and I would have breakfast and go through our Sotkari Ta practices together. Montor then traveled to the Fronidian capital, where he had an office at the Arandan embassy that was his home base for his tactical and liaison duties. Soon after he left, Foxor and Lasarta would arrive. I spent a few hours teaching lessons to Josher. Afterwards, Lasarta and I ran errands while Foxor stayed home with Josher. Once a week, Lasarta and I visited a salon together for pampering. We arrived back home in time to prepare dinner and waited for Montor's arrival. Some evenings, we played games before they left. Montor treated me with kindness, but there was still a vacuum between us.

I didn't interface with anyone else other than a Fronidian female named Colora whom I knew from my journal was a friend. When I first met her, I had one of the debilitating headaches and déjà vu moments, which were becoming more frequent. I realized how Vadira had reminded me of her. Colora also worked in the capital, called me frequently, and joined us for dinner a few times. Not having recalled a single concrete memory from my past, I was, in that aspect, still in limbo.

39

MONTOR

I walked in darkness
You are the light
Born of my seed
The same but different
A miracle of love
My son, my pride
Her gift to me

"Gift" from *Montor's Secret Stash of Poems*

Having Josher at home brought me such joy. He had grown so much in one revolution. On rest days, I took him and Mina to different outings. The third time that we visited a holographic room, I invited Foxor and Lasarta to join us. Josher preferred the warrior games and liked when I joined him to fight together against opponents. He demonstrated impressive agility and strength for a child his age. Our daily Sotkari Ta physical regimen had plenty to do with it, but I liked to think it was also genetics.

Of course it is. He takes after me.

"He reminds me so much of you at that age," said Foxor. "You always chose challenging games and sports that were well beyond what was deemed normal for your age and size."

My chest swelled with pride as my foster father voiced my own thoughts.

After the holographic rooms, we went to a traditional Arandan restaurant. Josher was chatty, bragging to everyone about the battle level he had reached in the games.

Lasarta side-glanced at me and said to him with a knowing smile, "You are like your father in more ways than one."

Josher did not catch her hidden joke.

"In which other ways, *Lo Ro*?"

We all laughed out loud, except Mina, who only smiled. Of course, old jokes were not the same for her anymore. We had become people she was just getting to know. It was hard enough for her to understand when we accidentally all dropped the Lostai and started talking in Arandan, but she was becoming more fluent. Spending time with Lasarta helped her deal with the frustration of her memory loss. Reading through her journal was difficult and emotional but did nothing to jog her memory.

Sadness had settled in Mina's eyes. I sensed she wished to return to normal marriage life, and I physically desired her more than ever. When I caressed her cheek or touched her hand, it took extreme effort to lock down my sexual energy. Still, neither of us were ready emotionally. She would not take that step without regaining her memory, and I did not want that either. There were other barriers. Negative thoughts bombarded my brain.

My male pride is injured. I am angry at her infidelity.

Might I somehow hurt her psychologically?

Is she just settling for me?

We finished our meal early, and the weather was pleasant, so we walked home the long way through the park. Josher spoke about which games he would play on our next visit to the holographic rooms.

"*Ta Ri*, next time we go, can we invite *Fa* Kindor? I would like him to see how far I have reached in the game."

Although I had forbidden Mina to talk to anyone about her relationship with Kindor, I had confessed it to Foxor because I shared all my secrets with him. If I knew Foxor well, he had shared it with Lasarta.

Does Josher notice the uncomfortable silence?

I did my best to disguise my irritation.

"I am afraid that will not be possible, son," I said.

"Why not?"

Mina jumped in to try to rescue the situation.

"Kindor is busy at a new job and cannot travel here at this time," she explained.

"I would like to call him. I am sure if I ask nicely, he will come. He loves me."

I clenched my fists but otherwise tried to hide my discomfort. Mina spotted a street vendor selling sweet pies and tried to distract Josher by asking him if he would like one. He was stubborn and insisted.

He gets that from her.

"Even if he cannot come, I would like to call him. I would like to call him right away when we get home."

"You will drop the subject right now," replied Mina in a stern voice.

Josher usually was a disciplined and respectful child, but every so often, he had his outbursts, especially relating to things he was passionate about. He yanked his hand out of hers and glared up at us.

"One day, I will be old enough to go places on my own and

call whoever I want," he snarled. Crossing his arms, he stomped ahead of us.

Very defiant for a boy who is not yet two revolutions old. That, he gets from me.

The incident with Josher and the unfulfilled sexual tension that was building up in me increased my crankiness as days went by. I retreated more and more into work to avoid subjecting Mina and the rest of the family to my bad mood. Immersing myself in the important strategic issues facing the United Rebel Front, I spent long hours at the office at the Arandan Embassy, sometimes missing dinners, and other nights, I did not even make it home.

Four lunar cycles had gone by since I found Mina and Josher. The Lostai had continued on the offensive. The United Rebel Front felt the pressure of defending Aranda, Sotkar, and Dit Lar from constant Lostai attacks. The Tormixians had begun to second-guess their decision to join the rebellion as the Lostai, in retaliation, were brutal in their treatment of civilians there. In addition, the Namson had lost some ground.

Commander Portars called me just as I was leaving the office with the hope of making it home in time for dinner. I got in the transport pod, punched in my location codes, and put the call on the viewer.

"Hello, Montor, is this a good time to talk? I know it is a little late."

"Yes, sir, now is fine if you do not mind that I speak from the transport pod. I am on my way home."

"Sure, I will be quick, Montor. Two hours ago, the Lostai breached the security array on the southwestern continent on Sotkar yet again. We are sending them reinforcements and hope to push them back. The reason I am calling you is because Kaonto believes there are still Fronidian Sotkari Ta spies working for the Lostai among his ranks. He thinks they may be leaking security intelligence."

"Yes, I also suspected this."

"He is asking if we can negotiate with the Fronidian government to get tracking and information on known Lostai sympathizers. The Fronidians have been reluctant to help with this given their strict personal privacy policies. Kaonto will have his new lieutenant contact you to coordinate. As you know, most of his inner circle were infected by the virus and are either dead or permanently injured."

"Yes, that is fine. What is his name?"

"Well, you know him well. It is Kindor."

Shermont! Am I understanding correctly?

"Kindor?" I heard the anger in my voice.

"Is everything all right, Montor?"

I took a deep breath to compose myself.

"I just do not think he is qualified. What does he know about military tactics and strategy?"

"Well, apparently, he learned a bit when he was under your command, and Kaonto seems to have a lot of respect for him. Is this going to be a problem?" Portars said, narrowing his eyes.

"No, sir."

Two days later, Kindor called me. The first time the notification buzzer sounded, I ignored it. The second time, I picked it up, and at the sight of his face, I cut the connection. The third time, we glared at each other for a few minutes. Finally, he began to gesticulate in Sotkari sign language.

"Greetings, Montor. I realize this is awkward, but we are both professionals and need to collaborate to defeat our common enemy."

"If you were here in person, I would break your neck, but I suppose at a distance we can figure things out," I answered.

"Before we get down to business, may I ask how Mina and Josher are doing?"

I slammed my hands on the console.

"No, you may not ask." I rolled my eyes, but despite my ire, I acquiesced. "*Shermont!* They are fine."

"Rest assured that I have not tried to contact Mina, and she has not reached out to me either."

If only I could reach through the viewer and reduce his arrogant Sotkari face to shreds. How presumptuous of him!

"I have no doubt about that. She feels even more betrayed than I do. You know, she has been reading a journal we found. When she got to the part about meeting you and your supposed friendship, she flung the tablet across the room."

I fully savored the pain in his eyes. He turned away from the screen. A few moments went by before he looked back.

"One more thing, Montor. I know I owe you an apology."

I could not believe my ears.

"An apology? An apology is what you offer when you accidentally bump into someone. There is no form of apology that can address what you did, and frankly, if I am to get through this conversation with you, I would rather not be reminded of it."

His eyes lowered for another uncomfortable moment. When he faced me again, all emotion had been erased from his face.

"Very well. Let us get to the matter at hand."

Having made it through our "salutations," we mapped out our strategy to petition the Fronidian government for records on their Sotkari Ta citizens so we could identify possible Lostai infiltrators. He also told me he left the *hanstoric* he used to transport from Dit Lar in a personal storage bin on Fronidia and gave me the access codes.

"Another pending matter is testing if the geomagnetic properties on some of Fronidia's mountainous areas can work to charge our *hanstorics* and create intergalactic transportals similar to the one on Dit Lar. If so, we could accelerate returning rescued hostages to their home worlds. Colora was not successful in securing such permission from the Fronidian government."

"The Fronidian government is all about increasing their planet's riches and economic power. We need to offer them something. I am sure if we demonstrate that they can benefit from the use of the transportals for their commercial purposes, they will allow us to test the *hanstoric* here. If it works, we can negotiate to give them free use of the technology in exchange for access to their Sotkari Ta records and that they allow us to use the transportals to rescue hostages," I replied.

"Yes, that makes sense. So, how do we proceed?"

"I have become friendly with the Secretary of Economic Development. She is half-Arandan, is sympathetic to our cause, and has considerable influence. If I can convince her, I am sure she will get the Parliament to approve."

"Hopefully, this will not be a lengthy process."

"Kindor, be careful with your tone. I do not take orders from you. To be quite honest, I detest even having to talk to you."

"I did not mean to imply that, but if we do not root out the Lostai infiltrators soon, I am afraid we might lose another continent to the Lostai."

"I will contact you in one week with an update. Is there anything else we need to discuss?"

"No."

I cut the connection without any polite goodbyes. Cracking my knuckles helped me control the urge to punch things. When I arrived home that evening, I shared an after-dinner drink with Foxor and told him how I was now forced to collaborate with Kindor.

"Son, I understand your discomfort, but try to imagine he is just another officer of the United Rebel Front."

"I see him, and I imagine them together, and then I imagine my hands around his neck. What would you do if another male took Lasarta to his bed?"

He stood and scowled.

"I would tear his heart out!" he shouted, but then he sat again and softened his tone. "Son, your relationship with Mina has been something out of the ordinary from the very beginning. You cannot apply our typical Arandan mentality, and I do not want to hurt you, but you are in part to blame."

"I know. I left her alone too long. If I had been there when the Lostai invaded Dit Lar, things might have been different."

"Unfortunately, yes, you left her and in the company of a male whom you knew loved her."

"I thought I was protecting her and Josher, but also I was too cocky. I never thought he would dare..."

"Kindor is a good person, but Mina without her memory resulted in too much temptation. I have no doubt he feels terrible about this too. That will be his punishment."

Hearing Foxor refer to that filthy bastard as a good person made me need another drink. I poured us two more glasses of brandy.

"Montor, there is something else I would like to discuss."

"Yes?" I asked.

"Two lunar cycles from today will mark the second revolution since Josher's birthdate, and he is still without his first amulet. It is unacceptable."

My face flushed with shame. I had forgotten about a cherished Arandan tradition. The celebration was equal in importance to a wedding.

"I, I do not know what to say. It has slipped my mind. I will see to it."

"We know you have been busy, and Mina is not familiar

with our customs. Lasarta and I will make the arrangements and consult with you from time to time to make sure you agree with all the details. The most important thing I need from you now is the invitation list. We will search for and propose appropriate venues, so you can select the one you prefer."

"I will get the invitation list to you in a few days."

At the end of the week, after putting Josher to bed, Foxor, Lasarta, Mina, and I sat down in the resting room to discuss the details of the celebration.

"Montor, we have three venues for you to choose from. Colora's Fronidia Member's Only, Bramoc Room here in this neighborhood, and the event room by the River Tooran."

"Mina, do you have a preference?" I asked.

"I wish I could be more helpful, but obviously, I don't know about these places. I am sure whatever you select is fine."

"OK, then I pick Colora's Member's Only. It is a beautiful venue and reminds me of the Member's Only in Renna One where I spent a lot of time. We can stay overnight and offer lodging for anyone else who would like to do the same."

"Next is the guest list," said Foxor.

I displayed my suggested list on the viewer.

"OK, so first, we need to make sure we have covered close family," said Foxor.

"Well, that would be us here," I said, some bitterness evident in my voice.

"Yes, true," agreed Foxor with a sigh. "Next, you have included the *Barinta* crew, Commander Portars, Commander Larmont, and the lieutenants that attended your wedding and the battles on Dit Lar and Sotkar. I see on the list your friend, Tzarst from the Namson planet and his family."

"Yes. I also have added my coworkers from the Arandan Embassy and the Fronidian government, such as the Secretary of Economic Development. The United Rebel Front needs their help, and the party is an excellent opportunity to get leaders from both sides together in a friendly environment," I said.

"OK. And that is the list. Are we missing anybody?" asked Foxor.

"I have a special request." We all turned to look at Mina. "I would like you to search for Tony, the person who told Kindor where to find me. I owe him my life. I would like to thank him myself."

I did not like the idea. Tony reminded me of Gio, but Mina was adamant, so I agreed. After thinking about it with a clear head, I acknowledged he deserved my gratitude too.

"I guess you purposely excluded Captain Sortomor," said Lasarta.

"Yes, that pompous idiot has no place in my son's celebration. He was rude to my wife. Oh, I almost forgot. We must add Kaonto and his son."

"I agree," continued Lasarta. "OK, so only one other person is glaringly missing—Kindor."

"That back-stabbing bastard is not coming anywhere near me or my family!" I shouted.

Affected by my outburst, Mina's nervous eyes darted from Foxor to Lasarta. She pressed her fist against her mouth but said nothing. Not knowing that Foxor and Lasarta were aware of what happened with Kindor, Mina was surprised I would be so open with my displeasure.

"Son, if I may give an opinion..." Foxor clasped his hands, and by the tone of his voice, I knew he would say something wise that I did not want to agree with. "People know how close Josher and Kindor have always been. They will question why you did not invite him. They may reach their own conclusions. The thing you are trying to conceal may actually become even more evident."

Foxor did his best to be cryptic with his choice of words, but an uncomfortable silence nevertheless followed. Mina stared at me with her mouth open in silent protest. She knew for sure by then that I had told them.

"We also need to select who will be Josher's *Ta Ro Masas*, the people who replace his parents in case of an emergency. It is an important part of the celebration," said Lasarta. "I remember when your parents designated Foxor and me, one of the proudest moments of my life."

Lasarta was not trying to change the subject. I knew exactly where she was going with this. Standing, I began to pace. Mina pressed the palms of her hands against her head. Now that what happened between her and Kindor was out in the open, we were both upset.

"Can it be you and Foxor?" asked Mina.

"No. We are expected to die before you. *Ta Ro Masas* should be someone close to your age that can take your place if you are missing," said Foxor.

"I am galaxies away from my planet," Mina interjected with tears in her eyes. "Other than Lasarta and Foxor, the only other close friend I have according to my journal is Colora. She is also an old friend of Montor's, so I propose her."

"Yes, I think that works. What about you, Montor? Do you agree with Colora?" asked Lasarta.

"Yes, of course I agree with Colora," I answered with a groan.

"Good. Now, we need to select a male who can be a father figure for Josher should something happen to you," said Foxor. He stood to meet my eyes. "I can only think of one person who would give his life for that boy as you would."

I turned away from them, shaking my head.

"This is unbelievable. That thought process is what got me to my present situation in the first place."

"Yes, and you were correct in thinking that way. Otherwise, your wife and son might have been captured or dead by now. Kindor has rescued them more than once. Remember, Zorla is out there getting more powerful. Your family still has enemies."

"So, you would have me designate that scum as Josher's *Ta Masa*? That means he would be like a brother to me. Seriously, how much further humiliation would you have me endure?"

Lasarta got to her feet to join Foxor and me.

"I know how you feel, but he is not going to stay around. He would only come for the ceremony. We will explain to him the significance of this role, so he knows what is expected in the event that something happens to you. After the party, he can go back to whatever it is he is doing these days," she said. "Mina, what do you think?"

Mina was still sitting. She looked up at me, and we made eye contact.

"I cannot agree with anything that will spoil this joyous event for Montor. Find someone else for that role. Montor also has a good relationship with Commander Portars. Maybe he could be a good choice."

"No, he is only a few years younger than me," Foxor answered.

Mina finally stood. She clenched her fists and spoke with a tremor in her voice.

"Listen to me. Find someone else. A fellow soldier, his Namson friend..." Her voice cracked and became higher-pitched. "Someone, anyone. I do not want Kindor and Montor near each other."

I walked to the balcony and stared out at the night sky. Mina tried to muffle her sobs, but I heard them. After several minutes of only hearing Mina cry, I turned to face the three of them.

"Foxor is right. Our family still has enemies. As I have admitted before, regardless of my problem with him, Kindor is the only one I would trust with the life of my son." I sighed, hating the decision I was about to make but knowing it was the right one. "OK, I agree for Kindor to be Josher's *Ta Masa* and that he attend the celebration. Mina, do not worry. Do not feel guilty. I will still enjoy this milestone in my son's life. The only thing I ask is that someone talk to Kindor about it. I want as little to do with him as possible."

Foxor turned to Mina, who was still covering her mouth as she shook her head, vehemently signaling she would not do it either.

"OK, Montor, give me his contact codes. I will call him and explain everything," said Foxor.

40

MINA

The ceremony where Montor and I would present Josher with his first amulet was called *Bendorai* in Arandan. We had the amulet custom made at a special Arandan artisanal jewelry shop.

"I would like the amulet fashioned in the traditional style," Montor said to the young attendant without bothering to check any of the items on display.

"Interesting," the attendant said. "Hardly anyone does that anymore. I hope you actually have an idea of what you want it to look like."

Montor's eyes narrowed.

"As a matter of fact, I do." He took off one of the amulets from the cord he wore around his neck and slammed it on the counter. "I want it to look like this, but with a jewel encrusted in the middle. Do you have a problem with that?"

The attendant adjusted his tone.

"No problem at all, sir. I will be right back with our precious stone collection."

I took the amulet in my hand to take a closer look. A

horrible pain pierced the area behind my eyes. It was as if a light had blinded me.

"Mina, what is it?"

"Sorry, nothing...just another one of my headaches...when I focused on the amulet. Is there something significant about it that would affect me?"

He sighed.

"I probably should not say anything."

"Please, tell me."

"This is the amulet you gave me on our wedding day. My mother had given it to my father on their wedding day. Before being executed, my father gave it to Foxor, who had secretly kept it all those years. He then gave it to you so you could present it to me. Do you remember any of this?"

I shook my head and a sad silence hung over us until the attendant returned. Montor selected an amber-colored stone. He cupped my chin and tilted my face up so that our eyes could meet.

"It matches your and Josher's eyes."

"It is beautiful."

We waited as the attendant formed the shiny silver-toned metal into a quarter-sized imperfect circle for a rustic look and encrusted the stone in the center. Engraved on one side around the circle was Montor's clan name, Ventamu. We needed to select a virtue for Josher to be engraved on the other side. Montor deferred that decision to me, and I chose Generosity. He would have preferred I pick something like Courage or Strength, but I had the feeling that Josher would have those in abundance anyway.

When we arrived back home, Foxor informed us that he had contacted Kindor about the ceremony for Josher and the role we were asking him to play.

"Kindor says he will accept coming to the celebration and taking on the role of *Ta Masa* with one condition."

Montor's eyes blazed with anger.

"That cocky Sotkari bastard! It is an honor, and he dares to impose conditions. You know, maybe I made the wrong decision."

"Calm down," said Foxor. "He only requests that you allow him to communicate via the viewer with Josher at least once each lunar cycle, and twice every revolution, he would like to take Josher on a special trip here in Fronidia. He says if he is to truly fill this role, he wants to continue the bond that he has established with the child."

I stepped in to give my opinion right away because Montor had that wild look he got when he was furious.

"I think it is a reasonable request. It will be good for Josher. He misses Kindor."

"OK, wonderful. I will finalize the details with Kindor," said Foxor in a rush before anyone changed their minds.

Montor rolled his eyes as he poured himself a drink.

The days leading up to the *Bendorai* ceremony required other decisions and preparations regarding the menu, the music, and the decor. I tried to help Foxor and Lasarta as much as possible as Montor spent little time at home. His work usually kept him at his office late, and some days, he stayed overnight. Colora picked me up one day to shop for what I would wear at the ceremony. She joked that I had been spending too much time with Lasarta and was afraid I might select something old-fashioned and frumpy. We decided on a yellow dress with a flowing skirt, a form-fitting top, and a plunging neckline. Intermittent headaches affected me all day. She said nothing, but I had the distinct feeling this was not the first time she had helped me to select clothing.

The day of the party, Colora came to do my and Lasarta's

hair and makeup. I did not want to do much with my hair, but she insisted I gather it in an updo so that the curls framed my face. She also gave me gold-toned jewelry and added small shiny pins to my hair. As I contemplated myself in the reverse viewer in my room, I couldn't help but remember that the last time I was dressed this fancy was when I went to the mining company party with Kindor. That night was the first time we had been intimate. I did my best to shake the memory out of my head. Something else disturbed me. It lasted only a moment, a flicker of an image in my mind of me in a white dress with my hair done up in a similar style.

Montor and Josher wore matching suits that included tight pants, fitted long-sleeved white shirts, and long open vests. I took a moment to appreciate how the outfit highlighted Montor's muscular physique.

He looks hot!

Another flicker. Longer in duration this time. An image of a silhouette matching his frame in front of a long line of people. Then me in the white dress again.

What's happening to me? Are my memories trying to surface?

We were the first to arrive at the venue. I knew from my journal that the only time I had been there before was when we were forced to hide from the Lostai. It was a luxurious waterfront hotel, restaurant, and dance hall. Lasarta and I checked with the kitchen and waiting staff to ensure everything was in order before we relaxed at our tables to wait for our guests. The musical band arrived and got set up on the stage. Guests started trickling in soon after.

In the week prior, I had put in longer hours of meditation to prepare myself mentally for the impact of meeting the other members of the *Barinta*. They would be happy to see me, but I wouldn't remember them at all. Montor told me he had advised everyone of my memory loss, but I still felt awkward. Then there was the whole Kindor factor. Montor promised he would be on his best behavior, but the thought of the three of us together was disconcerting.

The first to arrive were Commander Portars, Commander Larmont and his wife, and a group of Arandan lieutenants. Montor, Josher, and I walked hand in hand to greet them. Some of the females caressed my cheek, and some tapped my shoulder. The males only nodded, but all of them in one way or another stated how happy they were to see me and how much Josher had grown.

We had a waiter lead them to their pre-assigned tables while we remained near the entrance to greet the other guests as they arrived. Montor took advantage of a lull to gaze into my eyes.

"Mina, did I tell you already that you look stunning? I love your hair that way."

I offered him a shy smile.

"Thank you, and yes, you did."

He took my hand and kissed it.

Maybe this party will help us get closer.

The next guest was a young, handsome, dark-skinned man. At first, my chest tightened. Other than Gio, I had no memory of another human. The similarity ended there. This young man had a wide, genuine grin and gave me a bear hug. Montor rolled his eyes but then half-smiled as if he had tolerated this before.

"Mina, me happy fi see you. You look so nice. Last time we did deh here, tings did really bad."

From my journal entries, I guessed who this might be.

"Damari?" I asked.

"Yeah, nuh worry yourself. Montor did tell me bout your memory loss. Me hope you get betta soon."

Damari patted Josher on the head before being led away.

After Damari, another human man arrived accompanied by

a handsome male Fronidian. His eyes welled with tears when they met mine.

"Mina, I'm so sorry. I should never have gone along with any of Gio's plans," he said in English, his voice full of emotion.

Only one other human was on the guest list.

"Tony?"

"Yes."

I sensed Montor's heavy breathing.

I should keep things brief.

"Gio was an evil person, and yes, you shouldn't have assisted him in any way. But the fact is, I owe you a debt of gratitude. You saved my life when you told Kindor where to find me. I hope you enjoy yourself here today, and I'd like to keep in touch. If there is anything Montor and I can ever do to repay you, don't hesitate to call on us."

"That's very kind of you, Mina."

He nodded to Montor, and he and his companion moved on to be seated.

Montor's friend from the Namson planet, Tzarst, arrived right after Tony. Tzarst and his family were the most different-looking race that I had seen. Their features were froglike, and they didn't wear shoes. One of the last entries in my journal before Gio took me were about these kind, brave people and how Tzarst had agreed to take me to Montor, even against Montor's wishes.

Kindor arrived next with an Arandan female who covered half her face with a veil. It looked like part of her outfit, but I realized it was Officer Lorret, whose face had been scarred by the Lostai. In my journal, I mentioned that she and Kindor were friends. Before we could greet him formally, Josher ran to Kindor, and Kindor picked him up.

"*Fa* Kindor!!!"

I heard their voices in my mind in conference mode in Arandan.

"Son, how are you doing?"

"I am great, *Fa* Kindor. This whole party is for me! Do you know *Ro Ma* has showed me how to spell many new words and I am at the sixth level in—"

"That is wonderful, and I would like to know all about these words, but let me greet your parents. We shall have time later to talk some more."

By the time he finished his chat with Josher, my heart beat twice as fast as it should. I focused on slowing my breathing so that I could be composed when he put Josher down. His eyes ever so discreetly looked me over before meeting mine. Those few seconds felt like an eternity. Other than that, he showed no emotion. Montor tightened his grip on my hand.

"Hello, Mina," Kindor said, nodding to me in the same respectful way as the Arandan males had done.

"Hello, Kindor," was all I managed to reply because my stomach was in a spin. I so wanted this greeting to be over with and pretended that Josher's shirt collar needed straightening out.

Kindor extended his arm towards Montor for the Sotkari salutation. Through the corner of my eye, I checked Montor's reaction. He accepted and nodded back, his face like stone except for the slight tension I detected in his jawbone.

Montor and Officer Lorret greeted each other in Arandan, after which she looked to me and placed her hand on my shoulder.

"Mina, it is good to see you looking so beautiful." Her expression was sincere.

Finally, I found my words.

"Nice to see you too, Lorret. I am so glad you are here. I look forward to catching up with you later. The waiter will show you to your table. I hope you enjoy yourself."

Once they walked away, I couldn't help but let out an audible sigh of relief. Montor pursed his lips but said nothing.

Montor's coworkers walked in last, including the Fronidian Secretary of Economic Development. She arrived unaccompanied, rendering the males standing at the nearby bar dumbstruck when they saw her. Taller than the typical Fronidian, she flaunted a spectacular figure in a flesh-toned skin-tight body suit topped only by a sheer, see-through tunic. Instead of typical dark Fronidian eyes, hers were yellow and picked up light from the tiny gold crystals that adorned the tunic.

She must be bi-racial.

"Larioma, this is my wife, Mina."

We nodded to each other.

She smiled sweetly, never taking her eyes off Montor, while talking to me.

"Pleasure to meet you, Mina."

"The pleasure is mine," I replied, raising my voice a bit to try to get her to look at me and stop smiling at Montor. "The waiter will show you to your table."

Once all the guests arrived and were seated, we moved on to the ceremonial part of the evening. The Arandan priestess called Montor, Josher, and me to the stage. She addressed the group to explain that the purpose of our gathering was to officially present Josher as a member of his ancestral clan. My basic knowledge of the Arandan language allowed me to follow along. She requested that Kindor and Colora, the people we had designated as Josher's *Ta Ro Masas,* join us at the stage. They would become close to what I understood as godparents.

The priestess requested the cord with the amulet and said a prayer. She read the sides of the amulet and held it out for all to see.

"Today, in the tradition of our ancestors, we present to the community Josher, a proud member of the Ventamu clan. Their homeland is of beautiful coastlines and beaches. In our history, many leaders come from the Ventamu clan. His parents pray he will be an example of the virtue of generosity in his community."

I noticed some of the male Arandans shifted in their seats and made faces. Like Montor, they would have preferred what they deemed to be a more male-centric virtue. I smiled to myself when the priestess continued.

"I praise his parents for their wisdom in choosing the virtue of generosity. Most families ask for courage and strength. Our people will never lack those qualities. We do not need to pray for that, but our lack of love, kindness, and generosity for each other caused the civil wars that were our downfall. We have worked hard to regain our freedom. Let us not forget these hard-learned lessons. And let us remember we did not gain this freedom alone but through sharing with other races who are in our same battle."

Montor beamed and whispered something to the priestess.

"Montor says he is lucky to have a wife who, in her wisdom, made such a choice for their son."

Everyone cheered and fist pumped.

The priestess continued, "Josher's parents have also made the all-important decision to designate *Ta Ro Masas* for Josher, the people who will take their place as parents, should something happen to them."

She gestured towards Kindor and Colora.

Kindor used Arandan sign language.

"Josher, I am honored to accept being your *Ta Masa*, and here is a token of my affection and commitment." I sensed he had also transmitted the message telepathically to Josher.

He gave Josher a small shiny package that Josher was to open later. Josher's smile lit up the room. Even Montor, who had been very serious while Kindor signed, softened his expression. Colora also offered Josher a gift, speaking out loud in Arandan. Everyone cheered again, concluding the ceremonial portion of the evening.

A multi-course meal was served. As tradition required, Montor, Josher, and I were seated at a table with Colora, Kindor, Lorret, Foxor, and Lasarta. Montor and I ignored Kindor completely, but there were enough of us at the table engaged in friendly banter to avoid making it conspicuous. Once dinner concluded and the tables were cleared, a steady flow of wine, cocktails, and other beverages were served. The band began to play, and people were encouraged to get up from their seats, mingle, and dance. Some people congregated at the bar.

Montor went to chat with the soldiers and his coworkers. Josher was engrossed in a conversation with Kindor and Lorret. Colora, Foxor, Lasarta, and I took our drinks and walked around the property to take in the beautiful surroundings. Montor didn't come back to join us, remaining for a long while engaged with a group of both male and female Arandan soldiers. With the free flow of alcohol, some of the females became flirtatious, locking eyes with the males, standing close to them, touching their shoulders and chests. Montor was no exception when it came to being on the receiving end of such behavior.

I noticed the circle opened, and Larioma stepped in. Montor took her by the elbow, and they sauntered together around the room as he introduced her to the other guests. Finally, he made his way to where I was. He introduced her to Colora, Foxor, and Lasarta as they had not met her yet.

She offered Foxor a provocative smile while addressing Lasarta, "I have often wondered what it is about Arandan males. They only grow more distinguished and attractive with age, right?"

Lasarta smiled politely while Larioma winked at Foxor before Montor led her on to another group.

"She is quite a specimen," said Foxor following her with his eyes. "The statuesque beauty of an Arandan female combined with the flirtation of a Fronidian."

Lasarta pinched him, and both she and Colora gave him a nasty look.

"Oww! But, my dear, there is no female quite like you." he quickly corrected.

Lasarta's brows remained furrowed as she watched Montor lead Larioma across the room. Larioma tossed her head as she laughed at something Montor said and touched his arm. Everything about her oozed sensuality. Lasarta sent Foxor to get us more drinks. Once he was out of our earshot, Lasarta turned to me.

"Mina, you know I have never inquired about your private life with Montor, but now, I feel compelled to ask. How are things between you and him, you know?" she said with a suggestive expression.

I lowered my eyes and admitted, "Montor and I have slept in separate rooms since he brought me back."

Lasarta's eyes widened with concern.

"No, no, Mina. It is not good for your marriage to be in such a situation."

"We feel I should have my memory back before we resume normal married life."

"Mina, a male like Montor should not be allowed to build up that kind of...tension."

This was one of the few times that Lasarta annoyed me.

What the heck? A male like Montor? What about my "tension?"

I huffed and rolled my eyes but bit my tongue.

"Mina, have you recalled anything?" Colora asked, joining the conversation.

"No," I said, my shoulders dropping. "Even after reading my journal."

Colora remained pensive for a bit.

"Maybe you need something more sensory to jog your

memory. Wait here a minute. I am going to put in a song request."

A few minutes later, she returned, and so did Foxor with our drinks. The band started playing the song that Colora requested. It began with a solo drum and a soulful chant.

I caught my breath when a vision of me in a white dress dancing with Montor flashed in my mind. Closing my eyes, several other images appeared like windows in a video conference, causing me to become dazed and a little dizzy. I held on to Colora for fear that I'd fall, but the unbalanced feeling only lasted a few minutes. My temples throbbed as memories continued to flicker and flash.

"I remember, Colora. I remember." I whispered.

She grabbed me by the shoulders.

"What, Mina, what?"

"This song and some other things."

I rubbed the area on my arm where his name was tattooed and remembered exactly the moment it happened. The excitement felt like electricity in my veins.

"Well, do not waste any time. Tell Montor. It is the news he has been waiting for!"

Lasarta and Foxor nodded in agreement.

I suppose now is as good a time as any. Time to stop living in limbo. Plus, I really want to dance with him.

I focused my mind to identify his light and sent him a telepathic message.

"Montor, I would like to dance this song with you."

I searched the room and saw that he excused himself from the group he was talking with, came over, and extended his hand to me.

"Sweetness, will you honor me with this dance?"

People cheered as we moved to the dance floor. Flutes followed the drums. Montor pulled me close. My heartbeat fluttered like hummingbird wings.

"This song has brought back memories," I whispered, searching his eyes.

"Mina, I am enjoying this dance with you, but you do not have to put up this act for me. I imagine Colora told you that this was our first dance," he said with a bit of a smirk.

"She did not tell me. That is not the only thing."

Somehow, I knew the moves and steps to this dance. Eventually, the beat became sexy and hot. Like a crane dance, our movements were synchronized.

"OK, what else?" he asked.

His skeptical tone annoyed me, but I pushed that aside and focused on the memories bombarding my brain. I needed to talk to him about something very intimate that only he and I had shared.

"I am having like a...like a daydream right this minute of us in a beach house with a glass ceiling. The bedroom is decorated in red."

"Probably something you read in your journal." His voice still sounded unconvinced, but his eyes were widening with curiosity.

"You said you wanted to make love to me like an Arandan. You started with my feet and worked your way up. We fell off the bed. Those details are not in my journal. I can bring you my tablet if you do not believe me!"

"Mina." His jaw dropped, and his eyes glistened as he stroked my cheek. "That was our wedding night," he whispered.

This breakthrough brought tears to my eyes too. He bent over and kissed me, nibbling on my bottom lip. Foxor and Lasarta were also dancing, and she winked at me. We remained on the dance floor. With each new song, Montor's hands and movements made our dancing more intimate.

I'm ready to ditch the party and head to one of the hotel rooms.

The band took a break, and we all walked to the bar. I

grabbed Montor's hand and brought him with me as I called Lasarta aside.

"Lasarta, if Montor and I disappear for a while, can you and Foxor take care of Josher and wrap up the party?"

"Of course, my dear. We will take care of everything."

She barely finished speaking when Montor chimed in, "Come, Mina, let me show you around this property."

He led me towards the water. I took off my shoes. The sand felt cool on my feet. It took us a good fifteen minutes to reach the shoreline. Gazebos with canopy beds and flowing privacy curtains lined the beach. He chose one, picked up a banner that was tossed in the sand, and stood it up so it was visible from far away.

"This lets everyone know this gazebo is occupied," he said with a sly smile. He hadn't smiled like that in all the time since he had found me with Kindor.

We lay on the bed, and he didn't wait another minute to take me in his arms.

He brought my hand to his mouth and licked my palm.

Thighs pressed together, I said, "Mmm. That tickles."

He left a trail of kisses on my arm, collarbone, and cleavage, his warm breath arousing me even more. Finally, he groaned.

"I have been waiting so long for this moment."

"So have I, Montor."

He grabbed me by the shoulders and gazed in my eyes, urgency in his expression.

"Mina, this is important. In case you have any doubt, I have not shared a bed with any female other than you since the day we were married. I will not deny that I have at times been tempted, but I have remained faithful."

I nodded, my soul filled with guilt feelings because I couldn't say the same.

"I am so sorry, Montor...I..."

"Shhh...do not worry...there is no need, sweetness."

His hands moved to my back, and he unfastened the top part of my dress and pulled it down to my waist, exposing my breasts. He descended on them with a ravenous mouth.

"*Shermont*, they are so lovely."

I only moaned as my hips squirmed in anticipation of what was coming soon. He sat up, pulled off his vest, and tossed it aside. Frantic, I unbuttoned his shirt and unfastened his pants. He stood, kicked off his shoes, and pulled off his pants and underclothes. I turned facedown so he could unfasten the dress waistband and pull it completely off. He laid it carefully on a side table within the gazebo. A memory flash suggested that I should stay facedown. He kissed my back and traveled down to my butt and back up again. Sliding his hands underneath me, he cupped my breasts while separating my thighs with his.

"I guess you remember I like it this way the best, sweetness," he whispered.

One hand moved down and between my legs, stroking and tapping until his fingers were saturated. He positioned himself and entered me without hesitation. His body was a wall of hard muscles, and his thrusts were not gentle, but the pleasure rocked me, and I moved with him. It was quick, and he collapsed on me. I sighed, a little frustrated that it was over so fast.

We rolled to our sides, and he pulled me close, my back against his torso and his hand on my tummy. He fell asleep right away, but I stayed awake for a while longer stroking his arm.

Later in the early morning hours, he kissed my head and awakened me. I turned faceup, and he propped on his elbow to look at me.

"Mina, I love you. I want to sleep with you every night for the rest of my life. We will never be separated again."

"Montor, I want the same thing. I love you, too."

I reached over to coax his face towards mine. Our lips met. I wanted to kiss him forever.

He pulled away and looked deep in my eyes, his pupils enlarged, erasing most of the yellow.

"Mmm, I will take my time with you now," he said in a deep voice, covering my neck, breasts, and tummy with kisses.

He continued further down, sliding his hands down my thighs to raise and spread my legs. His tongue explored and taunted me, taking me almost to the edge of climax but not quite. We rolled and tumbled over each other, touching and tasting until we couldn't wait any longer. He pulled me up to a sitting position and held me in a tight embrace while entering me. I loved how completely connected we were, his energy burning throughout every inch of my body. His stamina seemed never-ending now, and I moaned and shouted his name as he grabbed my butt, assisting me in moving my body back and forth.

"Oh, Montor, you are driving me crazy."

"Good, Mina, good."

He laid me flat on the bed and pressed his body against mine, my cheek against his chest, his heartbeat a boom in my ear. Only the seconds between each thrust separated us, our hips grinding until my body clenched. Orgasms echoed and reverberated on my insides. Once he knew I was satiated, he let himself release into his climax.

My skin glistened with sweat, and our hearts wanted to burst out of our chests. He kissed me gently. My toes curled, and I ran my fingers through his hair, enjoying the lingering pleasure that still coursed through my body. Finally, our pulses settled down. We napped for a few hours, got dressed, and went to the hotel room where we had left our overnight bag. After showering together and changing into something comfortable, we headed to the dining area. Montor had contracted the kitchen staff to be ready to serve breakfast for those who had stayed overnight. We ordered hot tea and the quiche-like dish he made for me on our first trip together to Renna One. I remembered that and the pizza dish he also had made for me.

"Mina, do you remember everything?" he asked.

"No, things are just popping into my mind at random. I think we should have the doctor evaluate me and advise on how I should approach this, but I am so happy, Montor. I know now that I am on a journey to recapturing my memories. I feel like a whole person again."

He caressed my cheek, and I heard nearby footsteps. Foxor, Colora, Lasarta, and Josher joined us.

"You two disappeared on us last night," Colora said, elbowing me with a mischievous look.

"Who else stayed overnight?" asked Montor, trying to divert attention from our escapade.

"Just a few drunken lieutenants. Everyone else left once the party was over. We made sure everyone knew that you both were grateful for their attendance," answered Foxor.

"*Fa* Kindor said I should practice new words so I can show him how well I can spell them next time he calls," Josher said.

"So, he and Lorret left too?" I asked.

"Yes, they did, but he said he would contact us about the logistics of his calls with Josher. He was very thankful that you will allow him to continue his relationship with the boy," said Lasarta.

"Well, order your food. I am so hungry, I think I will have another serving," said Montor.

As we ate, everyone shared their impressions of the ceremony and party.

"I must say, one of the best *Bendorai* I have attended," exclaimed Foxor.

Montor leaned over and caressed my cheek.

"I will always remember this day as so much more. It is the

true day that my wife came back to me, the day I regained my family. I will never allow anything to break our bond again."

I smiled while the rest fist pumped in approval. My soul was at peace. I looked forward to regaining all my memories, the beautiful and the ugly. I'd decide for myself the ones I wanted to forget, the ones I wanted to learn from, and the ones I wanted to treasure.

EPILOGUE – MONTOR

My soul said, endure
These are only the first steps
The journey is long
Our love is a destiny
I dare not question such things

"Steps" from *Montor's Secret Stash of Poems*

Doctor Kimara explained that the time had come to use meditation and hypnosis to help Mina sort out her random vision flashes into coherent memories. The prolonged process required daily doctor visits over two lunar cycles and was not without pain for Mina. Remembering her Earth family and life prior to being kidnapped brought Mina to her knees. Recalling Zorla and her time on Xixsted was also especially challenging. My chest filled with pride as Mina pushed through it all with the valor of an Arandan warrior while remaining a loving mother and wife to Josher and me.

I changed my work habits, making it home for dinner every night. When I needed extra time in the evenings for a work-related issue, I addressed it from home. Mina and I were making up for lost time. If it had been up to me, I would have stayed with her and Josher all day, every day.

I secured permission from the Fronidian government for testing the *hanstoric* in the electromagnetic caves of the southern hemisphere. Our United Rebel Front experts determined those Fronidian caves had similar properties as the crystalline caves in Dit Lar. The *hanstorics* could be recharged there to set up a trans-galactic transportal. Negotiations began regarding the terms of how to share the benefits of this new mode of space travel. The Fronidian government reluctantly started to provide information regarding Lostai sympathizers among their Sotkari Ta immigrant community. As part of the bargain, we agreed to extradite anyone we found to be a Lostai infiltrator back to Fronidia to stand trial. I would have preferred killing the filthy bastards on the spot but met them halfway in the negotiation. Kindor and his team began to analyze the information and identify infiltrators.

Kindor religiously called Josher a few times each lunar cycle. It irked me at first that my son looked forward to Kindor's calls as much as he did going to the holographic rooms with me, but eventually I agreed to allow Kindor to contact Josher as often as he wanted. I asked Foxor to liaison with Kindor. I wanted Mina and me to have as little contact with Kindor as possible.

The United Rebel Front and the Lostai Empire continued facing each other in battle on several planets: Sotkar, Tormix, the Namson planet, and Dit Lar. Keeping Aranda safe required constant border security and improvement of our shield technology. Renna One's splintered insurgencies remained separate from the United Rebel Front. In addition to trying to regain the regions they had lost, the Lostai engaged in a campaign to invade other less advanced planets in the galaxy and continued their search for races with embedded Sotkari Ta genes. I reached out to planetary governments across the adjacent sectors to join us in denouncing Lostai aggression.

While remaining in the hunt for the other Sotkari Transportals and Lostai prison camps across the galaxy, we continued to use Dit Lar and the new Fronidian transportals to send rescued hostages back to their home planets. I accompanied Mina to both transportals, where she trained United Rebel Front soldiers on the process. There were still lingering questions on what the display figures meant, but as long as the *hanstorics* were returned within two or three days for recharging, they proved to be a safe mode of travel. The Chaperone's traveling days were over, as were mine as the *Zateim* or battalion captain. I would continue to battle the Lostai from my office in my role as Strategic and Liaison Officer. Our highest priority was to preserve the sanctity and safety of our family.

Six lunar cycles after Mina regained all her memories, she confessed to me that she wanted to visit Earth again and try to see her children. I asked her to give me some time to get adjusted to the idea and plan how we would ensure her safety. I feared anything that might disturb the stability of our family. She agreed to wait a couple of lunar cycles before making that trip.

We also decided to try to have another child. Mina had her contraceptive surgery reversed, and then we went on a well-deserved family vacation. Our time together as a married couple became truly joyful. We traveled via *hanstoric* to a private island on Aranda and spent two weeks there, returning to our home in Fronidia late at night. The next morning, a call came in from Commander Portars as we ate our morning meal.

It was unusual for him to call me at home and at that early hour. I took the call on our dining room viewer.

"Montor, I see I have interrupted your meal. I am sorry."

"No worries, Commander. It is always good to hear from you."

"The only reason I contacted you at home is because we have received disturbing information from the Lostai Coroxt prison camp that we just liberated."

"Disturbing information?"

"Yes, there is an Earthian male among the rescued prisoners who claims to be Mina's husband." He cleared his throat. "Perhaps he is having trouble with the Lostai language since we all know Mina is widowed from her previous Earthian husband. Anyway, what most concerns me is that he says Zorla has Mina's Earthian daughter. I believe her name is pronounced *Aembuh*."

THE END of Book Two

Book Three Coming Soon: Is Mina's first husband, Joshua, really among the rescued prisoners? If so, how will Montor react? Do the Lostai have Mina's daughter, Amber? In the midst of a galactic war, Mina embarks on a search mission. What new allies and enemies will she encounter along the way?

LEXICON AND PLACES

Lexicon

- **Barinta** – (Arandan) collaboration, Montor assigned this name to his spacecraft
- **Bendorai** – (Arandan) ceremony that celebrates when a child is presented with their first amulet, usually one revolution (year) from their birth date
- **Bomar** – (Arandan) bread
- **Carinbo** – (Arandan) sleepy child, equivalent to "sleepyhead" in English
- **Fa** – (Arandan) shortened version of uncle, mainly used by young children
- **Faristo** – (Arandan) uncle
- **Goria** – (Arandan) large purple berry used in sweet pies and desserts
- **Gotumi** – (Arandan) vegetable native to Aranda considered a delicacy
- **Grem** – (Namson) dessert consisting of pockets of dough filled with sweet, macerated fruit

- **Grimah** – (Lostai) literally means "to mate" but used as a curse word equivalent to "damn it" or "fuck" in English
- **Hanstoric** – (Arandan) jumper, slang word that refers to the laptop-like device required to travel through space using the transportal
- **Jonjuri** – (Arandan) victory
- **Jouter** – (Fronidian) A dish of vegetables and grains topped with fish, served in an individual crockpot
- **Kantarext** – (Sotkari) curse word equivalent to "damn" in English
- **Lirinium** – (Lostai) the hardest metal known to the Lostai
- **Lo Ro** – (Arandan) shortened version of grandmother, mainly used by young children
- **Lo Romasta** – (Arandan) grandmother
- **Lo Ta** – (Arandan) shortened version of grandfather, mainly used by young children
- **Lo Taristo** – (Arandan) grandfather
- **Lorin** – (Namson) deep-fried mashed tubers filled with ground fowl
- **Marz** – (Namson) province
- **Mizora** – (Lostai) phaser rifle
- **Namit** – (Arandan) please
- **Ro Ma** – (Arandan) shortened version of mother, mainly used by young children
- **Ro Masa** – (Arandan) as part of the Bendorai ceremony, the person designated to take the place of the mother of a child in the event something happens to the parent, equivalent to "godmother" in English
- **Romasta** – (Arandan) mother
- **Sa veranttay** – (Fronidian) term of endearment used by Fronidian females towards males they care about,

equivalent to "beloved and handsome male" in English.

- **Santrock** – (Namson) domesticated beast mounted to play the Namson sport of "vernit"
- **Shermont** – (Arandan) curse word equivalent to "stinky feces" or "shit" in English
- **So** – (Arandan) shortened version of aunt, mainly used by young children
- **Somasta** – (Arandan) aunt
- **Stampu** – (Arandan) highly intoxicating beverage consumed in small shots
- **Ta Masa** – (Arandan) as part of the Bendorai ceremony, the person designated to take the place of the father of a child in the event something happens to the parent, equivalent to "godfather" in English
- **Ta Ri** – (Arandan) shortened version of father, mainly used by young children
- **Taristo** – (Arandan) father
- **Teronix** – (Arandan) dough pockets filled with savory vegetables in a tasty broth
- **Tomdarox** – (Arandan) animal with black fur that looks like a large bear with red eyes.
- **Vatimex** – (Fronidian) Fronidian martial art
- **Vernit** – (Namson) sport played by the Namson, players mount a domesticated beast and throw balls to their teammates, the object of the game is to get a ball over a goal
- **Vimor** – (Arandan) small, deadly pistol that delivers narrow, radioactive beams with precision
- **Vona** – (Lostai) small craft known for maneuverability and strong plasma beam weaponry capable of destroying larger vessels
- **Vormey** – (Arandan) wine

- **Yomoso** – (Arandan) strong, bitter coffee-like beverage
- **Yomurati** – (Arandan) to help or rescue
- **Zateim** – (Namson) Chieftain
- **Zirem** – (Lostai) long rod used as a weapon to deliver painful electric burns
- **Zorinto** – (Namson) intoxicating beverage made from fermented grain and sour juice

Places

- **Aranda** – planet in the Soma Quadrant plagued by civil war and later invaded by the Lostai. It is characterized by red oceans, pink sand, and a mustard-colored sky. Aranda becomes the birthplace of the United Rebel Front, an insurgency against Lostai rule.
- **Dit Lar** – small planet near Sotkar in the Morex Quadrant with breathable atmosphere. It is the location of a transportal that allows immediate travel across galaxies
- **Frazin** – small Fronidian village that borders an exotic vacation spot called Jamboran
- **Fro Gantar** – Fronidian capital city
- **Fron Onta Space Station** – one of Fronidia's largest space stations, providing docking for several thousand different types of spacecraft, transport pods, and shuttles
- **Fronidia** – technologically advanced planet in the Soma Quadrant focused on economic power and influence. Friendly towards refugees. Prefers to remain neutral as much as possible towards belligerent planets and/or factions within the

quadrant. Many Sotkari Ta that fled Sotkar after the Lostai invasion settled in Fronidia.

- **Losarex** – territory in the Southwestern continent of Sotkar that remained under Lostai control after the United Rebel Front uprising
- **Losta** – planet in the Morex Quadrant whose government is focused on increasing their empire and military might throughout the galaxy.
- **Marimbo Tu** – small island on Sotkar, Sotkari insurgency home base
- **Mastazo** – Fronidian province where a large refugee center is located
- **Members Only** – a venue that offers dining, dancing, and lodging with guaranteed privacy owned by Colora and Jortan, one is located in Fronidia, another in Renna One and a third on another planet within the Soma Quadrant
- **Namson** – planet at the outer edge of the galaxy, taken over by the Lostai, home to a race of frog-like people, many of who have embedded Sotkari Ta genes
- **Nexori** – Lostai military station in the Morex Quadrant
- **Penstarox** – a remote island on Aranda, home base of the Arandan rebellion
- **Renna One** – planet in the Soma Quadrant under Lostai control, famous for resorts and recreation, but also where Lostai employ slave labor at mining camps.
- **Rondarium** – A large Fronidian town near Zuntar where Josher was born
- **Rovera** – small Sotkari village
- **Solaro** – rural mountainous area on Sotkar where Kaya lived

- **Sotkar** – a planet in the Morex Quadrant, home to a people whose evolutionary transition resulted in some being born with telepathic and telekinetic abilities. The Lostai took advantage of the division between the Sotkari people to annex it to their Empire. Sotkari flora and fauna are characterized by their bioluminescence
- **Tan Aranda** – Arandan rebel home base located on the island of Penstarox
- **Tormix** – planet in the Morex Quadrant that eventually joins the United Rebel Front
- **Tremoxtar Mor** – a large island on planet Sotkar, home to many vacation and recreational resorts
- **Ventamu** – The name of the Arandan coastal country (and clan) where Montor is from. All people from Ventamu carry that as their surname.
- **Wayont** – remote Fronidian mining town
- **Xixsted** – Lostai science station located on the third moon of Losta (the Lostai home world)
- **Zalbadar** – small Fronidian city with a rest stop
- **Zamandi's Room** – An entertainment and restaurant establishment on Renna One that offers various bars, dancing and dining venues, and caters to the Soma Quadrant's rich and famous
- **Zuntar** – Fronidian village where Kindor and family lived and operated a restaurant

A NOTE FROM THE AUTHOR

Thank you for reading *Broken Bonds, The Curse of Sotkari Ta: Book Two*. Please consider taking a moment to write a review on Amazon, BookBub, and Goodreads. This means a lot to self-published authors such as me. I hope you have enjoyed the series so far. Be on the lookout for Book Three, which I expect to release in 2022. In the meantime, I would love to connect. Find me at:

My website: https://www.mariaaperez.com

Facebook private fan group: https://www.facebook.com/groups/mariasfederationoffriends

Facebook Page: https://www.facebook.com/MariaAPerez. Author

Twitter: https://twitter.com/MariaAPerez1

ACKNOWLEDGMENTS

The Curse of Sotkari Ta series represents a milestone in my life that has been long in the making. First and foremost, I am thankful that God has given me the opportunity to achieve my dream of becoming a published author. Next, I need to recognize the many people who helped me take the stories in my head and share them with readers.

Big hugs of gratitude to my husband, who supported me when I decided to take an early retirement, giving me the time and space to devote to my writing. He works hard so I can stay at home and follow my dream. He's always steadfast by my side. I love you, honey!

My sons were patient when I demanded the TV be turned down and understanding of my other quirks during all the days, weeks, months, and, yes, years that I've devoted to this series. They also offered objective opinions on the cover art and back cover blurbs. My love for you is beyond all galaxies and star systems.

My friend, Joanna, is a space opera fan, just like me. In addition to being my very first alpha reader, she has been a great cheerleader and advisor along the way. I am very grateful to my sisters, Sylvia and Wilma, and my best friend, TP, who also alpha read my books. Their different perspectives helped me mold the early versions of my story into something beta readers could work with. I can't thank them enough for the motivation they offered along the way. Thanks also to my beta readers, Ed Hormazabal (@EHormazabal_W) and Bailee Taylor (https://www.fiverr.com/baileetaylor), for their valuable feedback, helping me flesh out my characters and inspiring me to make the story better. Thank you to my nieces, Alondra, for helping me proofread, and Erika, for her input on the cover and back cover blurbs. You're both awesome. Many thanks to my ARC readers, especially Kelley, who was exceptionally thorough and expeditious.

I am deeply thankful to my editor, Stephanie Hoogstad, for her beta reading, her excellent editorial guidance and for taking the time to review other pieces of the puzzle. I couldn't have done this without her.

Thank you to my cover designer, Christian Bentulan. You patiently held my hand each step of the way and brought my characters and theme to life.

I must give a shout-out to my #WritingCommunity and #vss365 tweeps for welcoming me into their Twitter groups and for their advice and encouragement. Stephi Simone's guidance has been extremely helpful in several aspects of my writing projects including the Jamaican patois dialogue used by the character, Damari. I am so grateful for her friendship. A very special thanks to Migs (@OminousHallways), who wrote the beautiful introductory poem and collaborated with me on the poem titled *Surrender* featured in Chapter 10. He earned my trust early on, and I consider him a friend.

Big thanks to the talented Sam Steel (@SamJournals) for allowing me to include his poem *Scroll* in Chapter 25. I enjoy our collaborations on #draftfolderfriday.

I am lucky to have been blessed with two sets of parents: my biological parents and my aunt and uncle. I am grateful for their love and for teaching me the meaning of family, hard work, perseverance and generosity.

Last, but not least, I thank the readers, current and future. I hope you enjoy my stories for many years to come.

AUTHOR'S BIO

Maria A. Perez was born in Yonkers, NY, and grew up in New York City. She also lived in Puerto Rico and now resides in Boca Raton, Florida. She holds a Bachelor's in Business and has spent a successful career in Corporate America working in Accounting and Finance. Early retirement has allowed Maria to focus on her dream of writing and becoming a published author. She is married with two young adult sons and a labradoodle daughter. Maria enjoys reading all genres, although she's partial to dystopian, space opera and romance series such as *The Hunger Games*, *The Expanse* and *Outlander*. A diehard "Trekkie" and *Star Wars* fan, she is fascinated with the possibility of what is out there in unexplored space and the potential of the human race.

Follow Maria on her:

Website: https://www.mariaaperez.com

Facebook private fan group: https://www.facebook.com/groups/mariasfederationoffriends

Facebook Page: https://www.facebook.com/MariaAPerez.Author

Twitter: https://twitter.com/MariaAPerez1

CPSIA information can be obtained
at www.ICGtesting.com
Printed in the USA
BVHW030047231121
622233BV00021B/20

9 781735 113326